P9-AEW-895

COLUMBUS

A ROMANCE

BOOKS BY RAFAEL SABATINI

BY RAFAEL SABATINI

Columbus

A ROMANCE

HOUGHTON MIFFLIN COMPANY · BOSTON

The Riverside Press Cambridge

1942

The Riverside Press
CAMBRIDGE · MASSACHUSETTS
PRINTED IN THE U.S.A.

CONTENTS

Contents

COLUMBUS

A ROMANCE

I

 THE WAYFARER

A MAN and a boy climbed the slope from the estuary of the Tinto by a sandy path that wound through a straggling growth of pine trees. It was the eventide of a winter's day at about the time that the Spanish Sovereigns were moving to the investment of Granada, which informs you that these events fell out in the closing decade of the fifteenth century.

From the long line of dunes below them, the Arenas Gordas, stretching away for miles towards Cadiz, the sand was tossed and whirled like spindrift by a bitter wind that blew from the southwest. Beyond, the storm-lashed Atlantic was grey under grey skies.

The man was well above the common height, broad-shouldered and long-limbed, fashioned in lines of great athletic vigour. From under a plain round hat his hair, red, thick and glossy, hung to the nape of his neck. Grey eyes shone clear in a weathered face whose patrician mould and stamp of pride were at odds with the shabbiness of his wear. A surcoat of homespun, once black but faded now to a mournful greenish hue, clothed him to the knees, and was caught about his middle by a belt of plain leather. From this a dagger hung on his right hip and a leather scrip on his left thigh. His hose was of coarse black wool; he was roughly shod, and he carried his meagre gear bundled in a cloak and slung from his shoulder by a staff of quince wood. His age was little beyond the middle thirties.

The boy, a sturdy child of seven or eight, clinging to his right hand, looked up to ask, 'Is it much farther?'

He spoke in Portuguese, and was answered by his sire in the same tongue, on a note that was half-bitter, half-whimsical.

'Now, God avail me, child, that is a question I've been asking myself these ten years, and never found the answer yet.' Then, abruptly changing to the commonplace, he added: 'No, no. See. We are almost there.'

A turn of the path had brought into view a long, low building, irregularly quadrangular, starkly white against the black wall of pine trees that screened it from the east. From the heart of it sprouted upwards like a burnt-red mushroom the circular tiled roof of a chapel.

'For tonight that should be the end of our journey. If I am fortunate, Diego, it may also be a beginning.' He resumed his whimsical tone, as if thinking aloud rather than addressing another. 'The Prior, I am told, is a man of learning who commands the ear of a Queen, having once been her confessor. To confess a woman is commonly to hold her afterwards in a measure of subjection. One of the lesser mysteries of our mysterious life. But we walk delicately, asking nothing. In this world, my child, to ask is to be denied and avoided. It's a lesson you'll learn later. In order to possess what you lack, study to let none suspect that you seek it. Display to them, rather, the advantages to themselves of persuading you to accept it. They will then be eager to bestow. It is too subtle, Diego, for your innocent mind. Indeed, for long it eluded even mine, which is far from innocent. We go to test it now upon this good Franciscan.'

It is among the obiter dicta of the good Franciscan of whom he spoke, Frey Juan Perez, who was Prior of the Convent of La Rabida, that the temper of a man's soul is commonly displayed in his voice. It is possible that Frey Juan's was more subtly attuned than the common ear. It is possible that his wide experience as a confessor — in which capacity he commonly heard without seeing, so that his consciousness would be centred in his hearing — had led him to discover a definite affinity between the spiritual qualities and the tone and pitch of voice of a penitent whose countenance was rendered invisible to him by the screen of the confessional.

Be that as it may, certain it is that but for this settled conviction of Frey Juan's our wayfarer would not so easily have attained his ends.

The Prior was pacing the courtyard at about the hour of compline, which is to say at sunset. The Borgia Pope whose special devotion to the Virgin was to originate the Angelus had not yet ascended Saint Peter's throne. As Frey Juan paced, breviary in hand, reading with moving lips, as is canonically prescribed, the office of the day, his attention was disturbed by a voice addressing the lay-brother who kept the gate.

'Of your charity, my brother, a little bread and a cup of water for this weary child.'

There was nothing in the actual words, commonplace enough at a convent doorway, to claim the Prior's notice; but the voice, and, more than the voice, the contrast between the conscious pride that rang through its veiling huskiness and the humility of the request it uttered, might have compelled the attention of an ear even less sensitive than Frey Juan's. Its accent was definitely foreign, and the dignity of its intonation gathered increase perhaps from the precision with which a cultured man must be expressing himself in a language other than his own.

Frey Juan, whom we are not to acquit of a very human curiosity, especially in any matter that promised distraction from the gentle monotony of life at La Rabida, closed his breviary upon his forefinger, and stepped round an angle of the courtyard to view the speaker.

At a glance he recognized how perfectly the voice went with the man whom he beheld. He discovered power spiritual and physical as much in his shapely height and upright carriage as in his shaven face with its strong line of jaw and acquiline nose. But it was chiefly his eyes that held the Prior: full eyes of a clear grey, luminous as those of a visionary or a mystic, eyes whose steady gaze few men could find it easy to support. He had set down his bundle on the stone bench at the gate. But neither that nor the rest of the stranger's shabby details could obscure in Frey Juan's discerning scrutiny the man's inherent distinction. Beside him, the child on whose behalf he sought that meagre hospitality gazed upwards in round-eyed wistfulness at the approaching Prior.

Frey Juan advanced with a clatter of loose sandals, a barrel of a man in a grey frock. His face was long and pallid, with a deal of loose flesh about it, but made genial by the humour in the eyes and about the heavy-lipped mouth. He greeted the stranger with a kindly smile, and in formal Latin, to test perhaps his scholarship, or perhaps his faith, for that aquiline nose above the full lips need not be Christian.

'Pax Domini sit tecum.'

To which the wayfarer answered formally, with a grave inclination of his proud head: 'Et cum spirito tuo.'

'You are a traveller,' quoth the Prior unnecessarily, whilst the lay-brother stood aside in self-effacement.

'A traveller. Newly landed here from Lisbon.'

'Do you go far tonight?'

'Only as far as Huelva.'

'Only?' Frey Juan raised his thick brows. 'It is a good ten miles. And by night. Do you know the way?'

The wayfarer smiled. 'Direction should suffice for one trained to find his way through the trackless ocean.'

The Prior caught a vaunting note in that answer. It prompted his next question. 'A great traveller?'

'Judge if I may so describe myself. I've sailed as far as northern Thule and southern Guinea, and eastwards to the Golden Horn.'

The Prior sucked in his breath, and scanned the man more shrewdly, as if suspicious of a claim so vast. The scrutiny must have reassured him, for at once he grew cordial.

'That is to have touched the very boundaries of the world.'

'Of the known world, perhaps. But not of the actual world. Not by many a thousand miles.'

'How can you assert that, never having seen it?'

'How can your paternity assert that there is a heaven and a hell, never having seen them?'

'By faith and revelation,' was the grave answer.

'Just so. And in my case to faith and revelation I may add cosmography and mathematics.'

'Ah!' Frey Juan's prominent eyes considered him with a deepening interest. 'Come you in, sir, in God's name. It is draughty here, and the evening chill. Close the gate, Innocencio. Come you in, sir. We were shamed if we had no better hospitality than that of your modest prayer.' He took the stranger by the sleeve to draw him on. 'What is your name, sir?'

'Colon. Cristobal Colon.'

Again Frey Juan's shrewd eyes scrutinized the Semitic lines of that lofty countenance. There were New Christians of that name, and he could call to mind more than one consigned by the Holy Office to the fire as relapsed Judaizers.

'Your way of life?' he asked.

'I am a mariner and a cosmographer by trade.'

'A cosmographer!' The tone implied that the Prior's interest was increased by the description; as, indeed, it was; for Frey Juan was a scholar whose wide studies included, as Colon had been informed, the provoking mysteries of cosmography.

A bell began to toll. Lights from the leaded Gothic windows that overlooked the courtyard, the windows of the chapel, beat dimly upon the lingering daylight.

'It is the hour of vespers,' said Frey Juan. 'So I must leave you. Innocencio will conduct you to our guest-chamber. We shall see each other again at supper. Meanwhile we shall supply the needs of your child. It is understood that you spend the night with us.'

'You are very good to a stranger, Sir Prior,' was Colon's acknowledgment of an invitation upon which he had counted, and for which he had angled in his vaunting self-description.

Frey Juan, no less disingenuous, was content to answer by a wave of deprecation. For, kindly man though he was, it was not kindness only that prompted the hospitality. If he knew his world, this was no ordinary traveller. There might be profit in talk with such a man; and if not profit, at least entertainment such as came too rarely into Frey Juan's present claustral life.

The lay-brother held a door; but Colon hung back, to express himself in terms that reassured the Prior on the score of his faith.

'To rest is less urgent than to give thanks to God and Our Lady for having led my steps to so hospitable a house. By your leave, Father, I will go with you to vespers. For the tender little one it is different. If our brother will take him meanwhile in his care, it will deepen my obligation.'

He stooped to speak to the child, who, born and bred in Portugal, had stood intent but puzzled by this talk in unknown Castilian. What he said, holding the promise of refreshment, sent the lad eagerly to the lay-brother's side. From the Gothic portal of the chapel his father watched him go, with eyes that were tender. Then he turned abruptly.

'I keep your reverence.'

With a kindly smile the Prior waved him on into the little chapel of Our Lady of Rabida, whose image enjoyed miraculous fame as a prophylactic against madness.

The bell ceased. The officiating friar was already at the altar, and leaving Colon in the empty nave, Frey Juan went on and up to take his place in the choir.

2

Dixit Dominus Domino meo:
sede a dextris meis.' The Gregorian chant swelled up, and
Frey Juan, peering through the luminous mist sent up by the
tapers into the twilight beyond, was gratified to see his kneeling guest in an attitude of rapt devotion.

Anon, because of the interest aroused in him, the Prior was
not content that supper should be served to the stranger in the
bare hall where charity was dispensed to casual wayfarers, but,
treating him as an honoured guest, bade him to his own table.

Colon accepted the in ation as his due, without surprise or
hesitation, and the brethren ranged at the trestles set against
the walls along the refectory's length, furtively observed this
meanly garbed stranger striding beside the Prior with the
proud carriage of a prince, and asked themselves what hidalgo
might be honouring their house.

Up that long bleak hall Frey Juan conducted him to the
Prior's table on a shallow dais across the end of it, surmounted
by a fresco of The Last Supper so crudely painted as to be presumed the work of one of the friars. Another fresco no less

crude, of Saint Francis receiving the stigmata, adorned the ceiling, now dimly revealed in the light of a six-beaked oil lamp suspended from it. For the rest two Dukes of Medina Celi, painted in life-size and as if their limbs and trunks and heads were made of wood, scowled at each other across the hall from walls that were coated with the whitewash which the Arab had brought to Spain. The windows, square and barred, were set along the northern wall, at a height which admitting light afforded no distracting view of the outer world.

The food was plain but good: fish fresh from the port below in a pungent stew, followed by a broth of veal. There was wheaten bread and a sharp but wholesome wine of Palos, from the vineyards on the western slopes beyond the pinewoods.

They ate to the drone of a friar's voice, reading from a stone pulpit in the southern wall, a chapter from a 'Vita et Gesta' of Saint Francis.

Colon was seated on the Prior's right with the almoner on his other side. On Frey Juan's left the Sub-Prior and the master of the novices completed the group at the Prior's table. Seen through the misty light from the candlebranch that graced it, the grey lines of the minorites below looked ghostly in the crepuscular gloom enshrouding them.

When at last the reading ceased they stirred into life, and in that hour of relaxation a subdued hum of talk arose. To the Prior's table came a dish of fruit, sleek oranges, dried figs of Smyrna and some half-withered apples, besides a flagon of Malmsey. Frey Juan brimmed a cup for his guest, perhaps with intent to loosen a tongue that should have much to tell. After that, as he still sat bemused, the Prior ventured to spur him by a direct question.

'And so, sir, having voyaged far and wide you are now come to rest here in Huelva.' Thick-lipped, he lisped a little in his speech.

Colon roused himself. 'To rest?' His tone derided the suggestion. 'This is but a stage in a new journey. I may stay some days there, with a relative of my wife, who is now in the peace of God. Then I go forth again on my travels.' And he added almost under his breath: 'Like Cartaphilus, and perhaps as vainly.'

'Cartaphilus?' The Prior searched his memory. 'I do not think I have heard of him.'

'The cobbler of Jerusalem who spat upon Our Lord, and who is doomed to walk the earth until the Saviour comes again.'

Frey Juan showed him a shocked countenance. 'Sir, that is a bitter comparison.'

'Worse. It is a blasphemy wrenched from me by impatience. Am I not named Cristobal? Is there no omen to hearten me in such a name? Cristobal. Christum ferens. Bearer of Christ. That is my mission. For that was I born. For that am I chosen. To bear the knowledge of Him to lands as yet unknown.'

The Prior's eyes were round with inquiry. But before he could give it utterance, the Sub-Prior on his left inclined his head to murmur to him. The Prior assented by a nod, and a general rising followed for the 'Deo gratias' which the Sub-Prior pronounced.

Colon, however, was not to go with the departing friars. As they trooped out, Frey Juan resumed his seat in the high chair, and with a hand on his guest's sleeve drew him down to sit again beside him. 'We need not hasten,' he said, and re-filled Colon's cup with the sweet Malmsey.

'You spoke, sir, of lands as yet unknown. What lands be these? Have you in mind the Atlantis of Plato, or the Island of the Seven Cities?'

Colon's eyes were lowered so that Frey Juan might not detect their sudden gleam at the very question he desired, the question that suggested that the scholarly friar who might influence a queen was caught already in the web of interest his guest was spinning.

'Your reverence jests. Yet, was Plato's Atlantis such a fable? May not the Fortunate Isles and the Azores be remnants of it? And may there not be still other, greater remnants in seas as yet uncharted?'

'These are, then, your unknown lands?'

'No. I have no such speculative things in mind. I seek the great empire in the west, which I know to be of more definite existence, and with which I will endow the crown that may be given grace to support my quest.'

A sudden vehemence in him first startled the Prior; then its histrionic note drew a smile to his pursy lips. He scoffed good-naturedly.

'You know of the existence of these lands. You know, you say. You have seen them, then?'

'With the eyes of the soul. With the eyes of the intellect with which God's grace has endowed me to the end that I may spread in them the knowledge of Him. So clear my vision, reverend sir, that I have charted these lands.'

It was not for a man of Frey Juan's faith to mock at visions. Yet of visionaries, being a practical man, he was naturally suspicious.

'I am, myself, a humble student of cosmography and philosophy, yet I may be a dullard. For such knowledge as I possess does not explain how that may be charted which has not been seen.'

'Ptolemy had not seen the world he charted.'

'But he possessed evidence to guide him.'

'So do I. And more than evidence. Your paternity will admit that it is by logical inference from the known that we proceed to discover the unknown. Were it not so philosophy must stand arrested.'

'In matters of the spirit that may be true. In matters physical I am not so clear, and I must prefer evidence to imaginings, however logically founded.'

'Then let me urge such evidence as exists. Storms blowing from the west have borne to the shores of Porto Santo oddly carved timbers that have never known the touch of iron, great pines such as do not grow in the Azores, and huge canes, so monstrous that they will hold gallons of wine in a single section. Some of these may be seen in Lisbon now, where they are preserved. And there is more. Much more.'

He paused a moment, as if collecting himself; actually, in order to observe his host. Discerning a rapt attention in that full pallid face, he sat forward and began his exposition, his tone quiet, level and precise.

'Two hundred years ago a Venetian traveller, Marco Polo by name, journeyed farther east than any European before or since. He reached Cathay and the dominions of the Grand Khan, a monarch of fabulous wealth.'

'I know, I know,' Frey Juan interposed. 'I possess a copy of his book. I have mentioned that these are matters of which I, too, am a humble student.'

'You possess his book!' There was a sudden eagerness in Colon's face that brought to it an increase of youth. 'That spares me a deal. I did not know,' he lied, 'that I talk to one already enlightened.'

'You are not to flatter me, my son,' said Frey Juan, not innocent perhaps of irony. 'What did you find in Marco Polo that I have lacked the wit to discover?'

'Your paternity will recall the allusion to the Island of Zipangu, known by the people of Mangi — the farthest point he, himself, had reached — to be situated fifteen hundred miles farther to the east.' Frey Juan's nod encouraged him to continue. 'You will remember the fabulous abundance of the gold in those regions. Its sources, he says, are inexhaustible. So common is the metal that the very roof of the king's palace is covered with plates of it, as we cover ours with lead. He tells us, too, of the great abundance of precious stones and pearls, and in particular of a pink pearl of great size.'

'Vanitas vanitatis,' the Prior deprecated.

'Not, by your leave, if well applied. Not if employed for the furtherance of worthy ends. Wealth is not mere vanity then; and here is wealth beyond all European dreams.'

The very thought of it seemed to plunge him into a state of contemplation from which he was impatiently aroused by Frey Juan.

'But what has this Zipangu of Marco Polo to do with your discoveries? You spoke of lands across the western ocean. Assuming all the eastern marvels of Marco Polo to be true, how are they evidence of your western lands?'

'Your paternity believes the earth to be a sphere?' He took an orange from the dish, and held it up. 'Like this.'

'That is now the general belief among philosophers.'

'And you accept, of course, the division of its circumference into three hundred and sixty degrees?'

'A mathematical convention. That offers no difficulty. And then?'

'Of these three hundred and sixty degrees the known world includes but some two hundred and eighty. That is a fact upon which all cosmographers agree. Thus, the known lands from the westernmost point, say Lisbon, to the extreme of the charted eastern lands leave still some eighty degrees — nearly a quarter of the earth's total — to be accounted for.'

The Prior made a dubious lip. 'We are told that it is all a waste of water, so storm-tossed and wild that there can be no hope to navigate it.'

Colon's eyes flashed scorn. 'A tale of weaklings who dare not make the attempt. There were also fables of an impassable belt of flame along the equinoctial line, a superstition which Portuguese navigators along the coast of Africa have derided.

'Give me your attention, reverend sir. Here, then, is Lisbon.' He marked a point upon the orange. 'And here the uttermost point of Cathay: a vast distance of some fourteen thousand miles by my own measurement of the degree, which on this parallel I compute to be of fifty miles.

'Now, if instead of travelling east by land, we travel west by water, thus' — and his finger now went leftwards round the orange from the point where he had placed Lisbon — 'we come, within eighty degrees, to the same charted point. Your paternity will perceive that it is not merely a paradox to say that we may reach the east by travelling west. To the golden Zipangu of Polo the distance by the west cannot be above four thousand miles. Thus far we go by evidence. Inference justifies the belief that Zipangu is by no means the farthest limit of the Indies. It is merely as far as the Venetian's knowledge went. There must be other islands, other lands, an empire that awaits possession.'

With such ardour had he made his exposition that Frey Juan was touched by something of his fire. The simple homely demonstration with the orange had disclosed one of those obvious facts which until indicated can elude the acutest mind. The Prior had been swept almost helplessly along by the strong current of the young cosmographer's enthusiasm. But here of a sudden he perceived an obstacle, to which his sanity must cling lest he be carried utterly away.

'Wait. Wait. You say there must be other lands. That is to go farther than I dare follow you, my son. It is no more than your belief, a belief in which you may be deceived.'

Colon's exaltation was not cooled. Rather, being fanned, it

flamed more hotly. 'If it were only that, it would not be an inference. And a well-founded inference your paternity shall
acknowledge it. It is based no longer on mathematics, but on
theology. We have it upon the authority of the Prophet
Esdras that the world is six parts land to one of water. Apply
that here, and tell me where I am at fault: Or let it pass unheeded. Leave out of account my imagined lands, which
would halve the distance.' He dropped the orange back into
its dish. 'It still remains that the Indies lie within four thousand miles of us to westward.'

'And is that naught?' The Prior was suddenly aghast at the
vision that rose before his eyes. 'Four thousand miles of empty
waters holding perils known to God alone. The very thought is
terrifying. Where is the courage that would so adventure itself
into the unknown?'

'It is here.' Colon smote his breast. He sat erect, all pride,
the glow of his eyes fanatical. 'The Lord, who with so palpable
a hand opened my understanding, so that reason, mathematics and charts are as naught to my inspiration, opened up
also my desire and endowed me with the spirit necessary to an
instrument of the Divine Will.'

The force in him was one to bludgeon reason, the confidence
a fire in which to consume all doubt. Frey Juan, already won
by Colon's cosmography and logic, found himself now subdued
into participation in the man's fanatical assurance.

'In my vanity — for which God forgive me — I have
thought that I had some learning. But you reveal me to myself a mere groper in these mysteries.' He hung his head in
thought for a moment. Colon, sipping his Malmsey, watched
him like a cat.

Suddenly the Prior asked: 'Whence are you, sir? For from
your speech it is clear that you are not of Spain.'

Colon hesitated before giving an answer that was yet no

answer. 'I am from the Court of His Highness King John of Portugal, and on my way to France.'

'To France? What do you seek there?'

'I do not seek. I offer. I offer this empire of which I have spoken.' He alluded to it as to something already in his possession.

'But to France?' Frey Juan's face was blank. 'Why to France?'

'Once I offered it to Spain, and was left to the judgment of a churchman, which was like sending me to a mariner for a judgment on theology. Then I went to Portugal, and wasted time upon learned dullards whose armour of prejudice I had no arts to pierce. There, as in Spain, there was none to sponsor me, and the lesson I have learnt is that without sponsoring a man but wastes his time in seeking the ear of the rulers of these kingdoms. There is no land upon which I would more gladly bestow these treasures than upon Spain. There is no sovereign I would more gladly serve than Isabel of Castile. But how am I to reach Her Highness? If I commanded an interest powerful enough to deserve her ear, intelligent enough to perceive the value of what I bring, and persuasive enough to induce her to receive me, then . . . why, then I should be content to stay. But where am I to find such a friend?'

Absently the Prior's forefinger was tracing a circle on the oaken table with a drop of spilled wine.

Covertly watching him, after a momentary pause, Colon answered his own question. 'I command no such friend in Spain. That is why I seek the King of France. If I fail with him, too, then I shall challenge fortune in England. You begin to perceive, perhaps, why I liken myself to the errant Jew, Cartaphilus.'

Still the Prior's forefinger continued its absent-minded tracing.

'Who knows?' he murmured at last.

'Who knows what, reverend sir?'

'Eh? Ah! Whether you are wise. Sleep brings counsel, they say. Let us sleep on this, and talk again.'

Colon was content to leave it there. Not much had been achieved, perhaps, and yet enough to give him hope that he had not wasted time in coming to La Rabida.

3

 THE SPONSOR

Nothing in years of his peaceful conventional life had kindled such a fever in Frey Juan as the words and person of Cristobal Colon. He spent, as he afterwards confessed, a night in which distracting wakeful thoughts alternated with fantastic dreams of golden-roofed Zipangu — by which name it is universally accepted that Marco Polo designates Japan — and of glittering jewelled islands dense with monstrous canes that gushed forth wine when tapped. It distressed his Spanish soul that empire over such lands should be lost to the Sovereigns, who had such need of treasure to repair the ravages of their war against the Infidel. His feelings in the matter were at once patriotic and personal. It was natural that having once been the confessor of Queen Isabel, his devotion to her was not merely that of a loyal subject; it included an affectionate paternal regard, reciprocated in her, he liked to believe, by a measure of filial piety. Representations from him on behalf of his odd guest might induce her to give the man's claims that consideration which Colon complained had formerly been denied them.

Pondering this as he lay wakeful on his hard pallet, the good
Prior was ready to perceive the hand of God in the strange
chance that had brought Colon to La Rabida. He was not to
suspect that here was no chance at all; that Colon, as coldly
calculating in furthering his aims as he was fiery in expounding
them, well aware of Frey Juan's interest in cosmography and of
the link that bound him to the Queen, had made his way of
deliberate intent to the convent, there to dangle a bait before
the Franciscan's eyes. The Prior's curiosity, aroused by the
ring of the wayfarer's sonorous voice, had simplified the course.
Had it been lacking — and it is clear that Colon cannot have
counted upon it — the request for a little bread and a drink of
water for his child would have been followed by a prayer for a
night's lodging. In the course of that he must have made an
opportunity for just such an interview as Frey Juan's interest
had spontaneously supplied.

Suspecting none of this, the Prior asked himself was there a
miraculous quality, a divine intervention, in the sequel to the
hospitality he had offered. It was, however, in the nature of
Frey Juan to temper enthusiasm with prudence. Before com-
mitting himself to sponsoring Colon's case, he would seek confirmation by others, more competent to judge, of the faith the
man inspired in him.

The others whom he had in mind were Garcia Fernandez, a
physician of Palos whose learning extended far beyond the
healer's arts, and Martin Alonso Pinzon, a wealthy merchant
who had followed the sea, who owned some ships, and who was
known for a mariner of great experience.

To his persuasions that Colon should postpone departure
for at least another day, his guest yielded with a lofty air of be-
stowing favours, and on that second night after supper, when
little Diego was abed, the four assembled in the Prior's cell.
They crowded the narrow little room, whose furniture in-

cluded no more than three chairs, a table, a writing-pulpit and
Frey Juan's truckle-bed, with two shelves of books against the
whitewashed wall.

There Colon was invited to repeat the exposition with
which he had entertained Frey Juan last night. He came to it
with hints of a vague reluctance, be it to weary these gentlemen, be it to weary himself. But having begun, and being
caught up in the glow of his own ardour, the manifestly eager
attention of his audience came to feed it. Expounding, he left
his chair to pace the narrow limits of the cell, fiery of eye and
liberal of gesture. He spoke in withering scorn of those who
had disdained his gifts and with confidence of the irresistible
power within him ultimately to open purblind eyes to a dazzling vision of those gifts.

Already before he came to those details which had so impressed Frey Juan, both the physician and the merchant were
held by that power, which Bishop Las Casas, who knew him,
tells us that Colon possessed, easily to command the love of all
who beheld him.

Fernandez, the physician, lean and long, with a head shaped
like an egg and as bald under his skull-cap, combed a straggling beard with bony fingers as he listened, his pale eyes wide,
his body hunched within the black gabardine that clothed it.
Shred by shred the scepticism in which he had come was being
ruthlessly stripped from him.

Pinzon, on the other hand, yielded himself up readily to that
fierce sorcery. He had come in unsuspected eagerness to the
Prior's invitation because the matters upon which he was told
that he was to hear this voyager were matters that had long
lain within his own speculations. A square, vigorous hairy
man in the prime of life, bow-legged, with eyes vividly blue
under thick black eyebrows, he had something of the mariner's
traditional easy, hearty manner. His lips showed very red

within the black beard, but the mouth was too pinched and small for generosity. His sober affluence was advertised in a wine-coloured surcoat of velvet edged with lynx fur and the boots of fine Cordovan leather that cased his sturdy legs.

By the time the exposition reached its end, these two who had been brought to sit in judgment scarcely needed for their conviction that Colon should unfold a chart on which to the known world he had added those territories of whose existence he was persuaded by his own inner light, besides Marco Polo and the Prophet Esdras. Nevertheless over that map, spread upon the Prior's table, they came reverently to pore at his bidding.

Fernandez from his studies, and Pinzon from his wide experience, were able to appraise not merely its clear perfection as a piece of cartography, but, save in one detail, its scrupulous exactitude in delineating the known world.

Upon this detail the old physician fastened. 'Your chart gives two hundred and thirty degrees of the earth's circumference to the distance from Lisbon to the eastern end of the Indies. That does not accord, I think, with Ptolemy.'

Colon received the criticism as if he welcomed it. 'Nor yet with Marinus of Tyre, whom Ptolemy corrected, just as Ptolemy stands corrected here. I correct him also, you'll observe, in the position of Thule, which I, having sailed beyond it, found farther to the west than Ptolemy judged it.'

But Fernandez insisted. 'That is your authority. Your sufficient authority. But for the position you give to India what authority exists?'

It was a moment before Colon replied, and then he spoke with a slow reluctance, as if something more were being dragged from him than he cared to give.

'You'll have heard of Toscanelli of Florence?'

'Paolo del Pozzo Toscanelli? What student of cosmography has not?'

Well might Fernandez ask the question, for the name of Toscanelli, lately dead, was famous among cultured men as that of the greatest mathematician and physicist that had ever lived.

Pinzon's deep voice boomed in: 'Who has not, indeed?'

'He is my authority. The computation that corrects Ptolemy's is his as well as mine.' Brusquely he added: 'But what matter even if it be in error? What matter if the golden Zipangu should lie some fewer or some more degrees in either direction? What is that to the main issue? It needs not the word of a Toscanelli to establish that whether we go east or west upon a sphere, ultimately the same point must be reached.'

'It may not need his word, as you say, but your case would be immeasurably strengthened if you could show that this great mathematician holds the same opinion.'

'I can show it.' He spoke hastily, and would have recalled the words, for it offended his vanity that it should be supposed that his conclusions had been inspired by another.

The sudden, almost startled interest created by his assertion drove him to explanation.

'As soon as I could formulate my theories, I submitted them to Toscanelli. He wrote to me, not only fully approving of them, but sending me a chart of his own, which in the main corresponds with the one before you.'

Frey Juan leaned forward eagerly. 'You possess that chart?'

'That and the letter setting forth the arguments that justify it.'

'Those,' said Fernandez, 'are very valuable documents. I do not think a man lives with learning enough to dispute Toscanelli's conclusions.'

Bluntly vehement, Pinzon swore by God and Our Lady that for him so much was not necessary. Master Colon's speculations had pierced the very heart of truth.

The Prior, sprawling on the truckle-bed, purred now with satisfaction, declaring that it could not be God's will that Spain, where He was so faithfully served, should lose the power and credit to accrue from discoveries vaster than any the Portuguese navigators had made.

From Colon, however, these protests evoked no further response. On the contrary, his manner became coldly forbidding.

'Spain has had her opportunity, and has neglected it. Engrossed in the conquest of a province from the Moors, the Sovereigns could not see the empire with which I offered to endow their crown. In Portugal a king who looked with favour on my plans left decision to a Jew astronomer, a doctor and a churchman, a motley commission that rejected me, as I believe from malice. That is why I look afield. Too many years already have I lost.' He folded his map with an air of finality.

But the astute Pinzon, who knew his world far better than the other two, was less susceptible to awe of personalities. He asked himself why, if this man's decision to go to France were as irrevocable as he pretended, he should have been at the trouble now of so full an exposition of his theories. In Pinzon's view, what Colon sought whilst seeming to disdain it, was assistance in the execution of his tremendous aims. And so Pinzon addressed himself to the persuasion which he guessed to be invited.

He would be unworthy, he vowed, of the name of Spaniard if, believing what they had now heard, he should neglect to endeavour to secure for Spain the possessions that would result from their discovery.

'I thank you, sir,' was the lofty answer, 'for this ready faith in me.'

Pinzon, however, would not leave it there. 'It is so solid, so much in accord with notions that have been mine, that I could even wish to bear some share in the adventure, to set some stake upon it. Give it thought, sir. Let us talk of it again.' There was about him an eagerness scarcely veiled. 'I could muster a ship or two and the means to equip them. Give it thought.'

'Again I thank you. But this is no matter for private enterprise.'

'Why not? Why should such benefits be for pinces only?'

'Because such undertakings need the authority of a crown behind them. The control of lands beyond the seas and of the riches they may yield demand the forces that only a monarch can supply. If it were not so I should not have wasted all these years in battering upon the doors of princes, suffering denial at the hands of numbskull doorkeepers.'

The Prior, out of sympathy with, indeed momentarily dismayed by, Pinzon's urgings and relieved to hear them thus repelled, bestirred himself to intervene. 'There I might assist you. Especially now that I know of the formidable weapon with which you are armed. I mean this Toscanelli chart. Humble as I am, I could perhaps command the ear of Queen Isabel. For the piety and goodness of Her Highness maintains in her a kindness for one who was once her confessor.'

'Ah!' said Colon, as if this were news to him.

Inscrutable he listened whilst Frey Juan pleaded now, echoing Pinzon's sentiments that it were shameful in any Spaniard to suffer so great a thing to be lost to Spain and go to the magnification of any other kingdom. Let Master Colon be patient yet a little while. Having waited years, let him now wait but some few weeks. Tomorrow, if Colon consented, Frey Juan would ride out to seek the Court, before Granada or wherever it might be, to use with Her Highness such influence as by her goodness he possessed, to the end that she might accord an audience to Colon, and hear his proposals from his own lips.

Frey Juan would be as speedy as lay in human power, and in the meantime at La Rabida Master Colon would be well cared for with his child.

The note of intercession deepened in the friar's voice as he proceeded. He became almost lachrymose in his fervent endeavour to break through the cold aloofness in which the tall adventurer stood mantled.

When he ceased at last, his plump hands joined as if in prayer, Colon fetched a sigh. 'You tempt me sorely, good father,' he said, and turned away. He paced to the window followed by two pairs of anxious eyes, the Prior's and the physician's. In the glance of the merchant Pinzon, who knew his world and the ways of bargainers, there was less anxiety than shrewd mistrust.

At the room's end Colon slowly turned. He tossed his red head, and, majesty incarnate in a shabby coat, he conferred the favour asked.

'Impossible to refuse what is so graciously offered. Be it as you wish, Sir Prior.'

The Prior bore down upon him, smiling his gratitude. Behind him Martin Alonso laughed outright. Frey Juan supposed it an expression of pure joy, as well it may have been, for there is joy in seeing fulfilled the predictions of our judgment.

4

 THE NEGLECTED
SUITOR

The Prior of La Rabida pro-
cured himself a mule, and set out upon the following morning
for the Vega of Granada, where the Sovereigns had sat down
to invest the last Saracen stronghold.

The high confidence in which he went was not misplaced.
Queen Isabel received her ghostly father with all the gracious-
ness and piety due from a ghostly daughter. She listened to
his tale, and being infected with something of his enthusiasm,
yielded to his prayer, summoned her treasurer and bade him
count out twenty thousand maravedis for the equipment and
travelling expenses of Colon. Thus she dismissed the triumphant Franciscan to bring the man to audience.

Here was a promptitude beyond all the friar's hopes. He
made haste back to La Rabida with his news.

'The Queen, our wise and virtuous lady, has given heed to
the prayer of this poor friar. Do yourself justice now, and the
world is yours.'

Colon, incredulous at the swift and easy success attending
the gamester's throw upon which he had come to La Rabida,

lost no time in setting out. His son was to remain in the convent's care until he could take order about him.

At the moment of departure he was sought again by Martin Alonso Pinzon, who put forth an extreme geniality.

'I come to wish you fortune and to felicitate you upon this ready grant of audience. I swear you could have had no better ambassador.'

'I am as sensible of it as I am of this your courtesy.'

'It is no mere courtesy. After all, I have had my part in this success.' Answering the question in Colon's glance, he went on: 'Do me right, sir. It was my support of your views that sent Frey Juan to plead with the Queen.'

It was as if he urged a claim, a pettiness by which Colon was none too favourably impressed. But he dissembled his faint scorn.

'You leave me in your debt, sir.'

Martin Alonso laughed with a display of strong teeth behind the red lips within his black beard. 'It's a debt, faith, you may find it profitable to discharge. Bear in mind, sir, that I am ready to support your project. I love a hazard, and I would set a stake on this. I can command ships, as I have told you.'

'You enhearten me.' Colon was a model of cold courtesy. 'But, as I thought that I made clear, the enterprise is too vast. for private purses, else it had not been so long delayed.'

'Yet you may come to find that a private purse might bear some share in it. Why should it not, even though the Crown should offer the main support?'

'To me it seems that if I am supported by the Crown, the Crown will bear the cost.'

'But perhaps not all of it.' Martin Alonso was becoming importunate. He smiled, but there was a keenness almost of anxiety in his eyes. 'The royal treasury is under sore strain in

these days. The war has made a heavy drain upon it. The
Sovereigns may favour you, and yet hesitate on the score of
the expense. A little help might then be welcome. All I ask
is that you remember me should that be so, or,' he added
slyly, 'if you saw the chance to make it so. After all, as I have
said, it would be no more than my due, for my part in sending
Frey Juan to court.'

'I will remember,' said Colon.

But as he rode away it was in the determination to forget.
He wanted no partners, least of all an acquisitive merchant
who for the paltry purse that he might bring to it would not
merely claim a share of the profit but strive also to filch some
of the glory.

Accounting his trials now behind him, his shabbiness
sloughed, and clad by the Queen's bounty in a manner to set
off his natural graces, he came without delay to court under
the aegis of Frey Juan Perez.

The Franciscan's words were in his memory: 'The Queen,
our wise and virtuous lady, has given heed to the prayer of
this poor friar. Do yourself justice now and the world is yours.'

It was an enheartening assurance, and for what depended
upon himself Colon entertained no doubt. He would do himself the fullest justice, as Frey Juan should see.

And so, when he was brought to audience in the Alcazar in
the white city of Cordoba, it was no cringing suppliant that
the Sovereigns beheld. Conscious that his russet doublet and
the open mulberry surcoat with its hanging sleeves became
him well, he bore himself with the swaggering confidence of
one who is master of his fate.

Had the result depended upon the Queen alone, it might
have followed quickly; for though a woman of much sense and
calm judgment, she was still a woman, and so could hardly
remain indifferent to the appeal of the dominant masculinity

of this tawny-haired man with the eager, magnetic, youthful eyes and that power Las Casas mentions of commanding affection. But King Ferdinand was there, hard and wary, the shrewdest prince in Europe and the most calculating. A man in the late thirties, squarely and strongly built, but of only middle height, he was of a rather lumpy fresh-coloured countenance, fair-haired and with light prominent eyes. Those eyes looked with little favour upon the natural majesty and princely carriage of the adventurer whom Frey Juan presented.

Their Highnesses received Colon in a gracious chamber of the Alcazar, lighted by twin-arched windows and hung in the stamped and subtly coloured leather for which the Moors of Cordoba were famous, its marble floor spread with rich Eastern rugs. Two ladies waited upon the Queen, standing behind her tall chair, the handsome young Marchioness of Moya and the Countess of Escalona. The King was attended by his Lord Chamberlain, Andres Cabrera, Marquis of Moya, of whom it was said that his goat's eyes justified his name; by Don Luis de Santangel, the grey-bearded and benign Chancellor of Aragon; and by Hernando de Talavera, Prior of the Prado, a tall ascetic friar in the white habit and black cloak of a Hieronymite.

All these, like most of those who filled the high offices about the Sovereigns, were New Christians, men of Jewish blood, who, having risen to eminence by the talents of their race, were sowing an envy that was beginning to express itself in that ferocity of persecution of which the Holy Office of the Inquisition was to be the agent.

Colon by his very name may have led them to regard him as one of themselves, and certainly, had he looked, he would have detected a sympathetic warmth in the eyes of Santangel and Cabrera. Talavera, however, remained coldly aloof, his

glance lowered. Uncompromisingly honest, as he conceived
honesty, he would adopt hostility rather than yield to feeble
prejudice on racial grounds.

At the outset Colon gave little heed to these satellites. His
eyes and attention were on the Queen, at whose elbow Frey
Juan Perez had come to take an unobtrusive stand. He beheld a light-complexioned woman of forty of the middle
height, her shape and countenance moderately plump, whose
blue eyes gave him kindly encouragement. A certain homeli-
ness was not to be dissembled even by the richness of her
ermine-lined cloak of crimson satin so profusely slashed as to
display in gleams the cloth of gold of the gown she wore beneath it. In the belt of white leather at her waist smouldered
the fire of a balas ruby of the size of a tennis ball.

She addressed him in gentle terms, and in her placid voice
he caught a hint of the authority that dwelt in her. She spoke
in commendation of the ideas by which the Prior of La Rabida
had told them that he was inspired, and she assured him that
it was her wish to know more of this service which he believed
that it lay in his power to render to the Crowns of Castile and
Aragon.

His head high, his voice resonant he was prompt to answer.
'I kiss Your Highness's feet, and thank you for the occasion
so graciously accorded me. I bring you the promise of discoveries before which those which have brought increase of
dignity and power to the Crown of Portugal will look small
and mean.'

'A high promise,' croaked the King, and Colon could not
be certain that he did not sneer. Not on that account, however, was he perturbed.

'High, indeed, sire. But no higher than by God's grace and
guidance I shall soar.'

'Say on. Say on,' said the King, and now the sneer was
plain. 'Let us hear you.'

Colon inclined that proud head of his, which His Highness accounted too stiffly held, and launched himself in terms that had been well rehearsed upon a recital of his cosmographical theories. But he had not gone far before Ferdinand's harsh voice and rapid speech broke in upon him.

'Yes, yes. All this we have heard already from the Prior of La Rabida. It is his clear statement of your beliefs that has prompted Her Highness to grant you audience at a time when, as you should know, our crusade against the Infidel in Spain is giving us abundant preoccupation.'

A lesser man, one more imbued with the respect of persons, would have been put out of countenance. Colon was merely spurred to a greater assurance.

'The wealth of the Indies which I trust to lay at the foot of your throne, the inexhaustible wells of it to which I shall open your royal way, will repair the ravages of that conflict and supply resources for its triumphant conclusion, or for its extension even to a deliverance of the Holy Sepulchre, itself.'

He could have said nothing better calculated to kindle enthusiasm in Queen Isabel and bring her under the spell of the magic that he used. But to the King it was almost a contradiction, a challenge. With a sceptical smile on his full lips he forestalled any answer from the Queen.

'Do not let us forget that you speak of things seen so far only with the eye of faith.'

'What, then, is faith, sire?' Colon permitted himself to ask, but by answering at once let it be seen that the question was no more than rhetorical. 'It is the power to recognize by the inner light of inspiration those things of which the evidence is not tangible.'

'This has more the sound of theology than cosmography.' Ferdinand looked over his shoulder at Talavera with a crooked smile. 'What do you say to that, Sir Prior? It lies rather in your province than in mine.'

The friar raised his bowed head. His voice was grave and cold.

'As a definition of faith I have no quarrel with it.'

'For myself,' said the Queen, 'whilst no theologian, I have never heard it defined better.'

'Yet,' Ferdinand objected, turning to her in all courtesy, 'in such a matter an ounce of experience is worth a pound of faith. And of actual experience admittedly there is none to support the claims of Master Colon.'

Instead of answering, herself, the Queen invited Colon to furnish the reply.

'You hear His Highness.'

Colon lowered his eyes; his tone was almost wistful. 'I can but ask what is experience, and answer that it is no more than the foundation upon which those have ever built who have been endowed with the divine gift of imagination.'

'That is obscure enough to be profound,' said Ferdinand, 'but it takes us nowhere.'

'By your leave, Highness, at least it points the way. By applying the gift of imagination, by imagining the unknown from the known — the experienced — has man risen by stages upwards from a primeval brutish ignorance.'

His Highness began to show irritation. This man was more subtle and elusive than was proper in disputing with a prince. He made an impatient noise. 'We move here in the realm of the intangible, a realm of dreams.'

Colon threw up his head as if affronted. There was an almost fanatical glow in his clear eyes. 'Dreams!' he echoed. His voice soared and vibrated with power. 'All things are dreams before they become reality. The world itself was a dream before it was created, a dream in the mind of God.'

It was as if he had cast a burning brand amongst them. The King's jaw fell; Talavera's brow was dark; Frey Juan looked scared. In every other face, including the Queen's, Colon beheld only a flattering wonder, whilst from Santangel's full dark eyes he caught a look of warm, amused approval.

The King spoke, slowly for once. 'I trust, sir, that you are not floundering into heresy in the heat of argument.' And again his glance invited Talavera to pronounce.

The Prior of the Prado shook his head, his lean face forbidding.

'I do not discover heresy. No. And yet' — he directly addressed Colon — 'you go perilously deep, sir.'

'It is my way, Sir Prior.'

'Undaunted by the peril?' the friar sternly challenged him.

Colon rejoiced that it was the priest who had asked the question, for in answering the priest he could put his scorn into laughter, as he would not dare in answering the King. 'If I were easily daunted, reverend sir,' he laughed, 'I should not be offering to sail into the unknown and defy the terrors with which superstition fills it.'

His Highness deemed it time to set a term to the audience.

'It is not your audacity, sir, that is in doubt,' he said, and the calm comment had the ring of a reproof. 'If that were all we might be ready to employ you. As it is . . . it happens that I am by nature slow to take a man's own valuation of the wares he offers.'

'It is not in my mind that we should do that,' said the Queen. 'But neither will we reject the project because of our incompetence to judge it. Master Colon, His Highness and I will take counsel and consider the appointing of a junta of learned men to examine your claims, and to advise us upon them.'

Remembering how he had fared in Portugal at the hands of a junta stuffed with learning and frozen in the ignorance of its limitations, Colon's heart would have turned heavy had not the Queen added:

'I shall look to see you soon again, Master Colon. Meanwhile you will remain at court. My treasurer, Don Alonso de Quintanilla, shall have orders to provide.'

On that promise he had taken his dismissal, and if he departed in a confidence less high than that in which he had come, yet at least he could bear with him the assurance that he had left a favourable impression on the Queen.

Of his favourable impression upon the others he was soon to be assured. First there was Quintanilla, in whose house, by the Queen's disposition, he was lodged, and by whom he was more than cordially welcomed. There was more than his attractiveness to conquer the favour of Quintanilla. The finances of the two kingdoms were depleted to exhaustion by the Moorish war, and the Treasurer of Castile was sorely harassed in his need to provide supplies. By sharpening the persecution of the Jews to the extent of giving the Holy Office a freer hand in the pursuit of the wretched converts who relapsed into Judaism and suffered consequently, with the loss of their lives, the confiscation of their property, the ship of state was being kept precariously afloat. To buoy it up further there were the heavy loans made by such great Jews as Abarbanel and Senior, who sought desperately to deflect the greater persecution which their prescience told them that greed might presently let loose — a persecution not to be confined to relapsing Marranos, who by becoming Christians had brought themselves within the jurisdiction of the Holy Office, but to include in its remorseless sweep all the Children of Israel. If those succeeded who even now were pressing the Sovereigns to decree the expulsion of the Jews whilst compelling them to leave all property behind, the wealth thus harvested might resolve all difficulties. But in the meantime the difficulties remained to harass the Treasurer of Castile. Therefore was he the more eager for first-hand news of this man who proposed to unlock for Spain the vast treasury of the East, and, because of his hopes, the readier to lend him credit and support.

Then there was the Chancellor of Aragon, Luis de Santangel, whose countenance had shown how deeply he was moved by Colon's bearing at the royal audience. At heart he too was moved by considerations similar to those of Quintanilla. Beholding in Colon a potential saviour of Israel in Spain, he was as ready to believe him the instrument of God as Colon was ready to believe it of himself. For although Santangel had received Christian baptism and practised now the Christian faith, his heart remained with the people of his race. Indeed, so ill had he concealed it that once he had been made to feel the talons of the Holy Office of Saragossa, and compelled to do public penance in his shirt. Only the high value which the Sovereigns set upon his services and the great affection in which they held him had preserved him from worse.

Santangel sought Colon that very day at the house of Quintanilla, took both his hands in a long firm clasp, and looked deep into his eyes.

'I make haste,' he said, 'to proclaim myself your friend before your deeds shall have earned you so many that I shall be lost amongst them.'

'Which being translated, Don Luis, means that out of the goodness of your soul you desire to give me courage.'

'It means much more. It means that I foresee a great destiny for you, and that by you Spain is to be magnified.'

Colon smiled crookedly. 'I would the King had perceived it as clearly. Then he might have been less hostile.'

'That was not hostility. It was caution. The King is slow to reach decisions.'

'And I thought him quick to decide that I am a charlatan.'

Don Luis was shocked. 'Never believe that. His scepticism was to test your quality, and you rang true under the test. Those are the Queen's own words, my friend. So take heart in the assurance that your patience will not long be tried. You'll sup with me tonight, and you too, Don Alonso. Your good friend Frey Juan will be with us, breaking for once the rigours of Saint Francis. Tomorrow you are to wait upon the Marchioness of Moya. She desires your better acquaintance. When I tell you that she has more influence with the Queen than any person living, you'll see that you are civil to her. But, faith, there's little need to enjoin it. Her beauty will do that to one whom I judge to have an eye for beauty.'

The eye which Santangel so truly described was feasted to the full next day upon Beatriz de Bobadilla, Marchioness of Moya, when Don Luis conducted him to her mansion on the Ronda, overlooking the majestic Guadalquivir.

He went in the glory of russet doublet and mulberry surcoat, his red mane sedulously dressed, and in his clear mariner's eyes a glow of high confidence borrowed from the shape his fortunes were at last assuming. It was a glow that deepened when he contemplated her and met in her soft glances the approval in him of a shapeliness that matched her own.

Yesterday at the audience he had admiringly observed her. He had not been a man, or, at least, not the man he was, had he overlooked her. But yesterday there had been so much else to command his attention, whilst now there was nothing to deflect the delight his eye might take in her. A woman in the glory of her young maturity, she was fashioned on stately lines, tall and superbly made. Her black hair and the oval face beneath were framed in a pointed and stiffened silken coif that was edged with jewelwork. Her lips were moist and red, and there was a caressing languor in the regard of her dark eyes. Her high-waisted gown was of yellow silk with a broad hem of blue. Cut square and low, it revealed a glory of white throat.

Santangel, benign and fatherly, presented Colon.

'Marchioness, I beg our discoverer to kiss your hand.'

She chose to take the phrase literally, and held out to him the fairest hand he had ever seen; the texture of it to his finger-tips and lips was as the texture of satin. His lips dwelt in fervour upon it for longer than was quite seemly.

'Shall I prophesy for you?' she said, with a smile. 'It is that Spain will yet desire to be as free of your hand as you make free with mine.'

'A prophecy to intoxicate me, madam.'

'I do not judge you easily intoxicated?'

'Not easily. No. But when the wine is sweet and rich I take my chance of it.'

'With a full confidence in yourself. You do not lack for that, as we saw yesterday.'

'Yesterday, madam, I was but a navigator, rehearsing what his trade had taught him.'

'Oh!' Her fine brows arched upwards. 'And today?'

'Today the humblest suitor for your favour.'

'Yet I had not supposed you humble.'

'It was not my honour yesterday to be addressing you.'

Gently she rallied him. 'Fie, sir! That is to set me above the Queen.'

'Have mercy, madam. Do not provoke me into high treason.'

'That were, indeed, folly. For in the Queen you have made a sure friend, upon whose support you may rely.'

'It is more than I dared hope.'

'But why?' He felt the ardour of her glance upon him. 'The Queen is a woman, after all, and loves audacity in a man. Like the King, she discerned no lack of it in you.'

'To support me she had need to discern something more: that I can fulfil no less than I promise.'

'If you doubt it, you do poor justice to your arts of persuasion. Does he not, Don Luis?'

'If he doubts it,' said Don Luis so dryly that he set them laughing.

'You need not,' she assured Colon, 'nor need you doubt that I shall fail to keep you in the Queen's mind.'

'For that it is not only I who will have cause to thank you,' said he, with a full recovery of his normal swagger. 'Queen Isabel, herself, and all Spain will be in your debt.'

'Now,' she laughed, 'I hear the voice of the man of yesterday, the high note that brings us all into submission. For the rest, Master Colon, it is not with the debt to me of Spain that I shall be concerned.'

Thus for a full hour they talked with more covert fencing in their words than Don Luis approved. When he had kissed her hand in leave-taking:

'Count us your friends,' she bade him, 'and dispose of our house as if it were your own.'

Outside in the spring sunshine, on the Ronda, Santangel took him by the arm. He used a gentle, friendly tone.

'As a foreigner, Master Colon, you may be in danger of mistaking words which we Spaniards utter in merely formal courtesy, and which could be acted upon only to our dismay.'

Colon laughed. 'You mean that Spanish courtesy offers everything, counting upon a like courtesy to accept nothing.'

'Since you understand it so well, you will not overvalue the Marchioness's words.'

'Nor undervalue her gracious kindness.'

'I am by no means sure that it would not be more prudent.' He hugged the arm closer. 'Doña Beatriz de Bobadilla is the Queen's dearest friend, of great influence with her and an intimacy to which none other is admitted. Yet there's a prudishness in Queen Isabel that would not condone light conduct even in her dearest friend. That is something to be remembered. The other thing is Cabrera.' Santangel hesitated a moment, with a sidelong glance at his companion. Quickly and softly he added, 'He is one of ours.'

Colon was mystified. 'One of ours?'

'A New Christian,' Don Luis explained. 'Marquis of Moya and a power in the land as you behold him, he is yet the son of Rabbi David of Cuenca.'

Light came to Colon. It revealed, first, that he was assumed by Santangel to be a Marrano; second, that because of this the wife of a Marrano must be sacred to him. Now, despite his hispanicized name, and something in his cast of countenance to justify the assumption, a Marrano Colon was not. Yet perceiving that to deny it might jeopardize the goodwill towards him of a man whose esteem he valued and upon whose support he counted, opportunism prompted him to be disingenuously non-committal.

'I see,' was all he said.

'You'll forgive what would be a liberty if it were not rooted in regard for you.'

'I were a clown if I did not thank you.' Then Colon laughed. 'Oh, but be easy, sir. Cristobal Colon is not the man to let passion touch his destiny. My mission is too great to yield to human weakness.'

'Your mission may be. But are you?' wondered the Chancellor. 'Move circumspectly here, my friend, if you would prosper.'

Days of great consequence had followed for Colon, days of confident waiting, in which he took the eyes of the courtly throng in the antechambers of the Alcazar, and was proudly conscious that he took it. He had travelled far from the humble little house in the Vico Dritto di Ponticello in Genoa, where he was born, but no farther, he opined, than his deserts gave him the right. From this conviction came a poise to match his inches and his patrician countenance. Men nudged one another as he passed, and ever and anon, he would catch an awed whisper of his name. Haughty grandes, hidalgos who accounted themselves fashioned of different fibre from those that made up the members of the common herd, princes of the Church, great captains and men of state sought his acquaintance and used him with deference. For him more than one lovely lady cast aside Castilian reticence and allowed languid eyes to express a yearning admiration. He was enhanced by a certain mystery that attached to him. Shrewdly aware of its value, he did nothing to dissipate it. None could speak with certainty of his origin. By some he was accounted a Portuguese, by others a Ligurian noble. Some related that he was of a learning that was the pride of the University of Pavia, where it was said that he had studied; by others it was asserted that he was a great fighting seaman who had made himself the terror of Islam in the Mediterranean; others, again, explained that, boldest of navigators, he had sailed his ships into seas no other keels had ploughed. In one particular only were all agreed: his looks, his princely bearing, made human by a touch of swagger, his easy address and graceful speech, coloured by a foreign accent which yet did not impair its fluency, all went to convey an impression of his high birth and consequence.

These days, in which he loftily rubbed shoulders with the great, were probably the happiest he had ever known, warming him with that sense that at last he filled in life the place that became him. He knew no impatiences then, for, as has been said, whilst one may travel pleasantly there is little haste to arrive. Unfortunately this pleasant travelling did not last.

Imperceptibly the aura that had been set aglow about him
began to grow dim with the passage of weeks in which nothing
happened. The Queen's intimate, the Marchioness of Moya,
might still address him in public with an eagerness in her dark
eyes which she did not trouble to conceal. Cabrera, following
his wife's lead, might miss no chance of marking his regard,
and the dignified Santangel, by many accounted the most influential man in the two kingdoms, might use him publicly
with an almost paternal affection. Upon the court in general
he began to perceive that he grew stale, and this led him to
invoke the assistance of the Marchioness, to the end that she
might exert the omnipotence at court derived from the great
love the Queen was known to bear her.

With this intent, he sought her one day at her palace on the
Ronda, to be received with gentle reproaches for having made
himself so long expected there.

'It is, madam, that I lacked the presumption to suspect it.'

'It is for a discoverer to make discoveries,' she told him, and
so opened a door to the suit he came to make.

'I am, alas, a discoverer in danger of lying becalmed, forgotten.'

'Not by me, at least, my friend. If it depended upon me or
my reminders to the Queen, you would have a fleet of ships by
now. I have even been rebuked for my insistence.'

He displayed contrition. 'Madam! That I should be the
cause of that!'

'I have no quarrel with the cause,' she assured him with
such warmth that Santangel's warning and his own vaunt
were alike forgotten.

'I shall study to deserve this favour. You shame me that I
should come to importune you with my affairs.'

'Your shame should be that they supply the only reason for
your visit!'

'It would be so if I were not glad that to make my prayer provide the occasion.'

'Prayer? Lord, sir, I am no saint to be prayed to.'

'Am I to believe that when I have but the evidence of my eyes?'

'And what do they show you?' She was challenging.

'More loveliness than seems mortal, or than they can calmly endure.' He took her hand again, and for a moment she let it lie in his grasp. Her eyes were troubled. In their dark depths there was an appeal he could not read, and something of fear, aroused by his too impetuous ardour. They were as the eyes of one who about to leap, pauses appalled by the width of the chasm.

Her voice came to him in a soft murmur. 'Señor Cristobal, do not let us glide into a folly we should both repent. Your hopes of the Queen's favour . . .'

'Must yield at need,' he interrupted hotly, 'to more imperious hopes.'

'Those are not for us, Cristobal. Let us be wise in time, my friend.'

Yet the low, caressing tone was not calculated to restrain him.

'Wise! What, then, is wisdom?' he cried, and would passionately have answered his own question, but that she forestalled him.

'It is not to jeopardize the good we may possess for an illusion of something better that is unattainable.' It was as a prayer to him to help her to be strong. 'There are some things that I can give,' she continued, 'and those I give without stint. Be content. To seek more would be to lose all. For both of us.'

He sighed, mastering himself, and bowed his red head. 'It must ever be as you command.' He released her hand. 'I am not to trouble you, but to serve you.'

The tenderness of her glance was deepened by the humility of that obedient surrender. And then their sanity was completely restored to them by the entrance of Cabrera.

He advanced, a short, ungainly figure on his crooked legs, a friendly smile in his goat's eyes, and he used Colon with a warm consideration. He was still pleasant when Colon had left.

'Decidedly I must do what I can to promote the wishes of our navigator,' said he. 'He knows how to engage my interest.'

'I am glad to hear it.'

'And surely not surprised. You'll not find it odd that I should do my best to help him aboard a ship and have him sailing to the Indies or to perdition.'

'Lord, Andres! Will you be jealous?'

'I will not,' laughed Cabrera. 'It's to save myself that detestable emotion that I'll labour to have our gentleman weigh anchor at the earliest.'

She laughed without embarrassment. 'I shall do nothing to discourage you. He wishes himself at sea, and since I wish him well, must I not also wish him at sea? We'll labour to that end.'

She was so ingenuously frank and so lovely that Cabrera was content to be amused. Yet there was a sincerity under his jesting answer. 'He'll not wish himself at sea more fervently than I do. There is too much of him.'

It followed out of this that two or three days later, meeting Colon in one of the galleries of the Alcazar, Santangel was the bearer of reassuring news.

'There are more friends working for you than you may suppose. Here is Cabrera gone near to embroiling himself with the King by pestering him on your behalf. You see, he added, 'the wisdom of my advice that you be circumspect with the delectable Marchioness. It bears fruit in Cabrera's friendly interest in you.'

'And makes him anxious to be rid of me,' said Colon, sardonic. 'But if the fruit is to exasperate His Highness, how shall that profit me?'

'There is some profit for you with the Queen at least. Cabrera pleaded with them both, and Her Highness this morning bids me assure you that your affairs will soon be in train. If they have been so long delayed it is because of preoccupations with this war, to which are now added troubles with the King of France.'

'The Devil take the King of France, then.'

'That is not all.' The Chancellor's face grew set in lines of sternness. 'Torquemada is clamouring for a bill of expulsion against the Jews.'

'May Satan toast him over his own faggots.'

Santangel shrank in horror. 'Sh! In God's name! Men have gone to the fire for less. Here passion will not serve. Patience. Patience is the only armour.'

'I am empanoplied in it cap-à-pie. It begins to irk my bones.'

It was to irk them further yet. The Sovereigns quitted Cordoba to return to the camp in the Vega of Granada. The court followed, and Colon went with the court. He went with it to Seville, and thence in the winter to Salamanca, where at least he made a new and powerful friend in the learned Dominican Frey Diego Deza, the Prior of Saint Esteban, who was the preceptor of the young Prince Juan. Deza's keen approving interest in Colon's project revived for a season his drooping hopes. Deza added his weighty urgings to those with which Colon's other few friends kept the matter before the Sovereigns. And something might now have come of it, but that a rebellion in Galicia demanded quelling and distracted thought from all other matters.

Plunged back into despair by this fresh postponement, Colon swore that because he was divinely inspired all the legions of hell were in arms against him.

And now, a year and more after that exultant journey from Palos at the Queen's command, he was back in Cordoba, still waiting, still following the court, but fallen into such neglect that the Queen had forgotten to offer him his old lodging and he had been too proud to seek it unbidden. Thus, on Santangel's recommendation, he had hired himself a room over the shop of Bensabat, the tailor, in the Calle Atayud, narrowest and most crooked of streets in that city of narrow crooked streets.

The royal mind, engrossed in warlike preparations for the final conquest of Granada, could spare no thought for the schemes and dreams of navigators, whence it had followed that, cooling his heels about the royal antechambers, this man once regarded as a portent was now become an object of derision. His notion of reaching the Indies by the west which once had inspired awe was now so much a subject for mockery that six months ago already a witling had expressed it in a quatrain:

> Colon declares he finds it best
> To reach the east by going west.
> I nothing doubt he's found as well
> The road to heaven lies through hell.

The silly lampoon had enjoyed a vogue in a court which welcomed weapons of ridicule. It had reached the ears of the lordly Messer Federigo Mocenigo, Venetian Ambassador to the Sovereigns of Castile and Aragon, and thence it had followed that whilst Colon gloomed about the Court of Spain neglected and forgotten, he came to excite a deal of anxious thought in other unsuspected quarters.

In distant Venice a pattern of sinister design was being woven into the warp of his destiny.

 THE DOGE

VENICE at the zenith of her might and wealth, with Cyprus lately added to her wide possessions, holding the gateway, and therefore a monopoly of the commerce, between east and west, was ruled at this time by Agostino Barbarigo, a doge who under an elegant, gay, almost flippant exterior, masked a shrewdness seldom equalled by any holder of his office and a hard patriotism that would count no sacrifice — at least no sacrifice of others — too great to ensure that the Most Serene Republic should lose no fraction of her enviable power. With this aim he enjoined great diligence of observation and report in the agents he maintained at every court of Europe.

From Spain Messer Mocenigo sent news that brought him some disquiet, presenting him with the recurrence of a problem which once already he had solved. It was in his thoughts, although as yet he gave it no expression, as he sat with his brother-in-law Silvestro Sarasin, who was the senior of the dread Council of Three, the Inquisitors of State.

They occupied the gilded room of the ducal palace which

Barbarigo made peculiarly his own, and which he had hired
Carpaccio to embellish for him with subjects calculated to
please his fastidious, sensuous eyes.

It was the contemplation of the latest acquisition from that
magic brush, a bathing Dian, that struck from Sarasin a spark
of the humour that was characteristic of him. He was a fellow of gross shape, short and corpulent, yellow as a Turk, with
a double chin that was like the dewlap of an ox.

'If your allegorical bride were more of this fashion I could
find it in my heart to envy you the dogeship. Madam Leda,
I suppose.' He sighed. 'One understands that a god should
condescend to be a swan.'

'Not Leda. No. Diana. In lusting after her you risk the
fate of Actaeon, if not at her hands at least at those of my
sister.'

Sarasin was scornful. 'You overrate the family authority.
Virginia is a prudent wife to me. She has no sight for things
which it might trouble her to see.'

'Poor soul! You doom her, then, to perpetual blindness.'

'Devil take Your Serenity,' said Sarasin, but without resentment, 'and your opinion of me.'

They were men of an age, in the early fifties; but whilst
Sarasin's corpulence betrayed every year of it, the Doge,
light-haired, tall and slimly elegant in a houppelande of sky-
blue satin, still conveyed an illusion of youth. He had risen,
and stood with his thumbs hooked into the golden cord that
girdled him, his fair, narrow face sardonically smiling.

'What opinion do your lewd ways encourage? They tell me
that you are not above being seen at this new theatre Ruzzante has set up on Santi Giovanni e Paolo. Is that becoming
in an Inquisitor of State?'

Sarasin's prominent blue eyes goggled at his brother-in-law.

'They tell you? Who are they? Your spies, I suppose.

None else would recognize me. I may not be above going there, but I am above being seen there. I go cloaked and masked. And I'm not to be reproved for it; for I count it within the functions of my office.'

The claim was reasonable enough. This theatre which Angelo Ruzzante had opened, and which was attracting crowds of pleasure-seekers, was in the nature of an innovation. It was known as the Hall of the Horse — la Sala del Cavallo — presumably because situated in the little square where Colleoni rode in Verrocchio's lately unveiled equestrian statue, a bronze colossus of terrifying beauty.

'You can be diligent, I know, when duty jumps with inclination,' the Doge mocked him. 'What do you find there?'

'Nothing for official disapproval. They mime and play some comedies no more lascivious than I have seen performed at the Patriarch's Palace. There is a funambulist who terrifies you by his antics on a rope, an Eastern juggler, a fire-eater, and a girl like a houri in a Muslim's dream of Paradise.'

'My poor deluded sister! And what does she do, this houri out of Paradise?'

'She dances an outlandish Saracen dance, a saraband, to the accompaniment of queer clacking things like chestnuts, appropriately called castanets. Moorish, as the dance, I believe they are. Also she sings to the guitar, like a nightingale, alluring as one of the sirens that troubled Ulysses.'

Barbarigo laughed. 'A houri, a nightingale, a siren! Whence is this prodigy?'

'From Spain, they tell me. Her songs are Spanish: Andalusian, with odd cadences that quicken a man's blood.'

The Doge's flippancy vanished. 'From Spain? Ha! It happens to be of Spain I had to talk to you.' He sauntered, straight and elegant, to the window and back, drew a chair to the side of his walnut writing-table, adorned with heads of imps and cherubs that were gems of wood-carving, and paused. 'I have news from Spain that I find disquieting.'

Sarasin sat up. 'Concerned with Naples?'

'No, no. There's nothing there to give us thought. This is a menace vague as yet, but the more dangerous because impalpable, a thing with which, if it were to come, there would be no grappling. It arose once before; two years ago, in Portugal. I was able then to stifle it. It was not easy and it was costly. This time it may prove impossible.'

'A menace, do you say?'

Barbarigo sat down, and crossed his shapely legs, which seemed to have been kneaded into their dark blue creaseless hose from which the skirts of the houppelande had fallen away. He leaned forward, an elbow on his knee.

'There is adrift in the world a rascal Ligurian adventurer — and God knows no good ever came out of Liguria — who claims to hold the key to a sea route to the Indies by the west.'

Sarasin displayed contemptuous relief. 'A madman.' He sat back again, breathing scorn. 'A fable.'

But Barbarigo added, slowly so as to be the more impressive, 'That key was supplied to him by Toscanelli of Florence.'

'Toscanelli!' The inquisitor was startled. 'Bah! Did Toscanelli die a dotard, then?'

'Oh, no. There has been no subtler mathematician in the world. In this matter he took for his starting-point the discoveries of our own Marco Polo, and thence, by application of his mathematical knowledge and skill, he drew up a chart. This supported by a letter setting forth the arguments he sent to our Ligurian — a rogue name Colombo, Cristoforo Colombo, then in Portugal.'

'How do you know this? And why should Toscanelli deal with rogues?'

'This Colombo is a sometime navigator who was living

then by making charts, a matter in which I understand that
he is highly skilled. My information is that he had dreamed
of such a thing's being possible and had applied to Toscanelli
for an opinion. It was a dream that happened to coincide
with certain conclusions Toscanelli had drawn from his re-
searches. The Florentine supplied the opinion and a chart
with the rash enthusiasm and vanity of a man of science who
can perceive only the beauty of his own discoveries, recking
nothing of the mischief they may work in practice.

'With that chart Colombo sought King John in Portugal.
The name and authority of Toscanelli won him attention
where otherwise he could never have been suffered to cross
the royal threshold. King John, a patron of discoverers, since
he has grown rich by them, sent him before a commission of
men whose competence he trusted. Fortunately, like all
commissions, this one proceeded leisurely; and so my agents,
who had informed me of all this, were able to go to work as I
commanded. We bought two of the commissioners. The
third, a Jew, we were unable to corrupt. Maybe this Colombo
is, himself, a Jew. I do not know. Anyway, his only supporter
was outvoted, and the chart and letter were consigned to the
dust and neglect of things forgotten.

'But lately from Spain comes word to me that this adventurer, having hispanicized his name and calling himself
Colon, is at work again, this time at the Court of the Spanish
Sovereigns. So far he has made little progress because the
Moorish war absorbs attention. But once Granada falls the
rogue may have a hearing. There are strong influences at
work for him, and Spain may well covet some of the power
and wealth that discovery has brought to Portugal.'

There the Doge ceased, leaving Sarasin puzzled by the
earnestness he had used. 'But what then?' he asked. 'What
is it to us that Spain should profit in that way?'

'You have not understood, or else you have forgotten that
I began by saying that this discovery is of a sea-route to the
Indies by the west. If that were realized what would become
of our Venetian opulence, built up and maintained by the
monopoly of the Eastern trade which passes through our
marts?'

At last Sarasin understood. 'God save us!' He sat up,
pulling at his fat nether lip.

Barbarigo uncrossed his legs, and rose. 'You perceive the
problem. What is the solution? Bribes may not suffice this
time. Queen Isabel is shrewd, and Ferdinand grasping. They
may judge the matter for themselves, or appoint men I cannot reach.'

Sarasin's eyes narrowed. 'The solution is simple. Men are
mortal, God be thanked. You can reach this man Colombo.'
His tone left little doubt of his meaning. 'Expediency justifies
these things.'

But the Doge shook his fair head. 'It is not so simple. If it
were I should not be exercised. The man is nothing. It is the
chart and the letter that matter. Unless we possess those they
remain the real menace whether in the hands of Colombo or
another. Until we possess them Venice will never be secure
from it. In Portugal I first tried the direct method. But my
agents blundered. Colombo was set upon one night in Lisbon.
He's a stout man of his hands, and whilst he was defending
himself others came to his assistance. Forewarned by that, he
deposited the documents in the chancellery. There I supposed
them to lie buried after the commission had rejected his proposal. Somehow he has regained possession of them. But we
can be certain that he'll not again expose himself to being
robbed of them by violence.'

Sarasin considered. 'It's a matter for the Grand Council,'
he opined at last.

'If I am powerless, so is the Grand Council; so are the Ten.'

'Why so? The Republic might buy him. He will have his price.'

'That, too, has been tried. He mocked the man who tried it. "Where is the gold that can compass it?" he asked. "If you held an empire in your grasp would you accept less than an empire in exchange?" Thus the needy rascal in his confident insolence.'

Sarasin's fertility of mind was not yet exhausted. 'Then outbid Spain for him. Hire him to make the voyage for Venice.'

'How should that profit us? Once he had opened the trail, all the world might follow it.'

'Would there not be compensation in the lands he might discover, in this empire of which he talks?'

'I could not trust to that. What we hold is certain, and it's a substance we'll not relinquish for a shadow.'

'Why, then, I am baffled.'

'As I am at the moment. But a way there must be to thwart this down-at-heel, or else my next espousal of the sea will be a mockery. Give thought to it, as I am doing. And meanwhile ... Chut!' He set a long forefinger to his lips. 'No word of this to any man.'

6

THE novel theatre set up by Ruzzante in the Sala del Cavallo was prospering. Increasing patrician patronage was elbowing out the vulgar throngs that at first had flocked to it, and daily its benches were being occupied more and more by all that was best and noblest in Venice.

Among its most assiduous patrons was that very splendid, carnal gentleman Don Ramon de Aguilar, Count of Arias, envoy of Castile and Aragon to the Most Serene Republic. Careless of opinions, in a Castilian pride which included Venetians in the contempt of all who were not Spanish, he went there openly and, unlike Sarasin, unmasked, making no secret of the fact that La Gitanilla was the magnet that drew him thither. Once her interlude had been performed he would depart, indifferent even to Ruzzante's funambulist who drew such exquisite shudders from the crowd. The very charitable may have opined that he was drawn by the songs of his native land, those languorous Andalusian laments, rather than by the singer. But if all the truth is to be told, Don

Ramon had no ear for music. Of beauty he knew only that which his eyes could appraise, and to those dark, hot eyes of his a feast was spread by La Gitanilla's incomparable sinuous grace.

It was natural that he should wish to reward the delight she gave a fellow-countryman, and so he would send her flowers procured from the mainland, boxes of exotic comfits and even a trinket or two. Imposing himself by virtue of his rank and office upon Ruzzante, he was supplied occasion to visit her behind the scenes, but only to find her here as circumspect and formal as upon the stage she could be reckless and abandoned.

It was at an early interview that, misconceiving her reticences and anxious to set her at her ease, he protested: 'Child, you are not to stand in awe of me.'

'Why should I?' she had coolly answered him. 'You are a great hidalgo, a great lord, to be sure. But you are not God, and I go in awe of none other.'

It would have been disconcerting to one who was by no means persuaded that he was without attributes of divinity, had he not been reassured by the reflexion that this was a mere trick of the trade of a minx who knew how to spur desire. So the poor man parried the artful stroke with a laugh.

'I would I were as sure that you are not a goddess.'

But her persistent insensibility began to irritate a vanity swollen by too many easy conquests.

She continued to receive his visits in her dressing-room because, as Ruzzante informed her, it would be perilous to deny so great a gentleman. But not all his arts, nor the splendour and still youthful beauty of his person, could pierce the wall she raised about her.

Don Ramon grew impatient. Coyness was to be suffered and humoured to a point; but beyond that point it became tiresome. He was considering peremptory ways of ending it when, one morning, as he was putting the last touches to a careful toilet, his personal body-servant, a young Moor still named Yakoub although he had been baptized, brought him word that a lady calling herself La Gitanilla was begging to be received by his excellency.

There was a twitch of his excellency's vilely loose mouth, deplorable feature of an otherwise darkly handsome, narrow face. Then with a slow, sly smile at his image in the mirror, he went to greet his unexpected visitor.

She awaited him in the long room of the mezzanine, whose balcony overlooked the Canal Grande, agleam in the sunshine of that February morning. She advanced to meet his splendour — he was all in sulphur yellow — eagerness breaking through the veil of her timidity.

'It is kind of your excellency to receive me.'

'Kind?' He was deprecatory. 'Adorable Beatriz, have you ever found me other?'

'That is what emboldens me.'

'It asks little boldness to perform what is welcomed. Will you not put off your cloak?'

Obediently she doffed the brown hooded mantle that shrouded her from head to heel, and stood forth in a sheathing gown of a lighter brown that revealed her supple grace. Her more than moderate height was increased in appearance by the high waist from which was hung the long tongue of a scarlet, gold-edged girdle. Her head was bare save for the net of fine gold thread that confined the coils of her lustrous chestnut hair.

Don Ramon contemplated her with discriminating eyes. He considered the fine texture of her skin on face and throat, of a warm ivory pallor, flushed now on the cheekbones by a quickened stirring of her blood. He pondered the lissom shape and the swell of her breast that was heaving gently under the stress of an emotion which he found flattering. Above all he admired the easy proud grace of her carriage and the splendid poise with which the dancer's art had endowed her perfect body. This was no common slut of the trestles, no gipsy wench such as her theatre-name implied. There must be, he thought, good Castilian blood in the veins that looked so delicately blue against the whiteness of her throat. How else should she come by that air of pride, that placid self-command, that almost patrician dignity? Here, indeed, was a woman worthy of his fastidious discernment.

Clear hazel eyes regarded him steadily from under thin dark brows.

'I come to you as a suppliant,' she told him. Her voice was low and veiled by a seductive huskiness.

'Not here,' he answered gallantly. 'Never here. Here you may command.'

Her glance fell away from the glow of his eyes. 'It is to the envoy of the Spanish Sovereigns that I make my prayer.'

'Then I thank God that I am the Spanish envoy. Will you not sit?'

He led her by the hand to a divan that faced the windows. With studied artificial deference he remained standing, his own shoulders to the light.

Some of her calm was being lost in anxiety. 'It is a matter of your excellency's office. It concerns a Spaniard, a subject of our Sovereigns in fact, my brother.'

'You have a brother? Here in Venice? Well, well; tell me the case.'

She told it as smoothly as her anxiety permitted. A week ago, at Gennaro's tavern in the Merceria there had been a brawl in which daggers had been drawn, and a gentleman of the House of Morosini had been stabbed. In the confusion, as they were carrying him out, her brother who was present had picked up a poniard from the floor. It was a rich weapon, with jewels in the hilt, and her brother — she faltered here in shame — had been tempted to keep it. Two days ago he had sold it to a Hebrew goldsmith near San Moisè. It had been recognized as Morosini's, and as a consequence last night her brother had been arrested.

Don Ramon looked grave. 'In so clear a case I do not see what we can do. Your unfortunate brother, standing convicted of theft, is beyond an ambassador's protection.'

The flush vanished from her face. In its pallor her eyes became deep pools of fear. 'It . . . it is hardly a theft,' she pleaded weakly. 'He found the dagger on the ground.'

'But he sold it. A madness. Does he not know the severity of the Republic's laws?'

'How should he, being a Castilian?'

'But theft is theft, in Venice or Castile. Was he in need that he should have run this dreadful risk?'

'Scarcely that, since I have worked for both of us.' There was a hint of bitterness in the reply. 'But perhaps I stinted him. He has been softly bred, and he craved more than I was able to supply from my poor earnings.'

'You move me deeply,' Don Ramon commiserated, and then asked, 'What was it brought you to Italy?'

To hold his sympathy, since she must cling to the hope that out of it he might yet be moved to help her, she used an utter frankness. She had left Spain at her brother's urgent pleadings. He was in trouble there. He had killed a man in Cordoba. Oh, but quite honourably, in a fair encounter. But the man was of a powerful family, and the Alcalde had been made active. His alguaziles were hunting her brother. So he must go. Because she loved him, knew him weak and shiftless, feared for him if he went alone, and also because

there was nothing in Spain to hold her, she had consented to
go with him. She counted upon such arts as she possessed to
earn a livelihood for both. They had landed at Genoa a year
ago, and thence through Milan, Pavia and Bergamo she had
sung and danced her way to Venice. 'And now,' she ended
her lamentable tale, 'unless your excellency can help us,
Pablo will . . .' She broke off with a little shiver of sheer
wretchedness.

He was as unmoved by the peril of a worthless brother who
in his view deserved the worst that might befall him, as he
was stirred by the spectacle of her distressed loveliness. 'A
way must be found. He must not be left to the mercies of the
Most Serene.'

Don Ramon sank, as he spoke, to the divan beside her, and
his fine jewelled hand came to rest lightly and soothingly
upon her shoulder. 'Officially I am without power to intervene. But personally it is another matter. After all, I have
some weight. Depend that every ounce of it shall be employed.'

'I bless you for the hope you give me.' Her breath had
quickened, the flush was creeping back into her cheeks.

'Oh, I give you more than hope. I give you certainty. It
will matter less — far less — to the Serene Republic to punish
an obscure offender than to gratify the envoy of Spain even
when he is unofficial. So shed no tears, child, from those
heavenly eyes. Your brother will be restored to you very
soon. My word on it. His name is Pablo, is it?'

'Pablo de Arana.' She swung to face him in a surge of
gratitude with a movement of intoxicating grace. She was
radiant with relief. 'May Our Lady recompense you.'

'Our Lady!' His excellency made a wry face. Then he
laughed. 'Must I wait then until I get to heaven? I am human, faith, and look for something in this world.'

He saw the radiance perish from her countenance as she turned away, and for a moment he observed her in frowning annoyance. Abruptly he took her by the chin and turned her face again so that he could look into her eyes. He saw the mingled fear and scorn that glared from them; he sensed the sudden iciness that enveloped her; and the poor man was at a loss to understand it.

'Why, my Gitanilla, what is this? Will you shrink from me who am ready to pawn my credit for you? May I die but I deserve better from you. Must you act the prude with me?'

'I am not acting,' she told him, a blaze of pride in her eyes. 'Your excellency overlooks that I may be a virtuous woman.'

Annoyance made him brutal. 'Virtue that exhibits itself in dancing! The poor pretence. Bah!' He released her chin, and rose. 'I do not press myself where I am not welcome.'

It was artful enough to cast her into fresh panic. 'My lord! My lord! Let yourself be noble in this, and God will repay the charity you do me.'

He looked down upon her with a sneer. 'Is Heaven, then, to pay your debts for you? In that case let Heaven save your brother from mutilation, or the galleys, or even death.'

She shuddered. 'This is to be pitiless,' she moaned.

'What pity do I owe you? What pity do you show me? Is it not pitiless to scorn the love that burns me? Do you guess nothing of the jealousy that torments me when others feast their eyes upon you in the dance? I would wrest you from all that, and wear you for my own. I shall be returning soon to Spain. I will take you back with me, to live under my protection. And for your brother ... I have said what I can do, and will.'

Virtuous as she claimed to be, yet she knew her world. Bitterly had she been schooled in its evil ways in the last two years or so, in which she had depended for a livelihood upon her art and her beauty. If on the one hand they had maintained her, on the other they had made her an object for the constant insult of foul and soiling gallantries. She had withstood them, and in withstanding them her nature had hardened, so that now, mistress of wit and guile with which to repel them, they left her indifferent. She had, in her own phrase, acquired arts that enabled her to walk undefiled through the world's filth. Yet here, given a clear choice between her brother's life and her own defilement, those arts could not avail her. She must stoop to baser ones if she were to save at once poor Pablo and herself. She must cheat this man with promises, to be repudiated when he had done his part. Scruples she stifled with the assurance that a vile fellow who could so seek to profit by a woman's distress and urgent need, deserved no better than vile treatment.

With averted head, so that he might not read the shame in her eyes, she gave him his answer. 'Save Pablo, my lord, and then . . .' She faltered into silence.

He came close. She had a sense that he hovered over her like a vulture over the moribund. His breath fanned her cheek. 'And then?'

Her senses revolted. 'Oh, can't you do it without bargaining?'

It was a shock to him who had thought her on the point of yielding. 'So cold!' he reproached her, with a touch of bitterness. 'So stony! Gitanilla! Gitanita! Are you, then, flesh; or are you granite?'

She drew away from him, her breast in tumult, dissembling her disgust.

'I am a woman in sore distress!' she cried, hoping yet to arouse his chivalry.

She took up her cloak. He strode to hold it for her, and in adjusting it to her shoulders, stooped to sear her white neck with his hot lips.

The shudder with which she tore herself from his light grip infuriated him. 'Do you hope to move me by cruelty to generosity?' he mocked her. 'Come to me again when you see the folly of that.'

She fled without answering, leaving him thoughtful. He was dissatisfied with his own conduct of the affair. Somewhere he had blundered. There had been a moment in which she had softened, and he had failed to take advantage of it. That she would come again he was persuaded. Meanwhile, he would prepare the way for her brother's deliverance, and confronting her with the certainty of it as a result of his endeavours profit by the gratitude it must earn him. She was clearly of those with whom a man would best serve his interests by a show of disinterestedness. And, anyway, it was worth a gamble.

7

 INQUISITORS OF STATE

Iᴛ ᴡᴀꜱ among the wise enact-
ments of the Most Serene Republic that her Doge should
hold no communications with any representative of a foreign
power. In this as in many other things, however, Agostino
Barbarigo was a law unto himself, and whilst officially, as
Doge, he dared not transcend the rule or receive any envoy at
the Ducal Palace, unofficially, as man and in his family resi-
dence, he permitted himself sub rosa relations with some of
them, amongst whom was Don Ramon de Aguilar. If he
violated the spirit whilst observing the letter of the law, he
accounted himself justified by the services he was thus permitted, from time to time, to render to the State.

Therefore it was not from the Ambassador's gilded barge
with its richly liveried watermen, but from a private gondola,
that Don Ramon alighted on the steps of the Barbarigo
Palace on the Canal Grande within an hour of his interview
with La Gitanilla.

Sarasin was again with his brother-in-law when the envoy
was ushered into a room of splendours to which the East had

richly contributed. Notwithstanding the inquisitor's presence, and after formal compliments, the Spaniard came straight to the matter.

'I am a suppliant. I seek a particular favour at Your Serenity's hands.'

His Serenity, spuriously juvenile in a scarlet tunic that fell in short pleats from the waist, with one leg scarlet and the other white, and a little scarlet gold-broidered cap on his fair locks, bowed gracefully. 'It is accorded, excellency, so that it lies within my power.'

'All things lie there. And this, after all, is but a little thing. There's a poor knave, a countryman of mine, who is in trouble with the law over the matter of a dagger. He found it, and accounted himself at liberty to sell it. That ranks as theft, of course; but on the score of his ignorance I hope Your Serenity will be lenient with the poor devil.'

Sarasin, asprawl in the room's best chair, put up his eyebrows, whilst the Doge stood frowning, fingering his shaven chin.

'We are not easy with thieves in Venice,' he demurred.

'Oh, I am aware of it. But this is scarcely a theft. The fellow did not steal — not deliberately steal — the dagger. He found it. If Your Serenity could find it possible to order that the offence be overlooked, I will undertake that no one suffers loss, and you will leave me profoundly in your debt.'

'Why, if you put it so . . .' The Doge waved a graceful hand. 'Though you leave me wondering what can be the interest of the Count of Arias in so poor a knave.'

Don Ramon not only deemed frankness best, but accounted it of a kind to have amusing weight with the jocund Barbarigo. 'My interest is not in him, but in his sister, the lovely Gitanilla. She has been to beg my intercession, an advocate to make a saint of a devil or a devil of a saint.'

'And which has she made of you?'

Don Ramon laughed. 'I am but flesh, and the flesh is weak. It is not in me to resist a lovely woman.'

'Given, I suppose,' mumbled Sarasin, 'that it is not in her to resist your excellency.'

'I am not so ungallant as to neglect opportunity. Do you blame me, sir?'

'Not I. Not I.' Shivers of mirth agitated Sarasin's corpulence. 'Having seen La Gitanilla, I'd release all the thieves in Venice on those terms.'

'My sister, you see,' said Barbarigo, 'is not fortunate in her husband. As for this poor thief, why I must prove the anxiety I have ever professed to serve your excellency. Since the rogue's a foreigner, and provided there is naught else against him . . .'

'There is naught else, I am sure.'

'Why, then, on the condition that he leaves the territory of the Republic at once, I see no obstacle to ordering his enlargement. What is his name?'

'Pablo de Arana,' said Don Ramon, and he was voluble as only a Spaniard can be in his thanks.

When he had departed, Sarasin heaved himself up. 'If your sister is unfortunate in her husband, so is the Adriatic. What does one say of a Doge who is without reverence for the law?'

'The lex suprema is the welfare of the State,' said the smiling Doge. 'Lesser ones may yield to it.'

'God save us! And the welfare of the State is served by letting a thief go free. I must go to school again.'

'If it places the Ambassador of Spain under an obligation to me at this present time. Have you forgotten what I told you about Messer Christofero Colombo, the Liguarian navigator?'

Sarasin stared. 'How can Arias help you there?'

'I do not know. Not yet. But I neglect no thread, however mean. To secure this one, by all means let him have his thief — oh, and his dancing girl.'

'The thief if you will. As for the Gitanilla, the poor child deserves a better fate.'

'An Inquisitor of State, for instance. A pity she did not know it. She might have sought your interest instead of Don Ramon's. You are not fortunate, Silvestro, in your low pursuits.'

'Not so fortunate as Don Ramon. No. Ah, well! What matter a thief more or less in a world of thieves?'

But on the next day, Sarasin was of a very different mind.

He came panting and sweating from haste and excitement into the Doge's room in the Ducal Palace, and peremptorily demanded the dismissal of a secretary who was at work with Barbarigo.

'What now?' wondered the Doge, when they were alone. 'Has the Sultan Bajazet declared war?'

'The Devil take Bajazet. It's this Spanish rogue, Arana. I hear from Messer Grande that you've signed an order for his release.'

'Irregular of me,' agreed the flippant Doge. 'But was it not what yesterday I promised that love-sick envoy?'

'Fortunately with the condition that there would be nothing but this theft against him. A report on him has come before the Three. It is learnt that Arana came here from Milan, and there are suspicions that he may be a spy in the pay of Duke Lodovico.'

Barbarigo's gesture was disdainful. 'A spy in the pay of Milan? That is not likely. The relations between Duke Lodovico and Spain are no better than between him and us.'

'Don't let that be dust in your eyes. In spying all things are possible. My report is from Gallina, and he's as shrewd an agent as we possess. So that this is no miserable question of a larceny, but of an offence against the State. This man does not belong to Messer Grande. He belongs to the inquisitors. He belongs to me.'

'To you?' Amusement gleamed in the Doge's eyes. 'To you, eh? Come, come, Silvestro. Are you to play Don Ramon's game with the Gitanilla, holding her thief of a brother as your pawn?'

'I do not like the jest. Have I ever used my office to further my own ends? Let us be serious. This man is not to be released; at least, not until we've put him to the question.'

The Doge set aside his flippancy; but this because the jest so lightly uttered had set a seed in his mind. After a frowning pause, the wraith of a smile tightened his lips.

'But, of course, as you say, this is no longer a petty question of a theft. Such suspicions, however unlikely to be justified, must be investigated.' He sighed. 'I fear that we must disappoint Don Ramon. Regrettable, but then ... best examine this Spanish rascal without delay. But no torture to begin with, Silvestro. And you had better question the girl at the same time.'

That same afternoon two burly warders descended to the foul dank dungeon of the Pozzi, under the Ducal Palace, to hale thence the Spanish prisoner, a wretched fellow sapped in nerve and body by hard living, and now reduced by forty-eight hours of confinement in that loathly unlighted hole to the mere wreckage of a man.

Huddled on a wooden shelf that served him for a couch, he had been denied all sleep by horror of the rats that invaded the place when the water came to film and befoul the stone floor with the rise of the tide in the lagoons. He screamed at sight of the warders, who looked gigantic and grim in the feeble light of the turnkey's lantern, conceiving them to be the strangler and his mate.

They soothed his panic, and conducted him above stairs and by a noble gallery to the little audience chamber of the dread Three.

Impassive in their leather bucket seats of judgment at the polished table, they received him, Sarasin, the Red Inquisitor, mantled in scarlet, between his two black colleagues.

Blinking and scared, Pablo de Arana stood before them, cadaverous of aspect, with blood-injected eyes, a black stubble of beard on his leaden cheeks. The lingering slime and filth from his dungeon made him repulsive, and perhaps something more, for Sarasin made great play with a pomander-ball to his nostrils whilst grimly inspecting him.

The theft of the dagger was touched upon, and summarily dismissed by one of the black inquisitors as not being a matter for this august tribunal. Since the offence was established, Pablo might look forward, he was told, either to the loss of his right hand or a long term at the oars of the Republic's galleys. That, however, was matter for a lesser court. The Three had to deal with something graver far.

Thereupon it was Sarasin who took up the interrogation.

Did the prisoner admit that he came to Venice from Milan? He did. What, then, was he doing in Milan, and what was the precise business upon which he left it to come to Venice? Warned that prevarication would be useless, that the tribunal possessed the means to twist or burn the truth from the most recalcitrant, he was invited to seek leniency by frankness.

He told a whimpering tale, obscured and complicated by his invocation of every saint in the calendar in turn to bear witness to his truth, of having no business in Venice save the safeguarding of his sister Beatriz Enriquez de Arana, known as La Gitanilla.

Sarasin was facetiously sarcastic. 'Quis custodiet ipsos custodes?' he wondered for the amusement of his colleagues. 'A custodian, thou? I should pity any woman guarded by such a watchdog. But no matter for that. What we desire to know is why you could not do this safeguarding in Milan.'

Pablo was voluble. He would willingly have done so. But Messer Angelo Ruzzante had heard her sing and seen her dance on a trestle stage in a square of the Ambrosian city, and had tempted her to Venice with the promise of good money.

Sarasin caressed his double chin. 'And that was all? Think well before you answer. There was no other inducement to come to the lagoons?'

There was none. He came because he could not allow his sister to come alone, exposed to all the temptations and pursuits that beset the path of a cantatrice. He took Saint James of Compostella to witness that this was true, and so enable the Red Inquisitor again to amuse the court.

'I doubt if Saint James of Compostella can be induced to leave the peace of God to come and testify for such a mouldy rogue. But your Ruzzante shall be brought before us, and also the woman. After we have heard how far they confirm your tale, we'll make a beginning with you.' He waved a plump hand. 'Take him away.'

Ruzzante, examined that same afternoon by the Three, confirmed the prisoner's story. A personable man of some culture and a ready wit, his testimony did Pablo good service.

After Ruzzante came the Gitanilla, summoned and escorted from her lodging by an agent of the tribunal.

She stood before them straight and lithe, in a fear so well dissembled that she seemed almost bold.

The trend of the questions, which completely ignored the matter of the theft, came to increase her alarm. Commanding herself, she answered them in a low, steady voice, through whose huskiness rang undertones of the melodious quality with which she enchanted audiences. Upon the ears of these three elderly men its magic seemed to have no power. Coldly, now from one, now from another of the Black Inquisitors fell the questions, whilst Sarasin sat back, his elbows on the arms of his chair, observing her over his joined finger-tips.

To questions upon what she had done in Milan and why she had left it for Venice her answers were ready, as they were when she was pressed to say whether her brother showed himself eager that she accept Ruzzante's proposals, whether he had not actually displayed anxiety to do so. Equally ready was she in naming their Milanese associates. When, however, they shifted their questions from Milan to Spain, and demanded to be told for what reason she and her brother had left it, having something to conceal she faltered, fell into contradiction, and when ruthlessly pressed admitted that her brother was a fugitive from justice.

At last, those inscrutable men were bringing the examination to a close when a narrow door behind them opened to frame a resplendent golden figure. It was Barbarigo, himself, coming from a meeting of the Grand Council, still arrayed in the ducal chlamys, his fair locks crowned by the corno, the stiff, humped golden cap of his high office.

His delicate hand, outstretched to stay the inquisitors from rising, signed to them to continue, whilst he remained standing, just within the doorway, having closed the door.

Thence his shrewd eyes pondered the witness, marvelling to behold, either in garb or countenance, so little to betray her station. She stood, a slender blue pillar in her mantle, the hood thrown back from her dark head. In the glowing eyes under the broad smooth brow he saw the fierce pride behind which her fears were hidden. He observed the sensitive, generous mouth and softly rounded chin, and told himself that the face possessed not only beauty, but bore the imprint of a quality that any noble woman might have envied. Whilst he could understand the spell she had cast over Don Ramon de Aguilar, yet his fastidiousness was nauseated at the thought of such a woman falling a victim to such a profligate. If he knew aught of human nature, the quality he detected in her was a power to subdue men to her will such as Saint Anthony himself would have been troubled to withstand.

When presently her dismissal came from Sarasin, he observed with approval the dignity with which this poor cantatrice inclined her head in acknowledgment.

Then at last he spoke. 'Let her be detained in the antechamber.'

As the door closed upon her, Sarasin looked round at him in surprise. But here Barbarigo was official, and the brother-in-law was lost in the Doge. He came round to face the inquisitors. 'What are your findings?'

'Little enough,' Sarasin informed him. 'The prisoner is a worthless dog on whom that woman wastes her devotion. He lives on her, and she would go to the rack for him.' His glance questioned his colleagues, and was answered by murmurs of ready agreement. 'Therefore,' he continued, 'her testimony is of no value, save that it agrees with Ruzzante's, as his does with the prisoner's own answers. Yet there may be things which neither the girl nor Ruzzante knows. After all, Gallina is our shrewdest and most zealous agent, and his grounds for suspecting this Arana of practising with ——'

The Doge had heard enough. 'No matter. You may sift that at your leisure.' He stood pondering, chin in hand. 'She would go to the rack for him, eh? So I, too, should judge her. There is fire enough under that cool skin of hers. Let us use her gently. It may comfort her to see this brother. And it may be fruitful.'

'If Your Serenity orders it, I'll have him brought to her.'

'Not so. Not so. Rather, let her be taken to him.'

Aghast, one of the inquisitors blinked. 'He is in the Pozzi, Serenity.'

Barbarigo smiled darkly. 'Just so. That is where she should see him.'

8

BROTHER AND SISTER

Pablo de arana, back in his dungeon, crushed by an even greater apprehension than had been his before his examination by the Three, was roused from a dejected torpor by the clank and rasp of a key, the opening of the door and a feeble yellow glow of light.

Crouching on his plank, he glared like a scared animal; then, as his sight cleared, he started up, beholding his sister.

The warder set his lantern down beside her on the uppermost of the three steps that led down to the stone floor. She came down a step, and then recoiled, appalled by the foulness of the floor. The movement drew a guffaw from the gaoler. 'Aye! Not so dainty as a lady's parlour. But there he is. My orders, mistress, are to leave you with him for ten minutes.'

The door clanged again, and brother and sister were alone.

It was a moment before either spoke. Hoarsely at last he croaked her name.

'Beatriz! Why are you here?'

The wretched sight of him was blurred for her by a mist of tears.

'My poor Pablo!'

The sob that broke her voice, chilling him with fresh dread, brought uppermost the creature's egotism. 'Well may you pity me, in the pass to which you have brought me.'

'Oh, Pablo! Pablo!' she cried, and the reproach in her voice was a goad to his humour.

'Pablo! Pablo!' he mimicked her. 'That's your way of denying it. You'll say it wasn't by your wishes that we came to this cursed Venice. Were we not well off in Milan? Did you not earn enough there to satisfy your selfish greed?'

The lament might drive a sword through her, but it could not take her by surprise. She was inured to earning nothing but reproaches in return for her unstinting service to him. She accepted with the same resignation with which she would have accepted a physical affliction in him, holding it something that sprang from a weakness in his nature for which he was not accountable. Like all egotists he had ever been obsessed by a sense of martyrdom. He laboured under an abiding sense of wrong, and found ever other than in himself the blame for misfortune that his failings procured him.

His present plaint, however, was too extravagantly unjust for resignation. 'That is not true, Pablo,' she defended herself. 'Think! Yourself you urged me to accept Ruzzante's proposals.'

'Knowing your nature, your pretensions. What peace should I have had if I'd opposed you?'

Very gently she remonstrated, 'Pablo, dear, was it I who stole the poniard?'

But not all her gentleness of tone could prevent the words from driving him to fury. 'Body of God!' he snarled. 'I did not steal it. I found it. Must you lie so that you can reproach me? And I never should have been driven to sell the cursed thing if you had not stinted me. Your grasping avarice is the

cause of all this trouble. And now that I'm in the grasp of
these Venetian dogs they must be inventing other things
against me. O God! Born unlucky. That's what I am.
Dogged through life by ill luck. Is there anything I haven't
suffered?' He took his head in his hands, and groaned in self-
pity. 'But you don't answer me. Why are you here?'

'The Inquisitors of State permit me to visit you.'

'With what purpose? So that you may gloat over the state
to which you've brought me? They are to put me to the
question. Did they tell you? Do you know what it means?
Do you know how the hoist wrenches a man's bones from their
sockets?' He ended on a scream. 'Mother of God!' Again he
sank his face into his grimy hands.

Pity, conquering repugnance, brought her to step down
into the foul ooze of the floor, so that she might soothe his
terrors. But he writhed himself free of her enfolding arms.
'This does not help me.'

'I am doing what I can,' she told him. 'I went to Don
Ramon de Aguilar, to beg him to claim you as a subject of
Spain, to use the influence of his office for you.'

'Don Ramon?' He lowered his hands, to look at her. In
the lantern light his eyes gleamed hope and cunning. 'Don
Ramon, eh! Vive Dios, that was well thought. Aye, you
should be able to work upon him. He had an eye to you.'
He clutched her wrist. 'What did he say?'

Her voice was toneless. 'He offered a bargain. A shameful
bargain.'

'Shameful!' His grip tightened. There was alarm in his
voice: 'What then? What then? Shameful would be to leave
your brother in this hell. Virgin Most Holy! Will you always
play the cursed prude — even in this extremity?'

Because he felt her shrink from him his voice soared hoarsely
in passion. 'Shall I be racked and broken, or maybe strangled,

because you're dainty? Have you no bowels, girl? Having
brought me down to this, will you leave me to perish when at
so little cost you can rescue me?'

'A little cost!'

'What then? What is it, after all? If you had any true
feeling for me ——'

She interrupted him. 'Feeling? Oh God! What can I do?'

'What can you do? You know what you can do. You can't
deny me.' He patted her shoulder, suddenly fond and brotherly. 'God will requite you, Beatriz, as I shall. Once out of
this you'll find me different. I'll live for you. At need I'd
give my life for you. Seek Don Ramon again. Lose no time.
Spare no persuasions with him.'

The gaoler, opening the door, mercifully put an end to her
agony. 'It is time, mistress. You are required to go.'

Pablo became all slobbering fondness in his farewells. She
was his dear good sister, the best sister man ever had. He
trusted her, confident that she would work his salvation.

At last she was following the gaoler up the narrow stone
stairs on dragging feet that were befouled and sodden from
the dungeon's slime. It occurred to her that her soul was in
much the same case. Her pity for Pablo, the long-standing
habit of protecting him, fought with her loathing of his callous
indifference to the sacrifice asked of her. She sought excuses
for him in his inherent weakness of body and spirit, haunted
as he was by terror of a dread ordeal that dwarfed all else.

9

Aᴛ ᴛʜᴇ stairhead the gaoler surprised her with the announcement that she was awaited by His Serenity.

With no more than half her wits about her she suffered him to lead her along that gallery, up a noble staircase by richly frescoed walls, down yet another gallery flooded by sunshine, to a door of carved panels enriched by gilding. Admitted by a sleek silken chamberlain, she was given a moment's pause in an anteroom, and then ushered into the gilded ducal chamber whose gothic windows looked out over the blue waters of Saint Mark's Basin and the shipping anchored there.

Here Barbarigo awaited her, no longer in his official robes. He had put off the cloth of gold of the ducal chlamys, but was scarcely less arresting in a flowing houppelande of black with broad silver arabesques, over a short crimson tunic and crimson hose.

By the condescension of setting a chair for her he diminished the awe with which the man and the office alike inspired her.

'Pray sit, madonna.' His voice, like the title he bestowed upon her, implied a flattering deference. His glance enveloped her, from the eyes made haggard by the brief visit to the Pozzi, to the foulness on her shoes and the hem of her gown. All this his fastidiousness deplored.

'By Your Serenity's leave,' she responded, taking the seat he offered. She sat upright, with a statue's rigidity, her bare hands folded in her lap, and waited.

His Serenity remained standing. 'You have seen your brother, madonna?'

'I have seen him.'

He sighed. 'I grieve that you should have been pained by the necessity. Such sights are not for a woman's gentle eyes. And I commiserate you, too, in the affliction with which you are visited by your brother's peril. Believe that I could desire to relieve it.'

'Your Serenity is gracious.' She spoke with an effort. This man inspired dread. In his willowy elegance, his light movements, his silken voice, she detected something sinister and feline.

'In this matter now of being an agent of the Milanese ——'

'It is false,' she was so rash as to interrupt him. 'A wild suspicion. It has no foundation. It can have none.'

'You assure me of that?'

'I swear it.'

'I do not hesitate to believe you.' She gasped relief too soon. 'Unfortunately the Inquisitors of State are more difficult to satisfy. They may test him on the hoist. Even if he withstands that, there will remain this matter of the theft. For that he should lose his hand. But as slaves are wanted for the Republic's oars he may be sent to the galleys for the remainder of his life.'

She came to her feet in a white heat of passion. 'I perceive that Your Serenity mocks me.'

'I?' His lightness vanished. 'Saint Mark! I hope I am incapable of that. No, no.' A gentle hand on her shoulder pressed her down again to the chair. 'On the contrary.' He moved away with his sauntering gait, and turned again. 'I sent for you to offer you your brother's freedom.'

She said no word, but watched him with dilating eyes. And he added after a pause: 'Without concerning myself whether he is innocent or guilty.'

She continued silently to fix him with her stare, waiting in increasing surprise and suspicion. He sauntered back, and came to a halt squarely before her, considering her again with his air of faint, detestable amusement. 'That should earn your gratitude.'

'Assuredly, my lord,' she choked.

Gently he asked: 'And you will afford me proof of it?'

She shivered and for a moment closed her eyes. Again she seemed to hear Don Ramon's hateful wooing. It stirred her to hot revolt.

'Must it always be the same? Because my necessities compel me to sing and dance for men's delight, is it to be presumed that there are no bounds to what I will do in the same cause? Must the credit of virtue be denied me?'

There was a protesting weariness in Barbarigo's faint smile.

'You go too fast and too far. Unless I gave you that credit, madonna, I should have no proposals for you. You are a very beautiful woman, a fact which will hardly have escaped your notice. Beauty, however, is not enough. It is because allied with it I perceive — or else I am a poor judge — a noble pride that guards your virtue and keeps you pure, that I account you irresistible to any man upon whom you set your will.'

She found all this bewildering. 'I do not understand.'

'You shall. It is not for myself that I require your service. It is for the State.

'Listen. At the Court of Spain, in Cordoba, or Seville, or wherever it may be, there is a needy adventurer in possession of a chart, from an Italian hand, to which he has no genuine right. By means of this chart and a letter of directions that goes with it, it is in this man's power to do great injury to Venice. Obtain them for me, and in exchange you shall have the life and liberty of your brother.'

She stared, white-faced, wide-eyed. 'In exchange? But what means have I of obtaining these things?'

'All that I ask of you is the will. The rest you possess. Such beauty as yours, madonna, is a currency that purchases most things from most men; and this man, as I've informed myself, is no anchorite.'

She was in deepest distress, and some revulsion. After all, this was not so different from Don Ramon's proposal. The price, in the end, remained the same, and in the ears of her memory rang Pablo's prayer to her to pay it. 'But how am I to reach this man, to reach the Court of Spain?' she weakly asked.

'That shall be our care. You will be well assisted, and generously supplied. Come, madonna. What do you say?'

She wrung her hands. Her generous lips writhed scornfully. She had thought the price the same as Don Ramon's; but now she perceived here an added infamy of betrayal.

Watching her keenly with his languid eyes the Doge repeated, 'What do you say?'

'No!' She came to her feet. She was passionate. 'It should not be asked of me. To be a decoy! That is an infamy.'

Barbarigo spread his hands. 'I do not press it. Some other must serve my turn. If I have offended you, forgive me. The notion sprang from my commiseration of your case, from my desire to ease your affliction on the score of your unhappy brother.'

'Merciful God!' she moaned. 'Can you show me no pity?'

'If I could give you — freely give you — your brother's life and liberty, he would be with you now. But not even the Doge can set aside the law unless he can show that he does so for the sake of some advantage to the State. Short of that I fear that your brother is doomed to a gallerian's fate, unless they mercifully strangle him.'

She cried out in pain, swaying where she stood. 'Mother in Heaven, help me! Tell me what I should have to do, my lord. Tell me more. Tell me all.'

'Of course. Of course you shall be told. Meanwhile you know enough for a decision.'

'If I were to try, and yet fail?' she asked in a tone of yielding. 'I do not even know if the thing is possible. You have not told me enough.'

What else he told her was of such effect that Don Ramon de Aguilar, visiting the Sala del Cavallo that same night, was disappointed of his hopes of seeing La Gitanilla and could obtain no explanation of it from Ruzzante. All that Ruzzante could regretfully tell him was that she was not there and that he did not know if she would come again.

Perplexed he called upon the Doge next morning for his answer in the matter of Pablo de Arana, hoping in this connection to have some word of her.

He was kept waiting, which annoyed a person of his consequence.

Whilst impatiently he paced the antechamber, a large, florid, goggle-eyed gentleman, showily dressed, emerged from the Doge's room, and gravely saluted him.

He looked down his nose, and his acknowledgment of the greeting was barely perceptible. He knew that the fellow under his exaggerated patrician exterior and in spite of patrician pretensions was a secret agent of the Council of

Three, and he was by no means sure that it sorted with his dignity even to acknowledge the greeting of a creature who pursued such a vocation.

But the man, whose name he knew to be della Rocca, came striding towards him.

'I am required to yield place to your excellency.' He was almost patronising. 'His Serenity will receive you at once.'

Silently cursing his impudence, Don Ramon followed the usher whom Rocca beckoned.

The Doge received him with regrets.

'Alas, my friend, in this affair of Pablo de Arana, I find myself without power to help you. There appears to be more against him than a mere matter of larceny. The unfortunate man is in the hands of the Inquisitors of State.' Don Ramon took this to explain the presence of the agent of the secret tribunal. 'In their proceedings,' Barbarigo continued, 'not even the Doge can intervene. But as, anyway, they have required his sister to leave Venice, I must suppose that your interest in his affair will be less acute. I hope so.'

Barbarigo smiled his pleasant smile into the envoy's countenance, and the Spaniard was left wondering whether there was a note of mockery in the expression of regret on which the Doge closed the matter, or whether the bitterness of a thwarted man made him imagine it.

 THE RESCUE

Cristobal Colon idled in his lodging over the shop of the Marrano tailor Bensabat, reviewing the past and pondering the future, and discovering no satisfaction in either.

They were at the end of May, and the white city of Cordoba lay baking under the ardent Andalusian sun. Soon the mountains that screened the city from the north would be covered again as with snow by the blossoms of the orange-trees that covered the long slopes, and the gardens of the Alcazar would be aflame with flowering pomegranates.

Through the open window the sounds of the street came up to him on the tepid air: the tinkle of mule-bells, the cry of a water-seller, the voices and laughter of children, the whirr of a spinning-wheel industriously plied in a doorway across the street.

Disgruntled, he lounged on a day-bed of interlaced leather in that small, low-ceilinged room, from which an alcove containing his bed was shut off by a curtain of faded tapestry.

The furniture was mean and scanty. An oaken table of di-

minutive conventual design stood in the middle of the bare
floor. A rude clothes-press of chestnut-wood was ranged
against a wall; a plain, low coffer of the same timber stood beneath the latticed window. A couple of straight chairs, their
seats of interlaced leather like the day-bed, completed the
mean equipment.

For only adornment of the roughly plastered, whitewashed
walls there hung above the day-bed a brass oval set in an
eight-pointed star as wide as the length of a man's hand and as
long as it was wide. The oval panel bore a craftily painted picture of Our Lady. Ending at the waist, it was mantled in ul-
tramarine over a rust-coloured corsage; fair-skinned and gold-
en-headed, the face was one of delicately featured youthful-
ness. It was Colon's own property, purchased years ago in
Italy, as much because of his devotion to the Virgin as for the
sake of the feminine sweetness it expressed. It was the work of
one Sandro Filipepi, known as Botticelli, who was greatly es-
teemed in Rome. It had been with Colon ever since on all his
travels, and it had looked serenely down upon him at his
prayers, even as he hoped that Our Lady, Herself, might look.

With brooding eyes he considered his surroundings, and
found them poorly adapted to a man of his ambitions, or to
one who moved at ease in courts. Though, to tell the truth, he
no longer moved at ease at the Court of Spain; indeed, since
the return to Cordoba he scarcely moved there at all. He had
grown conscious that men still nudged one another as he
passed, as they had nudged one another on his first appearance
eighteen months ago, but with this difference now, that the
nudges were accompanied by contemptuous smiles. He had
wearied of blinding himself to these slights. He had even begun to fear that the control in which he curbed a temper by no
means cool might slip from him and betray him into a rashness
to justify the malevolence that mocked him. Because of this,

and because his fine doublet of russet brocade had worn as
threadbare as his patience, he had discontinued a futile attendance at a court in which the war with the Moors, political
chicanery with France and the spirit of persecution afoot
against the Jews left no room for consideration of his lofty
enterprise.

Thus in his jaundiced mood he began to think that it was
time to make an end. His quarterly stipend had been sent him
that morning by Quintanilla, and reckless of the dishonesty of
the thought, he was considering buying himself a mule and
setting out for France, there to begin again. But who could
say that in France a like frustration might not await him?
Frustration was his portion. The powers of evil were at work
to delude him with hopes before raising obstacles to their fulfilment. Who would care if he went? Probably the Court would
not even remark his absence.

There he checked. Two there were, at least, to whom such a
step would bring regret: Santangel, who held him in such
warm esteem, and the Marchioness of Moya. On the thought
of the Marchioness of Moya he lingered in a day-dream. In
what esteem did she hold him? His imagination conjured a
vision so vivid as to seem palpable: the languorous smile on
the moist red lips, the intent yearning eyes that seemed to look
deep into his soul, the noble shape, the white, alluring throat.
A sensitive, sensuous woman whom he might have taken to be
a solace to the loneliness that was inevitable to such a temperament as his. But there were barriers between them; barriers
which he might have broken down but for considerations not
only of honour, but of the master-interest of his existence. A
want of circumspection in that quarter might have jeopardized
his chances with the Sovereigns. So he had practised circumspection, but in a vain hope, as it now seemed to him.

A step upon the crazy, creaking stairs dispelled her image.

It was as if she, herself, had fled in alarm before this intrusion. Someone rapped on his door. Without rising, he bawled a command to enter, and looked over his shoulder to see who came.

In a bound he was on his feet, as the portly figure of Don Luis de Santangel filling the doorway, ushered with obsequious gestures by old Bensabat.

The Chancellor came forward, the door was closed, and the little room seemed rendered more bare and shabby by his presence and the sober richness of his apparel. 'You hide yourself, Cristobal,' was his reproachful greeting.

Colon took the proffered hand. 'It is more profitable than to display myself for the amusement of apes.'

'Out of humour, eh?' Don Luis tapped Colon's cheek lightly with two fingers.

'Unreasonably, you'll say.'

'Oh, reasonably enough. But I bring you news.'

'That the Sovereigns are moving upon Granada, that they have decided to make war on France, that they preside at the battle raged with gold by Abarbanel against the rack and fire of Frey Tomas de Torquemada. I know it all, you see.'

Santangel smiled tolerantly. 'There happens to be something more to-day. Your friend, Frey Diego Deza, has come to court. He asks for you, and he has stormed the Queen on your behalf. He dares, with a Dominican's audacity, to reproach her for her neglect of you after what she promised. The Moya supported him, and between them they have so shaken Her Highness that messengers have gone to Salamanca, to summon the doctors who are to sit in judgment upon your theories. Do I give you news?'

'You announce a miracle. As well as my need to perform one, so as to give sight to souls that are blind.'

'I believe you equal to performing it.' Santangel sat down

on the day-bed, leaving Colon standing. 'Meanwhile, I've said that Deza asks for you. It were ungracious and unwise to neglect so good a friend.'

'I've rubbed myself shabby against the doors of antechambers. In a world that values the coat above the man I must go shamed.'

'That is provided for. Bensabat is putting the last stitches in a coat of brocade that every fop will envy you. Never look so fierce. Men speak of you as my friend, and a shabby friend diminishes a man's own credit. So forgive the liberty.'

'If the coat has been made for me, then, by Saint Ferdinand, I'll pay for it.'

'So you shall if you insist: out of the treasures of the Indies, on your return. God avail me! Can't your pride accept a gift from an old man that loves you?'

Colon became humble. 'I am so much in your debt already.'

'For what, pray? What have you had from me besides faith?'

'If there were nothing else, would that be nothing? Who else has given me as much?'

'I could name one or two. And now there is Diego Deza imperilling his favour on your behalf. The good man does not fight for you alone. A fervent Christian and a Dominican, he is nonetheless a converso. He looks to this discovery of the Indies and its treasure to stay the present persecution of the Jews.' Between question and assertion he added: 'You'll wait upon him to-morrow at the Alcazar. His effort must not be lost.'

'You urge it out of the same compassion.'

'And you should yield for the same reason if you had no other.'

Colon confessed that he would be not only a curmudgeon but a fool if he did not hasten to return thanks for this rescue from oblivion, and the following morning found him in the halls of the ancient Moorish palace, braving the covert sneers of the courtly throng in a splendour of black and gold that restored him some of his swagger.

Some may have wondered whether they had sneered too soon when they saw him in close and imtimate talk with the influential Dominican who was the prince's tutor.

Diego Deza, a little paunchy man with a brown fringe of hair about his tonsure, and pale short-sighted eyes in a face that was round and red and glossy, went his ways at last leaving Colon enheartened by assurances that soon now there would be an end to his long season of waiting.

In this good mood the Count of Villamarga found him; a tall sallow gentleman, this, whose black velvet cloak bore in red embroidery the lily-hilted sword of a knight of Saint James of Compostella. He had for companion a large florid man, with fair hair and prominent blue eyes, whom he presented as Messer Andrea Rocca, a gentleman in the following of the Venetian envoy to the Court of Spain, newly arrived in Cordoba.

Colon, caring nothing for either of them and lacking excuse to leave them, was constrained by courtesy to stand and receive their idle chatter. Matters were only half improved when Villamarga, with a lift of the hand to a passing courtier, excused himself.

'Give me leave to say a word to Don Ignacio,' he begged, and was gone.

Alone with Colon, the Venetian became effusive in Italian. 'Our native tongue should better serve between us. Spanish is a language in which I grope a clumsy way.' Under Colon's haughty stare he laughed. 'I hoped that you would remember me, Messer Cristoforo. But I see that you do not. Indeed, why should you? My part in the affair was of so little account,

whilst you were the hero of it. I speak of the sea-fight at
Tunis, ten years ago, when your worthiness's valour achieved
the rout of the Turkish galleys.'

'You were at Tunis?'

Della Rocca sighed and smiled in one. 'That you should ask
it! I was an officer serving under Captain Lamba, that other
great Genoese. I have often thought of you since and wondered how you prospered. Conceive my surprise to see you
here. And Villamarga tells me of a great enterprise ahead of
you in Spanish service. On my life, I envy those that sail with
you. What honour to share the undertaking, and what honour
to serve under so great a captain!'

To parry the effusive flattery Colon spoke lightly. 'My
difficulty is to persuade the world of it.'

'So thinks your modesty, sir. You'll never lack for followers.'

'I was thinking of ships. They are less easy to come by.'

'Ships?' The Venetian took him by the arm familiarly, and
drew him away to the seclusion of a window embrasure. 'I
understood from Villamarga that the Sovereigns are to provide
the ships. But if there is room for any other share in the venture, why, sir, I am not so wealthy but that I should welcome
such a chance to increase my possessions, yet wealthy enough
to provide one ship. And like me there should be many.'

He paused there, his prominent eyes intently questioning.
Colon was reminded of Pinzon, who at La Rabida had made a
similar proposal, a proof, indeed, that there were others, as
della Rocca said.

His answer now was much what it had been to Pinzon, that
this thing could not be undertaken save with the weight and
authority of a crown behind it. Before they could carry the
discussion further, a blare of trumpets came to herald the arrival of the Sovereigns.

Through the lofty double doors under the cusped Moorish arches at the hall's end, the royal couple entered, preceded by two chamberlains. King Ferdinand, a rather sombre figure in a dark velvet gown that fell to his heels, a flat cap of black velvet on his fair head, was attended by the tall, elegant figure of the Cardinal of Spain, by the portly Duke of Medina Sidonia in black, and by the black and white gauntness of Hernando de Talavera. Queen Isabel, sedate and placid, her train borne by a stripling page, with a castle escutcheoned in gold on the breast of his short red doublet, was followed by the Marchioness of Moya and Medina Sidonia's deep-bosomed Duchess.

They advanced slowly through the lane that opened before them in the courtier throng, with occasional pauses for a word here or there with one or another of those who made up the attendance.

It fell to Colon, who was not expecting it, to be thus honoured by the Queen.

'Ah, sir navigator, you have been much in our thoughts. You have waited too long, but you may look now to hear from us soon.'

He bowed low. 'I kiss Your Highness's feet.'

Under the battery of eyes that were turned upon him as she passed on, he was careful to mask his elation, blessing his brocade and its donor for the figure that he cut.

The bright eyes of the Marchioness of Moya saluted him with a smile as she moved on in the Queen's wake, whereby the warmth in his breast was so much increased that he wanted to laugh at the sidelong scowl he got from Talavera.

Rocca's hand was on his arm. The Italian's voice was sibilant in his ear.

'A word in passing from the Queen, and a smile from the loveliest lady of the Court! Did I not say that you suffer from an excess of modesty?'

Colon, made gay by this fresh ignition of hopes that had been almost spent, laughed lightly. 'I suffer from many things, but not from that, as you would say if you knew me better.'

'To know you better, sir, is what I most desire. I shall look for you soon again here.'

And so, with compliments they parted.

II

THE AGENTS

In the best room, above stairs, in Cordoba's best inn, the Fonda del Leon, the florid and flamboyant Messer della Rocca held forth with more than a touch of vainglory to an audience of one.

'I brimmed him a full cup of the wine of flattery, and in his conceit he quaffed it to the dregs.' He quoted himself: '"I was in the fight at Tunis, where your worthiness's valour accomplished the rout of the Turkish galleys."' And again: '"This enterprise ahead of you: what honour to bear a part in it! What honour to serve under so great a captain!"' He gulped it so that he almost choked himself. 'It led me to offer to supply a ship. If he should yet succumb to that temptation, I might reasonably ask him to let me see his charts, and so we might find a short cut to our ends.'

He paused there for applause. But it did not come. His audience, a short square man, built like an ape for power rather than grace, was not by nature prodigal of applause. There was so much bone in his face, and so brown was it, that it looked as if carved of walnut. Small eyes, like beads of jet, pierced the speaker with a steady look in which there was some contempt.

'To the Devil with subtleties. Our orders are definite enough, and we'll keep to them.'

Rocca was tolerant. 'You can't complain that I haven't opened the way to it. Now that I've worked on his vanity to make him my friend, the rest should be easy. A warm man, if I'm a judge. We'll keep to our orders, of course. But it need not prevent me from believing that the direct method would save a deal of time and trouble. Six inches of steel well placed between the ribs one evening, and ——'

'And all might very well be lost if the chart were not upon him, as it wouldn't be. The first thing to discover is where it is. He may have deposited it in the chancellery, as he did in Lisbon. In that case a deal of art will be necessary on the part of Beatriz. If on the other hand he keeps it by him, then we may use your direct methods. But first we must be sure. A false step and we ruin all by forewarning him. As Messer Sarasin made clear, the man is naught, the chart is all. You should remember that.'

'I've said that I'll keep to the letter of the instructions.'

'You had better.'

'But time may defeat us. It is growing very short. That is what you do not know and Messer Sarasin did not take into account. I have it from Villamarga that the Sovereigns are about to become active in the matter. There's a commission of Salamanca doctors being assembled to sit in judgment upon it.'

Momentarily the other's attention quickened. It faded again at once. 'A royal commission? And you ask if we have time? Bah! Royal commissions travel swift as snails, and never arrive. It is reassuring.'

'I am glad to hear it.'

'I am not saying that we should be dilatory. Precisely what relations have you established with this navigator?'

Della Rocca gave him details.

'A good beginning,' he was approved. 'Now let it rest for a couple of days.' He was issuing orders rather than advice, and his flat voice had the ring of authority. For this man, who bore the ridiculous name of Gallina and whose godparents, either with a sense of humour or the utter lack of it, had christened him Galeazzo, regarded by the Inquisitors of State as their shrewdest agent, had been entrusted with the conduct of the affair. It was Rocca's part to act as his coadjutor. Because of the difference between them, and because each possessed qualities which the other lacked, they might be said to complement each other, which was the very reason why Sarasin had associated them. Rocca, showy in dress and airy in manner, well able to carry off his assumption of gentility, could move in courts without appearing out of place. Gallina, of coarser fibre and ruder appearance and manner, was of wider experience and proved ability in handling the darker business of the Inquisitors of State.

Rocca accepted his instructions. 'At your pleasure.' Then he asked: 'What of the girl?'

'She has settled with her Morisco, as she expected. She had worked for him before, and brought custom to his eating-house. He is glad to have her back.'

'Then all goes excellently. What's for dinner?'

They were still at table in that upper room when La Gitanilla arrived.

She entered without ceremony, and they greeted her with none, not troubling to rise. She came forward, moving with her easy grace, thrusting back the hood that overshadowed her face. She unfastened and cast off her cloak, and took the chair at the foot of the table across which the two agents faced each other.

Her simple gown of clinging black, without adornments, stressed the pallor of her cheeks. There were dark stains under the hazel eyes, and a faint air of weariness hung about her, heightening the appeal of her unusual beauty.

'Gallina tells me that you have made your arrangements,' said Rocca.

She nodded. 'It was not as easy as I thought. The times have changed since I was last in Cordoba. The Holy Office grows more vigilant of Moriscoes and Marranos, and Zagarte is nervous of the Dominican Brotherhood.' From her scornful drawl it might have been supposed that she was not, herself, a Christian. 'He thinks it as well to supply what the Holy Office must approve. So he supplies a mystery — "The Martyrdom of Saint Sebastian." At first the good fool refused to introduce a profane interlude into this sacred spectacle. He was filled with horror; not at the profanity, but at the sacrifice of so rare a chance of profit.' She laughed on a note of some hardness. 'With Cordoba full of soldiery, it would make his fortune to have me sing and dance for him again, whilst at present there are few who come to see his mystery, and those few eat little and drink less. He suffered, poor devil. He sweated in refusing me.'

'In refusing you?' cried Rocca. 'But . . .'

'Oh, be easy.' She was derisive. 'I overcame his difficulties for him. I have woven myself into his mystery. I am to be Irene, a young Christian who rescues Sebastian from death, and is herself martyred. I am to replace the lout of a boy who plays the part at present.'

Rocca looked none too pleased. 'And do you think to forward matters by a nun-like mummery?'

'Nun-like! Vive Dios! I am to sing and dance. Is that nun-like?'

'In a mystery?'

'It supplies the occasion. My song will be a lament over the body of Sebastian, to the tune of *Debajo de mi Ventana*, which Venice loved to hear.'

Rocca goggled at her in horror. 'You'll end in the fire, girl.'

'The piety of my words shall be my shield. Have no alarm. And my dance, too, shall be of the most pious.'

'Piety in a dance!' Rocca's horror increased. 'Holiness in hell.'

She laughed at him. 'We contrive it in Spain. You may see the seises in Holy Week danced before the high altar in the Cathedral of Seville.'

Gallina grinned. 'An amazing country in which anything seems possible. This may serve.'

'So far as the Holy Office is concerned, Zagarte has no doubts. So you need have none. So far as this man Colon is concerned ... Is he ... What manner of man is he?'

Rocca answered her. 'Inflammable as sulphur. There's a whisper at court that his ardours all but brought him to ruin over the lovely Marchioness of Moya. Oh, a warm man, my dear. You've an easy task.'

'Easy?' Suddenly grave, she looked at him with dislike.

'Yes, easy. He'll be wax in the hands of a girl of your spirit.'

She continued to frown upon his jovial, laughing face.

'It was in my mind to ask Zagarte to have a new mystery composed. The story of Samson. To the Philistine Delilah a dance would have come more naturally, a dance of allurement.' There was bitterness in her tone, which escaped Rocca. He swore in his enthusiasm. 'Cospetto! That was well conceived. Nothing could serve better.'

He was warming to it when a sneer from Gallina that was like a blow came to enlighten him.

'She mocks you, you fool.'

Rocca's prominent eyes were grave in wounded disapproval.

'Nay, sirs,' she told them, with a curl of her lip. 'If I mock, I mock myself.'

Gallina condemned her. 'That's no proper spirit to bring to the work.'

'So that I perform it, what does the spirit matter to you? Give me to drink.'

He poured wine for her, to which she added water from an unglazed amphora of baked clay.

 AT ZAGARTE'S

Lured thither by the flamboyant Messer della Rocca, Colon sauntered with him in the gardens of the Alcazar.

They took their idle way by an avenue of fragrant orange-trees, which, close-set and overarching, coolly shaded them from the blazing Andalusian sun.

The Venetian, displaying himself a great talker, worked hard to ingratiate himself. He knew how to be subtly flattering as much by allusions as by the deferential court he paid to his companion. He succeeded the more readily because Colon, uplifted by the new hope of a speedy shaping of his affairs, was in amiable mood, and because, however little he might be disposed to avail himself of the offer, yet a man who proposed to supply ships at need was clearly not a man to be treated lightly.

The talk was of all things, from voyages to the known limits of the world, by way of deeds of arms now doing, to the land of Spain and its folk. Having thus, by easy stages, reached the Spaniards, it was natural enough that Messer Rocca, this jovial savourer of life, should linger over Spanish women.

'They blend,' he declared, 'the Orient with the Occident, and so achieve a perfection dangerous to men, like ourselves, from other lands. Have you not found them so?'

'No more dangerous than are all women,' Colon admitted. 'They trouble a man's peace of mind.'

Rocca was amused. He took Colon by the arm confidentially. 'Only when reluctant to satisfy our longings, and that's a complaint I cannot bring against the ardent women of Spain.'

'Since you find them lovelier than others I can understand it.'

'But do not you? If you do not, let me convert you. Here in Cordoba I can show you a pearl of womanhood that it would be hard to match outside of Andalusia. You know Zagarte's eating-house. You don't? How long have you been in Cordoba? No matter. There are, then, two excellent things with which I can make you acquainted. Sup with me there this evening after witnessing a mystery-play that's performed daily in Zagarte's courtyard. My pearl of womanhood is displayed in it.'

So it fell out that in the late afternoon, Rocca, reinforced now by Gallina, whom he presented as a fellow-countryman and a merchant, conducted Colon down the Calle de Almodovar. It was a busy thoroughfare of houses whose uniformly white walls were broken at intervals by the gateways to their patios. Through the wrought-iron scrollwork of the gates there were inviting glimpses of courtyards where fountains played under cool green foliage. Above them windows that opened upon the street were guarded by ironwork that bellied outwards, and here and there a balcony was gay with flowers.

There was bustling movement all about them, in which many were moving on the same errand, folk of various degrees, humble in the main, but with a sprinkling of sedate merchants, and here and there a stiff hidalgo, who took the wall of all the others. A string of pack-mules, gay with bells and tassels of coloured wool, clattered by. A water-seller's donkey with a barrel slung upon either flank was urged along by a bare-legged lad with his incessant raucous shout of 'Agua!' There were noisy girls of the people in flaming shawls, with roguish liquid questing eyes, exchanging railleries with passing men-at-arms; and there were noble ladies, discreetly hooded, attended each by a duenna or a liveried page.

Through this moving press came Colon with his escorting Venetians to Zagarte's eating-house, proclaimed by a gilt shield above the gateway, emblazoned with a bunch of grapes. A knot of citizens stood about it, and about these some beggars flitted, whining. Rocca opened a way with his elbows, quelling resentful looks by his haughty stare. The gatekeeper bestirred himself to clear the entrance for them, and within the deep archway of the gate Zagarte, himself, came forward to receive them. A little brown Morisco, keen-eyed, sharp-nosed and wide-mouthed, he was all white. From waist to neck he was clothed only in his shirt, and whatever he may have worn below was covered by a spotless apron.

He washed his hands in the air as he bowed, addressing Messer Rocca by name. He had reserved the best room for his lordship. If their nobilities would give themselves the trouble of following, he would conduct them. He hoped that his mystery-play would amuse them. It was well liked, even by nobilities of the Court, who honoured him with their patronage.

Talking ever, displaying his white, even teeth in his effusiveness, he led the way across the spacious courtyard, protected by an awning of green canvas from the ardours of the sun. At one end a platform had been raised on trestles for the players. Immediately below this, a dozen or more rows of forms were ranged and already occupied; behind them the court was cleared to give standing room to the remainder and humbler section of the public. Here, too, some groups of townsfolk had already gathered and were noisy. Facing the platform on the first floor there was a gallery for diners, glazed for their protection in winter or in bad weather, but standing open now. The other two walls bore windows on the ground and first floors, some eight in all. These were the windows of lesser rooms for diners who desired them and could afford to be private. It was to one of these on the ground floor and near the stage that the Morisco conducted his illustrious patrons. Its furnishings were of the simplest: a table in mid-chamber, another for the service, ranged against the wall, and four chairs. But the scoured boards of the floor were strewn with slim branches of fragrant rosemary and lemon verbena.

An Andalusian girl in bright colours, gipsy-tinted, sloe-eyed and saucy, assisted Zagarte to place the chairs in the window. Being assured that for the moment their lordships lacked nothing beyond the wine-flagon and cups placed on the side-table for their refreshment, the Morisco and his girl withdrew.

From their window they observed the motley crowd below. Three other windows, draped in red damask like their own, were occupied by ladies and gentlemen whom Colon recognized as attached to the Court. Plainly, then, in yielding to Rocca's invitation he had not derogated from a proper dignity in one who enjoyed the countenance of the Sovereigns.

Rocca chatted gaily in the little time of waiting. Gallina, grim, taciturn and contemptuous, watched the comings and goings below from very force of habit, paid no heed to Rocca's chatter and left Colon wondering why so dull a curmudgeon should have been included in the party.

At last fell the knocks demanding silence, the audience settled down with a rustle and the mystery began.

A tall stripling in the morion and breastplate of a Spanish archer took the stage with a swagger and announced himself a centurion of the Imperial Guard, named Sebastian, held in esteem by the Emperor Diocletian and in such high favour by the gods that he might confidently hope soon to be made a tribune.

An early Christian in the guise of a grey friar, his historical identity so vague that yesterday two men had almost killed each other in a dispute as to whether he was Saint Peter or Saint Paul, overhearing the young man's boasts, came forward to denounce, in a voice of thunder, as false the gods whom he invoked.

Altercation followed in which Sebastian, beginning arrogantly, was gradually subdued by arguments bellowed from the friar's powerful lungs, gradually brought to such conviction of their unanswerable truth that he fell upon his knees, imploring to be taken into the Christian faith.

Sprinkling him with water from a bucket that had been thoughtfully provided, the friar pronounced over him the words of baptism. It was still doing when, to surprise the ritual, a fat man in a red gabardine, with a brass circlet on his brows, appeared upon the stage followed by two more soldiers in Spanish accoutrements. Revealing himself to be the Emperor Diocletian, he furiously upbraided Sebastian for his apostasy, and passionately pleaded with him to return to the gods of Rome. His grossness and the pertly defiant answers of Sebastian swept the simple-minded audience with an approving hilarity, chilled when the Emperor in a final explosion of wrath ordered Sebastian to be put to death.

Six more soldiers came to the Emperor's call. The centurion was stripped of his breastplate and strapped to the column,

with his back to the audience. Half the soldiers remained by
the pillar to guard the pinioned martyr; the other half,
ranged in a file, shot at him with arbalests, to the loud indignation of the spectators, but it was not clear whether this
was at the act or because denied the morbid satisfaction of
seeing the quarrels take effect. All that the public was permitted to see was the hero sagging more and more limply in
his bonds, until in the end, announcing that it was finished
and that thus would he deal with every Christian dog,
Diocletian stamped off with his soldiery.

Then, whilst the martyred centurion hung inanimate, the
tinkle of a guitar was heard, to which presently was joined a
voice, a woman's voice, rich and full and indescribably sweet.
The lilt of the song was lively and gay, and a people of
emotions, readily stirred by music, so far surrendered to the
spell of it that Sebastian and his martyrdom were forgotten.

Two stanzas were heard before the mysterious singer made
her appearance, coming slowly around the screens. A moment
she stood poised there, still singing, as if for the love of it and
out of the sheer joy of life.

Tightly swathed in white draperies that revealed every line
and curve of a lithe body that was a miracle of grace, she held
herself for a long moment with head thrown back in an attitude of exultant challenge that made men catch their breath.
Then as her roving glance alighted on the martyr in his bonds,
her song broke off abruptly on a cry of horror. She was
suddenly transformed. She became an incarnation of pity-
ing woe, and thus swept the audience back into the drama
which her coming had interrupted.

She ran forward to loosen the cords that held Sebastian,
whereupon he fell clear of the pillar and lay on his back. It
was now seen that a dozen arbalest-bolts were sticking in his
doublet. She set aside her guitar, and in graceful movements,

kneeling beside him, she piteously ministered to him. She drew out the shafts, opened the breast of his doublet, and with a cloth set herself to stanch his imagined wounds. Still kneeling, she reached for her guitar again. Once more the liquid voice soared to enthral her listeners. She sang the passionate love lament *Debajo de mi Ventana*, with which she had intoxicated the Venetians, but with the words so cunningly adapted that it became the pious elegy of a Christian virgin over the body of a martyr.

Whether the audience was moved by the dramatic implications of the song, or merely by the voice and charm of the singer, to such enthusiasm was it moved that peace could not be restored until she had repeated the performance.

After that it was not clear whether the shooting of Sebastian had not completely extinguished him, or whether the flood of melody poured over him had wrought the miracle of resurrecting him. The audience may have found the latter explanation the more credible when Sebastian sat up to thank and bless his rescuer for her ministrations.

She had no more than time to tell him that her name was Irene and that she was a Christian maid, when Diocletian froze all hearts by striding on again in fury to surprise them. Sebastian was carried off to be put to death elsewhere by more effective means, and Irene was given to choose between sharing his fate and offering incense to the gods. Being a songstress the appropriate god for her in Diocletian's view was Apollo. Accordingly soldiers dragged in a wooden altar surmounted by a laurel-crowned bust, and a smoking thurible was thrust upon Irene.

She stood a moment before the Emperor whilst he recited the details of the horrible fate in store for her if she refused. Then, as if appalled, she began her thurifer's saraband, symbolizing her hesitations between the fear of martyrdom and the glories to follow upon it. Commencing very slowly, with movements that were little more than posturings of terror and appeal, her dancing gradually gathered pace until it became a whirling exultation that revealed every supple grace of a body that would have been an inspiration to Phidias. At its climax she checked abruptly on tiptoe, flung the censer in the face of the god, and then lightly, as if there had been no flesh and bone within the silks that swathed her, she sank down into an inanimate amorphous heap at the feet of Diocletian. On the Emperor's verification that she had inexplicably expired, and on his awed wonder of whether the Christian God who had cheated him of his prey might not be more powerful than the gods of Rome, the mystery closed.

Whilst the spectators, delighted with Irene, yelled her name in acclamation and flung a shower of blancos and maravedis upon the stage in substantial witness to their enthusiasm, Colon, who, leaning from the window, had watched her every movement with absorption, sank back in his chair bemused, and released a sigh.

Rocca who had furtively watched his intentness laughed outright.

'Well?' he asked. 'Was I justified? Have you ever in all your travels seen a sweeter piece of flesh?'

'Entrancing,' Colon agreed. 'Divine.'

'Oh, not divine. Human, God be thanked. Divine would make her too inaccessible, and already she's inaccessible enough. As modest as she's desirable. As much a Christian virgin in life as on the trestles.'

Zagarte came in to hope that their nobilities had been entertained and to ask if it was now their pleasure to sup.

From the courtyard below arose the hubbub of departure. They quitted the window, and Rocca ordered Zagarte to serve.

'If your supper is as toothsome as your Irene, you'll have won a patron in my noble friend here.'

The little Morisco bowed with a flash of teeth. He would not disappoint them. They should have of his best, an olla of pigeons over which their worships would lick their fingers.

'You would add a relish to it if you were to bring the incomparable Irene to sup with us, eh, Ser Cristoforo?'

Colon awoke from his absorption. He reared his tawny head, and there was an eagerness in his eyes. 'Oh! Could it be?' And he looked at Zagarte.

The Morisco no longer smiled; his eyes were solemn, his lips pursed.

'It were a great honour for her. But your nobilities will not hold it against me if she refuses. Others have invited her, but she never accepts. There's a cursed prudishness in this Beatriz Enriquez.'

'Others?' Rocca frowned. 'Others, perhaps. But we are not as others. We are of the Court. Tell your Beatriz that, my good Zagarte. Tell her that. Tell her how much it weighs with you, how much her own interests will be served by civility to persons of our condition.'

Colon got up, and came from the window. 'Nay, nay. Use no constraint. That the girl adds virtue to beauty is to be respected.'

'Ah! If I might assure her of that.' Zagarte's expression was more hopeful.

'Saint Ferdinand!' cried Colon. 'For what do you take us, then? Are we common troopers or savages? If she comes she will have no cause to complain of us.' And because Rocca laughed, he added sharply, 'I'll answer for it.'

Zagarte bowed. 'Be sure I'll do what I can.'

When he had gone upon his errand Gallina sneered. 'These airs and pretences in a vulgar dancing-girl!'

Colon looked into that wooden face with dislike. 'A dancing-girl. But not vulgar, if you know the meaning of the word.'

'I know that, and more. Enough not to be easily fooled. Bah! A trick of the girl's, or else of the Morisco's, so as to make her the more desired.' And he added, with a finger to his nose: 'Experto loquor. What do you wager that she will not come?'

'I may hope that she will not refuse a civil invitation.'

'Or be disappointed if we are over civil.'

'A misogynist,' Rocca explained him. 'Forgive him.'

'No misogynist. No. But not a fool either. I've a nose for frailty no matter which of its several masks it wears.'

Thus again he provoked Colon. 'Sir, if your nose perceive frailty there, it's lost its sense of smell.'

Rocca smiled upon them, and the smile at least was genuine, for all was shaping as he could wish. He entered upon an altercation with Gallina, violently disagreeing with his cynical outlook. They were still at that comedy when Zagarte returned ushering La Gitanilla.

'My lords, I have explained to her that an invitation from gentlemen of the Court of the Sovereigns is no less than a command.'

'And to commands, of course, I must bow,' said she, with a little smile of irony, and a dignity that no lady of the Court could have bettered.

She was still in her clinging draperies of white, but covered now by a mantle of blue silk, and above her left ear she had thrust a tuft of pomegranate blossoms, startlingly red against her dark chestnut hair.

'We are fortunate,' said Rocca, 'to find you so obedient.' He went on to name himself and his companions, indicating them with a noble breadth of gesture.

Gravely she acknowledged each in turn. On Colon her eyes lingered an instant inscrutably.

Colon bowed as he might have bowed to a princess, self-contained and without hint of gallantry. 'I count myself happy in this opportunity to thank you for the delight you have given us.'

She did not choose to be gracious. 'I do not sing and dance for thanks. I am paid for it.'

'Every artist worthy of payment lives on the earnings of his art, but pursues it because naught else is worth pursuing. I thought — I hoped — that it might be so with you.'

'You hoped it? Why?'

'Because to give joy by exhibiting such gifts should itself be a joy.'

She gave him a long look before replying. 'You speak as if you were, yourself, an artist.'

'An artist, no. But a man driven by the same irresistible impulse of inspiration.'

'Whereas I am irresistibly driven by the impulse of necessity. And that is to be devil-driven.'

Gallina looked at Rocca with a lift of the brows.

'You imply,' said Colon, 'a mystery within your mystery, the mystery of Irene rather than of Saint Sebastian.'

Rocca broke in. 'Say the mystery of womanhood, which no man can fathom.'

'Do not complain of it,' said she. 'If you could fathom it your interest in her would be lost. And what should you be then?'

Zagarte came in bearing a great covered dish. Gallina pointed to it.

'On the subject of mysteries, my friends, here is one of Zagarte's ollas.'

The Morisco set the dish on the side-table. 'No mystery, noble sirs. An accomplishment; an excellence; a perfection. Regale your noble nostrils with these essences.' And he whisked away the lid, to release the steam that arose from a stew of pigeons.

'Facilis descensus,' laughed Colon. 'Thus we come head-long from things of the spirit to things of the flesh.'

'Give thanks,' growled Gallina. 'You have not the air of an anchorite nourished on herbs and prayers.'

'Why, no. I take what comes, being all human weakness.'

The serving-wench came in with platters, and after her a boy staggering under the weight of a basket of flagons.

Colon set a chair at the table, and his smile invited La Gitanilla to sit. 'We keep you standing,' he deplored.

Their eyes met, and some of the pride that smouldered in hers was softened by the deference blending with admiration in his glance. Quietly she thanked him, sat down and loosed her mantle. Still he hovered about her. He cut bread for her, and poured wine from one of the flagons the boy had set upon the table. She acknowledged the attention.

'A welcome privilege,' he murmured.

'Said the serpent when he offered Eve the apple,' Rocca mocked. 'Beware of him, sweet Eve. Never so seductive as when humble.'

'I have a good ear,' she answered lightly.

'Faith, then,' said Rocca, drawing up his chair, 'I haven't come to Spain in vain.'

'Why did you come?' she asked him.

'To behold you. Would not that be reason enough, Master Colon?'

'Reason enough to cross the world.'

'Lord!' she cried. 'Is any woman worth so long a journey?'

'I never met another of whom it might be said.'

The answer, by its solemnity, disconcerted her. Under his grave eyes she appeared momentarily distressed. She recovered on a strained laugh.

'But you'll have met a good many to whom you said it.'

'May this be my last cup of wine if that is true.'

'Quoth the serpent,' she laughed, and watched him curiously as he drank.

'Oh, a master of all the gallantries,' mumbled Gallina with his mouth full.

'Yet scorning falsehood.' Colon set down his empty cup.

'Why scorn it?' wondered Rocca. 'A legitimate weapon in war, and therefore in love, which is a sort of war.'

'I perceive no parallel,' Colon disagreed.

'Is it possible? What is love but an engagement between assailant and assailed, besieger and besieged? Am I wrong, divine Beatriz?'

'I hope so. Perhaps Master Colon will tell us. There should be knowledge of such matters under that red thatch.'

'I'll tell you that he is grossly wrong. What he describes is but a poor travesty of love. Something that merely wears the mask of it.'

'Let us then hear Master Colon on love,' said Gallina. 'I've often wondered what it really is.'

'You ask me to define the indefinable, the mysterious force beyond control of will, that draws two beings together irresistibly to their fulfilment.'

Gallina laughed his unpleasant jeering laugh. 'For something that you pronounce indefinable that is not bad.'

Colon shook his head. 'It is still too vague. But at least it dismisses the notion of antagonism.'

'I do not want it dismissed,' objected Rocca. 'Antagonism is the very spice of love. I am sure that Beatriz agrees with me.'

'Why should you be? It is to imply experience, and the implication does not flatter me.'

'What? Saint Mark! You were never given that face and shape for a nunnery, or to play the nun in the world.'

Her brows darkened. 'My face and shape are not the whole of me.'

Irrepressible, Rocca guffawed. 'But enough for me or any man, eh, Master Colon?'

'For any man whose discernment goes no further,' Colon rebuked him, to the malicious amusement of Gallina.

Rocca gaped. 'Why? What else is to discern?'

'If you must ask you would not understand the answer.'

'If you knew it you would not be evasive. Lord! I have no patience with your subtleties. A man should be content with what his five senses reveal to him.'

Colon laughed to ease the suspicion of tension. 'That may be wisdom: to think with the eyes, rather than to see with the mind. Perhaps I should save myself trouble if I adopted it. And yet, what would life be without trouble? It is the striving that brings a savour to it.'

'Successful striving,' Beatriz quietly corrected.

'All striving carries the hope of success. Without it there is only surrender, which is death.'

She considered him with eyes that were grown friendly. 'It is good to be a man,' she said, on a note of sadness. 'To have the shaping of one's fate.'

'How few succeed!' said he.

'But all may strive, and you have said that the striving is all.'

Then Rocca broke in. 'Devil take your solemnities. Are we here to be gay, or to make philosophy?'

To be gay he applied himself in his boisterous fashion. But he was indifferently supported. Gallina lacked the art of light chatter. Beatriz sat bemused, as if a veil had descended upon her spirit, and Colon, quietly absorbed in her, contributed little to hilarity.

In the end Rocca was provoked into admonishing him.

'Master Colon, the disadvantage of thinking with your eyes is that all the world may read your thoughts.'

'Since they dishonour none, what matter?'

Beatriz emptied her glass, and rose. 'I'll fetch my guitar, so that I may repay so generous an entertainment with a song.'

'We ask no payment, mistress,' Gallina protested.

'You shall receive it, none the less.'

She was gone, and Rocca turned, lugubrious, to Colon. 'I've served myself ill by bringing you. I had hopes, myself, in that quarter, and you've extinguished them. The girl had no eyes for any but you.'

Colon looked him squarely between the eyes. 'If you mean her honestly I'll embarrass you no further.'

'Honestly!' crowed Rocca, and Gallina laughed with him. 'A dancing-girl!'

Colon shrugged, disdaining argument. He was finding this shrill, coarsely flamboyant Venetian insupportable. Gallina cut in with his eternal sneer. 'This good Rocca has enjoyed such easy triumphs that he has ceased to believe in virtue. But I am of your mind, sir, that if he were to put his fortunes to the test with this child, his vanity might take a fall.'

'Is that a challenge?' Rocca demanded.

'For shame, sir,' Colon rebuked him. 'Is this a subject for a wager?'

'Cospetto! If you take it so seriously, I'll leave you a clear field, my friend. That and my blessing.'

'You mistake me,' Colon was beginning, but got no further, for Beatriz re-entered.

Two little songs she sang for them, little plaintive love-songs in the minor key so dear to Andalusians, in which tears and laughter were so intermingled that Colon's heart was wrung by them.

At parting, whilst Rocca and Gallina were busy with
Zagarte, he stood over her murmuring, 'May I come again
to hear you sing, to see you dance?'

She sat with her head bowed over the guitar in her lap.
'It needs no permission of mine. Zagarte will make you
welcome.'

'Will not you?'

She looked up, straight into his eyes, and he detected something akin to a cloud in hers. Then her glance fell away again.
'Does that matter?'

'So much that if you will not, I shall not come.'

She laughed softly, but without mirth. 'Then it were un-
dutiful to Zagarte to deny you.'

'I care nothing for that.'

'How insistent you are!' She sighed. 'But that is the way
of you. Is it not?' And then, before he could answer, she had
added: 'I'll make you welcome. Yes, Why should I not?'

13

Rocca was none too pleased with her. He came back that night to Zagarte's, where she had her lodging. Gallina, who did not entirely trust his methods, came with him, to employ a curb at need.

'Look now, my girl,' Rocca told her, 'this is no case for aping the great lady and affecting prudery. You know what's to do.'

She measured his inches with a curling lip. 'Isn't there harlotry enough in what I do, without adopting the manner of it, too?'

He stared in annoyance. 'A fine spirit in which to go to work. Very fine. But think a little less of your dignity and a little more of Pablo de Arana rotting in the Pozzi with the rats for company.'

This turned her livid. 'You hulking piece of cowardice. Must you add to my torment so as to serve your foul ends more speedily? Isn't what I do vile enough to satisfy your vileness and your masters' without ——'

'Look you, my girl,' he stormed in, 'that's no way to speak of His Serenity.'

'Sh!' Gallina hissed at him. 'Do you want all Cordoba to
hear you? Impatience never accomplished anything.'

'Can we afford patience, with time pressing as it is? Once
the junta ——'

'Quiet!' Gallina thrust him aside, and faced the girl, setting
a hand on her shoulder.

She squirmed away from under his touch. 'Say what you
have to say without pawing me.'

'Oh, a dainty piece,' sneered Rocca.

But Gallina was unmoved. 'It is just that the sooner this
thing is done, the better for us all, Beatriz, your brother included. To-night it seemed to us that you wasted time. Still,
it was a beginning. When next he comes be a little less . . .
aloof. That's all.' And he took leave in the current terms:
'Remain with God.'

Mechanically she answered, 'Go with God.'

Outside, however, Rocca vented his annoyance. 'Why
check me when I would have spurred her?'

'Because I prefer that the girl should go about it in her
own way.' And he quoted the proverb: 'Chi va sano . . . Who
goes slowly goes safely and goes far.'

'Or else he never arrives at all. But have it your own way.'

After that there was no further pressure upon Beatriz to
bring her victim to the net. Nor was pressure necessary where
the victim proved so ready and willing to entangle himself.
The very reticence that Beatriz had employed, yielding to her
nature, was the chief allurement, where the beckoning wan-
tonness that Rocca so crudely urged would have repelled the
victim.

The circumstances of the moment, too, rendered him vul-
nerable to allurement. Inflammable of temperament, as
Rocca judged him, the passion aroused in him by the Marchioness of Moya, from being curbed, had brought him a

yearning solitude of soul. His life at court, and the neglect into which he had fallen there, had increased this sense of solitude, bringing him an overwhelming loneliness. Beatriz had been brought into his life at a moment when his heart was aching from emptiness.

It was not a moment in which he could have withstood, had he desired to do so, the appeal to his senses of so much beauty and grace in one who seemed to hold out to him the promise of that fond companionship that might heal this loneliness in which he moved.

He could not wait beyond the morrow to fulfil his promise to visit Zagarte's again. Once more, and now alone, he occupied that same room, and from its window watched her every movement with avid, hungry eyes.

Afterwards, in response to the invitation he had sent her by Zagarte, she came to him, and if she hesitated, and demurred a little upon finding him alone, yet in the end she yielded to his respectful insistence that again she should remain to sup with him.

It was no more than a beginning. On the next day, and the next after that, he was again at Zagarte's, and Beatriz was supping with him, in an intimacy that grew apace and yet was kept within rigidly decorous bounds, which he made no attempt to overstep.

Because she was restrained by her very nature from exerting any conscious allurement, she played the greater havoc with his senses. Whilst gently gracious in word and attitude, there was no hint of archness in her manner. And whilst when he exerted himself to amuse her, her soft laughter was not withheld, yet there was a hint of sadness in it that smote the heart. She was as one who laughs despite herself in time of mourning, with the ache of bereavement ever behind the laughter.

It led him once to say, 'If I read you aright, mistress, the world has not been kind to you.'

'Is the world ever kind?' she evaded.

'Ah! You have marked its hardness, have you?'

'Being alone, with none to shield me from it.'

He was grave. 'Yet your own nature should have been your sufficient shield. But alone? How does that happen?'

'Is it so uncommon?'

'To be alone, yes. Though not to be lonely.'

'I am both,' she told him, and then, as if it were an indiscretion to be covered, 'but why talk of me?'

He was not yet to be put off. 'But have you, then, no kin?'

'None to avail me. I have two brothers. Both are wanderers. Neither is in Spain. Now tell me of yourself.'

'A host's duty is to amuse his guest. And my history is not amusing.'

'Not amusing? When you are of the court?'

'Ah, but no courtier. A suitor merely. A patient, unsatisfied suitor; of all things the dullest.'

'What is your suit?'

'A small matter to the Sovereigns. So small that they keep overlooking it. A matter of a ship or two with which to sail the unknown. I am by trade a navigator.'

'An engaging trade.'

'When you navigate. I rust in harbour, rigged with patience that the years are rotting, wasting myself by faith in promises that have proved as water; eating out my heart in loneliness in foreign lands.' He smiled into her sombre eyes. 'We have that in common it seems, you and I. Our loneliness should make a bond between us. A healing bond.'

Momentarily her eyes fled away from his, as if scared. Then they came back, to meet again his yearning, wistful gaze.

'A bond? But a mariner's bonds are soon loosened.'

'Even if it were so, there may be sweetness and comfort in them whilst they endure.'

'Leaving heartbreak behind them when they end.' There was scorn in her smile. 'Is there wisdom for a woman in such bonds?'

'It is folly to refuse a fleeting joy in a life in which all joys are fleeting.'

'Once I believed it, and took the joy that offered without heed of the sorrow that might follow.'

'You have suffered,' he said gently. 'One reads it in your eyes.'

'Nor is it yet in the past. I eat now the bitter fruit that grew from intoxicating blossoms.'

'That is the common lot of man.'

'And of woman still more commonly. But whither do we stray? This is not gay. Let me fill your cup.' With a sudden gaiety she poured for him. Thereafter constrained by her questions he entertained her with talk of his voyages, of marvels seen in distant lands, and of perils met upon the sea. Thus, from the past, she brought him to the present and the future.

'Tell me now of this voyage you project. This voyage into what you call the unknown.'

'Since it is into the unknown, what can there be to tell?'

But she would not suffer him to laugh it off. 'The unknown? That is but a word. It will be known to you, else how should you think to sail in it?'

'By groping my way, as we do in the dark.'

'Do you mean that you go into seas as yet uncharted?' There was suspense in her round-eyed gaze.

He smiled upon her wonder. 'Oh, there is a chart. A chart of sorts.'

'A chart of the unknown? How can that be? Tell me of it.'
She sat forward, elbows on the table, her face in her hands,
her regard intent, a quickening heave to her breast.

'What can I tell you of it? It exists, drawn by the pen of
imagination in the hand of reason.'

'That should be a strange chart. Like a portrait of someone the painter never saw. I would give much to see it.'

He was amused. 'Why? What do you conceive a chart to
be? It's no matter of sea and land scapes, but just lines,
some straight, some curved. So much gibberish to such eyes
as yours. Enough!' There was a peremptoriness in word and
gesture as he swept the matter away. 'You know all of me
that matters, and I naught of you. Why,' he asked, 'do you
sail under false colours?'

She sat back suddenly, aghast. 'False colours?' she echoed,
faltering, a green pallor about her lips.

'Calling yourself La Gitanilla,' he explained, 'when clearly
you are not gipsy born.'

Her gasping laugh was of relief. 'Oh! That!' she rallied
her scared wits. 'Neither was I born a dancing-girl. Being
this, I take a name that suits the trade.'

'Why do you pursue it?'

'Of necessity. I can spin and embroider and paint a little,
and it is fortunate that among the useless accomplishments of
a gentlewoman I include music and a natural aptitude to
dance.'

'Fortunate?' he questioned. 'I wonder.' His eyes were
grave. 'Is it quite fitting in a gentlewoman?'

'I did not say that I am one, but only that I possess the
accomplishments of one.'

'How else should you possess them?' He was impatient of
the implied denial. 'It needs no label to proclaim you.'

There was no further word of charts that day. The talk

having veered away from the subject would not return to it, nor was there any attempt from her to bring it back.

When at last he took his leave, he kissed her hand reverently as ever, and he made his usual prayer: 'You'll suffer me to come again?'

She laughed with a brave display of white, even teeth. 'What guile is masked in your humility!'

He laughed in his turn, shrugged and asked, 'Who is not guileful in approaching his ends?'

That sobered her suddenly. 'What are your ends with me?'

'Child, have I not told you? The bond in which to dispel our common loneliness. Nay. Never frown. Give it thought until we meet again.'

He went his ways without waiting for her answer, leaving her troubled and darkly pensive, in a state of dangerous pity for a victim who so readily bared his throat to the knife.

Himself he went so haunted by the thought of her that even the obsession of his project began to yield to it. For two days he did violence to his inclinations and kept away from Zagarte's. On the third day, which was Sunday, he attended with the court at High Mass in the Mezquita, as Cordoba's cathedral was still called, that vast mosque founded by Abderrahman, and since converted into a Christian temple.

He passed up the middle aisle of the nineteen aisles formed by a forest of eight hundred slender pillars of marble, of porphyry, of jasper, which carried the low horseshoe Moorish arches in alternating wedges of red and white. He reached the main Mihrab, where amid Moslem splendours was enthroned the Virgin of the Assumption. The thunder of Gregorian chorus rolled through the vaulted labyrinth, incense was heavy on the hot air.

On the very threshold of the Mihrab, kneeling by one of the pillars that in its slenderness and lack of height seemed symbolical of an Arab tent-pole, he found his devotions diluted by insistent thoughts of Beatriz. On the high altar, the very image of the Virgin, always the object of his special worship, seemed to assume the features and enigmatic smile of Beatriz.

He fought piously against the distraction, imploring Our Lady's aid in that combat. But presently chancing to look to his right, round the porphyry pillar that screened him on that side, he beheld Beatriz herself, a dozen yards away, on the edge of a neighbouring aisle. So unexpected was it that at first he deemed it a vision, an illusion created by the fever in his mind. And, indeed, something of the quality of a vision it must have possessed, for only the keenness of a lover's eye could have pierced the veiling draperies of long blue mantle and close-drawn hood. Unerring it was, for presently a movement of her head disclosed her features to him even in that muffled light.

He prayed no more that day. His devotions from that moment were for that kneeling blue-mantled figure; his hopes, no longer centred on his soul's salvation, were concerned with speaking to her when the Mass should be ended.

They were hopes that suffered frustration. Emerging by the great bronze doors into the Court of Oranges, where fountains gleamed in the sunlight and files of orange-trees formed aisles as if in continuation of those within the Mezquita, he found himself in a glittering group of courtiers. Before he could detach himself Santangel had surged beside him and taken his arm, and as they stepped aside to let the press flow on, Cabrera and his marchioness had joined them. She was never so much at ease with Colon as when her husband was present, as if then secure from too embarrassing a response. So now.

'My friend,' she hailed him, 'my dear Cristobal, I rejoice to know that the end of your long waiting is at hand.'

'As I do,' said Cabrera.

'Had it depended upon you, the end had been reached long since. I have much for which to thank you both.'

'Alas!' she sighed. 'Too little. I had the will, but it was left for Frey Diego Deza to display the power. At least, now that he has opened the door you may count upon me to see that it is not closed again until you are given satisfaction.'

Colon found himself wondering why he remained cool, why for the first time in their acquaintance her voice had lost its power to thrill him, her statuesque beauty to quicken his blood.

He addressed Cabrera. 'Your marchioness, my lord, is my guardian angel.'

Cabrera's goat's eyes were quizzical. 'The patron saint of all deserving men.'

'And the object of their veneration,' said Colon, but he spoke from the lips alone. His mind, following his eyes, was elsewhere. He had just seen Beatriz step forth from the portal of the Cathedral into the sunlight of the vast court, thronged now with loungers.

She moved with a demure stateliness, mantled and hooded, an agate rosary entwined in a Book of Hours between her gloved hands. At her heels, in attendance upon her, trotted a middle-aged Morisco woman, shrouded in a white burnouse.

Santangel and the Marchioness were talking, but Colon was no longer listening. His eyes were following Beatriz, and his soul was in his eyes. As she approached the first fountain a gallant in green put himself suddenly in her way, bowing until his cap swept the ground, in an exaggeration of courtesy that was an impudence. As she stepped aside the gallant stepped with her, so as to continue to bar her progress.

Colon stiffened, and the audible catch of his breath made his companions turn their eyes in the direction of his scowling glance.

Beatriz had stepped aside again, her head thrown up so suddenly that her hood was displaced and her profile revealed. Her lips moved rapidly, and Colon could imagine the blaze of pride from those hazel eyes, before which the importunate gentleman was recoiling with a sheepish grin of discomfiture.

'The dancing-girl from Zagarte's,' said the Marchioness, tonelessly.

It is to be doubted if Colon heard her, so absorbed was he. But as Beatriz resumed her way, his anger took expression. 'There's a fine fellow would be better for a cooling in the fountain.'

Cabrera was amused. 'But I'd counsel you not to administer it. He is the Count of Miraflor. A hidalgo of some weight.'

'Not so heavy but that I could lift him into it.'

'Why, Cristobal!' said the Marchioness, in a voice of gentle protest. 'Is it possible that you, too, are a worshipper at that tawdry shrine?'

He found it necessary to control resentment. 'I had not observed it to be either a shrine or tawdry,' he answered evenly.

'A dancing-girl!'

'Each of us is what he is from force of circumstances. They are few and enviable who can choose. Fewer still who can shape their destinies.'

There was a suspicion of tartness in the lady's smile. 'You make philosophy on her behalf.'

'If philosophy be, indeed, the love of knowledge. That child is forced to depend upon her throat and her feet for the means of life, with only her wits to shield her from the evils of the world.'

'You invite pity for her?'

'Not pity. No. Understanding. You observed her quality in her reception of that leering fop. He, too, no doubt, deemed her shrine a tawdry one.'

Cabrera laughed. 'In Heaven's name, Cristobal, not so loud, lest you suffer for your chivalry.'

'When I suffer for it, it will not be at such hands as those.'

'Your danger, rather,' said the Marchioness, 'might be at the hands of your chivalry's object. She is to be envied for her champion.' In tone and glance there was a frostiness that was new to him. She took her husband's arm, and inclined her head in leave-taking. 'Come, Andrés.'

Colon bowed low. 'I kiss your hands, madam, and yours, sir.'

Santangel's hand was on his arm as they departed. Beatriz by now was out of sight. The Chancellor chuckled softly. 'There is nothing here to surprise or vex you, Cristobal. The ardours which the Marchioness is conscious of having aroused in you have marked you for her own: a sort of spiritual possession. It does not flatter her to discover that others less exalted may deflect your devotion. Not reasonable. No. But feminine.'

Colon was out of temper. 'If I have made an enemy of her I must deplore it. But I would not mend it.'

'By my life, has this dancing-girl, then, so firm a hold upon you?'

'Enough that I should resent scorn of her from any who owes a better fortune to the accident of birth. Beatriz Enriquez bears the stamp of gentle blood. If she have it not, then I prize her worth still higher. She possesses that rarer thing: a natural nobility.'

'As I've a soul to save, I begin to suspect her of possessing witchcraft.'

'It's a jest to you.'

'No jest at all. For on the voyage that lies ahead of you a woman might be heavy ballast.'

'Or, perhaps, an inspiration.'

'Oh, if it were really that...' Santangel shrugged his broad shoulders. 'After all, perhaps it is saner to love a woman of flesh and blood than waste yourself in a lenten passion for a lady who to you might as well be a painted saint in a cathedral window.'

'I think that is how I should reason if instinct did not save me the trouble.' More thoughtfully he added, 'I should be sorry to make an enemy of the Marchioness of Moya.'

'Oh! As to that, she may deplore that you cast an eye elsewhere, but what would she be admitting if she were actively to resent it? Give yourself peace, and come home to dine with me.'

They moved down the court towards the Gate of Pardon, Santangel saluted on every hand by those who still idled there, with an occasional greeting for Colon, whom rumour was re-establishing. But not even these reflections of the reviving royal favour could relieve the gloom in which he moved. The implications of the Marchioness of Moya's words had too deeply ruffled his spirit.

14

T HAT uneasy spirit of Colon's
was further to be ruffled on the morrow at Zagarte's.

To his usual invitation Beatriz returned by the Morisco the
answer that she could not come, and begged him to excuse
her. He was in no mood to do so.

'What the devil's this?' he blazed.

Zagarte spread his hands, and hunched his shoulders.
'Mugerices. Womanishnesses. Vapours. What can I do?'

'Perhaps there is something I can do. Where is she?'

'She has a temper, excellency. She can be a wild-cat if
provoked.'

'Let us provoke her, then. Lead the way.'

She had her dwelling, as he now discovered, in two rooms
on the upper floor. One of these served her as bower and
dressing-room, a diminutive bedchamber leading from it.
There was some luxury in its equipment. An Eastern carpet
clothed half the floor, a Moorish divan spread with bright
cushions was set against one of the walls. She rose from this
when Colon appeared, tall and more than ordinarily master-

ful, in the doorway. That she should deny herself to him was
as a spur to drive him headlong.

'How, sir? I sent word . . .'

'I know what word you sent.' He closed the door, shutting
out Zagarte. 'It was no word to send me. Why am I denied?'

'Is your pleasure alone to be considered between us?'

'Not if it ceases to be your pleasure, too. Come, Beatriz,
there must be some good reason to refuse me.'

'You acquire rights over me, I think. I have not conceded
them.' She sank to the divan again, rather wearily. She was
in a state of only half understanding her own mind, and therefore only half understood the comedy it prompted her to play.
'It would be best for both of us if you kept to your fine friends
at court.'

'Beatriz! What is this?'

'The best advice that I can give you.' She did not look at
him. 'That was a very beautiful lady, yesterday, at the
Mezquita; and a very exalted one; the Queen's friend. Fitter
company for you than I.'

He came close, and set a knee on the divan beside her, thus
lowering himself to her seated level. 'Is it possible that you
do me the honour to be jealous?'

'Jealous? Yes. But of my repute. I am no fine gentleman's
toy.'

'I am no fine gentleman. Just a rather lonely man who
loves you.'

This was a thrust at her vitals, to rob her, by its suddenness,
of breath. There was a look almost of fear in the eyes she
slowly raised to his. Then she assumed resentment, like an
armour. 'Of what do you talk? You have known me scarcely
a week.'

'That is just the time I have loved you, Beatriz, so utterly
that it is impossible you should not be aware of it. It has

revived my courage, dispelled my loneliness, gilded a drab world for me. You are to me not merely a woman, but the incarnation of all womanhood, which I worship because of my two mothers, who were women, the one on earth and the One in Heaven.'

She was staring at him now in awe. Tears were gathering in her eyes, evoked as much by the actual words he used as by the reverence vibrating in his voice. Her lovely mouth was tremulous. Then as if to combat the weakness to which he was reducing her, she laughed. 'The Devil can lend a man an angel's tongue for the undoing of a woman.'

'Is it possible that you believe it of me?'

'Whatever life may have denied me, it has cruelly supplied me with discernment.'

'Not if you can discern no better in me. This, my Beatriz, is pure perversity.' His arms went round her as he spoke, and he drew her close.

For a moment, taken by surprise, she let him have his will. Then, as his lips touched her cheek, she broke the spell of it. Battling wildly she thrust him from her. 'No!' she cried, and again, 'No!'

'Beatriz,' he pleaded, 'why will you deny your heart?'

'My heart? What do you know of my heart?'

'What my own tells me.'

She hung her head, and taking this for the end of resistance he enfolded her in his arms again. Holding her, he slipped down to sit beside her. 'You are glad, Beatriz? Say that you are glad, my dear.' His lips found her neck, and as if he had stung her she started again out of his embrace.

'Ah, but you go too fast,' she protested. 'Give me time. Give me time.' She was pleading passionately in an agitation that bewildered him.

'Time? Life is so brief. There is so little time to waste.'

'I . . . I must be sure,' she evaded desperately.

'Of me?'

'Of myself. Ah, leave me now. I implore it of the regard you say you have for me.'

She was in such agitation — an agitation as plain to him as it was incomprehensible — that consideration left him no choice.

He rose, urbane and gentle. 'I do not understand what should distress you so. But I'll not press you now. You shall tell me when next I come.'

He stooped to kiss her hand, and was gone.

Zagarte came upon her some moments later crouched on the divan, in tears. His wide mouth tightened. 'What's this? Has that long rascal mishandled you?'

'No, no. And you are not so to speak of him.'

'That will depend upon the occasion that he gives me. In your place, Beatriz, I'd be wasting no time on him. By what they tell me he's a man of no substance for all his fine airs: a hanger-on at court, a place-seeker, a foreign adventurer. He'll mean you no good. An enterprising rogue with the women, I gather. They do say that the Marchioness of Moya ——'

She let him go no further. 'Enough of your evil tongue, Zagarte. You'll lose it one of these days through want of caution. Leave me alone. Go.'

'Curb your impatiences, my girl. I haven't yet told you why I came. There's a very noble hidalgo asking to see you.'

'I'll not see anyone.'

'Tcha! Tcha! Listen, girl. This is not a nobleman to be denied. He is nephew of the Inquisitor General of Cordoba. He is newly home from an embassy abroad, and he claims to be an old friend of yours, the Count of Arias.'

Her eyes went wide in her tear-stained face. 'Who?'

Zagarte rubbed his hands. 'I see that you know him.'

'I do. And the more reason not to see him.'

'Now, now, my dear. Be reasonable. He is ——'

'I know what he is. He answers to the description you supplied of Master Colon.'

'But so different a case. So great a hidalgo. Come, now. What shall I tell him?'

'To go to the devil.'

'Is that a message I can carry?' Zagarte was annoyed.

'Soften it as you please so long as you understand that that is what I mean.' Zagarte raised his hands in protest, and opened his mouth to plead. 'Not another word!' She sprang up so fiercely that the little Morisco recoiled before her. 'Go! Out of here!'

He backed away to the door. He was grinning without mirth. 'Oh, curb your furies. I'll do what I can. I'll tell him you are indisposed. Impossible to take a high hand with a gentleman of his quality.'

He went out grumbling that only the men of the Muslim faith from which he had apostatized understood the proper treament of women.

To Beatriz the unexpected presence in Cordoba of Don Ramon came acutely to remind her of her brother in the Pozzi. Had the Venetian agents, who were her present masters, desired a spur to drive her to the fulfilment of their aims, they could hardly have discovered a better one than this; whilst, on the other hand, had Fate desired to increase to the pitch of anguish her loathing of the task before her, it could not have done it better than by Colon's impassioned wooing.

For to-night, at least, she had disposed of Don Ramon. He had accepted the excuses offered by Zagarte. But he came back on the morrow, and having witnessed her performance in the mystery, was not again to be put off by any plea of indisposition.

Harassed, Zagarte sought Beatriz with the envoy's demand
that she receive him.

'Not now or ever. Tell him so,' was her answer.

'I dare not.' Zagarte was grim. 'Understand that. I dare
not. I have already dared too much. I dared to tell him that
I knew you would not see him. He was very short. He was
not to be denied, he said, and I'd best contrive that you
receive him, or it would be the worse for me. Come, now,
Beatriz,' he coaxed. 'Why deny to a hidalgo, a grande of
Spain, favours of which you can be prodigal to a nobody?
There's no manner of sense in you.'

'I will not be pestered by this beast.'

Zagarte became viperish in his despair. 'You'll sing and
dance here no more, then.'

She laughed at him. 'Who will be the loser? How many
came to see your mystery before I joined it?'

'We shall both be the losers. But for me, at any rate, it
will be less of a loss than having them find heresy in these
mummeries. I don't want to take part in an auto-da-fé.
That's what this Count of Arias hints might happen. Don't
you see? I'm only a poor devil of a Morisco.' In fervent intercession he added: 'A little reasonableness, Beatriz! For both
our sakes.'

He had said enough. Whilst breathing hard in anger to
perceive the havoc that an unscrupulous Don Ramon had
power to make, yet concern for the Morisco conquered her.
'Very well,' she said, at last. 'Let him come.'

But her consent almost increased Zagarte's anxieties, so
grimly was it delivered. 'You'll receive him agreeably?'

'So that he comes you will have done your part. The rest
is my affair.'

So Don Ramon was brought, all unconsciously to play out
his little part as a pawn in the hand of Destiny.

He stood for a silent moment in the doorway, surveying her with a quizzical smile on his narrow face. He wore a surcoat of darkest olive on which faint arabesques were wrought in thread of gold. Loosely shaped and full-skirted, with wide sleeves that hung to his knees, it gave bulk to his too slender figure. A flat velvet cap of the same colour, with a black plume clasped by a jewelled buckle, adorned his dark head.

Wearying of his stare, standing in stiff defiance before her mirror, she challenged him. 'What do you seek, sir, that you are so importunate?'

He came forward, his manner easy, his loose mouth smiling. 'I can understand that you should be afraid to receive me . . .'

'Afraid!'

' . . . after your breach of faith with me in Venice. That, my dear Beatriz, was not the way to treat a friend who was at great pains to serve you.' His smile became reproachful. 'However, God be thanked I am not by nature vindictive. I bear no malice. At least, none from which amiability will not shield you.'

He took her weakly surrendered hand, and raised it to his lips. In recovering it she answered him tonelessly. 'I broke no faith. There was no faith pledged. You offered me a bargain — a sordid bargain. That is all.'

'How ungrateful! And how untrue.' His tone continued easy. 'Although you promised nothing I did all that I could. I saw the Doge. I pleaded with him, even with some sacrifice of my ambassadorial dignity, and I actually won his promise to release your unhappy brother. Unfortunately, afterwards, so he told me, he discovered reasons — reasons of state — that made it impossible for him to fulfil his promise. But to deny me thanks for what I did! That is not nice, Beatriz. And it was not nice to quit Venice without a word to me, after the proofs I had given of my devotion. It was ungenerous.'

'You sought to profit by my need,' she reminded him. 'But that is in the past.'

'Well said. We'll agree to turn the page, and do better in the future.'

'It will save trouble, Don Ramon,' she told him coldly, 'if you will understand that I have no more concern in your future than in your past.'

'It would break my heart to believe you.'

'Break it, then, and go. You intrude upon me.'

'So hateful, am I?' But he still smiled, and it was this smile that awakened her fear and loathing. He found himself a chair, sat down and crossed his shapely, green-clad legs.

'You did not hear me. I asked you to go.'

He shook his head in tolerant reproach. 'So regrettable between old friends. So improper. So undreamed by me, solicitous to serve you now, as I would have served you before.'

'I ask no service of you, Don Ramon, and I need none.'

'Do not be too sure. This mystery, now, in which you are performing. It touches dangerously upon holy things. It may even be that it is not without suspicion of heresy, and some might judge that the part you play is tainted with blasphemy. These are matters for the Holy Office, and it is perhaps unfortunate that Zagarte should be a Morisco, on all of whom the inquisitors keep a suspicious eye. Enchanting though you would be doing penance in your shift, candle in hand, yet I should deplore the spectacle. And there might be worse to follow. You begin to perceive how necessary as a friend I might prove to you?'

He smiled upon the horror that glared at him from her white face, understanding but the half of it.

'If it were really so?' she asked him.

'How could I help you, do you mean?' He threw back his surcoat, revealing the red lily-hilted dagger embroidered on the left breast of his doublet. 'Not only am I a lay-tertiary of Saint Dominic, but the Inquisitor of Cordoba, Frey Pedro Martinez de Barrio, is my uncle. My testimony to your unstinting piety would be a sure shield to guard you. Now you will understand that——'

'That the influence that could be used to protect me could also be used to accuse me. That is what I am to understand. Is it not? Let us be quite clear, Don Ramon.'

Under the stark contempt of her glance he preserved his detestably smiling demeanour. 'What is there to anger you? After all, I give you flattering proof of the insistence of my devotion.' Less amiably, he added: 'In Venice I was cheated of my dearest hopes. I do not readily submit to that. Nor do I readily relinquish that upon which I have set my heart.' He rose, and moved towards her. His manner changed again to one of pleading conciliation. 'Why will you force me, Beatriz, to woo in such ungracious terms, when all I ask is to lavish upon you the treasures of my tenderness?'

An altercation beyond the door came to interrupt him. Zagarte's voice was raised in expostulation. 'But I tell your worship that it is not seemly,' to which a peremptory voice made answer: 'Out of my way, Zagarte. Out of my way!' Then the door was flung open and a tall figure in black and gold surveyed them from the threshold.

There was a mutually staring pause. 'What do you want here?' Don Ramon at last demanded.

The poise of the intruder's tawny head became more arrogant, the brows were raised above steely eyes.

'Well, sir? Do you hear me? What do you want? Who are you?'

Colon closed the door. 'The question is rather: who and what are you that you should ask me?'

'I am the Count of Arias!' was the truculently shouted

answer. He expected the name to produce an impression. But it evidently completely failed.

'Is that all? By your bellowing I might suppose you to be Captain Matamoros.'

To Don Ramon this was incredible. 'You are insolent, sir.'

'That is to match your insolence. My concern is with this lady. Not with you.'

'You should have the grace to see that you intrude. At some other time Mistress Beatriz may see you, if she so pleases.' He waved an angry hand in dismissal.

But Colon refused to be dismissed. 'I do not understand that you give orders here.'

'It is time you did, then; and also that I do not usually give them in vain.'

'The Devil take you and your orders. I am not concerned with what usually happens to them, or with you, whatever you may be.' Colon's eyes swept past the furious noblemen to Beatriz where she stood, frozen still by the menace of Don Ramon's last words to her. A glance of wild entreaty from her came further to bewilder him, whilst Don Ramon was raging.

'You shall discover who and what I am, to your cost. Out of here!' Again Don Ramon pointed to the door. 'Out of here! At once!'

Ignoring him, Colon continued to look beyond him at Beatriz. He spoke quietly. 'Whether I go or stay is for Mistress Beatriz to say.'

She stirred at last, and, distraught, answered wildly, as her newborn fear of Don Ramon dictated. 'Oh, go, go! Please go!'

This was to dumbfound him. He pondered her with eyes that reflected the hurt to his soul. Thus until Don Ramon roused him.

'You have heard.'

'I have heard,' said Colon slowly.

'Then why do you wait? Out of here, you rascal.'

Colon's precariously balanced temper was overthrown. It was only outwardly that he preserved a show of calm. 'I do not like "rascal,"' he said, and swept his cap across Don Ramon's white face. As Don Ramon fell back, anger blending with amazement that anyone should have the audacity to strike him, the other added: 'I am Colon. Cristobal Colon. Anyone will tell you where I am to be found.'

Don Ramon was in a slobber of rage.

'You shall hear from me. You shall be schooled, you dog. Be sure that you shall be schooled.'

But already the door was slamming upon Colon's departure. Don Ramon swung livid and trembling to Beatriz. 'Who is he? Who is that scoundrel?'

But now, anger, mastering her, too, broke down her circumspection.

'Go,' she ordered him. 'Leave me. Go! You've done harm enough.'

'Eh?' He croaked. 'By God and His Saints, I've done harm, have I? That is to follow. Enough harm to settle the account in full. To dare to strike me. Me!' He flung about the room noisily inarticulate, adding by his violence to her distraction. 'By the living God, it's the last blow he'll ever strike in this world.'

His quaking fury terrified her.

'What do you mean?' she cried. 'What will you do?'

'Do?' He laughed unpleasantly. 'My lads will know what to do. You'll have a friend the fewer when they have done with him.'

She seized his arm in panic. 'Mother of God! What do you mean?'

'Haven't I made it clear? Do you think a man may live who can boast that he has struck me?'

'You will do murder!' she gasped in a terror so manifest that it had the effect of staying his passion. For a long moment he considered her with speculative eyes. 'We'll discuss it,' he said presently, and drew her to the divan. 'Sit down, and listen.'

15

Colon, emerging furiously from Zagarte's, almost collided with a large gaudy man who seized him by the arm to arrest him. An Italian voice haled him out of his angry absorption.

'Gesumaria, Ser Cristoforo! Whither so blindly?'

'Not now. Not now.' Colon disengaged his arm. 'Give me leave.' And he plunged away.

Rocca, fingering his chin, watched the tall figure until it disappeared round a twist of the crooked street. His brow darkened. 'The devil!' he said aloud, and went purposefully in. He needed reassurance that no folly on the part of Beatriz had created some breach between her and Colon.

He crossed the courtyard unheeded, and went briskly up the stairs. But along the corridor to her door he trod like a cat, from the instinct which his trade had developed in him. At the door itself he paused. A man's voice reached him.

'Realize, adorable Beatriz, that it is as profitable to be my friend as it is deadly to be my enemy.'

It was enough to assure Rocca that his coming was timely.

He rapped on a panel, and without further ceremony lifted the latch and went in.

On the divan sat Beatriz in distress, her shoulders hunched. Over her — like a monstrous spider in Rocca's indignant eyes — stood the long olive-green elegance of Don Ramon.

Rocca affected surprise. 'God forgive me, I believe that I intrude. Oh, your pardon, madam.'

If he really meant to withdraw, he was stayed by Beatriz, with the eagerness of relief. 'But come in. Come in. His excellency is just taking leave.'

Don Ramon's countenance, darkened by this fresh intrusion, was darkened further by that dismissal. He had flung no more than a cursory glance over his shoulder at the newcomer. Deeply annoyed though he might be, he had no wish to embroil himself again. Enough already that day had his dignity suffered. He elected to be haughtily distant.

'I shall return, at a more convenient time. When you are less occupied with other visitors.'

He waited a moment, but receiving no reply he turned to go, and so came face to face with Rocca, whom he had last seen in Doge Barbarigo's antechamber.

There was mutual recognition and mutual surprise. Rocca, well schooled in dissimulation, scarcely blinked. But Don Ramon, with nothing to conceal, sharply threw up his head. 'Why, sir . . . I know you. You are from Venice.'

Rocca bowed, without trace of his consuming anxiety. Denial would be worse than idle. He must carry this by impudence.

'Your lordship's memory flatters me.' It was his hope that Don Ramon's memory would not reach too far. 'I was attached there to the chancellery.'

'The chancellery? I knew you as an agent of the Inquisitors of State.'

Liking it less and less, Rocca preserved his practised calm. 'Oh! In very special matters only. And now you see me in the following of the Venetian envoy to the Sovereigns of Castile and Aragon.'

'An odd promotion.' Don Ramon looked with narrowed eyes from the Venetian to Beatriz. 'Very odd.'

'We are old friends, Beatriz and I,' Rocca explained, 'from her days in Venice.'

'I do not doubt that. I am not doubting it at all. An agent of the Three would no doubt find some usefulness in such a friendship. Perhaps even in Cordoba. You leave me wondering.'

'Sir, I've said that in Cordoba I am attached to the Venetian envoy.'

'To be sure you said so. Yes,' he answered with a sneer on his loose mouth. 'And I ask myself in what capacity. Well, well! I take my leave.'

He bowed with a cool formality, and went out.

Beatriz, who had risen, and Rocca stood looking at each other, with no word spoken until Don Ramon's footsteps had faded in the corridor. Then Rocca's lips took an unpleasant twist.

'That's a meeting that would have been better avoided. I wonder what's in the popinjay's mind.' Then, abandoning conjecture, he came to the matter of the visit. 'What trouble was he threatening you?'

'The worst. He'll discover heresy or blasphemy or both in my part in the mystery. He's nephew of the Grand Inquisitor of Cordoba, and, himself, a lay-tertiary of Saint Dominic. His word, he tells me, can send me to the fire.'

'A hot wooer, faith! An ardent gentleman.' Rocca was sardonic. 'And with Colon? What occurred?'

'An altercation. Not much in itself. But enough to make that devil swear to have Colon's throat cut.'

'So, so! Handy with both steel and fire. A gentleman of
parts. We must take order about him.' He was suddenly
anxious. 'Colon went off in fury. He has not broken with you
on that fool's account?'

She relieved his fears by telling him what had passed.

'That should be soon mended when Colon knows with what
the dog was threatening you.'

'He must know it at once. He must be warned.'

'And you mean to go, yourself, and warn him. Excellent!
It's an opportunity not to be neglected. The very occasion
for tenderness. It should advance matters between you by a
long stride. Don't you see?'

'I see,' she answered heavily.

'To it, then. Why so glum? Nothing could have fallen out
better.' He displayed a faint excitement. 'He's lodged at
Bensabat's, the tailor in the Calle Atayud. By my soul, Don
Ramon may prove to have done us the best of services. It's
well said that all evil doesn't come to hurt us. Away with
you, then. Find Colon. It's a heaven-sent chance to find at the
same time the thing we seek.'

That prospect took him off in good humour. But he was
thoughtful again by the time he reached the Fonda del Leon
and Messer Gallina, and there poured out his tale.

'This damned popinjay,' he ended, 'comes blundering into
our plans like a bumblebee into a spider's web.'

Gallina's dark wooden face remained inscrutable. He sat
at table, with papers before him, at the interrupted task of
preparing by candlelight a report for the Council of Three.

'He is certainly inconvenient. In fact dangerous. Damnably
dangerous. But at least we are warned in time. So far no
harm is done.'

'But how long shall we be able to say that? His recognizing
me for an agent of the Three is bad enough. That in his mind

he is linking Beatriz with me as another agent is still worse. He scarcely troubled to conceal his suspicions. A word from him to the Corregidor of Cordoba, and we should be asked to account for ourselves.'

'Do you suppose I don't perceive it? That he should come between Colon and Beatriz is nothing. That breach is soon healed in the case of a man as love-sick as Colon. And such healings make for expansiveness. But if Beatriz were arrested with you as a Venetian agent...' He shrugged. 'Your image was very apt, Rocca. A bumblebee in a spider's web.' He sat back, fingering his square chin, his eyes veiled. 'He's extremely inconvenient, our Don Ramon de Aguilar, this hidalgo who commands fire and steel in such abundance.' He made the comment dispassionately. 'Where does the fool live, do you know?'

'That's soon discovered. But to what end?'

Gallina sat up again. 'The only end.' He drew a sheet of paper forward, and took up his pen.

'Wait.' The quill scratched and spluttered for some moments. 'There.' He held out the sheet on which he had written:

> My lord: — You have left me in such terror that I cannot bear it longer. I cannot sleep until I've made my peace with you. I implore you to come to me at once, and believe me your servant who kisses your hands and will deny you nothing.

Rocca frowned over it. 'I see. But the writing?'

'Is it likely that he will know her hand?'

'No. That's true,' Rocca slowly agreed. He returned the sheet. 'It wants her name to it.'

But Gallina shook his head, and on his tight mouth there was that smile of his that was always akin to a sneer. 'For that jackanapes it requires no signature. For others it would be too much.' He folded the sheet, sealed it with a blob of wax, and wrote the superscription. 'Now order supper,' he commanded. 'This must wait awhile.'

At an hour that night by when Cordoba was disposing itself for sleep, and wayfarers in its narrow streets were scarce, a man muffled in a dark burnouse knocked at the gates of a Moorish palace on the Ronda with an urgent message which he was ordered to deliver to Don Ramon de Aguilar in person.

The porter admitted him to a courtyard where the glow of a lantern faintly gilded the bubbling water of a fountain. Thence, after a spell of waiting, he was conducted to the hall, where Don Ramon himself stood to receive him.

'What is your message? Whence are you?'

The messenger's face remained invisible in his hood. But his salaam and the Arab garment that enfolded him announced him to Don Ramon and to the porter alike for a Mudejar. In silence he proffered his letter.

Don Ramon broke the seal and stepped under the three-beaked lamp that hung from the ceiling, so that he might have light by which to read. A gleam leapt from his eyes and a flush of colour to his sallow cheek.

'A hat and cloak, Gonzalo.' He was peremptory.

'I have leave to go, excellency?' murmured the messenger.

'Yes. No. Wait.'

The elderly porter was settling the cloak on his master's shoulders. 'Shall I summon Salvador or Martin to accompany your lordship?'

'No. This Mudejar will serve for escort. I may not be returning to-night. My arms.'

Gonzalo girt him with a belt carrying sword and dagger; then, ordering the messenger to follow, Don Ramon set out.

They emerged upon the wide Ronda, facing the broad Guadalquivir. It was a clear soft, starlit summer night, and the moon in the last quarter, riding high, flung shafts of silver athwart the black bosom of the river and turned to silver flakes the ripples that broke over the wheels of the Arab water-mills. The Ronda was deserted, and the only sound that broke the silence of the night was the distant tinkle of a guitar.

Don Ramon swung to the left and went off in the direction of the great Moorish Bridge, whose six arches were black pits of shadow. He moved at speed in his joyous eagerness to respond to the unexpected invitation he had received.

Whatever may have been false in the note that had lured him forth, it conveyed at least a faithful impression of the affliction of its supposed author. It was an affliction that sprang from two merging sources: her deep trouble at the manner of Colon's departure and the inferences dishonouring to herself in which he must have accepted his dismissal, and the still deeper trouble sown by Don Ramon's threats to Colon's life.

Rocca had promised to take order. But what order could he take against one so powerful as the Count of Arias, and whatever it might be, would it be taken in time?

She was at once cold with dread of what might happen to Colon and hot with shame of his probable present thoughts of her. It was not to be endured. There could be no peace from these emotions until she had warned him and explained herself.

In the end, without thought for herself or the dangers that might lurk by night in those streets for an unescorted woman, she had gone forth without even troubling to summon her Morisco woman to attend her. To the Calle Atayud the distance was short, the streets were almost empty, and of the few she met none heeded her.

The entrance to Bensabat's shop was by a door on the left of the courtyard, immediately within its iron gate. She found the bell-chain, and in answer to the tinkling summons the tailor's door was opened, sending a rhomb of light across the gloom. Into this hobbled the bent, aproned shape of Bensabat. He came to peer at her through the bars of the gate.

'I am seeking Master Colon. It is urgent.' She was out of breath from the haste she had made, and from apprehension of two moving shadows vaguely seen in a doorway across the street.

'Master Colon? Ohé!' he cackled, and drew the bolt. 'Come you in. Come you in.' He pointed to a dark doorway, farther down the yard on the left. 'In there. His door is at the head of the stairs.'

She thanked him, hastened on, climbed the stairs and knocked.

'Enter!' a voice answered.

She lifted the latch, and the door yielded.

Colon sat in shirt and breeches at his table, and by the light of two candles in tall wooden sconces was at work with coloured inks upon a large chart. At least, that was the purpose of his sitting there. Actually the ink was drying on the quill he held. He was gnawing the feathered end of it, and his brooding eyes saw nothing of the chart before him. What he saw was the face of Beatriz, white and distorted by some emotion that baffled him, whilst an echo of her voice rang in his ears to wound and anger him with its harsh, urgent 'Go! Go!'

As the latch clicked and the door of his humble room swung slowly inwards, creaking on its hinges, he looked round, and imagined for a moment that he was still at his visions. Timid, hesitant, Beatriz stood framed in the doorway.

He flung down his pen, and started up.

'May I come in?' she asked, and without waiting for his answer did so, closing the door and coming forward.

They stood at last eye to eye with the table between them, her lips tremulous, her breast heaving in agitation, he, outwardly calm and stern, waiting. Speech poured from her breathlessly. 'You understood — did you not? — why I bade you go. You saw — did you not? — that I was under constraint?'

Out of his pain he answered hurtfully. 'It is natural, I suppose, with your kind, to prefer a grande of Spain to such as I am.'

'My kind! What is my kind? No matter. You say that to be cruel. You want to punish me for what you suppose was an offence against you.'

'What would you have me suppose it?'

'What it was. What you might have seen if you had faith in me. Is it difficult to understand that I had no thought but fear for you?'

'You do not flatter me by such needless fears.'

'Needless? Oh, not needless. If it were I should not now be here.'

'I am asking myself why you are.'

There was a touch of fierceness in her answer. 'To warn you. That man left me swearing that his bullies would deal with you. You know who and what he is, and the infamous power he wields. Bitter, evil, vindictive, he will not scruple to use it as he threatens, and he accounts himself beyond the reach of consequences. That is why I am here: to warn you, so that you may guard yourself against his malice.'

He stood a moment thoughtful, looking at her. 'What,' he asked at last, 'is he to you, this man, that he permits himself the airs of a master?'

Her smile was bitter. 'At least not what you have done me the wrong to suppose. If he were I should not be driven to come to you. Oh, don't you see?' she broke out passionately. 'I never more fervently wished to keep you beside me, never more urgently needed you than when for your safety's sake — with no thought but that — I bade you go. Don't you see?'

The fervour of her appeal brought him round the table to her side. He set an arm about her shoulders, and drew her against him.

'I am dull at times,' he said, in penitence. 'Culpably dull. In my soul I have been angry with you. I miscalled you. I conceived that you despised the heart I offered.'

'You had only the appearances by which to judge. That is why I am so urgent to come and correct them.'

'I should have seen further.'

'Yes.' Her eyes were wistful. 'You should have understood that what you saw was but one of the indignities to which I am subject in my way of life.'

'Why do you follow it?'

'Do you ask me that again? I must answer as before. For bread. It is all that I can do, short of shutting myself in a convent.'

'You were never born for it.'

'Do I know for what I was born? I was not born to poverty. But misfortune has brought me to it, none the less.'

'This must end, Beatriz.' He was resolute. 'Your Don Ramon has shown me the urgency where I perceived only the necessity. God knows I have little to bestow save my devotion. But soon now, this will be mended, and what I have and am I offer you, Beatriz; and my name shall shelter you if you will have it.'

'If I will have it?' she echoed, as if she did not understand.

'If you will marry me, my dear.'

He felt her body tremble against him, and there was a long pause before she spoke. 'You offer me that!' Her voice was

low, and laden with wonder. Then, suddenly, she broke
away from him, and confronted him squarely, her eyes tragic.
'Oh, what do you know of me?' she cried, and flung wide her
arms, as if offering herself for his closer inspection.

She bewildered him. 'I know that you are my woman; that
I love you, Beatriz.'

'God pity me!' she wailed.

'Beatriz!' He advanced, holding out his arms; then checked
as she recoiled before him.

'No, no.' She turned aside, and with uncertain steps, like
a blind person, she crossed to his day-bed, and sank to it
listlessly, her hands limp in her lap. 'It is impossible, Cristobal.
Impossible.'

His bewilderment deepening, he came to lean over her.
'Impossible?'

There was a distraction of grief in her answer. 'What would
I not give to make it possible! That you think of me so is the
greatest treasure I shall ever possess. I am yours, Cristobal,
for as long as I live. I will love you and serve you with all
that I have and am.'

'But then . . .'

'I am already married, Cristobal.'

He straightened himself abruptly, and fell back a pace,
agape.

'Married! You are married?'

'Three years ago at the Pentecost,' she answered miserably,
'when I was eighteen, and a poor, innocent fool who believed
no evil of anyone.'

'And your husband?'

'I have no husband. That is the only mercy Fate has shown
me. The man I married is a gallerian serving a life sentence
on the galleys of Castile. He was a poor debauched profligate,
who ended as such rogues end, by stabbing a man with whom

he quarrelled over a good-for-nothing woman. It happened that the wounded man survived. Because of this, and because the galleys are always in need of oars, Enriquez was allowed to live instead of being garrotted, to toil at the oar until he dies. But between him and me the bond tied by the Church abides, and so ...' She broke off, spread her hands in a pathetic little gesture of misery, and let them fall again in helplessness.

Stricken, he sank to the couch beside her. He set an arm about her shoulders and drew her close. 'Poor child! Oh, what can one say to you?'

'Nothing, Cristobal. There is nothing more to say. Best let me go. Right out of your life. I came into it for no good ...'

'That, never.' His vehemence stifled the confession that emotion was wringing from her. 'Never. Never. That you cannot marry does not alter my resolve to make you my care. More than ever do you show me the necessity.'

'Ah, if you knew. If you knew everything. Listen.'

But again he interrupted her. 'I know enough. I know all that matters. I know that I love you, and you have confessed that you love me.'

'So truly!' she protested on a note of passion. 'But ——'

'There is nothing else to concern us. I began by saying that I have nothing. But I believe myself to stand on Fortune's threshold, that soon I shall be amongst the greatest in the land. Wealth and power will be mine to set you where you should be.' He drew her squarely to him, enfolding her hungrily. 'Beatriz!' He bent and kissed her lips. But no sooner had she let him have his way than alarm awoke in her.

'Let me go now,' she begged him. 'Ah, let me go. Let me go!'

Obediently he released her. 'Let me get my coat, and I will escort you home.'

She stayed him in the act of rising. 'No.' There was not only firmness, but a sudden alarm in her denial. 'Have you forgotten why I am here? What brought me? You are not to go forth alone at night.'

'Bah!' he laughed.

'I am serious. You do not know the Count of Arias. Nor have I told you all. As I came I saw two men lurking in a doorway across the street. I do not know that they are Don Ramon's bullies. But I fear it.'

'I shall go armed,' he promised, to reassure her.

'That may suffice in the daytime, if you are watchful. But never at night. Promise me that you will not stir forth alone.'

'That would be intolerable.'

'Promise me,' she insisted. 'If you love me, promise me. If you will not think of yourself, think of me. If anything happened to you where should I find me a protector?'

'A protector whom you protect,' he laughed. 'A fine guardian, that.'

But behind his laughter there was seriousness. The possibility of being cut off, weighed now for the first time by this man of strong vitality, started a sudden train of thought, a fresh concern for her. If that were to happen, be it by the agency of Don Ramon, be it by some other, what, indeed, would then become of her for whom he had made himself responsible? Some provision must be made. He had little to leave, yet something there was that he could do to benefit her in such a case. He took a swift resolve.

'Listen, Beatriz. There's a word I must say before you go. As for this Don Ramon, be sure that I shall know how to guard myself. He serves, however, to remind me that I am mortal, and there is something for which I should provide.'

He went to take from the wall the brass panel that bore the picture of the Madonna, and from the concave back of it he removed a key. With this he unlocked the coffer under the window, raised the lid, and withdrew a slender tin case, a half-yard in length by a foot or so wide. He held it up. 'You see this case?'

She nodded without speaking, staring fixedly.

He replaced it, closed and locked the coffer, and came back to sit beside her.

'It is my legacy to you,' he said. 'It contains all that I possess of value. But its value should be great. It is a chart, and with that chart a full declaration of the facts and judgments upon which it is drawn.'

She was rigid, her hands clenched, striving with her rising agitation. 'Should anything ever happen to me, Beatriz,' he continued quietly, 'here is what you must do. You will take that case, and deliver it to Don Luis de Santangel, the Chancellor of Aragon. I will tell Bensabat that in any such case you are to be made free of my few possessions here.'

Her sudden clutch upon his wrist interrupted him. 'No, no!' It was a cry of pain.

'Wait,' he said. 'Hear me out. With the chart I shall enclose a letter for Don Luis de Santangel, directing him to sell to the Sovereigns these means to enable another to carry out the discoveries by which I look to magnify the wealth and power of Spain. Don Luis, I know, will do his best so that half of the price obtained should enable you to live in ease and dignity; the other half will go to my little son, who is now at Palos, at the Convent of La Rabida.'

'Mother of God!' she cried out, in such consternation that he swung fully to face her.

She was staring at him with tragic eyes; eyes of a startling blackness in the pallor of her face. Meeting his glance, she was torn by a sudden violent sob; then, lowering her head, she abandoned herself to a passion of weeping.

For a moment he sat appalled. 'Why, Beatriz! Beatriz!'
He took her in his arms. 'Why, child, what need is there for
this? I merely take the common prudent measures against
the unlikely case that I should not be at hand to shelter and
provide for you.'

'Oh, the shame of it! The shame of it!' she sobbed.

'Shame? Where is the shame?'

'In my worthlessness. I am so worthless.'

He held her close. 'To me worth more than all the wealth
of the Indies that await me.'

'You don't understand.' She looked up piteously. Then, in
a convulsive movement, she flung her arms round his neck,
and drew his head down upon her breast.

Pillowing it there, his arms enlacing her slender graceful
body, he yielded himself to the thrall of an ecstasy such as he
had never known.

16

Aᴅᴍɪᴛᴛᴇᴅ by Colon, old Bensa-
bat shuffled into his guest's room as was his morning habit,
bearing on a copper tray a frugal breakfast of bread, cheese,
olives, dried figs and a jug of the heavy dark wine of Malaga.

Having set it on a corner of the table, which was still spread
with the map on which the coming of Beatriz had interrupted
Colon's work last night, the old man looked round, and his
glance alighted on a woman's blue cloak that lay across the
day-bed. His face discreetly blank, he looked up at Colon,
who stood beside him in shirt and breeches. He bowed a
creaking back. 'A good morning to your worship.'

'Good morning to you, Juan.'

Bensabat waved a gnarled hand to indicate the tray. 'Your
worship is served. And there's a letter from His Excellency
Don Luis de Santangel brought by a messenger.'

Colon nodded. Bensabat lingered, his little eyes straying
furtively to the alcove, the curtains of which remained closely
drawn. 'Nothing else your worship requires this morning?'

'Nothing else, Juan.'

'Ah! There's a deal of news abroad. They do say that the Sovereigns will be leaving Cordoba in a day or two, to return to the Vega. Fresh troops have arrived there. The siege is to be pressed hard, they say, so as to make sure that the Cross replaces the Crescent on Granada before Christmas.'

'Ah!' Colon nodded vaguely. He waited for Bensabat to go.

'There's bad news, too,' the tailor babbled on. 'A hidalgo was fished out of the river this morning, as dead as Mahomet, with his head cracked. A very noble hidalgo; the Count of Arias, nephew of the Inquisitor-General of Cordoba.'

Colon was conscious of a momentarily quickened pulse. He was conscious, too — or else he imagined it — of a faint sound from beyond the curtains of the alcove. Outwardly, however, he remained unmoved, and the sound, if really audible, would hardly have reached Bensabat's deaf ears.

'Poor gentleman,' he said. 'God rest him!'

'Amen, sir! Amen!' The tailor crossed himself with New-Christian ostentation. 'It isn't rightly known whether he broke his head in falling, or whether it was broken for him before throwing him in. A handsome, lustful gentleman, the Count of Arias, with a back to set a coat off to perfection. He'll be greatly missed.'

'Not a doubt,' said Colon, and grew ribald:

> 'A handsome body clothed a soul as fair
> And wore a doublet with a princely air.'

'God save us, sir!' Bensabat was scandalized. 'Do you make a jest of it?'

'A jest? An epitaph.' He took up the letter from the tray. 'You have leave, Juan.'

Bensabat, perceiving at last his dismissal, shambled out.

He had scarcely gone when the curtains of the alcove, which had been an object of such deep interest to him, were swept apart and Beatriz came breathless to join Colon.

'I heard,' she panted, her eyes grave.

'The Count of Arias?' He looked down at the glossy chestnut head that reached to his shoulder, and put an arm round her. 'Poor man! I'll have a Mass said for his soul. I owe him that for supplying the occasion of your coming to me last night, to warn me.'

'Unnecessarily, as we now know.'

'Unnecessarily, but happily. Or do you regret it?'

'No,' she answered soberly. 'I shall never regret it.'

'I vow to God you shall never have reason.' He stooped to kiss her. 'You are now my care. Sit here.' He placed a chair for her, swept the chart away to the day-bed, and drew the tray before her. 'Break your fast, child. It's poor fare. But the Indies still await discovery.'

There was an air of blitheness about him, as if he had recaptured his first youth. Straight and vigorous, he moved resilient as a panther. His grey eyes were light and eager. He hovered about her, quick and gay, talking the while.

'It's but a poor lodging, this. But such as it is it offers you a haven in your need, as will henceforth whatever lodging may be mine. When I return from the lands of the Grand Khan, where the roofs are tiled with gold, you shall be housed in splendours worthy of you. Until then beautify these poor shards for me by freely making use of them.'

He paused to pour wine for her. 'Why so solemn, my Beatriz?'

'Listening to you makes me solemn.'

'I talk awry, then. I want to see you smile. You are not unhappy? You have no misgivings for entrusting yourself to such a vagabond?'

'My dear!' she cried, in repudiation.

'If that means that you have not, then all is well.' He began to eat. Munching, he tore open, at last, the letter, and an added brightness shone in his eyes.

'The Salamanca doctors of whom I was telling you last night have arrived in Cordoba to sit in judgment on me. I am to go before them at once. The Sovereigns want the matter decided before they return to the Vega. Not tomorrow, says Don Luis, for it is the Feast of Corpus Christi. And — ha! — the astute Chancellor counsels me to carry a candle in the procession, so that I may make sure of the favour of Frey Diego Deza and the other theologians who are to judge me. Theologians to pronounce upon cosmography! Laugh, Beatriz. Oblige me by laughing. For this is as humorous as a cosmographer would be preaching the sermon in an auto-da-fé.'

Yet neither then nor after did he find it easy to amuse her. She ate and drank but little, and that little in preoccupation, for which at last he chided her. 'There is something on your mind, Beatriz.'

She smiled by an effort. 'The thought that I must be going,' she prevaricated. 'It is time that you smuggled me out of this. It grows late. Zagarte will be wondering.' She rose.

He helped her into her cloak. 'When shall I see you again, my dear?'

'Why, when you will. I shall be waiting for you until you come.'

'There is so much still to say between us. So much that perhaps it will never all be said.'

He kissed her, and closely hooded she slipped away.

She reached Zagarte's, and across the courtyard, deserted at that morning hour, she sped to the staircase, and so gained her room.

She opened her door, and checked, startled by the sight of a man seated at her table. He raised his grizzled head and disclosed the sardonic, bony face of Gallina. He rose with an eagerness unusual to his inscrutability.

'What are you doing here?' she demanded sternly.

'Waiting for you, my dear. And for what I hope you'll have brought me.'

Thus brutally was the haunting horror that she had been madly striving, and even succeeding, to exclude from her tormented mind, thrust suddenly, as it were naked, under her notice.

'I bring you nothing,' she told him, choking.

'How? Nothing? Nothing?' His beady eyes never left her face. They seemed to possess a queer, paralyzing power. 'Close the door,' he bade her, and was mechanically obeyed. 'Come now, my girl, you went to warn and stayed to kiss. Surely not quite in vain. Not if I know you at all; and I think I do.' He waited a moment, ever watchful. 'Well?'

'I have told you that I bring you nothing.'

'Ah!' He moved slowly towards her. 'But why this defiant air? What does it mean?' He was suddenly beside her, and she found her wrist in a grip that made her wince. His bony face was close to hers, and never had his beady eyes looked quite so evil. 'You aren't thinking of playing us false, little fool? You haven't by chance fallen like a ninny into the pit you dug for him? You haven't been abandoning yourself to silly emotions?'

'Release my wrist,' she panted angrily.

He more than obeyed. He flung it from him in a gesture of disgust. 'You silly slut! I am answered. It is what I half-suspected when Rocca told me last night of your terrors of what might be done to this rascal mariner by your other friend the Count of Arias.'

'Whom you've murdered,' she flung at him.

His glittering eyes did not waver in their steady contempt. 'Assume it if you please. But do not breathe it if you value your own breath. Leave that.' He was peremptory. 'Give

a thought instead to your brother, going mad in the Pozzi
with the fear of the cord, whilst waiting for his dutiful sister
to procure his deliverance. Trusting to her.'

Deathly white she crossed to the divan, and sank to it without answering. But Gallina pursued her ruthlessly. 'Will you
tell me that you've been cheated? That you've paid the price,
sacrificed your virtue, given yourself to that rascal's lusts, and
obtained nothing in return? Is that how it goes?'

'Oh, you are vile. Vile! Vile!'

'Miscall me to your heart's content, but let me understand.
Having given all, have you accomplished nothing? If so, why?
Let me know where we stand.'

Then, bending over her, he abandoned his sinister note.
He assumed instead a matter-of-fact tone. 'To me, after all,
it's no great matter what happens to your brother. But at
least be honest with us. Don't waste our time if you're no
longer concerned to save him, if you've decided to leave him
to his fate. The galleys. Or the strangler.'

'Pablo!' she wailed from her tortured conscience.

'Well?'

Cunningly goaded by this insistence upon her faithlessness,
yet she could not take the path along which he sought to
drive her; neither could she persist along the one she had
thought to tread. Either way led to betrayal, the one of her
lover, the other of her brother. Appalled before so horrible
a choice, she knew only the need to postpone, to temporize.

'Wait, wait.' She took her tormented head in her hands.
She spoke wildly, at random, to gain time. 'You expect the
impossible. How could I get possession of the chart whilst
he was there?'

Had she looked at him, the sudden gleam in his cunning
eyes must have warned her of how much he was inferring.
His tone was suddenly softened. 'Why not? Why not?' So
as to test his inference, he drew a bow at a venture. 'Since,

at least, you've discovered where he hides his chart, that is something.' He paused, watching her closely. As there was no denial, he added the probing question: 'When can you use this knowledge?'

This, however, pressed her too sharply. She answered in fierce rebellion. 'Never! I shall never use it. Never.'

He drew breath audibly, and straightened himself. He was smiling, confirmed now in his assumption.

'But what a waste,' he protested, 'since you possess the knowledge. Having gone so far — not to go just a little further and so deliver your unhappy brother.'

'You are answered. I have told you.'

'Yes. You have told me. You have certainly told me.'

She no longer heeded him. He stood a moment, then abruptly crossed to the door, and was gone, leaving her crouched on the divan, her head in her hands, her vision blurred by anguish.

He went back to the Fonda del Leon to await Rocca, who did not return until high noon, and who came in such bubbling excitement that Gallina must allow it to pour itself out without attempting to dam the flow. The source of it was in the discovery just made at court that the junta of doctors had arrived from Salamanca. It was to sit immediately. Not tomorrow, because tomorrow was the Feast of Corpus Christi. But possibly on Friday, or perhaps Saturday and certainly not later than next week, the Sovereigns being now in haste to leave for the Vega. Action, therefore, must be immediate. Beatriz must bestir herself that very day. She had been much too leisurely. But perhaps last night . . .

Gallina's malevolent smile at last made its appearance. 'Not so leisurely,' he interrupted. 'No. Much worse than that. The fool has tangled herself in her own web.' And he told him what had passed.

Rocca's prominent eyes bulged in a congested face. His

temper boiling up, he heaped infamies upon Beatriz until
Gallina checked him.

'Wait. Something is gained. She knows where he hides
the chart.'

'If she knows that, she may easily be brought to do the
rest.'

'Easily? Not with a girl of her spirit. Violence might only
exasperate her into betraying us to Colon.'

'And her brother, then?'

'There are fiercer loves than the sisterly kind. Haven't you
noticed it? We'll go cautiously and patiently. Sarasin is not
an indulgent employer.'

Rocca had fallen into thought. 'If she knows where he
hides it, that means that she has seen it. That puts an end
to doubts as to where it is. It must be in his lodging.'

Gallina sneered. 'You become acute, Rocca.'

Rocca left the sneer unheeded. 'In that case we know all
that we need.'

'Of course.' Gallina was still sneering. 'We have merely
to go and get it.'

'Just so,' said Rocca. 'And tomorrow is our opportunity.
Colon is to follow the court in the Corpus Christi procession.
We make sure of his absence for more than half a day.
Time and to spare in which to go through the effects in his
lodging.'

Gallina no longer sneered. 'And how do we enter it?'

'If I can't find a key to his door, I'll break the lock.'

'And his landlord, the tailor?'

'There's no likelihood that he will be at home. There's
not a converso in Cordoba will dare to make his Christianity
suspect by staying away from the procession. Nothing could
fall out better.'

Gallina reflected.

'I begin to believe you,' he said at last.

17

 CORPUS CHRISTI

Under the broiling Andalusian sun of June, in the vast Court of Oranges of the Mezquita, milled a motley human swarm made up of noble and simple, courtiers in silk and velvet, men-at-arms in steel, knights mantled in crimson or blue, ecclesiastics in black, friars in brown or grey or in white under flowing black cloaks, tabarded heralds and trumpeters in red and yellow. All this was being resolved into order by the Alcalde Mayor of Cordoba, Don Miguel de Escobedo.

Occasional arguments between the civil and ecclesiastical authorities, human stupidity and official impatiences, productive of a good deal of objurgation which none accounted out of place in those sacred precincts, delayed operations, so that the sun was high and the heat and reek becoming oppressive when at last at a signal from the Alcalde the trumpets wound a shrill flourish.

In instant response the bells of the Cathedral crashed forth from the belfry that once had been a minaret, and the great bronze doors were thrown open to give egress to the procession's noblest and essential part.

Whilst there was a general scurry and lighting of candles, one from another, the Alcalde Mayor, in black corselet and black morion crested by a deep comb of polished steel, passed briskly down the court.

Outside the red walls, which in their embattled massiveness suggested the enclosure of a fortress rather than a temple, his mounted alguaziles were ranged, waiting.

He mounted the horse one of his men held for him. At his word of command and a wave of the gloved hand that held his truncheon, the horsemen wheeled into double file, so as to form the head of the procession, and began to advance at a walking pace through the lines of spectators of both sexes that thronged the streets. Above their heads, at windows and balconies hung with tapestries, with cloth of gold or silver or with velvets, crowded those whose dwellings lent them this advantage.

The alguaziles paced sombrely forward in the sunshine flooding down from a sky that was like a dome of polished steel. In their wake, pouring from the Court of Oranges by the Gate of Pardon, headed by a Franciscan bearing a crucifix came some three score surpliced choristers, the sweet young voices of these boys intoning the *Veni Creator Spiritus*. They were followed by the Inquisitor-General of Cordoba, the sable banner of the Holy Office, charged with the green cross between the olive branch and the naked sword, borne before him by a Dominican friar. At his side walked the Provincial of the Dominicans, and after them came some fifty friars of their order, walking two by two and each bearing a lighted candle. A like number of lay tertiaries followed, all of them noble, bearing embroidered upon their black mantles the silver cross of Saint Dominic. There were more banners, more friars, of the Order of Saint Francis now, and then came a herald and six trumpeters, and the very heart of the procession was reached. High above the heads of the walking fraternities appeared as if enthroned the flaming figure of the Cardinal of Spain. He rode a milk-white mule, whose red housings fringed with gold trailed in the dust. From head to foot, from the toe of his shoe to the crown of his wide hat, he was a flame of vivid scarlet. A cloud of grooms and pages in his red liveries surged about him.

His approach was as a signal to the people to kneel to receive the blessing he dispensed from his raised right hand that was scarlet-clad like all the rest of him, the cardinalitial sapphire worn over the glove.

Kneeling, the people remained obedient to the bell that a surpliced acolyte was clanging. He advanced between two thurifers, who rhythmically swung their censers ahead of a great canopy of cloth of gold, borne on gilded poles by six bare-headed knights of Calatrava. Under the canopy the great golden monstrance was carried by a prelate in a cope of cloth of gold that was studded with gems. He was attended by four ecclesiastics in white surplices and crimson stoles, and flanked by files of candle-bearing friars.

Thurifers followed again; then another herald and more trumpeters, and King Ferdinand, bare-headed, as Grand Master of Alcantara, wearing over his gilded armour the white mantle with the red fleurdelisé cross of the order and followed by twenty knights similarly mantled.

After these came a long orderly train of gentlemen of the Court, headed by the Chancellors of Castile and Aragon, with grandes of Spain immediately following, and lesser folk composing the tail. Among these, distinguished by his height and bearing, dutifully walked Cristobal Colon.

Men-at-arms in steel came next, trailing pikes, and in their midst a colossal armoured figure of Saint George, swaying precariously on a great war-horse, and retained in the saddle by the grooms who held the figure's legs on either side.

Slowly and with many halts the long procession wound its way under the increasing ardour of the Andalusian sun, through the crowded crooked streets. It pursued an encircling course that brought it round and back by the Almo dovar, where in a pavilion that had been specially erected, the Queen and her ladies awaited it.

It would be a full three hours after its setting out before it re-entered the Court of Oranges, where part of it was disbanded, whilst the remainder went on into the Cathedral for the *Te Deum* that was to close the day's devotions.

Those three hours had been profitably spent by the Venetian agents.

Bensabat's shop was shut, as were all the shops of the city on that great feast-day. But the gate of his courtyard remained unlocked, and the street was deserted, all the world having gone to see the show. There was none to observe Gallina and Rocca as they passed in, nor would any have given it a thought even had they been seen.

They reached the head of the stairs, and the ingenious Rocca went to work with a collection of keys with which he came supplied. At the sixth attempt the lock responded and the door swung open.

Their search was not a long one. A few moments sufficed for an investigation of the contents of the clothes-press, whereafter they passed to the coffer under the window. This, locked as they found it, seemed more promising. Because none of his keys would fit, Rocca would have smashed the lock. But the more expert Gallina knew how to investigate its contents without leaving obvious traces. With Rocca's help he turned the coffer on its side, so as to examine the bottom. It consisted of no more than two planks of thin pinewood, attached by a half-score nails to the more solid chestnut sides. He went to work, using a stout dagger as a

lever. The nails yielded, and in a moment one of the planks
had been removed. Through this opening he drew out the
contents: some few articles of wear, some odd books, a couple
of rolls of parchment and a thin metal case. From this last
Gallina extracted a parchment folded almost to its exact size,
which, being opened out, proved to be a piece of cartography
of Colon's own. But amongst some other parchments, less
prominent from their smaller size, he came upon a chart that
bore Toscanelli's seal and signature, and with this the precious
Toscanelli letter setting forth the scientific justifications for
those parts of that chart which still remained assumptive.

Gallina's almost lipless mouth was stretched in a grin.
'Here we have it all.'

He closed and replaced the case, and with it, as best he
could, the contents of the coffer; then, having tapped the nails
of the plank into their original holes, so as to restore the
bottom to its first condition, he set the coffer upright again,
precisely as it had stood before, and with no sign of having
suffered violence.

In less than half an hour, even before the procession in
which Colon would be detained had left the Mezquita, the
two Venetians were on their way home in triumph.

In their room at the Fonda del Leon, exultant and in mutual
felicitations, Gallina locked away the precious documents in
a shallow iron box.

'His Serenity's gratitude should be worth at least a year's
pay,' he chuckled. 'The thing is done, and so very simply,
after all. As for Beatriz, the slut may hang herself in her
garters now. That is, if Colon doesn't strangle her when he
discovers the theft. We had better quit at once,' he added.
'To-morrow.'

But Rocca shook his head. 'It would not in any case be
possible. There are arrangements to be made, horses to hire,

and the like. With all Cordoba making holiday to-day, there is none to supply us. And, after all, there is no need for haste. We'll wait until we know the finding of the Salamanca doctors, so that we may report it to His Serenity.'

'That is not important.' Gallina was harshly impatient.

'Not in your view, perhaps. But it will be in the Doge's.'

'Delays are dangerous.'

'Where is the danger? A day or two will not matter. And His Serenity must account it desirable.'

Gallina yielded reluctantly. 'I shall know no peace,' he said, 'until we have taken ship at Malaga.'

18

Colon came late from the Mezquita, long after the last of the faithful had departed, and, his mind turning instantly from the sacred to the profane, he took his eager way to Zagarte's.

He found the eating-house thronged with holiday-makers. There was no place to spare either among the press in the courtyard witnessing the mystery or at the tables in the gallery packed by those who had come to eat and drink, whilst every window was occupied. Zagarte and his myrmidons, male and female, flitted breathless, panting and sweating, to minister to the wants of the patrons. The performance was already in mid-career, and Beatriz had just made her entrance.

Colon thrust with difficulty through those who stood elbow to elbow at the back of the court, and gained at last the entrance to the stairs. He went to await Beatriz in her room, which her Morisco woman was setting to rights when he entered.

Through the open window he could hear the voice of Beatriz, and it seemed to him that it lacked something of its usual irresistible vivacity. When at last she came he was quick to observe her dull-eyed pallor and a listlessness momentarily put off at sight of him. A flush of eagerness was spent almost before he had kissed her hand.

She dismissed her woman, and let herself rest a moment against him, smiling wanly into the concern of his countenance.

'I am a little weary, that is all,' she reassured him. 'I seemed barely to have the strength to dance to-day.'

His encircling arm was tenderly supporting her. 'That you should have to make sport for the mob!' he growled.

'It serves no good end, my friend, to inveigh against necessity.'

'It's a necessity that I have promised you shall cease. If to-morrow my affairs prosper, as I count, there will be no more of this for you. You will become my care.'

'Why should I burden you, Cristobal?'

'Why should I love you, Beatriz? Answer the one and the other is answered. All that I have aimed to do, which has been an end in itself, is now become no more than the means to an end.' He ran on. 'For an hour and more, after all had gone, I remained on my knees in the Mezquita, praying to Our Lady of the Assumption; praying for you and for me; praying for grace so to acquit myself to-morrow that I may finally deliver you from all this.'

She hung her head, her eyes suddenly moist.

'Do you pray for me to-night, Beatriz, in the sure knowledge that in praying for me you will be praying for yourself.'

'My dear, my dear!' She was softly weeping, the tears wrung from her by a torment that he could not guess. 'It needs no such knowledge to make me pray for you. Be sure that you shall always be in my prayers.'

'They will make me strong,' he said, and reverently kissed her.

When at last he left her, he went in a confidence that was
high even for so sanguine a temperament as his. He felt himself invested with a power that nothing could resist, a power
by which inevitably he must prevail to-morrow before the
junta.

This splendid confidence was with him in the morning
when, having broken his fast and prepared to leave for the
Alcazar, he went to assemble his few needs.

He unlocked the coffer and raised the lid, to discover its
tumbled contents. It gave him a moment's pause, but no
more. After all, there had been no tampering with the lock.
The disorder must be a result of his own haste and carelessness. He took up the case and extracted from it the large
chart which he had prepared and which he was to lay before
the doctors. This he rolled, and tied with a piece of ribbon.
Then he sought the Toscanelli chart and letter. Failure to
find them chilled him. He brought the case to the table,
emptied it out, and in dread went piece by piece through all
that it contained. The precious documents were missing.

He stood a moment perplexed and stricken; then he returned to the coffer, and feverishly dragged everything out of
it in a search that was equally fruitless.

He sat down, numbed and limp, to realize that he had been
robbed; it was not to be understood. He had found the coffer
locked as he had left it. Nevertheless certain it was that he
had been robbed; robbed, in this hour of hours, of the stoutest
of his weapons for the battle he was to wage. In chagrin and
rage he asked himself who could have done this thing, who
could even have known that he was possessed of that precious
chart. He had mentioned it to none — that is to say, to none
but Beatriz, and the thought of her in connection with this
loss was dismissed before it could even grow into a suspicion.

He could think only of the Portuguese. King John knew of

the existence of the chart. Was it possible that having learned
of Colon's suit at the Court of Spain, and fearing lest perhaps
the project which he had rejected should, after all, be well-
founded, and that Spain should profit by it, King John had
employed agents to commit this theft?

It would be of a piece with the meannesses he had suffered
at the hands of the King of Portugal. But he could not even
surmise when the theft might have been committed. It was
months since last he had looked at that chart.

For a while he sat there faint and sick under this cruel blow,
stricken at his high assurance of triumph. Gradually, however, his resilient nature shifted the focus of the situation, until
it appeared less desperate. After all, to what did his loss
amount? The Toscanelli documents were merely confirma-
tory of his own conclusions. Those conclusions had been
reached by arguments developed before ever Toscanelli had
been consulted, and by these arguments, overwhelming in
their total, he should carry conviction to any assembly of men
of learning.

He took heart afresh. If the shabby King of Portugal was
indeed the thief, he should find that he had stooped in vain
to this mean larceny.

By the time he came to the Alcazar his courage was as high
as ever, and was there to be further fortified not only by
Santangel's good wishes but by Frey Diego Deza's assurances
that Colon could count upon his suffrages. The paunchy,
benign little friar was on his way to the council chamber
where the junta was assembling when he paused in the anteroom for a word with the waiting Colon.

'Be confident of success, my son. Mine is not the only
voice upon which you can depend to-day.'

What need, he asked himself, to bewail his loss when without Toscanelli's support his arguments had carried conviction

to so acute a mind as Deza's? Upon that reassurance he dismissed his last misgiving, and took his way to the council chamber.

Thirteen men, of whom nine were ecclesiastics, composed the tribunal that was to pronounce upon his plan.

Seated along one side of a long table that was covered in red velvet and furnished with writing materials, they faced him when, outwardly composed, of an aspect so commanding that in itself it should compel men's confidence, he advanced into the vaulted room.

Frey Hernando de Talavera, now Bishop of Avila, who presided, occupied a high chair with carved arms, raised by some inches above the others, so as to enthrone him. On his immediate right sat Deza, on his left Don Rodrigo Maldonado, a navigator of experience now Governor of Salamanca. The other laymen were Don Matias Rezende, Admiral of the galleys of Aragon, and the two Chancellors, Quintanilla and Santangel. Of the remainder, five were in the white habit and black cloak of the order of Saint Dominic, all of them professors at the University of Salamanca; a sixth, Frey Hieronymo de Calahorra, in high repute as a mathematician, wore the grey fustian of Saint Francis. The last, a secular priest, was Don Juan de Fonseca, of whom Las Casas says that though a cleric and an archdean, he was very capable for worldly affairs, especially for recruiting soldiers and for manning fleets, for which reason the King and Queen always entrusted him with the fleets which were armed in their lifetime. A sufficient explanation, this, of his presence on the junta.

Facing the middle of the table, opposite to Talavera, a low armchair had been set, to which Colon was invited by a gracious wave of the bishop's slender, almost translucent hand.

He bowed to the assembled company, and took his seat,

with his rolled chart across his knees. At once Talavera addressed him.

'We are gathered here, sir, by command of Their Highnesses in order to hear your proposals in all detail, examining such proofs as you may have to urge, so that we may judge of their possibility of execution, and after full discussion report upon them to Their Highnesses. We can assure you, sir, of a sympathetic hearing, and we invite you to begin.'

Under no obligation to do so, Colon nevertheless rose. He possessed sufficient histrionic sense to realize what he would thus gain in dominance.

Beginning quietly and warming gradually to his task, he discoursed of the discoveries of Marco Polo and quoted from the Venetian's own account of his eastern travels, giving the position of Zipangu as some fifteen hundred miles beyond Polo's own eastern journeyings. Then, reminding them of the sphericity of the earth, of Ptolemy's theory, which all knowledge accumulated since had gone to confirm, he pointed out how irresistibly it followed that by sailing west, the Zipangu of Polo and lands beyond it must be reached. Independent evidence of the existence of such lands was supplied by objects drifting out of the west that had been washed up on the shores of the Azores: he spoke of those pieces of timber of a kind never seen in the known world, so carved that it was clear the work had not been done with iron; a monster pine-tree, the like of which did not grow in the known world; and he alluded to those canes, now at Lisbon, so gigantic that a gallon of wine might be contained between any two joints, which he supposed to be the giant reeds of which Ptolemy speaks.

He was jarred at this point by the first interruption. It came from Maldonado, and bore witness to the narrowly legal training of the man's mind.

'You speak now, sir, merely of things which you have seen,

or of which you have heard tell, but which you cannot show
us, and which, therefore, we are not to consider.'

Two or three heads were sagely wagged in agreement. That
and the interruption were as spurs to Colon's quick nature.
His grey eyes flamed upon Don Rodrigo.

'I speak, sirs, of things of whose existence you may readily
inform yourselves, things whose existence is generally known
to men who engage upon the study of such matters.'

He counted upon the weakness of human nature to ensure
silence, since the admission of further doubts must now serve
only to acknowledge ignorance.

After a moment's pause in which none attempted to answer
him, he resumed with an increase of confidence. Leaving the
realms of mathematics and physics, he passed to Scriptural
warrant for his next argument. He quoted the Prophet Esdras
as having revealed that God commanded that the waters be
gathered into the seventh part of the earth, and upon that
divinely inspired assertion he based the calculations which
established that land must be reached within a distance of
some seven hundred leagues to westward, that this land would
be the easternmost point of the Indies, as the chart he had
prepared would serve to show.

He unrolled his parchment, advanced to the table, and
spread it there before the presiding Bishop.

At Talavera's invitation, Deza and Don Rodrigo drew
closer so that they might study it with him. They had no
comment to offer, and the chart was passed on for study by
the other members of the junta. They pondered it, in twos
and threes, fingers pointing, lips whispering, heads wagging,
whilst Colon, waiting, returned to resume his seat.

At last, when the chart had come back to lie again before
Talavera, the Bishop's solemn dark eyes were levelled on
Colon. 'You will have something more to urge.'

'Have I not urged enough?' asked Colon with quiet deference.

'You have urged assumptions, backed, it is true, by arguments, but not, so far as I perceive, by evidence. We have
no such proofs as we are sent to seek.'

Colon came to his feet again. 'With submission, my Lord
Bishop, I think you have. Proof by deduction is a form of
proof known to every mathematician, and in a less degree to
every mariner.'

Talavera appealed to the Admiral. 'What do you say to
that, Don Matias?'

'I hold it a good answer, my lord. It is a sound argument,
accepting the sphericity of the earth, which to-day is beyond
doubt, that if we sail west, we must eventually reach the
ultimate boundaries of the land to the east of our starting-
point.'

From the table's end a harsh voice croaked with a touch
of derision. 'Can the sphericity of the earth establish the
puerile contention that land is distributed over every side of
it?' It was Calahorra, the Franciscan doctor, who spoke.
'Is it not manifest,' he pursued, 'that the ocean encircles the
land, that the land is bounded by the ocean, and that to sail
forth upon this is to sail without hope of return?'

'Yet,' said Colon quietly, 'men have sailed forth upon it.
Bold navigators in the service of Portugal have thereby brought
great credit, power and wealth to the Portuguese Crown.'

'Sailed forth upon it, do you say? Sailed along the edge
of it, keeping within sight of land, coasting Africa. A very
different matter.'

'And rounding the Cape of Torments, since renamed the
Cape of Good Hope,' Colon retorted. 'Thus sailing into seas
that superstition formerly peopled with monsters.'

'God give you a better understanding!' the Franciscan

bawled at him. 'That was still to sail along the ocean's edge; a very different matter from venturing out upon it, going westward across it.'

'A very different matter, indeed,' agreed another voice, to announce to Colon yet another adversary. It was Don Juan de Fonseca who had spoken, a bulky man of middle height, whose round, flat, yellow face made up with his bald, glossy yellow head the appearance of a bladder of lard that had been smeared with features.

Meanwhile the Franciscan was continuing: 'The very sphericity of the earth by which you set such store must render return impossible. For though you might sail down the slope of the seas, how could you ever hope to sail up it again?'

'Yes. Answer that,' Fonseca mocked him.

Colon permitted himself disdain. 'That is scarcely a matter for theologians. I invite those here who are mariners to say from their experience upon the seas how often they have seen a ship hull down upon the horizon — no more than her top-masts visible — which presently has come up into full view.'

He looked for confirmation to Maldonado and Rezende. Both nodded.

'That is certainly so,' said Don Rodrigo.

'A thing well known to every sailor,' added the Admiral.

The Franciscan owned defeat by a shrug. Fonseca, how-ever, would not yield. He was exacerbated into shrillness. 'An illusion. As much an illusion as the famous Isle of Saint Brandan, which many have seen, but none has ever reached. Who can deny it? To accept these theories is to accept the absurdity of the antipodes.'

'Is it an absurdity?' Colon asked him. 'Pliny as long ago as in his day was pronouncing the antipodes the great contest between the learned and the ignorant. If we are to dismiss as absurdities all those things which we cannot understand, how much of the world would be left?'

'Enough for sane men,' Fonseca answered him, and with that contemptuously abandoned the argument.

But it was not yet to be allowed to drop. It was taken up by one of the Dominicans, Frey Justino Vargas, a doctor of canon and civil law.

'The theory you advance, sir,' he urged in a mild voice, 'will not hang together unless we accept belief in the antipodes. To this, whatever cosmographers may say, a great father of the Church opposes a serious obstacle. Lactantius has raised the question whether there are any so foolish as to believe in the existence of men who walk with their heels upwards and their heads hanging down, or that there is a part of the world in which trees grow downwards and rain falls upwards.'

'Was he a mariner, this Lactantius?' Colon asked dryly.

The question sobered some countenances that were grinning and brought him a sharp rebuke from Talavera. 'You have heard, sir, that Lactantius was a father of the Church, a saintly man of almost evangelical authority.'

But Colon in his irritation was not to be put down. 'Upon matters evangelical, with which we are not now concerned.'

'You are at fault, sir. The great Saint Augustine has pronounced the doctrine of the antipodes to be at issue with our Faith. For to contend that there are inhabited lands on the opposite side of the earth would be to contend that there are peoples not descended from Adam, since it would have been impossible for them to have crossed the intervening ocean. This would be to contradict the Scriptures, which expressly declare that we are all descended from that first-created man.'

For a moment Colon stood baffled, caught, he felt, in a theological morass in which it might be dangerous to struggle. Yet struggle he must, or else own defeat; and he would incur the peril of fire for heresy rather than abandon the fight.

'Do the pronouncements of Saint Augustine rank as dogmas of the Church?' he asked, and for all the humility of his tone, he shocked them by the question.

'You speak,' Talavera sternly reminded him, 'of one of the great luminaries of our Faith.'

But here, unexpectedly, it was the erudite Deza, admittedly the greatest theologian present, who came to Colon's aid. He turned to Talavera.

'He is probably aware of that, my Lord Bishop,' he said quietly. 'What he asked was only if the pronouncements of Saint Augustine rank as dogmas. And to that the reply must be that they do not.' His myopic eyes twinkled as he peered round to see if any would have the temerity to find fault with him. 'We are not to hobble Master Colon by leaving him under the fear of stumbling into heresy.' He smiled at Colon, encouraging him to proceed.

'I thank you, Frey Diego. I have to say that there is something that Saint Augustine may have left out of account: mutations in the surface of the earth since the creation. Lands that are now beyond the ocean may once not have been so divided from those we know. There is Plato's lost continent of Atlantis, by some accounted a fable, but credited by others just as learned, who see in the Fortunate Isles fragments remaining from that continent's disruption. If Atlantis once existed — and who shall dare to say positively that it did not? — it may have supplied a bridge by which the children of Adam passed to those far-eastern lands, whose presence, much nearer to us on the west, I claim to demonstrate.'

Deza nodded. 'That is, indeed, something that may have escaped the notice of Saint Augustine.'

The Admiral had drawn the chart towards him and had been studying it. He now took up the examination. 'I'll not dispute with you, sir, that you offer a plausible case. But in my view it still remains no more than plausible. I take it that we are all acquainted with the writings of Marco Polo, and to an extent they would seem to justify you of your conclusions. But only to an extent. Beyond that we depend upon your mathematics.'

'By your leave, sir, there is more here than mathematics.' Colon drew himself up, his eyes kindled, he delivered himself in resonant tones with the voice of the mystic. 'There is the light vouchsafed to devout and earnest contemplation: the light of God's grace, which has illumined my mind to this discovery for His greater honour and glory.'

'Sir, sir!' cried Talavera, with a hand raised in protest. 'What are you claiming now?'

Far from quenching the fire in Colon, this was but fuel to it. His voice soared dominantly. 'What I know from the force astir within me. And it must prevail, so that our Holy Faith be spread through lands unknown and peoples yet unknown, however Satan may blunt men's wits against the truth I expound, and inspire them to withstand me.'

He paused a moment, dominant, majestic in his poise, meeting the sudden wonder and displeasure in which they received that tactless suggestion that they might possibly be Satan's agents. Then he concluded: 'King John of Portugal put to shame his sight, his hearing, and all his faculties, for I could not make him understand what I said. That was, I now see, the will of Heaven, to the end that I should bear this inestimable blessing to the Sovereigns of Spain, so worthy of it by their labours against the Saracen. They, with the vast wealth from these new lands at their command, will persevere in that work until the Holy Sepulchre shall have been delivered from the Infidel. That, noble and reverend sirs, is the end to which I am but an instrument in the Divine Hand, to fulfil the promise of that chart.'

Santangel, absorbing through eyes and ears every shade
and turn of that fiery address, was stirred by a secret amusement tempered by anxiety. He trembled lest this dear rogue
should overplay his part, overdo the histrionic magnetism
which he suspected him of deliberately exerting.

He was relieved of his fears by the half-cowed looks of the
junta when, ceasing on that high note, Colon stood before
them, his mien and attitude those of one who has flung down
a gage of battle.

So effectively had he subdued them that it was some
moments before any spoke. Then it was Fonseca's sneer that
shattered the spell he had woven.

'All this may be as you say. But at present we have no
more than your word for it.'

'As for all the rest.'

'As for all the rest. Just so. That is our difficulty.'

He would have continued, but that Talavera, cold, honest
man that he was, intervened, to check him.

'You make a high claim, Master Colon. It is for this junta
to determine whether you sustain it by what you have stated.'

He looked about him, and his glance settled finally upon
Deza, as if inviting the Prior of Saint Esteban to answer an
inquiry that was general. 'Are there any further questions?'

'For myself,' said Deza, answering the invitation of the
look, 'I am satisfied. Setting aside Master Colon's persuasion
that he is divinely inspired, which I by no means reject,
because it can be only by God's grace that men's minds are
so illumined, his cosmographical conclusions compel my
respect.'

The high repute of Deza's erudition precluded open contradiction. Only Fonseca, at the table's end, ventured by
the darkening of his countenance to express a scornful disapproval. The mild Dominican who had intervened before,

Frey Justino Vargas, was not, however, to be stifled even by Deza's great authority.

'The reverend and erudite Prior may be justified of his faith. But is faith enough in such a case as this? I recognize that proof of the existence of something which the eyes have not yet seen must of necessity be only inferential. But in accepting such inferences are we not to be governed by the recognized authority — or the lack of it — of those who draw them?'

'We may be governed,' Deza answered him, 'by the inferences themselves, by the effect of their impact upon our wits and our logic.'

'Agreed. Oh, agreed, most reverend Prior. But should not something more be required by us? We move here in a realm of speculation. The most that we dare to say is that from the arguments of Master Colon it is possible that these lands of his dreams may actually exist. We admit that these arguments are shrewd. But does even the great learning of which this junta disposes suffice to judge the competence of Master Colon?'

'In other words,' said Talavera, 'we should hesitate to accept Master Colon's conclusions because of his lack of established authority as a cosmographer and a mathematician.'

'That is my difficulty, my Lord Bishop.'

Colon stood hesitating. He was in prey to a mixture of emotions in which chagrin predominated. Abruptly he was brought face to face with the need to play his last card. Trump card though it was, he must ever have been reluctant to play it save in the last necessity, since to do so must diminish the lustre of conclusions independently reached, must make it appear that they were borrowed from another, instead of merely confirmed by that other's greater authority. Yet play it he must at last, if it had still remained in his possession.

Immeasurably was his chagrin increased now at the theft of
that card without which, as things were falling out, he might
fail to prevail against the opposition of these limited, preju-
diced intelligences.

And then the matter was taken out of his hands by Frey
Diego Deza.

'Happily,' he said, 'that difficulty does not exist. Master
Colon is supported by the authority of the greatest mathematician the world has known: Paolo del Pozzo Toscanelli.'

The announcement made a stir which Santangel thought
to increase by adding, 'And it was precisely because of this
support that Her Highness was moved to appoint this junta.'

Talavera looked bluntly at Colon. 'Why were we not told
of this before?' he complained.

'I did not perceive the need. I depended upon the cogency
of my arguments and upon the chart that is before you.'

'It will shorten discussion,' said Deza, 'if you submit the
chart you had from Toscanelli.'

'You have a chart in his hand?' exclaimed Talavera, and
the faces of Colon's opponents were seen to lengthen.

With rage under his outward composure, and with every
eye upon him, Colon answered truthfully, yet evading the
actual question. 'When first I formulated my theories, and
before submitting them to the Court of Portugal, I sought a
pronouncement upon them from Paolo Toscanelli. In expression of his full agreement he sent me a letter and a chart
that differs from the chart before you in one particular only.
I do not agree with him upon the distance westward. By my
computing, it is materially less.'

'No matter,' said Talavera. 'The main principle remains;
and it is upon the main principle that the word of that great
cosmographer is of weight.' He looked to right and left for a
confirmation that was nowhere now withheld.

'Of Toscanelli's agreement with that principle,' said Colon boldly, 'I have the honour to assure you.'

There was a pause, in which there was perceptible a lowering of the temperature as surprise first grew and then gave way to a vague suspicion. At last Talavera spoke.

'It is not your assurance that we ask, but the actual chart.'

Pressed thus, Colon stood at bay. 'Unhappily I am unable to lay it before you. It has been stolen from me.'

Again there was that ominous silent pause. He saw the widening of Santangel's eyes, the lengthening of Deza's ruddy face. Fonseca whispered to his neighbour.

'But, sir,' said Talavera, at last, in a voice that was entirely colourless, 'who would rob you of such a parchment?'

'There, my lord, you ask more than I can answer. Nor at the moment does it matter. I no longer possess it. But that I did possess it, and that it is precisely as I have stated, I here make solemn oath.'

Someone softly laughed. It was as a whiplash to Colon. He stiffened, the blood suffused his face, and his eyes flamed upon countenances that were blank when they were not scornful. For a moment his self-control slipped from him; but before he could speak Talavera was addressing him again, coldly judicial.

'Master Colon, since you came to Spain have you ever shown this chart to anyone?'

'Never. No.'

'So that Toscanelli being dead we have only your word for its existence?'

'That is all,' Colon admitted.

'And if I rightly understand Don Luis de Santangel, it was on the strength of this word of yours that Their Highnesses ordered this inquiry?'

'It may have influenced them. No more than that.'

'It would seem to follow, then,' put in Fonseca, 'that if
Their Highnesses had known that no such chart, in fact,
exists, this inquiry would never have been held.'

Colon was stung to heat. 'If the implication is that I misled Their Highnesses by pretences that were false, I resent
and reject it. False it would be to say that the chart does
not — or did not — exist. Rash to assume that, even if it did
not, Their Highnesses might not still have ordered my claims
to be examined. And I may add that in no case should I
have thought to produce it save to convince minds that attach
more importance to a name than to logic and mathematical
deductions.'

It was not a happy retort. It had an air of bluster that
must alienate any sympathy still lingering amongst them.
But exasperation was mastering him.

He met the eyes of Deza, who had been his stalwart advocate, and found them stern. Santangel and Quintanilla
showed troubled countenances. Elsewhere he met either inscrutability or open scorn.

There was yet a question from the Dominican jurist. 'You
said that you were at the Court of Portugal when you received
that chart and letter. Did you submit them to King John?'

'I did.'

The Dominican put up his brows. 'And yet King John was
not persuaded to support you with ships?'

'A fact,' said Colon, 'for which the Spanish Sovereigns if
wisely advised may have occasion to be thankful.'

Frey Justino Vargas was content to vouchsafe him a sour
smile in acknowledgment of that expiring flicker of the fire
they had damped.

Talavera waited yet a moment, and as no other offered to
speak, he cleared his throat to utter Colon's dismissal.

'If you have nothing to add, sir, we will come to our deliberations. You have leave to retire.'

Under the general mistrust of him which he now perceived, it required an effort of self-mastery to maintain an outward dignity of bearing. 'I have to repeat, my lord,' he said, 'that what I have told you of the Toscanelli documents is true, and of that I take God to be my witness. With that, sirs, I thank you for the patience with which you have heard me, and kiss your hands.'

He bowed solemnly to the assembly, and stalked out.

But before the door had closed upon him he overheard Fonseca's sibilant voice. 'I do not think, my Lord Bishop, that we need waste much time in our deliberations upon this imposture. It is plain that we have been assembled in consequence of a misrepresentation fortunately discovered in time.'

19

 THE REPORT

Colon's pride had stiffened and sustained him for just so long as their eyes were upon him, but not a moment longer.

As the doors of the council chamber closed behind him his body sagged from its erectness, and half-blinded by angry emotion he took a faltering way to a bench that was ranged against a wall.

A couple of pages were whispering in a corner. A stalwart guardsman with polished morion and ordered partisan stood like a statue before the door. These took no heed of him, and there were no others in that gloomy hall to observe the outward signs of his dejection. For although he sat there, with a vague thought of awaiting the end of the deliberations, it was rather out of the need of a word of explanation with Santangel than from any hope that the junta would find other than against him.

His broodings devoured the moments. Time went unperceived, and when the doors of the council chamber were thrown open to give passage to the men who had sat in judgment upon him, he was startled by the speed with which it seemed to him that their conclusions had been reached. A bare half-hour had they consumed, and not the half of that did it seem to him.

Talavera came first, walking between Maldonado and Rezende.

Instinctively Colon rose. His movement drew their eyes, which at once were averted again when they saw who stood there. They passed on, leaving him quivering as if they had struck him.

Next came Deza, walking alone, with bowed head; Deza, who had believed him, who had been convinced by him, and who had so stoutly championed his cause with the Sovereigns. Deza saw him too; and Deza too, passed on without a word or a sign, from which Colon could but gather that even Deza had come to regard him as a trickster who did not scruple to employ falsehood and mean artifice so as to buttress a weakness in his case.

The viperish Fonseca followed, in animated talk with the Dominican jurist, and now Colon cursed himself for having lingered in that antechamber, exposing himself to this humiliation of being ignored, unheeded.

At last Santangel appeared, walking in silence with Quintanilla. For a moment Colon trembled, lest Santangel, this dear warm friend to whom he owed so much, should also pass him by. That pain at least he was spared. Santangel quitted his companion's side, and careless of the eyes and opinions of others came straight across to Colon. His countenance was troubled. He spoke on a sigh and with a shake of his grey head.

'So far it has gone badly for you, my dear Cristobal. But it may yet be mended. After all, it may yet be possible to recover this chart.'

'I thank you at least for believing that it exists.'

'Why should I not?'

'Others discover a difficulty. Those gentlemen who go yonder ——'

Santangel's hand upon his shoulder interrupted him. 'The longer I live, Cristobal, the more I perceive how little charity there is in man.'

'That answers me. The junta is to report me a low, swindling trickster. In the words of Don Juan de Fonseca, my claim is an imposture.'

'Waste no thought or temper on that arrogant priest, nor on any of this. I will come to you presently. Go now.'

He patted Colon's shoulder encouragingly. But Colon was beyond encouragement. He went home in despair and shame.

On weary limbs he mounted the stairs to his lodging, opened the door, and checked under the lintel at sight of Beatriz seated before his table.

She sprang up to greet him, leaving a black lace mantilla to drape the chair. 'I had to come, Cristobal. To wait for you here and to have your news at the first moment. I have been so impatient. You have triumphed, my dear. I know you have.'

He came forward into the light from the window, and it revealed how drawn and haggard was his face. She shrank appalled.

'Cristobal!'

His smile was a grimace of pain. He thrust her back into the chair, went down on his knees beside her, and buried his face in her lap.

'It is finished,' he groaned. 'All is gone from me: hopes, credit, honour itself. Before night I shall have been reported to the Sovereigns as a lying mountebank. If they are merciful I shall be ordered to leave Spain, or else King Ferdinand, grudging the loss of the poor pittance they have paid me, may cast me into prison for having practised a cheat.'

She took the tawny head in her caressing, soothing hands. She questioned him breathlessly. He sat back on his heels, and looked at her. 'I have been robbed,' he said.

'Robbed?' Horror hushed her voice. It stared at him from her eyes. 'Of what? Of what have you been robbed?'

'Of everything.' He got to his feet again. 'Of everything but life. They leave me that so that despair and shame may feed upon it. I have been robbed of the weapons with which I could have bludgeoned sense into those Salamanca numskulls, those learned dolts, those vain priestly sceptics.'

He set himself to pace the room in long strides, like an angry panther, rehearsing for her the sneers, the innuendos with which he had been goaded into telling them of documents which, had he been able to produce them, must have commanded respect, but by the absence of which he was branded an impudent impostor.

She sat very still and white, her anguished eyes never leaving him as he swung to and fro in his pacing. At last he came to a halt before her, his lips bitter.

'That is the end of all my dreams, including that dear, proud dream of which you were the centre and pivot, my Beatriz. I must go on my travels again, go peddle my wares elsewhere, if even so much is worth while now that I have lost the surety without which princes will not give heed to what I offer.'

She set her elbows on the table, and took her head in her hands. She strove to recall the exact words which Gallina had wrung from her fears. It came to her that she had admitted knowing where Colon kept the chart. It was only a little thing; so little that at the time it had seemed nothing. But now she realized exactly how much she had unwittingly told that crafty Venetian.

She conquered the numbness that held her, and forced her-self to speak. 'When did you last see those parchments?'

'When? What do I know? I had not looked at them for weeks. Even when on Wednesday I enclosed in the case the letter for Santangel that made provision for you, I did not examine the case's contents, so sure was I that all was there.'

'Is it impossible that when last you handled the chart you did not replace it?'

'Impossible. I never kept it anywhere but in the case. Besides, I have searched everywhere.'

'You were absent all day yesterday,' she reminded him. 'Could it be that your lodging was entered then?'

'I found no sign of it. And yet' — he recollected some-thing — 'I remember a disorder in the coffer when I went to it this morning in which I could not think to have left it. I last opened it on the morning after you were here.' He reflected. 'It is possible that it was yesterday that I was robbed. Yet how? The coffer was locked as I left it. And who would know where I kept the key?'

'I knew.'

'You?' He stared. 'You mean that as I told you, so I might have told others. But I did not. And even you did not know which chart in the case was the valuable one.'

She wanted desperately to tell him, be the consequences what they might. 'Listen, Cristobal . . .' She raised her eyes, and met his haggard burning gaze. Her courage drained from her. Impossible to add to the torment he was suffering by an avowal which made her the agent, however unwilling, and unwitting at the end, of this betrayal.

'I am listening, my love.'

'Oh, nothing . . . nothing,' she faltered. 'An idle passing thought.'

He stooped and kissed her lips, nor heeded their cold unresponsiveness. Still leaning over her, he spoke in a voice of heartbreak. 'When I found you I needed you so much, Beatriz. And now that I need you so much more — as I have never needed anyone — I must renounce you.'

There was no response from her. She sat so still that she might have been deemed insensible but for the utter misery of her countenance.

A knock at the door brought the relief of an interruption.

Colon went to open, and found Santangel on the threshold. 'Don Luis!' He stood aside, to give the Chancellor passage.

Santangel came in; then, seeing Beatriz, he halted. 'I am perhaps inopportune?'

'Never that. This is a dear friend, Mistress Beatriz Enriquez, who comes to me in the hour when most friends abandon me.'

Don Luis uncovered, and bowed gravely. He recognized her for the dancing-girl whom Colon had defended from the scorn of the Marchioness of Moya. His shrewd eyes observed the disorder of her looks, and thought the better of her for it. Nor had he outlived a reverence for such beauty as that of Beatriz.

'It was urgent to let you know, Cristobal, that Their Highnesses will not give audience to the Bishop of Avila until this evening. I have dragged a promise from him that if the missing chart should be discovered before then, he will withhold the report now drawn.'

Colon's glance softened. 'May I die if ever I had a better friend.'

Santangel waved this away. 'The chart?' he asked. 'Have you thought, at least, by whom you might have been robbed?'

'I can think of none.'

'Surely, surely! Search your mind. Everything depends upon it, even your very honour. Remember the old maxim: *Cui bono fuerit?* Consider whom it might profit.'

'Some there may be. I had thought of the Portuguese. But only because none else occurred to me. A fantastic suspicion.'

Don Luis stamped about the room in exasperation. 'Under what need was Deza,' he cried, 'to drag in the name of Toscanelli? We might have done well enough without mention of that chart.'

'He meant to help me.'

Don Luis shook his head in deprecation. 'Oh, yes. He meant the best, as I did. And we achieved the worst. Even Deza, who was so much your friend, has turned against you now. Like the rest, he regards this tale of robbery as a subterfuge.'

Colon was shaken by a gust of rage. 'God avail me! What anxiety to think evil! What readiness to strip a poor devil of his honour! What jealousy of the favor a foreigner might earn with the Sovereigns! What joy will not be theirs in denouncing me a shameless impostor!'

Santangel's shoulders were bowed, his countenance a mask of sorrow. 'If you can give me no hope of finding those evidences...' He ended with a shrug, and a spell of silence followed.

Beatriz continued to sit with her elbows on the table, her chin on her clenched fists, wretchedness in every line of her drawn face. The urge to speak, to tell them what she knew, was stifled by fear of Colon's contempt.

'I'll go to the Queen,' said Don Luis, at last. 'Her heart is as tender as her mind is shrewd. Depend upon me to fight for you to the last.'

'Alas, my friend. I furnish you with no more than broken weapons.'

'We shall see. We shall see. Sustain your courage. I will come soon again. Perhaps tonight.'

When he had gone, Beatriz discovered that she, too, must go. They would be awaiting her now at Zagarte's. She was late already.

'Yes,' he grimly agreed. 'You must go. I am to be laughed at for my boastful talk of delivering you from that thraldom.'

She fled distracted, and was halfway to Zagarte's before she checked. What she lacked the courage to tell Colon, she could tell the Chancellor; and having told him she could vanish from the scene. On that thought, she stood arrested in the busy street, heeding neither those who jostled her nor those who paused to stare at the wildness of her looks. The thought became resolve. Zagarte, the mystery and the audience might go hang.

She turned, and then she checked again, a dreadful vision before her eyes. Her brother, Pablo, utterly forgotten in her present anguish, rose like a mournful ghost before her. For an instant she stood again in that dark, dank dungeon of the Pozzi, and beheld him gaunt and unkempt, passionately pleading with her to deliver him from that hell even at the cost of her chastity. The thought that now, having calculatedly worn Armida's girdle so as to accomplish his deliverance, she was to leave him to his hideous fate, doom him for his lifetime to the galleys, shook her resolve. The horror of choosing between her brother and her lover again confronted her. Only by betrayal and sacrifice of one of them could she avoid the betrayal and sacrifice of the other. Only by treachery could she mend treachery.

A passing soldier, jostling her intentionally and muttering a ribald invitation, brought her back to her surroundings. With a look that scorched him from her path, she sped away in the direction of the Mezquita.

Don Luis had his dwelling at the head of a street that ran beside the Cathedral's western wall, down towards the

river. The house stood back in a courtyard where palm trees
and aloes flourished about the marble basin of a bronze
fountain. A halberdier, guarding the gateway, was barring
her way to inquire her purpose when Santangel, himself,
emerged from the house.

Gracious and deferential, it was not in his nature to put her
off when she begged for a word with him.

'The moment is hardly well chosen. I am on my way to
the Alcazar. You will guess both my purpose and its urgency.'

'Your excellency will go the better furnished by what I have
to tell you.'

His kindly eyes searched that pale, eager face. 'Come with
me.' He led the way across the sunlit court into the cool
gloom of a stone hall, where lackeys sprang to minister. He
waved them away, and ushered her into a little waiting-room.

'What can you have to tell me?'

Her answer struck at the very heart of the matter. 'Who
the thieves are, and where they may be found.' Under the
amazement in his glance she hurried on. 'They are agents of
the Venetian Inquisitors of State. Two of them: and their
names are Rocca and Gallina. Rocca represents himself as
attached to the Venetian Embassy at the Court of the Sovereigns. They are lodged at the Fonda del Leon.'

He took a step towards her. 'How do you come to know
all this?'

'Must I tell you that?' The question rang in his ears like
a cry of pain. 'Is it not enough that you have their names?'

'If I am to act I should know more, particularly since one of
them, from what you tell me, can claim ambassadorial privileges.' And he added, 'Does Cristobal know this?'

'I have not dared to tell him.'

'Ah!' He raised his heavy brows. But his rich, deep voice
was very gentle. 'Why is that? Be quite frank with me, child.'

She stood for a moment in the hesitation of one who faces inevitable calamity, her eyes lowered, her body rocking a little, her hands twisting one within the other. Then with a sudden fierce defiance she plunged into her tale.

'In the Pozzi at Venice I have a brother, held a prisoner, rightly because of a theft, wrongly because suspected of being a spy of Aragon.'

From that beginning the whole miserable story flowed, whilst Santangel, immovable, inscrutable, scarcely seeming to breathe, stood listening and weighing every word.

'I know,' she told him at the end, 'how loathly I must appear to you; how loathly I am. I know that I deserve no mercy. Yet this I say, and take Our Lady of Sorrows to witness, that in what incautiously I allowed Gallina to learn from me, I had no thought of betraying Cristobal. For the love I had so vilely been hired to simulate had become a reality.'

'You do not need to protest it. You make it manifest.' Don Luis spoke softly, soothingly. 'My poor child! Yours was a cruel choice between your brother and your lover.'

'And — merciful Heaven! — how have I chosen?' she cried in anguish.

'As was just and right,' he firmly assured her. 'For your brother's plight no responsibility can lie upon you. His own courses brought him to it. He has no claim upon you to deliver him. In urging one he but adds to his offences. Cristobal, however, is caught in a snare in which you were used as the decoy. That he is your lover, that you love him, is nothing to the matter. Duty demands that at all costs you should deliver him.'

Wonder overspread her face at the revelation his reasoning brought her, and with that wonder a relief against which she must still be struggling. 'If I could believe that! What a burden of horror would not be lifted from me.'

'Would you put it to the test? Go and confess yourself.
There is not a priest would give you absolution until you had
made a reparation by undoing what you have done. So
dismiss an idle remorse. Go now. Leave me to act. I will
see the Alcalde-Mayor at once, so that order may be taken.'

'You will require my testimony for that.'

He shook his head, smiling a little. 'That is the last thing
I shall require. Your testimony would compel the Alcalde to
take action against you.'

'I know. That does not matter.'

His smile broadened, it became more tender before this
eagerness for reparatory martyrdom. 'Child, that would
mean your ruin, and at such a price Cristobal would not
thank me for the recovery of his honour. Leave this in my
hands. I shall contrive without you. Meanwhile, lose no
time in telling Cristobal. Tell him everything.'

She trembled. There was a frightened look in her eyes.
'I ... dare not. Not yet, at least.' On a thought she added:
'Would you ... would your excellency tell him? Then it will
be for him to do as he chooses with me.'

He considered. 'If you wish it. But, believe me, child, it
will come better from you.'

She wrung her hands. 'I dare not. At least, not until the
harm has been repaired, until the chart has been recovered.'

'Well, well! That is what chiefly matters. The rest we'll
leave for the moment. I'll lose no time.'

It did not prove as easy as Don Luis had counted. Don
Miguel de Escobedo, the High Justiciary of Cordoba, was a
punctilious gentleman, rigidly bound by the law's formalities.
He was not disposed to take action until his questions were
answered.

'It is idle to press me, Don Miguel,' Santangel protested.
'Assume that I have received the information under seal of
the confessional.'

'Since when have you been in holy orders, Don Luis?'

'It is not only the priest who hears confessions. I am pledged not to divulge the source of my information. Suppose that I could not obtain it without that pledge. Should I then have permitted this crime to go undiscovered and unpunished?'

'But where is the evidence of the crime?'

'My word.'

'Your word? But is it not, rather, the word of some person unknown?'

'Not unknown to me. Will that not satisfy you?'

'How can it? One of these men, you tell me, is in the following of the Venetian envoy. Even with full evidence I should be reluctant to meddle with a man in that position.' The Alcalde combed his grizzled beard. 'Unless action should be justified by results, my office would be in jeopardy. Couldn't you bring me an order from the Sovereigns?'

'No. But I can undertake that they'll approve you when it is done.'

'May I die if I know what to do. I'll send for the Corregidor.'

So the executive officer was fetched, a very military gentleman, named Don Xavier Pastor. When Santangel's requirements had been put to him, he proved a man of more ideas and fewer scruples than the Alcalde.

'A chart and a letter, eh?' He nodded, and added pertinently, 'If we find them on one or the other of these Venetians, how shall we prove that they do not belong to him?'

'Master Colon, no doubt, will tell you how to identify his property.'

'Then let us begin with Master Colon.'

'But after that?' demanded the Alcalde, shocked by his subordinate's lightness. 'One of these men, remember, is attached to an embassy.'

'Depend upon me not to act officially.' Don Xavier permitted himself to wink. 'We avoid embroiling ourselves. Trust me to be delicate.'

'If you blunder I shall disown you,' the Alcalde threatened.

'I shall deserve it,' laughed the Corregidor, whom Santangel was finding more and more a man after his own heart.

They went off.— Santangel and Don Xavier — to find Colon, the Corregidor being warned that on no account must he disclose that they already knew the identity of the thieves.

'I bring you hope, Cristobal,' Don Luis greeted him. 'Here is the Corregidor, who undertakes to recover your chart.'

'When we don't know who stole it?'

'That will be for us to discover,' said Don Xavier. There was a confident smile, which Colon thought fatuous, on his long lean face. 'Put your faith in us, sir. We have our ways in Cordoba.'

'Surprising ways if you can accomplish this.'

'With your assistance. How shall we know the chart is yours when we find it?'

'It goes with a letter, superscribed with my name, bearing the signature Paolo Toscanelli and his seal: a spread eagle under a ducal crown. The chart, in the same hand, bears the same seal and signature.'

'That is all I need. Look to hear from me soon again. God rest you, sir.' And he marched out.

'A very self-sufficient gentleman, liberal of promises,' was Colon's criticism, neither just nor grateful, for the Corregidor was on his way to the Fonda del Leon.

He went no farther than the landlord's parlour, where Quisada, who kept that prosperous house, met him with the respectful anxiety which a corregidor inspires.

'God save your worship.'

'God save you, Quisada. What rooms have you for hire?'

'None at the moment, sir, the Lord be praised. With Their Highnesses in Cordoba there is not a lodging empty.'

Don Xavier stroked his long black moustaches. 'That is vexatious, now. Will no guest be departing soon?'

'Oh, yes. To-morrow. My best room above stairs will be free.'

'That is certain? Who is your departing guest?'

'Two foreign gentlemen; Venetians. The mules are ordered for eight o'clock in the morning.'

'Mules?' The Corregidor was jocular. 'Do they ride to Venice?'

'Why, no, your worship. To Malaga, to take ship.'

'Of course, of course.' He laughed the point away. 'Their room may serve. If so you shall have word from me tonight.'

Thus, with all the information that he required, the Corregidor departed. Late that evening he went to report to the Alcalde, and found Santangel with him.

The Chancellor had come from the Alcazar a half-hour before in grim anxiety to know what was being done. He had been in attendance upon the Sovereigns when Talavera, accompanied by Deza, Fonseca and Maldonado, had presented to Their Highnesses the junta's report, which utterly condemned Colon's project.

'The idle dream of a reckless adventurer, who so as to impose himself did not scruple falsely to claim the support of a famous mathematician.' Thus Talavera.

The Queen's face had lengthened in disappointment. King Ferdinand's had almost brightened.

'A timely conclusion,' His Highness opined. 'With the final reduction of Granada before us, we have something other than dreams to engage us.' He turned, smiling, to the Queen. 'I have ever looked with misgiving, as you know, upon the enthusiasm this trickster's fantasy awakened in Your Highness. It was my fear that your credulity was being abused.'

The placidity of the Queen's countenance was momentarily disturbed. A faint flush that may have been of resentment swept like a cloud across it. For despite the courtesy of King Ferdinand's tone, she perceived in his words a tolerant derision that offended.

'Even at the risk of being mocked for that credulity,' she retorted, 'I will neglect no opportunity that might make for the greater power and glory of the realm of Castile which it has pleased God to place under my rule.'

'I trust, Madam, that I am no less sensible of the duties of my position. It is because of this that if err I must, I will err on the side of caution where Spanish lives and Spanish treasure are to be staked.'

'I do not doubt it,' she answered him. 'But too much caution may thwart achievement.' She turned to Talavera with something of challenge. 'You deliver this, my Lord Bishop, as the considered judgment of the junta?'

'Our considered judgment, Highness.'

'But not unanimous,' Santangel threw in. 'It is not mine.'

The Queen gave him a friendly glance, whilst His Highness laughed, with good-humoured mockery. 'You are not of much account as a cosmographer, Santangel.'

'But enough of a jurist, Highness, not to confuse negative with positive evidence.'

'That expresses my own feeling, Don Luis,' the Queen was quick to approve him, and turned again to Talavera. 'Why must you conclude that it is a falsehood that this chart was stolen?'

'Permit me to remind Your Highness that beyond Colon's word we have no evidence that it ever existed.'

'And beyond yours,' flashed Santangel, 'there is none that Colon did not speak the truth. A man's failure to supply proof of his statements is not in itself evidence that he lies.'

'Not in itself. No,' Talavera answered patiently. 'But in the circumstances it is significant that none has ever seen this chart. To allege theft of it when pressed to produce it is a convenient subterfuge for a trickster who had won a hearing by pretending to possess it.'

Her Highness manifested impatience. 'To what purpose such a pretence, since in the end it must be exposed?'

'So as to provide opportunity to present arguments by which he might dazzle and seduce us.'

'This is ingenious. Subtle, indeed. Yet it all proves nothing,' the Queen insisted, advocating, indeed, not Colon's cause, but her own. 'If there has been foolish credulity it has not been mine alone. Frey Diego, there, was won by Colon's arguments. Do they become worthless because he cannot produce this chart?'

'My belief in his theories, madam,' Deza defended himself, 'were rooted in my belief in the man, and influenced by the assertion that they had the support of Toscanelli. Before the junta he made no mention of Toscanelli. It was I who brought up the matter of the Florentine's chart when it seemed clear that Colon's unsupported arguments were not acceptable to judges who were dutifully cautious. I confess that I cannot avoid the grave suspicion aroused by his statement that he had been robbed of it.'

Santangel, perceiving the impression Deza's grave words had made, went in to combat it. 'That is a suspicion that I, at least, refuse to share. I recognize greatness when I see it, and Colon is too great a man to be a liar.'

King Ferdinand laughed. 'If I know anything of men, there is no such greatness. The opinion, Santangel, does more credit to your heart than to your head.'

'It is an opinion, Highness, that I shall yet hope to justify.'

'Not only credulous, but sanguine,' the King rallied him. 'Well, well. They are qualities that go together; but I had not thought to find them in a man of your sagacity. I think you will agree, madam, that until Don Luis discovers this justification we may leave the matter, and turn our minds to the more pressing business of Granada.'

The Queen sighed a reluctant assent, and with a rather wistful smile for Santangel prayed, if without confidence, that he might realize his hopes.

It was the end of the discussion, and with a sense that in the heat of it he had pledged some of his credit, Santangel sought the Alcalde again, to ascertain what had been done.

Thus the Corregidor found him there on his arrival. Don Xavier's manner was brisk and breezy. 'Everything is well in train,' he announced. 'The Venetians set out in the morning for Malaga, there to take ship for home. Their mules are ordered for eight o'clock. You will probably agree, Don Miguel, that this departure is a sort of admission that their work in Cordoba is done: that they have obtained what they sought here.'

The Alcalde agreed warmly. Santangel, however, was brought to exasperation. 'But perceiving this, have you done nothing more? These men must not leave Cordoba.'

The Corregidor grinned. 'I think they must. We have no warrant upon which to detain them, and as I understand it, we are not likely to have one.'

'Devil take me if I dare issue one on such evidence, against a man who is a member of an embassy,' the Alcalde agreed.

'But what then?' Don Luis demanded.

'If we can't prevent their departure,' said the Corregidor, with a sly smile, 'we can certainly prevent their arrival. The Malaga road is in bad repute, infested with brigands. But we can't be everywhere, Don Luis, with our alguaziles. If a couple of rash foreigners get themselves robbed, the State can't be held responsible. I think that is the way of it, Don Miguel. It will avoid any complications with the Venetian envoy.'

Santangel's relief permitted him to be jocular. 'You make me suspect that to be Corregidor of Cordoba is a profitable trade.'

 THE GIPSIES

THE departure of the two Venetians from Cordoba on that Saturday morning of early June was delayed by a congestion of the streets and of the road which, crossing the river by the Moorish Bridge, runs southeastward through the Campina. For it happened that on this same morning the Sovereigns, with imposing warlike pomp, were setting out for the camp in the Vega, to take in hand the last stage of the conquest of Granada.

The eyes of Cordoba had been rejoiced and its heart thrilled by that majestic parade. To the flourishes of trumpeters richly tabarded and under waving banners, Their Highnesses had ridden forth at the head of a long line of glittering knights. The King made a brave show in his gilded armour, and even Queen Isabel rode in a warrior's back-and-breast of black damascened steel inlaid with arabesques in gold.

The knightly phalanx was followed by a cavalcade of the Queen's ladies, on mules that were richly housed and tasselled, and after these came the Court functionaries, civil and ecclesiastic, and other members of the royal household,

with grooms and falconers at their tail. Next rode a troop
of men-at-arms, with bannerols fluttering from their lance-
heads, succeeded by a long column of pikemen in light body
armour, who marched four by four, trailing their ten-foot
pikes, and these again by a regiment of arbalesters, Swiss
mercenaries in short leather jackets shouldering their cross-
bows and armoured only on their breasts, so as to advertise
their boast that they never turned their backs upon the foe.
The rear was brought up by ox-wains, the foremost bearing
the clumsy siege lombards, the remainder laden with the
baggage, urged along by the lance-like goads of the lads who
marched beside them.

In dust and heat this army, cheered by the townsfolk,
wound its way from the Alcazar to the Moorish Bridge, and
over this set out on its journey to the camp in the pleasant
fertile Vega of Granada.

It would be an hour or so later, by when the way was clear
again, that Rocca and Gallina left Cordoba by that same
Moorish Bridge over the wide river, winding like glowing
amber in the morning sunlight about the golden sandbanks
of its course. The muleteer from whom they had hired their
beasts went a little ahead of them. They rode sedately on
well-groomed mules, the harness bedecked with coloured
tassels and hung with bells that tinkled gaily as they moved.

Under a spreading fig tree before a wineshop in the street
that intersected the huddle of low white houses forming the
bridgehead on the Campina bank, a half-dozen men, with a
deal of noisy chatter and laughter, were drinking a morning
cup. Their mules were tethered to the rings in the wall beside
the wineshop. They were of a rude aspect, men of the sierras,
with something in their lean activity of the wolves that
haunted the mountains. They were in fustian jackets, their
legs untidily cross-gartered. Gipsies, the muleteer contemptuously pronounced them.

Our Venetians trotted on, reaching the end of the suburb and the edge of the open country, where a crowd of beggars, attracted thither by the morning's cavalcade, whined for alms and sought to move compassion by exhibiting their sores. A mile or so farther, in the open lands of the Campina, there was a clatter of overtaking hooves behind them, and the muleteer ranged his travellers aside, to give passage to a little troop that moved at speed in a cloud of dust. He recognized them for the gipsies who had been drinking at the venta by the bridge, and said so, cursing them for the dust they raised, as they swept on, ever vociferous, to breast the next slope of that undulating country.

'May the Devil break their dirty necks,' was the muleteer's prayer when he set his mule going again.

They came at a gentle pace up the acclivity over the crest of which those wild riders had vanished. How completely they had vanished the Venetians did not realize until in their turn they reached the crest, and paused there to breathe their mounts.

In the depths of the shallow valley before them the yellow waters of the Guadajoz wound their sparkling way through smiling lands of a richer fertility. On their right a dark forest of beech and oak and chestnut trees in flower made a tall rampart for the grey road. On their left terraced vineyards broke the southern slope, falling away to rich green pastures, where herds of active Andalusian kine were browsing.

They ambled down the slope, splashed through the ford at the foot of it, and breasted the rise beyond. The trilling of a lark, high in the blue dome overhead, was the only sound in the silence of that countryside. But when they were midway up the hill a sudden shout rang out, three mounted men broke from the cover of the trees to range themselves across the path of the travellers. They were three of the gipsies, and their leader, a long, lean scarecrow in a wide-brimmed hat with a greasy black smear across his face that had much the effect of a mask, stood a half-mule's length ahead of his fellows.

Harshly he ordered the travellers to halt, which was, anyway, unnecessary, for they had halted already.

'Lord Jesus defend us!' gasped the muleteer.

But Gallina and Rocca, men who were not easily moved to fear, demanded truculently to know what was wanted of them.

The leading ruffian laughed. 'Just what you happen to have about you, noble sirs. Dismount, and lively.'

A noise behind made Gallina look over his shoulder. He found the other three in their rear, cutting off their retreat.

Rocca was profane. But Gallina wasted no breath. He lugged out his sword. 'Forward, Rocca! Cut the brigands down.'

The rowels of their spurs drew blood, and the maddened mules charged forward at the gallop, the Venetians standing in their stirrups with swords raised to strike.

The leading bandit took the cut of Gallina's blade on his staff, and on a whirling counter brought the length of quince-wood, that was tough as steel, across the Venetian's head. Protected only by a flat velvet cap, the blow rolled him senseless from the saddle, and it was mere good fortune that his feet left the stirrups.

Rocca fared no better. The fellow he charged swerved aside to avoid him, and swung his staff with terrific force at the forelegs of the Venetian's mule. The beast came down on its knees, and the abrupt check in full career catapulted Rocca into the road, to lie there as senseless as his companion.

He was the first to recover, and when this happened found himself in the cool gloom of the forest, on the mossy bank of a brook. The first thing his reopening eyes beheld was the muleteer roped to a tree; the next was Gallina, lying inert alongside of him. Then both were eclipsed by a brown, leering, lantern-jawed face at close quarters, and Rocca was aware of hands working upon his body. An attempt to rise informed him that he was tied at wrists and ankles, and he now made the further discovery that his doublet was gone. A voice was bidding the rogue that handled him make sure that he had no money belt.

'There's naught else,' the bandit answered. 'I've searched him to his mangy skin.'

'Go through the other pigeon, then.'

The ruffian moved away from Rocca, and the Venetian, to that extent liberated, turned on his side, glaring mute, impotent ferocity. Thus he was able to watch the leader who held and was searching his doublet. The fellow had emptied the pockets, and was now feeling the material between finger and thumb. To Rocca's increasing rage the man discovered the stiffness of the package that the Venetian had sewn between the velvet and the lining. He brought out a knife, and ripping the one from the other, drew forth a slim oilskin wallet. He dropped the doublet, opened the wallet and from it extracted what Rocca knew to be the Toscanelli chart and letter. He scanned them closely in turn, and replaced them in their wallet. This he pocketed; then, kicking the doublet across towards Rocca, he called off the man who was rifling Gallina.

'Leave that. It's no matter for him.' He swung on his heel briskly. 'Now, my lads, we'll be moving.'

Rocca found his voice. 'Wait!' he cried. 'Wait! Our money you may have. But the papers in that wallet are worthless to you. Leave me those.'

The bandit grinned. 'Worthless, eh? That'll be why you hid them. It'll need a scholar to tell me their worth. I'll be keeping them until I find one.'

Rocca struggled into a sitting posture, unconscious even of the ache in his bruised head. 'They're worthless, I tell you, to anyone but me.'

'And what may they be worth to you?'

'Ten thousand maravedis,' was the impatient, reckless answer.

'That means a hundred thousand at the least,' the fellow laughed. 'I thank you for telling me. I'll find me a buyer.'

'You'll run your neck into a halter in searching. Look, now. You shall have your hundred thousand maravedis.'

The rogue stared at him, and again loosed his odious guffaw.

'Where shall you find them?'

'In Cordoba. Come to me there tomorrow, and . . .'

'And run my neck into the halter you mentioned. Saint James! I'm a simpleton, to be sure.'

'Listen ——'

'You've told me enough. What I have I'll keep.'

But here Gallina, who, disregarded by Rocca, had not only recovered consciousness, but had taken a quick clear grasp of the situation, came into the discussion. 'A moment, my friend. A moment!' He paused to utter a groan of pain; then mastered himself, and went on: 'No good ever came of refusing to listen. Give my friend the wallet, and let him go back to Cordoba for the money. Hold me as a hostage until it's paid.'

But the bandit merely laughed. 'I've known men caught like that.' He shook his head. 'I am content with what I've got.'

He began to move away, when Rocca's voice, raised almost to a scream, arrested him again. 'Hi! You scoundrel thief! You'll be hanged for this. Give me back the wallet, and we'll lodge no complaint. But if you don't, I swear to ——'

'Quiet! You'd bear plaint, would you? There's a saying that dead men tell no tales. You'd best remember it before you provoke me into cracking your necks for you.'

He strode away, barking out orders. His manner, almost military, procured him a prompt obedience. Some of the gipsies untethered the mules, and led them away through the trees; others unbound the muleteer.

'You'll untie your patrons after we have left,' the leader told him. 'You may tramp back to Cordoba. It's not above three leagues. We'll take your mules. But you'll find them again at Lamego's venta by the Moorish Bridge.' He bowed to the Venetians with a flourish of his broad-brimmed hat. 'Remain with God, my masters.'

'The Devil go with you,' was Rocca's answering civility, spoken through his teeth.

In evil case, sore in body and sick in soul, the agents of the Three presently came out of the forest with the muleteer, and set out to make their way back to Cordoba on foot.

By the time they reached the Moorish Bridge the sun was already low. At the venta the muleteer called a halt, so that he might inquire for his beasts. The Venetians, weary, dusty and footsore, were glad of the chance to quench their raging thirst. They entered the noisome common-room, and Rocca, sinking limp to a greasy stool, called for wine in a voice that was hoarse from weariness and peremptory from irritation.

The vintner looked askance at their bedraggled condition and at the bloody bandage about Gallina's head. But because Gavilan, the muleteer, was known to him he was ready to serve them without questions.

Avidly they drank the sour wine, and Gavilan drank with them. He filled and drank again before he found the use of his tongue to ask for his mules.

'They came back three hours ago,' Lamego told him. 'I knew them for yours, and I've turned them into the field at the back.' Then at last he ventured the question: 'What has happened to you?'

'The devil has happened,' Rocca told him, in a raging voice. 'We've been robbed and flayed, as you can see. A cursed country this in which such things can happen. Who brought back the mules?'

'What do I know? A lad from the hills.'

'Would it be one of those merry gipsy lads that were drinking here this morning?'

The vintner thoughtfully scratched a cautious head. 'Nay, now. There were a many drinking here this morning after Their Highnesses rode out. I wouldn't remember.'

'I thought you wouldn't,' was Gallina's sour comment. 'And what way did he go, this lad, after he left the mules?'

'Nay, now, I never mark suc'h things. I serve my patrons, and trouble no more about them when they've gone with God.'

'A model host, in fact.'

But Rocca, in his evil mood, was not content to leave it there. 'Just the host for a country of thieves and cut-throats.'

'You've no call to say that of me, Master Foreigner. No, nor of Castile, which, as everyone knows, is the best-ordered land in the world. We've a hermandad to watch over the roads and keep them safe for travellers.'

'A hermandad! A brotherhood! Aye, a brotherhood of bandits. The only plaguy brotherhood we've seen on your Castilian roads.' The vintner withdrew in a scowling silence, and the muleteer went off through the house to find his beasts.

Rocca brimmed himself another can. 'I wonder,' he said, 'if hemlock tastes as vilely as this poison. Only thirst can ——' He checked there, staring ahead, jug in hand. Then he smashed the vessel down so violently upon the board that it broke, and the wine flooded table and floor. That, and the oath with which he came to his feet, made Gallina look round.

A man had just entered the wineshop, a tall, loose-limbed fellow in a fustian jacket, with cross-gartered legs, at sight of whom Gallina's beady eyes became beadier. It was the leader of the gipsy bandits who had that day assailed them.

'God avail us!' he ejaculated, and came to his feet in his turn, whilst Rocca, with the fierce, silent purposefulness of a hound, was already leaping at the newcomer.

The gipsy, thus assailed, flung him off with violence. 'Holá, drunkard! Devil take your embraces.'

'Brigand!' roared Rocca, and returned to the assault, reinforced by Gallina.

Together they fell upon the gipsy.

'You shall sweat blood, you rascal, for to-day's work,' Gallina promised him. 'We'll have your dirty neck in a halter.'

The man struggled wildly in their grasp. 'The Devil break your bones! Hi, landlord!' he panted. 'Hold off these murderers.'

They swayed in a writhing, fighting, gasping mass, across the earthen floor of the inn, raising the dust and knocking over a table at which a couple of peasants had been quietly drinking.

The gipsy went down with the Venetians on top of him, whilst the vintner danced about the group with angry remonstrance.

'Sirs! Sirs! For the love of Heaven! What's the meaning of it?'

Rocca, with a knee on the gipsy's stomach, gave him answer. 'This is one of the brigands who waylaid us. Call the watch whilst we hold him. Call the watch.'

'But you're mad, sirs,' the vintner protested. 'This is Master Ribera. He's no bandit.' He strove to pull them off their victim.

The gipsy renewed his struggles. 'Let me go, you crazy louts.' He raised his voice. 'Hi, there! Help! Help!' Then, louder still, he emitted the call that summoned the watch. 'Acuda el rey! Acuda el rey!'

The answer was miraculously prompt, and it came in strength. No fewer than four alguaziles surged, amazingly opportune, upon the threshold and clattered into the inn.

'What's here? What's happening?' demanded the leader, but waited for no answer before falling upon the Venetians. They beat them with the butts of their short halberts. 'Up, you rogues! Up! Do you want to kill the man?'

'A pair of crazy, drunken, foreign scoundrels,' whined the gipsy, 'manhandling a poor devil.'

Rocca, vainly trying to shake himself free of the grip of two alguaziles who had hauled him to his feet, delivered himself in breathless fury. 'We've been robbed on the highroad, and this is one of the brigands who robbed us.'

The gipsy sat up painfully, feeling himself, with a great show of concern for his limbs. 'They're drunk!' he cried. 'I haven't been out of Cordoba all day. I can bring a dozen to swear it. These rascals were killing me. They've broken some of my bones, I think. Ai! Ai!' With gasps of pain he gathered himself carefully up.

'Leave them to us, Master Ribera!' shouted the leading alguazil. 'They can give an account of themselves to the Corregidor. Come on, you scoundrels.'

'Keep a civil tongue,' fumed Rocca, 'or you'll repent it. Let us to the Corregidor, by all means. But bring that rascal along, too.'

'Do you give me orders now? The Devil burn you. Answer for yourself, Master Foreigner. That'll be enough for you: setting about honest Castilian folk, and miscalling them. Get along, there. Get along. March!'

'You fools ——' Rocca was beginning, when a prod in the small of his back from the butt of one of the pikes cut short his utterance and thrust him yelping forward: 'Get along, curse your garboil. You can talk to the Corregidor.'

Thus in ignominy and fury they were haled from the inn and away through the streets of Cordoba, with a tail of jeering urchins and idlers that increased steadily all the way to the market-place where the Corregidoria and the gaol were situated.

Into that gloomy building of heavily barred, unglazed windows the agents of the Three were conducted, and after their names had been taken and entered in a register, with a note of the plaint against them, they were locked in a stone cell that seemed to them no bigger than a dog kennel. It was entirely unfurnished, save for a heap of unclean straw that was to serve them for a bed. There, hungry, weary and savage, they began by cursing Spain and all Spaniards, and ended by cursing each other.

The Corregidor, who, they had been told, would see them in the morning, was at that moment with Don Luis de Santangel in the lodging over Bensabat's shop in the Calle Atayud.

They had discovered there a melancholy Colon in the act of packing his effects, preparatory to departure.

Santangel with a laugh commended these activities. 'That is wise. You will be journeying to the Vega tomorrow, as I shall. We will go together, Cristobal.'

Colon found the laughter out of season. 'I am for France, Don Luis.'

'And what should you do in France?'

'Hope that King Charles will be able to form a judgment without the help of a junta.'

'You've no faith, then, in our Corregidor. He has a word to say to you. That is why I have brought him.'

'I am grateful for his interest. But I perceive nothing that he can do.'

'Nothing more, perhaps,' said Don Xavier, advancing to the table. He slapped down two folded parchments. 'This, I think, is your lost property, sir.'

Colon held his breath as he pounced upon them. When next he looked up the weariness had been swept from his face. His eyes were full of light.

'You work miracles, then, in Cordoba?'

Don Xavier laughed. 'In a modest way. My alguaziles are brisk lads. Master Rocca has been so handled that there will be no ambassadorial complications. Don't ask me how. That must remain our secret.'

'What I ask you, sir, is how shall I reward your alguaziles?'

Still the Corregidor was merry. 'Never let that trouble you. The rascals have rewarded themselves. It's the State of Venice will have to bear the charges, as is just and proper; in fact, poetic.'

 THE MARCHIONESS

THE Chancellor of Aragon travelled in that state which became his quality and consequence. A dozen grooms, well mounted and well armed, with his blazon — azure, two chevrons argent — on the breast of their leather hacketons, served him for escort. A string of sumpter mules followed with his tents and baggage.

The little company rode south under the hot sun of June, and on the third day after leaving Cordoba it crossed the river Genil, and came out of dust and sultriness into the vast and miraculously green plain of the Vega and the breezes cooled by the snows of the Sierra Nevada. From the heights above the river they had viewed the Vega's emerald expanse, interlaced with the sparkling silver of the snow-fed tributaries of the Genil, whence it derived a fecundity and a beauty comparable in Saracen eyes with the Plain of Damascus.

In the distance ahead of them, on the south bank of the parent stream, where tall poplars stood like a hedge of giant spears, they beheld the many coloured tents of the Spanish camp, an immense, sprawling city of silk and canvas under a cloud of fluttering banners and waving standards. Far beyond it, on the heights, hazy in the distance, stood the towers and minarets of Granada, the last Moorish stronghold, dominated by the embattled walls of Alhambra the Red, and taking for background the massive escarpments of the sierra, whose snow-capped heights were rose-flushed and opalescent in the evening sun.

At Santangel's side Colon paused with him to view the opulent beauty of the prospect. Then they pushed on across the verdant plain, by vineyards and olive groves, by feathery acacia and flowering syringa, whose perfumes sweetened the breeze, beside acres of oats and of yellowing wheat, fields of gold splashed with the scarlet of poppies.

Colon rode in high hopes, among which, being human, was that of discomfiting those who had denounced him a trickster, flinging their malice in their teeth to shame them.

'Leave me to handle them,' Don Luis had insisted. 'I'll see their reverences choked with their own words. Your turn will follow.'

That had been settled between them before they left Cordoba. Where they had not agreed had been in the matter of Beatriz. Santangel had urged Colon to seek her at once, urged it with an insistence that surprised Colon by the interest in her which it suggested. Colon, however, had stood firm. He would not seek her until he could go to her with certain news. Meanwhile, to allay her anxieties, he sent her a note to inform her that his stolen property was recovered. Santangel struggled with a temptation to tell him the truth of what had occurred, but conquered it by the persuasion that the knowledge would come to him better in the form of a confession from Beatriz. Thus would the healing absolution be more certain.

They came at sunset to the outskirts of the vast encampment, the lines of ordnance and victualling carts, the herds of Andalusian and Arab horses, of mules and of donkeys, and the paddock of draught oxen. From the clamour and move-ment of this, they passed to the no less clamorous cluster of huts erected by the artisans; the smiths with their forges, the carpenters with their benches, the masons, rope-weavers and basket-makers, who made up the army of engineers to build bastions, causeways, bridges and what else was needed for the transport of the artillery, which was under the Queen's own active ingenious direction.

Beyond these outskirts of the camp, they passed up long avenues of tents, about which soldiers took their evening ease, the noise and bustle of the place augmented by the voices of bards and ballad-stringers, the cries of pedlars who with their pack-mules or donkeys circulated everywhere seeking trade. But there were no other camp-followers to be seen, and none of the harpies who habitually prey upon troopers. In the camp of the chaste and pious Isabel nothing awaited them but the whip.

Moving slowly through the press, they came at last to the heart of the encampment, where about a great clearance were pitched the gay silken pavilions of the Sovereigns and their court. Here were the purple tents of the warlike Cardinal of Spain, who brought two thousand men to swell the royal forces, those of the Duke of Medina-Sidonia, the Marquis of Cadiz and other grandes whose armed vassals were incor-porated in the Spanish host, each tent proclaimed by the banner waving over it.

Santangel made his way to the Marquis of Moya's pavilion, where the welcome given them by the Marchioness seemed to be rather on his companion's account than on his own.

'Now, this is well thought, Don Luis. For had you not brought our Cristobal, he might not have sought us for himself.'

Colon bowed low. 'I kiss your hands, madam. You'll have heard that I am in disgrace.'

'Which is just when friends may serve you.'

Cabrera was not slow to support her welcome of him. 'At the moment there is perhaps not much that we can do. But you shall command us, and we'll prove to you how little credit we attach to your detractors.'

'The Lord confound their malice,' said the lady piously.

'I come in the hope to do it, myself, madam.'

She shook her head. 'This is not the moment for arguments. I have tried them.'

'On my behalf?'

'Did you suppose my faith so easily destroyed? Or that I want for courage?'

'There is no virtue with which I do not credit you, madam.'

'I have none stronger than my faith in my own opinions. If you'll be guided by them, you'll postpone all suits. Her Highness is aggrieved. She feels herself humiliated in the eyes of the King, who has never smiled upon your project.'

'Now, that is excellent,' said Santangel, and rubbed his hands. 'Her Highness will be the more eager for Colon's rehabilitation.'

Cabrera was gloomy. 'You view it too lightly. Further insistence just now might be a provocation.'

But they refused to be dismayed. Santangel's smile grew broader. 'So it shall be for some. I mean it so to be. But not for Her Highness. We come with proofs, not arguments. The proofs the gentlemen of the junta said they would accept as definite — the missing chart and letter, the robbery of which they pronounced a palpable subterfuge — we have recovered them.'

'Vive Dios!' swore the Marquis, whilst his lady stared until laughter kindled in her splendid eyes.

'That will provide a resounding vindication.'

'At least it makes my honour safe,' said Colon.

'And all the rest.'

'Hardly the rest. Malice was content to crush me with this pretext. But had I been able to produce the chart the learned doctors would no doubt have found that it did not suffice.'

This gave her thought: amusing thought from which it resulted that she became the promoter of a conspiracy to confound Talavera and Fonseca, both of whom were with the Sovereigns.

'I stand as much in need of rehabilitation with the Queen as she with the King, and our Cristobal with both. So give me leave to handle this. You shall see what a jurist has been lost in Beatriz de Bobadilla.'

They stayed to a supper of eels and trout from the Genil and ortolans of the Vega, with a white wine of Estremadura, chilled in snow from the sierras. So gay were they over this repast that Colon, who knew the gaiety to be that of spirits generously exalted on his behalf, was paradoxically almost touched to melancholy.

After supper a groom lighted them to the royal pavilion of audience, over which floated the standard of the two kingdoms.

The King was at chess with the Bishop of Avila, whilst the Queen, at a table some distance away, was receiving a report from Captain Ramirez, her Master of the Ordnance, known as El Artillero. This was concerned with the new lombards that were to augment the royal artillery. Fonseca, that ecclesiastical man of war, was naturally in attendance. Although from head to foot he was in unadorned black and wore no weapons, yet since Nature had completely tonsured him there was nothing about him to denote the priest.

Ramirez was taking his leave when a page raised the heavy tapestries that shut off the vestibule, so as to give passage to the Marchioness, who as the Queen's intimate possessed the right of access at all hours.

Her Highness looked up from El Artillero's list. She had been scanning it by the light of a cluster of candles of perfumed wax in a massive silver candlebranch. She smiled a gentle welcome as the Marchioness came forward, splendid in blue velvet, the bodice cut square to make a brave display of her white throat. She advanced over the Eastern rugs that carpeted the richly furnished tent, to take the seat by the table to which Her Highness motioned her.

'You do not usually seek me so late, Beatriz. You had leave to remain absent.'

'But cause to be present. I have news for Your Highness. News of Colon.'

If she had overturned the candlebranch she could not have surprised them more. The King, overhearing across the tent, swung round in his chair. 'News that the rascal has left Spain, I hope.'

'Indeed, I am the bearer of no such evil tidings, sire.'

'Evil? I could bear worse. But, to be sure, you ever had a kindness for that long-legged put.'

The Bishop moved a piece. 'Check, sire,' he murmured.

'It's his mind that commands my respect, Highness,' said the Marchioness.

'Yet his legs are the better part of him,' laughed Ferdinand, and returned his attention to the game.

The Queen sighed. 'The worth of him has unfortunately been tested — by Don Juan here, among others.'

'I am fortunate to find Don Juan with Your Highness.'

Fonseca bowed, but there was no smile on his round, flat face.

'I have a hope,' the Marchioness continued lightly, 'that I may bring him to change his view on Master Colon.'

'Alas, madam, it is too solidly founded.'

'Solidly? Solid as sand, Don Juan.'

The King moved a piece in haste. 'What's that?' he shouted, and again looked over his shoulder. 'Are you still defending that unmasked impostor?'

'From the error of his judges, sire.'

'On my soul, you push your infatuation something far.'

'It is an infatuation for the good of Spain and the honour and glory of Your Highnesses.'

The Queen patted her hand. 'No one doubts your good intentions, Beatriz. But this matter has been judged.'

'And sentence passed,' Ferdinand flung in. 'It is *res judicata*.'

'Check, sire,' said the cold voice of the Bishop. 'It will be checkmate on the next move, I think.'

'Eh?' His Highness glowered at the board. 'To the Devil with Colon and this distracting chatter of him. The dog has lost me the game.'

The handsome eyes of the Marchioness were solemnly turned upon him.

'I could prove to Your Highness that more might be lost over Colon than a game of chess.'

'By Saint James, yes. A deal of time and patience.'

'Therefore,' the Queen admonished her, 'do not be adding to that loss.'

It was a mild rebuke that must have silenced any but the Marchioness of Moya. The Marchioness, however, was a beloved and privileged person.

'Would my love for you, madam, excuse my disobedience?'

Ferdinand heaved himself up, and stood square and solid, a frown between his blue eyes. 'In the name of Heaven, Beatriz, do you not perceive that there are no words to mend this broken thing?'

'I have not deserved Your Highness's attention. I spoke of proofs.'

'But proofs of what?' asked the Queen.

'That Colon was rashly judged.'

Ferdinand laughed. 'You're of a persistence that would shame a spider.'

'Give me leave, then, to spin my web.' She looked from Ferdinand to the Queen with an entreating smile.

'And now you are all siren,' the King laughed, whilst the Queen added questioningly, 'There is something in your mind, Beatriz?'

She took this for permission, and plunged boldly. 'I am fortunate to find here my Lord Bishop of Avila, who presided over the junta, and Don Juan de Fonseca, who bore so weighty a part in it.'

Talavera had risen with the King. His cold eyes pondered her in silence. Don Juan bowed, again, with a grace too courtly for a priest. 'You overestimate my worth, madam. My poor part was to unmask this man.'

'Of the mask your wits had fitted to him.'

'Not I, madam. Not I. But his own false hands.'

'Let that be the issue between us. Have I Your Highness's leave to come to it?'

The Queen sat back in her chair, perplexed by this strange eagerness. 'Oh, but let us hear you,' she consented. 'I don't doubt that Don Juan will make a good defence.'

The King lounged across to them. He chose to be amused. 'A joust, is it? As I live, Bishop, you'll be dragged into the lists before all's done.'

The Marchioness looked into Don Juan's round yellow face, dazzling him a little by the effulgence of her glance. 'You persuaded yourself and others — did you not? — that Master Colon's claim to have possessed a chart from the great Toscanelli was a falsehood.'

'I persuaded myself, Marchioness, do you say?' He was

smiling, unctuously confident. 'By your leave, it was Colon, himself, who persuaded us of that.'

'He told you that he was lying, did he?'

'By his methods,' Fonseca assented. 'They have been employed before by other tricksters. It is a common thing for men of no authority in themselves to pretend that for what they state they have behind them an authority that is beyond dispute. Thus this man dug a pit for himself. For when we asked him, as our duty was, for his proofs, he pretended that he had been robbed. A stale trick.'

'A stale trick? Where is the evidence that it was a trick at all?'

Ferdinand laughed outright. 'Lord, man! You will begin to see that to argue with a woman is to carry water in a basket.'

But Isabel frowned. 'Perhaps,' said she, 'Don Juan has nothing better in which to carry it. Let us hear him.'

Fonseca strove with his impatience. 'The evidence is in the irresistible inferences from the facts. It is not credible that had this man possessed such backing for his arguments he would not have produced them long before our insistence drove him into claiming that possession.'

'I see,' the Marchioness conceded, with apparent reluctance. 'I see.'

'God be praised,' the King mocked. 'Her eyes are opened.'

'Not quite, Highness. What I do not understand is why, if Colon's theories did not suffice to convince, identical theories put forward by another could have done so. No doubt I am but a foolish woman, but I cannot perceive the difference.'

It was Talavera, moving slowly towards them, who answered her.

'The difference, madam, is that which lies between the opinions of an ignorant visionary mariner and that of the most learned mathematician of his day.'

'Are you answered, Marchioness?' the King asked her.

'Indeed, sire, I am being buffeted at every turn.' She trilled good-humoured laughter at her own discomfiture. 'But surely, sirs,' she looked from Talavera to Fonseca, 'it is easy to show that you overstate this difference. You will hardly pretend that if Colon's arguments, which must have failed to persuade you, had actually been supported, as he foolishly asserted, you would have found in his favour.'

'That is no pretence, madam,' said Talavera sternly.

'What?' Her brows went up. Her countenance reflected a disturbed amazement. 'Can you assert, my lord, that if this misguided fellow could have produced the chart and the letter, he would have received your support?'

'I do assert it, madam,' said the Bishop firmly, and 'Undoubtedly, madam,' added Fonseca.

The Marchioness's laughter of unbelief visibly annoyed them both.

'It is easy to assert a thing the proof of which cannot be called for. You would be less glib, I think, if Colon's possession of those documents were still untested.'

'Madam!' cried the Bishop, in outraged protest.

'An error, Marchioness,' said Fonseca. 'An error gross and uncharitable. You will forgive the terms.'

'I find them mild,' laughed the King.

But the silent Queen was placidly watchful. Her shrewdness perceived that behind all this there was some definite purpose.

The Marchioness, returning to the attack, was no longer smiling.

'Gross and uncharitable! Fie, Don Juan! Yet I will own myself both if you will dare to say that were Colon at this moment to lay Toscanelli's chart before you, you would advise Their Highnesses to give him their support. Dare you?'

Fonseca goaded almost to the limits of endurance answered irritably: 'I have as good as said so already.'

'And you, my Lord Bishop?'

Talavera shrugged. 'The assertion is idle, superfluous. But if it will content you, madam, I make it without hesitation.'

Smiling again, and with something now of triumph in her smile, she turned to the Queen. 'Your Highness hears these reverend gentlemen. Have I bound them tightly enough?'

Fonseca was disturbed. 'Bound us, madam?'

'In the web that I warned you I was spinning. Perhaps you did not sufficiently heed the warning.'

The Queen sat forward. 'You have been mysterious long enough, Beatriz. Shall we now have some plain sense from you?'

'The plain sense of it, Highness, is that I hope I have made impotent the prejudice out of which these gentlemen pronounced Colon a trickster. It has pleased God that to confound them Colon should have recovered the chart and the letter that were stolen. He is here in the camp, waiting to lay them before Your Highnesses.'

22

 REHABILITATION

CRISTOBAL COLON stood before Their Highnesses in the golden candlelight of the royal pavilion.

Not only would Queen Isabel's sense of justice brook no delay, but she was moved, too, by her desire to justify her own earlier enthusiasm, which the finding of the junta had made to appear a foolish credulity.

Santangel and Cabrera had come in with Colon. The Marchioness of Moya, as Colon's sponsor now, stood midway between them and the table at which the Queen remained seated. The King, with Talavera and Fonseca, made a group immediately behind Her Highness. The Toscanelli parchments and Colon's own chart lay on the board before the Queen.

Santangel was speaking, at Her Highness's bidding, to his own share in the recovery of those documents. 'The thieves,' he was saying, 'were two agents of the Venetian Republic, one of whom had for some time been about Your Highnesses' Court, on a pretence of being attached to Messer Mocenigo,

the Republic's envoy. They were overtaken ten miles from
Cordoba, on their way to Malaga, and in order to avoid
complications with Venice, the matter was so handled by the
Corregidor as to appear an act of banditry.'

The King intervened harshly. 'That tale hardly makes
sense. What interest could Venice have in this?'

'Whether it makes sense or not, Highness, the facts are as
I state them, and as the Corregidor of Cordoba can witness.'

'And with submission, Highness,' Colon added, 'so much
sense does it make that it begins to explain the influences at
work against me in Portugal. The wealth and power of
Venice is built upon her commerce with the Indies. She
holds the only gateway to Europe for that trade. To reach
the Indies by the West is to shatter that monopoly.'

Ferdinand was thoughtful. 'Faith, that might be an explanation,' he acknowledged grudgingly.

The Queen looked up from the documents, which she had
been studying. 'I grieve, sir, that an injustice should have
been done you as much as I rejoice that you are fortunately
enabled to expose it.'

Fonseca, made daring by chagrin, ventured to interpose.
'It might be prudent, Highness, to make quite sure — if,
indeed, it is possible to make sure now that Toscanelli is
dead — that we are not being imposed upon by forgeries.'

The mockery of the Marchioness's low laugh brought the
blood to his yellow face and fury to his dark eyes. A wave of
the Queen's hand reproved her.

'The writing on the chart is in the same hand as the letter
with Toscanelli's signature, and both bear his seal.'

'These things may be counterfeited, Highness.'

'Faith,' Ferdinand agreed, 'that is not to be denied.'

The Queen turned in her chair, and looked up into Fonseca's
face. 'Are you suggesting that they have been? Speak up,
man. Let us have clarity. The question is a serious one.'

Emboldened by the King's support, Fonseca did not hesitate. 'As Your Highness says. It is in my mind that a man under a cloud, and so expert a penman as Master Colon's own chart proves him to be, might not be able to resist temptation.'

Colon laughed, which did not please the Queen. 'What is amusing you, sir?'

'The manner in which Don Juan covers his innuendo. It is like paint upon rotten timber. Give me leave to speak his mind for him. It is that I have forged these documents so as to make good my imposture.'

'And if I were to put it as plainly as that, how should you prove me wrong?'

'I should not. It would not be necessary. I might remind you, for instance, that a forger would have gone before the junta already armed with his forgeries. But I need not even urge that, unless you can show that the Venetian State knew that it was in my mind to commit these forgeries before it dispatched its agents to purloin them.'

Ferdinand loosed his laughter. Even the austere Talavera could not suppress an amusement that was general.

Fonseca's lips writhed. He bowed to the Sovereigns. 'My zeal for Your Highnesses makes pitfalls for me sometimes.'

'Oh, and for others,' said Colon, which did not make Fonseca love him any better.

'Hush, sir,' the Queen gently reproved him. 'At such a time you can spare some generosity. Take your charts. You have leave to go. But you shall wait on us again to-morrow.'

'I kiss Your Highnesses' feet,' he said, and departed well content.

In all that had passed the deepest impression upon the Queen, deeper even than the production of the Toscanelli chart, had been the Venetian attempt to become possessed of it, and Colon's explanation. No richer confirmation could have been supplied of her own wisdom in having from the first desired to sponsor the venture.

'They are shrewd, these Venetians,' she told King Ferdinand, when they conferred alone. 'And they foresee just such an aggrandisement of Spain as Colon promises, an aggrandisement at their own expense.'

'Is there not aggrandisement enough for us in the conquest of Granada?'

She shook her head. 'Sovereigns have a sacred trust. It is not for them to pause whilst any channel offers by which to magnify the country over which they have been called to rule.'

'True. But do not let us confuse dreams with realities. The lands to be reached by this western voyage are still no more than a dream.'

'The conquest of Granada was but a dream. Yet now it nears fulfillment.'

'Granada we can see. We know it for a reality that it exists. We cannot see these lands of Master Colon.'

'Not with the eyes of the flesh. But they are visible to the eyes of Colon's spirit: to his imagination.'

'It is just of this that I complain. Shall we risk lives and treasure, blood and gold, to prove that his imaginings are not vain?'

'To venture nothing is to accomplish nothing.'

'Yet what have we to venture? This war has drained our treasuries, and it may still drag on for months. We need every maravedi for what is yet to do.'

This, at least, was not to be gainsaid, wherefore the end of the matter was that when, obedient to the summons, Colon waited upon the Sovereigns on the morrow, it was to learn of yet another postponement of his hopes. But now, at least, there was a definite promise.

'We have well considered,' the Queen told him, 'and we are resolved to support your undertaking. It must wait, however, until Granada is conquered. Not until then will it be possible for us to take order about it. In the meantime Don Alonso de Quintanilla shall have our orders to continue to provide for your subsistence as generously as the state of our treasury will permit.'

It was less than he had hoped from that audience, yet not so little that he need despond.

'After all,' as Santangel told him afterwards, 'when a man has waited years, a few added weeks need not exasperate him.'

They sat alone in the Chancellor's silken tent. They had dined, and were still at table, the Chancellor busy with a dish of cherries. Colon fetched a sigh. 'I am still to be accounted young, yet my years have been so chilled by hope deferred that the snows are already settling on my head.' He lowered it to show the strands of grey that began to show in his luxuriant tawny mane.

'Look for no pity from me on that score. I have grown white in the service of princes.'

'A service to break the heart of a man. Granada!' Colon was scornful. 'A city. And its conquest is to delay the conquest of a world.'

'Be comforted. It will not delay it long. This war will not last out the year. The Sovereigns are carrying it with method.'

'I'll go wait the end of it in Cordoba with Beatriz. She will give me patience who has already given me so much.'

Santangel smiled pensively. 'More perhaps than you guess. Yes, go to her, Cristobal. She will be waiting for you. And . . .' He broke off, hesitating for a moment. Then added: 'Be gentle with the child.'

Colon's eyes widened in surprise. 'You may trust me to be that.'

23

THE CUP

OF

TRIBULATION

O<small>N THE</small> morning after their ig-
nominious consignment to that stone cell in Cordoba gaol,
the two Venetian agents were haled before the Corregidor to
render an account of themselves.

They stood before him blear-eyed from sleeplessness and
indignation, unkempt and flea-bitten, for although, themselves, they had gone supperless, they had furnished a banquet
for the tenants of the straw that supplied their bed. Nevertheless, Rocca at once launched forth upon an address which
he had spent much of the night in silently rehearsing. It was
sternly cropped in full flow by the saturnine Don Xavier.

'You are not to deafen me with your chatter. You are to
speak only to what I may ask you. You are now in Castile,
and in Castile we conduct our proceedings in an orderly
manner.' He turned to the notary beside him. 'Read them
the plaint.'

They listened gloomily to the account of the contumelious
conduct of which they were accused, and were asked at the
end if they denied it.

Rocca conceived this to be his cue for a second attempt at delivering his oration.

'We do not deny it. But I will beg your worship to ——'

His worship checked him there by raising his hand, whilst he directed the notary at his side. 'They do not deny it. Set that down. That is all I asked.'

'But, sir ——'

'That is all I asked,' the Corregidor thundered. He paused, and then continued on the awed silence he had produced. 'It is for the Alcalde to pass judgment on your offence. Remove the prisoners.'

'At least,' said Gallina, 'we may be allowed to send a letter?'

'Not until the Alcalde has pronounced upon your case, or until he chooses to permit it.'

'And when will that be?'

'In the Alcalde's own good time. Go with God.' He waved them away.

It was a full week before the Alcalde's good time arrived, and two starveling wretches were brought before him. The indescribably foul appearance to which they were by then reduced rendered the more ludicrous the lofty tone assumed by Rocca, his assertions that he was a gentleman in the following of the Venetian Ambassador, and his imperious demand that he should be permitted at once to communicate with the Ambassador.

'You are to understand,' the grave Alcalde told him, 'that ambassadorial privileges and immunities do not include those of robbing and maltreating the subjects of the Spanish Sovereigns.'

Rocca's answer was a denial that there had been any intention to rob anybody, and that they had, themselves, been cruelly robbed by the very man they were accused of assaulting. In this last particular the Alcalde informed them he was assured they were in error.

The Alcalde condescended to permit them to send their letter, and when a secretary from the Venetian Embassy had come in response to claim them, they were restored to freedom subject to payment of a fine out of which Ribera should be compensated. Further, the Alcalde consented to receive the details of the robbery of which they proclaimed themselves the victims, and promised to refer the matter to the Corregidor.

Their cup of tribulation, however, was not yet drained. It was the Venetian envoy who forced upon them the bitter dregs of it when in their unkempt and soiled condition they stood before him.

The lordly Federigo Mocenigo, a large and imposing man of fastidious habits, looked down his patrician nose at these bedraggled agents of the Three. He listened to their tale, manifesting no emotion beyond a mild and rather malicious amusement.

'You do not appear,' he drawled, 'to have acted with that prudence desirable in gentlemen of your office.' His tone did not attempt to dissemble his contempt for that same office.

Gallina's face remained as wooden as ever. But the once flamboyant Rocca, who from posturing as an embassy functionary had come to regard himself as of that standing, repelled the rebuke with heat.

'I deny, excellency, that we have wanted prudence. With great skill we carried our mission to a successful issue. But we do not enjoy immunity from the dangers of highway robbery, and we can hardly be reproved for having suffered it. It is not,' he added viciously, 'a robbery that leaves room for smiles.'

'You are presuming, I think, to argue with me,' said his excellency, blandly unreasonable. 'In your place I should have taken precautions against being robbed of something I had been at such pains to obtain. But I am not to instruct you in the conduct of your despicable trade.' His excellency's play with a handkerchief that had been sprinkled with orange-water implied that he found his visitors offensive to his nostrils. 'You exist as a necessary social evil, which, however, is by the way. I suppose that I am now to provide you with the means to repatriate yourselves.'

'It may be too soon, excellency,' Gallina stolidly objected, 'to conclude that our mission is ended, that our loss cannot be repaired. Our immediate need is for support in obtaining justice against the robbers and the recovery of our property.'

'Or at least of the chart,' added Rocca.

His excellency was languid. 'I see that you are to instruct me. I suppose that you possess minds. If so, pray exercise them. I am to make a plaint to the Alcalde-Mayor of Cordoba. And of what, pray, shall I tell him that you were robbed? Of property that bears on the face of it the evidence that you stole it. Is that your notion of what should now be done? And you, Messer Rocca, are represented as a member of my embassy. Shall I have the Alcalde remind me that *Qui facit per alium facit per se?* A nice position, that, for an envoy of the Most Serene Republic.' He dropped his manner of contemptuous banter, to become stern. 'You shall have the means to get you back to Venice at the least cost to the State, and the sooner you are out of Spain the less offensive I shall find you.'

The lordly Rocca's sense of his consequence as a confidential and trusted agent of the Three was outraged. 'Are we, then, to report to the Inquisitors of State that we were hindered by your excellency in the fulfillment of our mission?'

'Will you be impudent, you rogue? As for what you call your mission, there is more comfort for you than your blundering deserves. Your mission has been fulfilled in spite of you. From what I learn, the owner of the chart found himself without it at the critical hour, and has been dismissed. So that is the end of the matter. And, anyway, I have no intention of compromising the Most Serene. You shall be supplied with means to return home. That, I think, is all that I have to say to you.'

Thereupon, cowed and disgruntled, they were ushered out, to scour themselves of their filth, and return to their old quarters at the Fonda del Leon. There, being clothed once more with some appearance of decency, they reviewed in bitterness the situation.

Their fellowship in misfortune had not produced the common result of endearing them to each other. The blame for this lay chiefly on Gallina's acid tongue, and his disposition to put the blame on his companion for the delay in their departure.

'May calamity overtake Messer Mocenigo,' Rocca was grumbling. 'A fool in office, a numskull born to the purple who has never yet had to strive for his bread. Very easy for him to be high and mighty with men who risk their necks to serve the State.'

'It does not look,' Gallina complained, 'as if we should serve the State much longer.'

'May your croaking choke you. Shall we be blamed for having been robbed?'

'Men like us are always blamed when things go wrong. That's what we're for. No account is taken of mischance where we are concerned.'

'You harp on the mischance. I've told you more than once that mischance, or chance of any kind, had nothing to do with what happened to us. It was all deliberate. There are plenty of indications of it. I still ask myself why they didn't slit up the lining of your doublet as they did mine. And why did that ruffian call off his fellow whilst he was still searching you? There can be only one answer. Because the chart was what he wanted. Having found it, he didn't trouble to look further.'

Gallina remained unconvinced. 'It looks like it, I know. But if Colon knew that we had stolen the chart, he wouldn't have sent gipsies to rob us. He would have had us arrested.'

'I own that's a difficulty. But I am as sure that those gitanos knew what they were looking for as I am that it was that trull Beatriz who betrayed us.'

'In order to hang her brother, I suppose. Bah! How could she betray what she didn't know?'

Rocca looked at him with increasing dislike. 'I sometimes wonder, Gallina, that with rudimentary wits like yours you should ever have prospered in this trade. It's one of life's mysteries. The girl knew that you knew where the chart was. When it vanished, what could she suppose but that we had stolen it?'

'If that were so, then our next conclusion should be that it was the girl who set the gitanos upon us. That, at least, would make some sort of sense.'

Rocca crashed fist into palm in astonishment at this sudden, sneering revelation. 'By the Host, Gallina, that is the explanation. We had better act upon it.'

Gallina was startled into reflection. 'I'll not deny it's a possibility,' he admitted. 'I wonder that I didn't think of it before.' He got up. 'But how act upon it? What remains to be done now?'

'We might pay Beatriz a visit, and find out exactly where we stand, and what's become of the chart. We might yet recover it. Anyway, there are accounts to settle with that strumpet.'

They found her in her room at Zagarte's, busy upon a piece
of needlework. It wanted still some hours to the daily performance, the attendances at which had been greatly reduced
in the past week by the Court's departure from Cordoba.

She was singing quietly to herself as she plied her needle,
a little song that withered on her lips at sight of them.

'God save you, Beatriz,' Rocca gently greeted her. If sad-
coloured fustian replaced his ruined brocades, yet the flam-
boyance of his bearing was undiminished. He rolled forward,
Gallina shambling after him.

'God save you,' she answered, staring. 'I thought you were
gone.'

'Without taking leave of you?' He was falsely genial. 'How
suppose it?'

'And why suppose it?' wondered Gallina. 'With our work
still to do.'

She was considering them in a calm that was only apparent.
Inwardly she was striving with an instinctive sinister dread
which their presence had awakened.

'You don't answer,' said Gallina, coming to stand over her,
as grim as Rocca was pleasant. 'If you supposed that we had
gone, you must also have supposed that we had done the work
you were sent to do. Is that it?'

'That is what I supposed, naturally.'

His accusation followed, bluntly so as to surprise admission.
'And you played us false by telling Colon.'

She rose suddenly, with something of defiance in her mien.
'Why are you here? Why do you take this tone?'

'Answer me.' Gallina's sinewy hand on her shoulder thrust
her down again. 'Don't trifle with us, girl. To go back on
your bargain and refuse your help would have been one thing;
that lies between yourself and your brother. But actively to
hinder us by betrayal is quite another. And it is not a thing
we can suffer.'

'What do you want with me? I have done enough for your purposes.'

'Yes, and then undone it, so that it all has to be done over again. Where is Colon?'

'I don't know.'

'Don't lie to me, you slut. Where is Colon?'

'I tell you I don't know. I haven't seen him for over a week. Go. Leave me. I have no more to say to you.'

Gallina leaned further over her. 'It might come to pass,' he said, his voice softly sibilant, 'that you might have no more to say to anyone.'

She was staring up in deepening fear, when Rocca sank to the divan beside her, and motioned Gallina away. He set a coaxing hand on her arm. He took a gentle affectionate tone. 'Listen to me, Beatriz. We've played fair with you. Will you play us false now for the sake of this rascal who tricks you to his ends? Are you so infatuated as to forget that this is a man of courts, whose proper mates are among the hidalgos and hidalgas? At what do you suppose that he values a dancing girl but as the toy of an idle hour? Why, child, all Cordoba knows that the lovely Marchioness of Moya is his mistress. Is that the man for whose sake you will destroy your brother?'

'Why do you come here to torment me? What do you hope to gain by it?'

Whilst Gallina watched in silence, Rocca pursued his subtle course of cajolery. 'We want to help you. But for that you must help us. Even now it may not be too late. What's done may yet be undone. Ten days ago, on the road to Malaga, we were robbed of the chart. I needn't tell you that that was no ordinary robbery. Now what we want you to do is ——'

There Gallina's cry came harshly to interrupt him. 'In the name of hell, must you still be talking?'

It startled both Rocca and Beatriz. They looked up and

round to see that the door had opened, and that under the lintel stood Colon.

He advanced, leaving the door aswing behind him. He was very pale, a wry smile on his lips, a smouldering fire in his grey eyes. 'Pray continue to instruct the lady in her duties, Messer Rocca.'

Both Rocca and Beatriz, the Venetian's hand still upon her arm, came together to their feet and with Gallina stood eyeing Colon in a shocked silence.

'What? Nothing more to say? Well, well! Perhaps you have said enough. Certainly enough to enlighten a poor, blind fool named Cristobal Colon. Now that I understand I admire your courage, you rogues, that you should still linger in Cordoba with your impudent decoy.'

'God!' gasped Beatriz, clutching her breast.

Rocca's hand stole behind him. 'You'll measure your words, my lad.'

'Be sure I'll measure them. I'll use no more than I need for a warning. See that you're gone from Cordoba by this time to-morrow, all three of you, you vermin, or I shall know how to see you gaoled.'

'Is that your humour?' said Gallina.

'That is my humour. To have you gaoled for thieves. I hold the proof, and for witnesses I have the men who found my property upon you.'

Rocca was airy. 'It flatters my discernment to find things just as I had supposed.'

'Use that discernment to profit by my warning. You owe it to the unfortunate woman whose harlotry you used.'

He swung on his heel to go, and Beatriz, petrified between a consciousness of guilt and a consciousness that the situation damned her utterly, had no word to stay him.

She could not guess whether Colon had come already in-

formed by Santangel of her betrayal and refusing to perceive
a mitigation of it in her subsequent warning, or whether still
in ignorance he had inferred her part from the situation in
which he found her and the words he had overheard. In her
despair, however, it did not seem to her that it could matter
either way.

It was left for Rocca to answer. His hand came from
behind him, armed with the dagger that had hung upon his
hip. 'We thank you for the warning. It is timely.'

Gallina's hand was raised to arrest his less calculating
associate. Colon, however, sensed rather than heard the
swift attack. He wheeled to meet it no more than in time,
and it was purely the unreasoned act of lightning reflexes
that caught the Venetian's wrist as the blow descended.

Big and heavily built, Rocca was an active, powerful man,
who in the pursuit of his dangerous calling had held his own
against odds in many a rough-and-tumble. But Colon, too,
was a man of his hands, of unsuspected strength, whom turbulent years at sea had schooled in a prompt dexterity. He
swung the arm outwards with a wrenching twist that drove
a searing agony through the socket. Then, as Rocca swung
sideways, a leg was thrust behind his heels to trip him, and
brought him crashing to the ground, his right arm dislocated
and useless.

Already Gallina was leaping to the attack, for though his
cooler head might deplore the battle so rashly joined, there
was no alternative now but to pursue it. He too was armed,
and Colon, looking round for a weapon, caught up, for lack
of a better one, Beatriz's guitar from the chair on which it
stood near his hand. Swung like a battle-axe, with terrific
force, the back of it smote Gallina's face to stay his charge.
As he staggered under the blow, the instrument was swung
a second time, and it took him so violently across the crown

that his head went through both sides of it and remained en-
cased in it as in a pillory. He fell back blindly, knocking the
table over, and with the blood streaming down his lacerated
face, struggled wildly to deliver himself of that jagged
collar.

Rocca, faint with pain, had, nevertheless, recovered his
dagger with his left hand, and was in the act of rising, when a
vigorous kick sent him sprawling again.

Colon, going out backwards, hurtled into Zagarte, who
with a couple of lads and Beatriz's Morisco woman had been
drawn by the uproar. The scene wrung from him an excited
'Bismillah!' and the dismayed inquiry, 'By all the devils, what
is happening here?'

'These two assassins set upon me with their daggers. Summon the watch.'

Yet a third lad who was arriving sped away on that errand,
whilst Gallina, delivered at last of the guitar, which lay
smashed on the ground, staggered forward without attempting
to stanch the blood that dripped from his face, yet attempting
truculence, with Rocca limp and livid at his heels. Beyond
them, on the divan, wild-eyed, mute and gripped by horror,
crouched Beatriz.

Zagarte just inside the doorway was angrily meeting Gallina
with protests that never yet had such things happened in his
well-conducted house. Vainly did Gallina demand to be
allowed to pass.

'You shall pass when the alguaziles come for you. May I
die if I'll suffer anyone to use brothel manners here. Drawing
knives in my house, you bandits! The Corregidor shall school
you.'

Thus he and his lads held them until the alguaziles arrived.
They came promptly and in force, no fewer than four of
them, upon a tale that murder was being done. With their

high sense of duty, they marched off not only the Venetians, but Colon as well. It would be, said their leader, for the Corregidor to disentangle the matter and decide who were the assailants, who the assailed.

24

 THE FLIGHT

BEATRIZ, half-stunned by the events, was left there with Zagarte and her woman. Their kindly attempts to rouse her went unheeded.

'And the accursed dogs have broken your guitar,' the Morisco inveighed, regarding the wrecked instrument with rueful eyes.

She swept a hand wearily across her brow. 'No matter for the guitar, Zagarte. My singing is finished with it. I shall not want another.'

'How? Not want another?' His wide mouth fell open. 'What are you saying?'

Wearily she got up. 'Just that, Zagarte. It is finished, my friend. I won't sing again here, or anywhere.'

'Now, now, God avail us! Those misbegotten sons of dogs have shaken you. We'll give you a holiday to-day. To-morrow...'

She shook her head, a mournfulness to inspire compassion in her lovely face. 'There will be no to-morrow.' She put a hand on his arm. 'Have patience with me, Zagarte. Be kind. I can bear no more.'

The little man put an arm round her paternally. The wrinkles in his lean brown face deepened in concern. 'But this will pass. It will pass, Devil take it. A fine girl like you isn't so easily dismayed.'

'I'm not dismayed. I'm just broken. Broken like that guitar.'

'But what have they done to you, those scoundrels?' he demanded, and in his exasperation so far forgot his baptism as to have recourse to the objurgations of his early faith. 'May dogs defile their graves!'

'Oh, it is not what they have done. It is what life has done. What I have done. Pay me what is due to me, Zagarte, and let me go. I could be of no further use to you here.'

He swung from prayers to reproaches, and back again to prayers. Had she no heart? He had always been generous with her. She had reaped a liberal share of the takings. He might let her have even a little more. What was to become of his mystery?

'It was well enough before I came to it.'

'But since you've been in it, it can never be the same again.'

'You have been good to me, Zagarte, and that would count with me if anything could. But I must go.'

'Where will you go, child?'

'Away from Cordoba. Away from the life I've been living. That is all that matters.'

From this resolve no power on earth could move her. Zagarte's patrons were to know her no more. On the morrow, sad-eyed and wistful, she said farewell to the Morisco, and on a mule, with her packages slung behind her, accompanied only by her woman and the muleteer, she rode out of Cordoba by the Almodovar Gate, and took the westward road that leads to Seville.

At about the same hour the Corregidor from his seat of

judgment in the cheerless audience chamber of the Corregidoria, with the melancholy crucifix on the white wall behind him, was scowling down upon Rocca and Gallina.

Once again those two had known the cramped, foetid hospitality of Cordoba gaol, following upon some crude and brutal surgery performed on Rocca to reduce the dislocation of his shoulder.

Colon, by the favour of the Corregidor, so fully acquainted with the secret history behind this affair, appeared now not as a delinquent, but as the accuser.

Courteously invited by Don Xavier to state his case, he announced that he had it on the word of Don Luis de Santangel, who at need would confirm him, that these men were guilty of a theft of which some days ago he had been the victim. Coming upon them yesterday he had taxed them with it, whereupon they had drawn their daggers and assailed him, constraining him to employ force so as to defend his life.

Don Xavier cleared his throat, and delivered himself.

'From the information in our possession, we know the first part of that statement to be true. The rest is so natural a sequel that its truth is not to be doubted.' He directed a black scowl upon the prisoners. 'By the intervention of the envoy of the Most Serene Republic, and because at that time the proofs of your offence were not perhaps so conclusive as they are to-day, you were leniently dealt with. That lenience you have abused by renewing your criminal turbulence. It is, as before, for his excellency the Alcalde to pass judgment upon you. What judgment he will pass I cannot foretell. But since both of you are men of vigour and stout sinew, you may hope that he will take the view that a term of years on the bench of a galley is due from you to the justice of Castile.'

Whatever the Venetians may have expected, it was not this. Before that grim prospect both broke into speech,

Gallina protesting that men could not be treated with such manifest injustice without even being heard in their own defence; Rocca demanding again, as a person in the following of the Venetian envoy, to be allowed to communicate with Messer Mocenigo.

Don Xavier answered them with cruel waggishness. 'As for being heard on your defence, that is a matter for the Alcalde, who will certainly hear you. In Castile we deprive no man of his rights. It is only so as to spare you the torment of suspense that I have indicated what must follow, since no defence that you can offer could deceive us as to your offences or diminish their abominable character.

'As for an appeal to his excellency the Envoy of the Most Serene Republic, the Alcalde will probably agree with me that it is desirable to avoid the possibility of an intervention that might be a cause of friction between states. So go with God, both of you.'

When they had been hustled out, Don Xavier turned to Colon. 'Be sure they will not trouble you again. But tell me, sir, the alguaziles say that there was a woman present with them at Zagarte's, a dancing girl.'

Colon's heart trembled within him. But his answer was steady.

'That was mere chance. She is nowise concerned.'

To that extent he could be merciful to her whom he judged to have used him with so little mercy. But no more. Although he ached for her, yet he desired never to see her again. Finding her in the hour of his great need, he had joyously given her in return for the consolation she brought him, all that he had to give, all that there was of him. She had become more to him than any other living creature, not excepting even the beloved child he had left at La Rabida. In her his spirit had found a spirit upon which to lean. This union had made him strong, deepening the inspiration to a mighty achievement, rendered more glorious in prospect from the hope of laying at her feet the fruits of it. Now these feet were disclosed to him as of basest clay, planted in the foul mud of deceit and harlotry. He had enshrined — so that he might cherish her to the point of reverence — an ignoble decoy hired to delude and rob him. And she had robbed him of something more than a chart. She had robbed him of his last illusion, of the last shred of lingering faith in human love and human decency. Well, let her go, poor wretch. Her punishment would come upon her all too soon without action of his. It would spring naturally out of the infamy of her existence.

For him there remained still the discovery of new worlds. Let that high destiny suffice him. It was as well, perhaps, that he should travel his road without encumbrances, with the singleness of aim in the appointed task proper to one who was, as he believed, and had declared himself, an instrument in the hand of God for the service of Man.

Thus he sought solace for the bitterness in his heart, the aching loneliness in which he was left by the defection of Beatriz. But resignation came not so readily to his beckoning. For days he moped and fretted in idleness at Cordoba. More than once he had to do violence to himself to avoid the weakness of repairing to Zagarte's, where he supposed that Beatriz still displayed her incomparable grace in the saraband. To combat the temptation he would seek the Mezquita, and prostrate himself before the blue-and-white image of Our Lady of the Assumption, seeking in that unearthly devotion to escape the heartbreak of his frustrated earthly love.

At the end of an intolerable week, finding that Don Alonso de Quintanilla was leaving for the camp in the Vega, he took horse and rode in his train to rejoin the Court.

Mists were rising from the watercourses of the Vega at the

close of a summer day when they descended into the plain,
saluted from the distance by the roar of the Queen's lombards
that were pounding the Saracen walls with stone and iron.

Through the stir and bustle of the camp they came at dusk
to Santangel's luxurious pavilion, and there the welcome from
the elderly Chancellor warmed Colon's chilled heart like wine.

'You do well to show yourself, and so keep Their Highnesses
mindful of you. But what ails you?'

Santangel took him by the shoulders, and turned him so
that the light from the lamp on the camp table fell full upon
his haggard face. 'Are you ill?'

'In the soul of me,' said Colon, and told his wretched tale.
Santangel was aghast. 'And she made no defence?'

Colon misunderstood the indignation rumbling in that deep
voice. 'What defence could she make? I took them so un-
awares, in the very act of conspiring anew. I overheard too
much.'

'Too much! You did not overhear enough. You fool! Did
you never ask yourself upon what information we were able
so soon to recover your stolen property? Did it never cross
your mind that someone must have told us just where to seek
it?' Colon looked at him in bewilderment. 'It was Beatriz.
Beatriz Enriquez. Whom else should it have been? It was
by an inadvertence that she betrayed to Gallina that you
kept the chart at your lodging. But the moment she knew
that it had been stolen, she came to me and told me all.'

'To you?' Colon was still unconvinced. 'To you? But why
to you? Why not to me?'

'That's a long story, and a wretched ——'

'Besides,' Colon raged on, 'from what I overheard it was
plain that she was leagued with those scoundrels, that she
had been hired to decoy and betray me. That is not to be
denied.'

'It is not denied.' Santangel was sorrowful. 'But the price! The poor girl was no venal adventuress. They suborned her craftily, cruelly, using her natural love for a rascal brother who is in the clutches of the Venetian State. But the unhappy child came to love you, and when the need arose proved it; proved it terribly by sacrificing her brother for you. That is what she did when she denounced the thieves to me. That is the woman you are scorning; the woman of whom in your pride you would not seek an explanation; the woman whose heart is probably now broken.'

Colon sat down heavily. 'I shall go mad, I think. Why, if this is so, why did she not tell me?'

'What chance did you give her? You drew your horrible conclusions and ——'

'I mean, when she told you.'

'Can't you understand how she must shrink from so dreadful a confession, at least until the harm had been repaired?' He sighed. 'I might have told you, myself, before you returned to Cordoba. She asked me to tell you. But' — he shrugged — 'I thought it better to leave that for her. I thought it better that she should win absolution from you by confession.'

He took his head in his hands. 'Absolution!' Colon cried. 'But from what you tell me, it is I who stand in need of it.'

'God be praised that you perceive it.' Don Luis came to set a hand on Colon's shoulder. 'Lose no time here. Get back to Cordoba, and put an end to what she will be suffering. Make your peace with that unhappy child.'

'Do you suppose that I need urging?'

Thus, within five days of quitting Cordoba, Colon was back again, seeking her at Zagarte's, only to learn from the Morisco that she was gone. This was a check in full career.

'Gone? Gone where?'

Zagarte did not know. She had taken her belongings, and

left on the morning after the disturbance with the Venetians. There was the muleteer whom she had hired. He should be able to say whither he had conveyed her.

The muleteer, when Colon found him at his stables near the Gallegos Gate, informed him that he had left Beatriz at a convent near Palma del Rio, at the junction of the Genil with the Guadalquivir.

Colon set out upon the following morning, and rode the thirty miles to Palma in four hours, his impatience mounting with every league of the journey. He found the low white building of the convent, above the river, on a hillock reached through a thicket of ilex. The elderly, toothless lay-sister who opened to his knock eyed him with the suspicion she would bestow upon any gallant who came inquiring for a lady. When at last she had understood whom he sought, it was to answer him that Beatriz Enriquez had stayed but two days at the convent. Then she had left again, but whither she had gone, or even what road she had taken, the sister could not tell him. Perhaps in the town of Palma he might be able to discover it.

Within a couple of hours there was no muleteer or inn in Palma that he had not visited. But he could find no trace of her. He spent the night at an inn, and on the following morning set out again, to pursue the road that led south and west. At Lorna del Rio, at Tocino and at Guadajoz, and at every roadside tavern in between, he went inquiring, describing Beatriz and the Morisco woman who accompanied her. It all proved vain. No trace of her remained, and at last, despairing, he abandoned the quest and went back to Cordoba to enlist the aid of the Corregidor.

Don Xavier would spare no effort to oblige one who enjoyed the powerful protection of the Chancellor of Aragon. His alguaziles should set inquiries afoot in every district they visited. In this renewed hope Colon waited, lingering for weeks in Cordoba. Gradually, however, with the lack of news, his hopes withered, and his bitterness grew in considering the want of faith which had made him so prompt to convict Beatriz.

25

 TERMS

THAT summer the great camp in the Vega was consumed by fire. To house his army, King Ferdinand replaced it by a solid city of brick and stone, built in the shape of a cross, which he named Santa Fé. It was to be a symbol to the Moor that Spain was permanently established there.

The siege was sternly pressed, and at last at the New Year King Bobadil rode out to surrender. To receive this the Christian host went out from Santa Fé in glittering splendour, led forth by the Cardinal of Spain.

On the Feast of the Epiphany the silver cross that had been blessed in Rome rose to replace the fallen crescent on the Colmares Tower, flanked by the royal standards and the banner of Santiago.

With the proud consciousness that ten years of arduous warfare was at last ended and the overthrow of the Moor completed, the last of his jewels incorporated in the Spanish Crown, the Sovereigns rode into the Saracen stronghold, so sharply outlined against the mass of the sierra that sparkled white in the clear January sunshine.

Colon, a morose and weary ghost, came somewhere in the tail of that triumphant train. He was growing shabby again; but it was now from loss of interest in himself; and with it went loss of interest in others. He was no longer eager to rub shoulders with the great or exalted at finding in their company the place in life that properly belonged to him. The vanities of the world were all that he now discovered in it, and he was liberal only in his scorn of them. In scorn he pondered the occasion of this vast glittering cortège, of which he was so insignificant a fraction. This marching host with waving banners and blaring trumpets celebrated the conquest of a city, culminating the conquest of a little kingdom. A little thing indeed, compared with the conquests Colon could add to the Crown of Spain. It moved his contempt to contrast the great exultation of these Sovereigns with the cool apprehensive caution in which they approached an enterprise that would bring them not a city but a world.

Within Granada the Christian host wound its way upwards by a narrow sinuous street, whose white walls, following Arab custom, were broken by no windows, and came at last, by the great sculptured gateway crowned with stone pomegranates, to a broad steep avenue of elms and the tinkle of running water, everywhere decoratively used with such cunning by the Moors. Up this avenue they streamed to the wide terrace, at the foot of which the riders dismounted; and so, between the twin towers that form the Gate of Justice, they entered the fortress-palace of the Alhambra.

The transition from the stern blankness of the embattled red walls to the delicate tracery and marble beauties of the interior was one to dazzle the eye and amaze the spirit. A quadrangle where pillars that seemed too slight and delicate to carry their burden of arches of a tracery fine as lace enclosed the Court of Myrtles. Clipped, fragrant hedges from which this derived its name flanked a long basin of water that was of the clear colour of the tourmaline. Thence through the palace to the Court of Lions and the halls that open from it, all was a splendour of Eastern beauty, of colonnades, mosaics, glazed tiles, gilded vaulted ceilings of honeycomb design, marble pavements spread with silken rugs, and walls hung with tapestries from the looms of Persia and Damascus.

Colon passed with the throng into the vast Mexuar Hall, and into the Mosala beyond, where an altar had hurriedly been raised and consecrated, and where as a first act of thanksgiving a High Mass was sung by the Cardinal of Spain. Kneeling there, disregarded and lost in that courtly press, he asked himself if he should yet live to hear a *Te Deum* intoned in thanksgiving for the conquests which it lay in his power to make. If his hour was ever to come it was now. If there was any steadfastness in the word of princes, his long waiting should at last be ended.

Coming forth again after Mass into the graceful arcades that surrounded as with a cloister the Court of Lions, he found himself singled out by Doña Beatriz de Bobadilla and her husband.

'You wear too sad a countenance for a day of such rejoicing,' she chided him.

'What would you, madam? Waiting begets weariness, and weariness sadness.'

'But that is over. You have the promise of the Queen, who never broke a promise yet. If you had no other cause to rejoice in the conquest of Granada, you would still have that.'

'Promises are so easily forgotten.'

'Have you so little faith in your friends?'

'I have so few, and to these I fear to become importunate.'

'Us you would offend by such a fear,' Cabrera assured him.

'I hoped he might have guessed it,' laughed the Marchioness.

'But here's another promise for you. The Queen shall see you within the week.'

As she promised, it so fell out. On the following Monday, the fifth day after the entry into Granada, Don Lepe Peralta, the Queen's own alguazil, brought Colon a command to wait upon Her Highness.

She received him in the Cuarto Dorado, that rich chamber of the black-and-gold ceiling that had been a part of the harem of the Moslem kings. In a tall chair upholstered in red velvet, with a red velvet footstool to her feet, she sat enthroned, attended only by three of her ladies, the Marchioness of Moya, the Duchess of Medina-Sidonia and another.

The interview if brief was fruitful. To his formal assertion that he kissed her feet, she offered him her hand, and as he knelt, she gave him welcome.

'We have kept you waiting long, Master Colon; much longer than was our wish; but at last, now that the war is ended, I can redeem my promise. I have sent for you to assure you of this.'

Under that assurance and her kindly smile, he recovered something of the erstwhile swagger that had lately been eclipsed.

'Ignorance, Highness, has spoken of my project as a dream. But I dare to prophesy more happy success and durable renown for the Sovereigns who undertake this enterprise than ever was obtained by prince the most valorous and fortunate.'

It was as if he expressed his conviction that by comparison with what he went to do, this conquest of Granada which had delayed it should come to appear a deed of small significance.

'You are of a high confidence,' she told him. 'But perhaps no higher than the enterprise demands.'

'Nor higher than its fruits shall warrant,' answered he.

'May it be so for the greater glory of our Faith. To-morrow you shall treat with my agents what is yet to be settled, so that we may launch the undertaking.'

When at last she dismissed him, he went in better heart than he had known for months, finding in the imminence of action an anodyne for his abiding sorrow, a measure of blessed distraction from the tormenting thought of his lost Beatriz. In a lightened mood he returned to Santa Fé and the house of Don Alonso de Quintanilla, where he was again lodged.

To Santa Fé on the morrow came the Court, returning from Granada, and there that evening Colon was waited upon by those agents whom the Queen had mentioned. There were four of them, of whom Quintanilla, as the Chancellor and Accountant-General of Castile, was one. The other three were Hernando de Talavera, who moving from eminence to eminence was now Archbishop of Granada, Don Juan de Fonseca and the Admiral Don Matias de Rezende.

Colon sat down with them at a table in that spacious room, warmed by the fragrant fir-cones that smouldered in a brazier.

Talavera, dutifully representing a still mistrustful and reluctant King, opened the proceedings in a few words of austere and chilly courtesy. Then Rezende, as a man of practical experience in matters of the sea, desired to know what exactly would be Colon's requirements.

It was Colon's view that fewer than four ships well found and well manned, with a total complement of some two hundred and fifty hands, would hardly meet the needs of the undertaking. Here, at the very outset, he met opposition from Talavera, expressing the parsimonious nature of his master. Rezende, of whom the Archbishop had sought the information, had put the cost of such an expedition at forty to fifty thousand gold florins, whereupon the Archbishop's long face grew longer.

'Unless you can moderate that demand, sir, I fear that it will defeat your ends. All the world knows that the war has drained the treasury, and that at this moment Their Highnesses are harassed for supplies.'

Colon was aware of it, just as he was aware of the bitter struggle that was joined between the Inquisition and the Jews. The fiery, fanatical Torquemada was inveighing against the Judaizing practices attributed to the conversos, and clamouring for the wholesale expulsion of the Jews, on the ground that there would be no peace in Spain whilst they abode there. If the Jews were expelled, the property they must leave behind would enormously enrich the treasury, and in the temptation which this must offer the hard-pressed Sovereigns lay the strength of Torquemada. Aware of it, the Jews, championed by Abarbanel and Senior, whose admirable equipment of the army that had conquered Granada alone deserved the gratitude of the Sovereigns, were offering now a gift of thirty thousand ducats to cover the whole cost of the war. The matter hung thus in the balance. Torquemada was yet to make his terrible gesture of hurling the crucifix at the Sovereigns, bidding them sell Him again for thirty thousand pieces as Judas of old had sold Him for thirty. It was still the hope of such conversos as Santangel who stood high in the favour of the Sovereigns that the possibility of great wealth to accrue from Colon's adventure, allied with the gold now offered by the Jews, should outweigh the insidious prospect of replenishing the royal coffers by persecutive measures.

Meanwhile, until choice was made between the present alternatives, empty the treasury remained, and the fact must be recognized.

'Upon what equipment may I count, then?' Colon inquired.

Talavera was looking at Rezende, as if referring the matter to him, when Fonseca intervened. 'What need to adventure more than one ship?'

It was Colon's turn to look at Rezende in an appeal made eloquent by a little smile of scorn.

Rezende was prompt to shake his head. 'No, no. That is not practical. It is too perilous. Two ships at least, and that is not enough. With three I think that Master Colon might be content.'

'Be it so, then,' Colon agreed, 'provided that they are sound vessels and well found.'

Talavera made a note, and they passed on to ask him if he had considered what recompense he would require for his services. The readiness of his answer showed how well, indeed, he had considered it.

'One tenth of all gains resulting from my discoveries.'

'One tenth!' The Archbishop was taken aback, and did not dissemble it. 'One tenth!'

'You expect Their Highnesses to be munificent,' sneered Fonseca.

'Is that munificence? If so I'll be munificent with you. I'll give you ten maravedis for every hundred that you bring me.'

'There is no parallel,' said Talavera. 'In this it is Their Highnesses who provide the means.'

'Who adventure their gold,' added Fonseca, 'upon a gamble in which you adventure nothing.'

Colon answered him with the utmost mildness. 'Only my life, my skill and experience as a navigator, the courage to confront whatever perils may lurk in the unknown, and the idea upon which the whole enterprise is based. That is all that I bring to it, Don Juan. A modest contribution, for which I ask a modest tenth. If in addition I am to bear some part in the cost of equipment, let it be added that I receive an additional share in the same proportion.'

Fonseca's jaundiced look may have inspired Quintanilla to

anticipate him. 'In my view, sirs, we might agree to this, subject to approval by Their Highnesses.'

'Subject to that.' Fonseca stressed it.

'Very well,' said Talavera. 'That, then, I think, will be all.'

'All?' Colon raised his brows. 'All?' He looked from one to the other of them, and found their faces blank. 'Consider, sirs! That were to treat me as a hireling. This is no more than a beginning, my Lord Archbishop.'

'But what else can there be? What else could you require?'

'The title of Admiral in all the lands I may discover or acquire in the ocean, with the honours and prerogatives enjoyed in his district by the High Admiral of Castile.'

'God save us!' ejaculated Fonseca, whilst the others stared, and none in greater disgust than Don Rodrigo Rezende.

Undeterred, Colon went calmly on: 'And I shall require this office and honour not only for myself, but for my heirs forever.'

'What have your heirs to do with it?' asked Quintanilla.

'What any nobleman has to do with a title won by the deeds of a forefather.'

'Again I beg leave to say — there is no parallel!' cried Talavera.

'Of course not,' Fonseca scornfully supported him.

'I'll make it clearer. My discoveries will be a heritage to Spain forever, and as long as that heritage endures, so long is it just that I should have my portion of its yield. But since I am not immortal, that portion must go to my successors.'

Despite the faultless logic of the claim, it remained in their eyes detestable that a man of obscure and foreign birth should dare to make it.

'To yield you this,' Fonseca objected, 'would be to raise you to an eminence as great as was ever filled by any grande of Spain.'

'No grande of Spain has ever so well deserved it.'

'Mother of God! You talk of your discoveries as if they were already made.'

'Surely not. When they are made I shall require something more.'

'More?' Talavera frowned, and Rezende laughed. 'What more would be possible?'

'Viceroyalty over all the lands of my discovery, with all a viceroy's powers of life and death.'

There was a silence of stupefaction, broken at length by Fonseca's sneer. 'I suppose that only modesty prevents you from asking for the crown of Spain?'

Then the Archbishop contented himself with inquiring, on a note of irony: 'Have you any further demands, Master Colon?'

'None other occurs to me at present.'

'But you may think of something else when you've had time,' gibed Fonseca.

Talavera heaved a sigh. 'Let us give thanks that we have reached an end. I will be frank, sir. These demands far exceed anything to which I could recommend Their Highnesses to agree. My colleagues here will each use his own discretion as to that. Then it will be for the Sovereigns to pronounce. But I can hold out no hope to you unless you can materially moderate your views.'

The sarcasm of the cold level voice was as a scourge to Colon's pride. The scorn with which this rigidly upright but autocratic prelate sought to humble a presumption which he found insufferable, produced in Colon the very opposite effect.

He rose abruptly, and stood straight and tall, looking down his nose at them, proud as Lucifer himself. 'By no single jot will I abate my demands. That it should be suggested betrays unfitness to judge the glory of this enterprise. Give me leave, sirs.' With a haughtily careless bow, he turned and stalked out.

He left them in a gaping silence, from which Talavera was the first to recover. 'There goes an untamable spirit fed on dreams.'

'A presumptuous, insolent upstart, whose pride is an empty bubble,' was Fonseca's angry opinion.

'Let us,' Quintanilla gently rebuked the ecclesiastics, 'practise a little charity in our judgments.'

Talavera became almost heated. 'Charity, sir? Charity does not demand that arrogance be met by meekness, or that we stifle righteous indignation at the pride by which the angels fell.'

'Fortunately,' said Rezende, 'our concern is not with casuistry, but with the demands of a man who has a high sense of the value of what he has to sell. That he will not abate the price is what every huckster begins by saying. If Their Highnesses refuse to pay it, he may become more reasonable.'

'If?' questioned Talavera, so scandalized that he raised his voice. 'The question does not admit of doubt.'

He did not intend that it should; nor yet did Fonseca, however the motives inspiring them might differ.

It was a full week, in the many preoccupations concerned with Granada, to which were added the burning question of the Jews, before the Sovereigns were able to receive the report of the Archbishop and his three colleagues.

Quintanilla, who by his long association with Colon had been brought under the spell of the man's personality, alone had no arguments to offer. Rezende kept to his tolerant view that the price was one put forward as a basis for negotiation. But Fonseca displayed an acrid, and Talavera a cold, indignation.

'These are his demands,' he said. 'It needs not that I indicate their effrontery to Your Highnesses.'

Ferdinand laughed the terms to scorn. 'A shrewd dog, as I've always judged him. He would make sure of a certain gain with nothing to lose if he should fail to make good his boasts.'

But the Queen was thoughtful.

'He may lose his life,' she said, as Colon himself had said. 'He may never return from this dark voyage into the unknown.'

'Which is to say that our support of him is a gamble at a time when we can spare no pieces.'

'We are pledged already to support him.'

'We were. But his exorbitant demands relieve us of the pledge. To me it seems an intervention of Providence.'

'That, Highness, is how I view it,' said Talavera.

'An unfortunate view, I think,' the Queen rebuked them both. 'I could never regard Providence as supplying me with a pretext for dishonouring a promise.'

Talavera's attitude suggested a withdrawing within himself. But Fonseca could not conceal impatience.

'The question, Highness, is not one of dishonouring a promise, but of its being rendered impossible of fulfilment because of the conditions demanded. If this man were to ask for the crown of Spain as his reward, it would hardly be yielded to him because of a promise to support his venture.'

'But he has not asked for the crown of Spain.'

'True,' snapped the King. 'And we may marvel at his restraint. For he has only just stopped short of it. He is to be a viceroy, with all a viceroy's royal powers. Does our dignity permit us to grant that?'

The Queen sat, chin in hand, considering. Reading hesitation in this, and presuming upon the circumstance that he was now her confessor and ghostly adviser, Talavera struck in to support the King.

'Madam, with no concern but for the honour and dignity

of your crown, I declare it my considered view that so to magnify a nameless foreign adventurer would be derogatory to both. This triumph of the Cross over the Crescent has brought great and well-deserved lustre to your reign. Would Your Highness imperil that, incur the risk of tarnishing it by the ridicule that would fall upon your credulity if a man so exalted by you were ultimately to fail, as well he may?'

Her brows came together. Her eyes were cold. 'Is it possible that you are questioning me?'

He humbled himself before that stern reminder that even a Queen's confessor is still her subject. 'My zeal betrays me, Highness.'

'And not only your zeal. Your very arguments. Are they based on quicksand that they shift so easily? First it is the lack of money, and then it is the honours demanded by this man that supply a reason for his dismissal.'

The King intervened with laughter. 'Nay, madam. You shall not make a whipping-boy of my Lord Archbishop. Those inconsistencies are mine, which he loyally supports, perceiving them to be closely intertwined. This man asks too much. That is to be admitted. Is it dishonest in me to be glad that he does so, since that relieves us of burdens which I cannot think that we are in case to carry?'

She shook her head. 'It is a satisfaction that I cannot share. The enterprise is a fine and worthy one. If it should succeed it would enable us splendidly to serve God by spreading the True Faith among those who dwell in darkness.'

'If it succeed, madam,' murmured Talavera. 'But after all, at present it is but a dream.'

She looked at him with an odd smile. 'A dream? So it was said once before, to his face. You were present, my Lord Archbishop. Do you remember the answer that he made? You thought it almost heretical. An illuminating heresy.'

He flushed in silence under her indulgent mockery, and again the King intervened. 'Yet the Archbishop is right when he says that if we support Colon, and his dream remains unfulfilled, we are in danger of becoming a laughing-stock to the world.'

'I think this victory over the Moor, ending a struggle that has endured for years, makes us secure from easy ridicule. However' — she turned to those four counsellors, only one of whom had really expressed her own view — 'we have heard, I think, all that you can urge, sirs. It will now be for His Highness and me to determine. You have leave to go.'

Their Highnesses were a long time determining. The duel between the Queen's fidelity to her word and the King's cautious reluctance was long-drawn. And in all that time Colon continued to cool his heels in Santa Fé, scornful of the rejoicings all around him, wearied by its varied manifestations in which the Court and army took such unrestrained delight.

The early days of February were reached, and the first palpitations of spring were already stirring in the womb of the Vega before a compromise was reached permitting the Sovereigns to return Colon an answer by Talavera. The Queen, her strength of purpose maintained by her favourite, the Marchioness of Moya, who worked constantly and loyally for Colon, had prevailed to the extent of a counter-proposal's being offered.

Colon should have the one tenth he demanded for his life-time and the title of Admiral for the expedition. But his interest should perish with him, and no viceroyalty could be conferred, as this would raise a subject too near to the awful dignity of the throne itself.

This came so near to what Talavera could approve that he was a willing messenger. He stood in Quintanilla's house, and, tall and gaunt in the black-and-white monkish garb which he retained in spite of his archiepiscopal dignity, he delivered in his level emotionless voice the royal message.

Colon, standing even taller than the Archbishop, heard him with weary ears, and when he had spoken pondered him with weary eyes. It affronted him that after all this waiting the Sovereigns should send him a message instead of commanding him to audience.

'Is it possible,' he asked, 'that your lordship neglected to inform Their Highnesses that my demands admitted of no abatement?'

The ghost of a smile fled across the prelate's thin lips. 'Be sure that I informed them.'

'Then, my lord, you need not waste your time in waiting. I have nothing more to say.'

'How, sir?' Talavera was stirred to indignation. 'Is that an answer to return to a royal message?'

'You misapprehend me. It is I who have received an answer. I vow to it so completely that I shall be leaving Spain at once.'

Quintanilla, who was present, intervened solicitously. 'Never that, Colon. It would ruin you.'

Colon laughed. 'Ruin me? Oh, no. It is not I who will be ruined; the loss is Spain's.' He crossed to the door, and held it. 'My Lord Archbishop, I kiss your hands.'

Talavera started as if he had been prodded. 'I am dismissed, then, with no more than that.' He raised his shoulders.

'Take time to think,' Quintanilla begged Colon.

'All eternity could not change me. The man who offers such service as mine does not accept a hireling's wage.'

Talavera began to move towards the door. 'Blessed are the meek,' he said with sarcasm.

'For they shall be trodden underfoot,' Colon completed. 'I know.'

Talavera checked, and his eyes kindled. 'Blasphemer!'

'Your lordship's servant.' Still holding the door, Colon inclined his head.

The Archbishop reached the threshold. There he paused, and looked Colon steadily between the eyes. 'To so proud a man the opinion of a poor friar can matter little. But I take the view that Their Highnesses are to be felicitated upon your refusal.'

'Your lordship does not state it accurately. The refusal is not mine but Their Highnesses'.'

'God be with you,' said the Archbishop, passing out.

'God be with your lordship,' answered Colon tartly, to add after the door had closed, 'but the Devil take you, nevertheless.'

As he came slowly back, Quintanilla's dark velvety eyes were full of sorrow. 'Ah, Colon! To fling all away like this!'

'An incredible folly in Their Highnesses.'

'Their folly?' Quintanilla was scandalized. 'I speak of yours.'

'You conceive that I have no pride, no sense of what I offer, or of what is due to me. Am I not even worth an audience, that messages are sent to me by a stiff-necked priest, so purblind that he rejoices in my discomfiture?' His passion increased. 'If the light of God's grace endowed me with a vision denied to other men, can the Divine Will suffer it to be frustrated? It would be blasphemy to think it. Be sure that others will profit by the parsimony of the Spanish Sovereigns.'

By this mood he reduced Quintanilla to despair, and then left him, to go in quest of Santangel. He afflicted the Chancellor by his woes, and still more by his resolve to depart at once from Spain.

'Your unfaltering goodness to me, Don Luis, is the only happy memory that I carry away.'

'Where will you go?' Santangel asked him.

Out of the depths of his chagrin Colon still reared his head with unabated pride. 'To enrich France by the gifts that Spain rejects.'

Santangel paced the luxurious room, resplendent with the Moorish treasures that Granada had yielded him. 'This must not be. Can you yield nothing of your demands?'

'What I offer is worth far more than I have asked. I am refused. So there is nothing now to keep me.'

Santangel came to stand over him where he sat. 'And Beatriz?' he asked softly.

The grey eyes clouded. 'An added reason for my going.'

'An abandonment of hope.'

'Hopes that remain unfulfilled are better abandoned. They supply only pain.'

'And is there no pain in despair? What else is the abandonment of hope? As long as you are in Spain the chance of finding her again will always exist. You must not go. I will do what I can to induce the Queen to grant you another audience.'

'Have I not had audiences enough? Procrastinations, postponements, slights, juntas to examine and insult me, branding me a mountebank, juntas to arrange conditions, and now, finally, a cold message by an insolent cleric, offering me a journeyman's wages. That is enough, I think.' He stood up. 'I am for Cordoba, to assemble the few rags I left with Bensabat, and then I shall set out for France.'

'Will you wait, at least, until I have seen the Queen?'

Colon shook his head. 'Not even your sweet concern can conquer me. I am weary of offering service as one asks for alms.'

There were no arguments to turn him from that proud resolve, and on the morrow he slipped quietly away, Santangel and Quintanilla being the only witnesses of his departure. He was dejected at the end, so dejected that he would stay to take leave of none of the few to whom he owed it, but begged Don Luis to be his deputy with them.

Santangel was brought to the verge of tears as he watched him ride away into the mists of that February morning. Only now, perhaps, in the thought that he was never likely to see him again, did he realize how much that stalwart dreamer had come to count for in his life. This was like parting with a son.

He heaved a grievous sigh. 'Poor lad! He deserves better of Fate than this.'

'Perhaps,' said Quintanilla, who was not, himself, unmoved. 'But he raises barriers by his intractable pride.'

Santangel turned impatiently. 'If we had been vouchsafed his vision it may be that our pride would not be less.'

He went off, taking little heed of the noisy, jostling crowd that thronged this main street of Santa Fé, to convey Colon's valedictory messages to Cabrera and the Marchioness.

They were breaking their fast when he came upon them in their house, adjacent to that which did duty as royal palace. Resentment tinctured their concern at the news he brought.

'That he should go without a word to us!' the Marchioness exclaimed.

Santangel excused him. 'The poor fellow carries a broken heart under a show of proud confidence. His only allusion to it was when he charged me to tell you that he would not add to his pain by coming to take leave of you.'

'You should not have permitted his departure.'

'I did what I could.'

'He must be brought back,' said Cabrera. 'Suppose that France were to profit by our sluggishness.'

The Marchioness rose. 'Come with me, Don Luis. We will see the Queen together.'

There was no hour at which the favourite was denied admission, and the Queen received her now in her tiring-room. She was seated before her mirror, two of her ladies in attendance, selecting a jewelled caul for her head from a casket at her elbow, a coffer covered in rose brocade and clamped by bands of gold.

She smiled through the mirror at the Marchioness. 'You are early, Beatriz.'

'I kiss Your Highness's hands.' And without preamble she added: 'Colon has left Santa Fé. He is going to France.'

The Queen sat thoughtfully frowning for a moment. Then she set down the caul, and slewed herself half round on the stool, so as to face the Marchioness. 'Ah! It is hardly what I expected in spite of what the Archbishop told me. A proud, intractable man, I fear.' She sighed. 'Still, if that is his decision, he must abide by it.'

'The decision is scarcely his, madam. Rather was it Your Highness's in refusing his conditions.'

'Do you know what his conditions were?'

'I do, madam.'

'And you think we should have accepted them?' The Queen smiled. 'I am sorry to deserve your disapproval, Beatriz.'

'Oh, madam!' Doña Beatriz protested, and then added: 'But is it wise to allow him to depart? Don Luis is in the antechamber. Will Your Highness receive him?'

She reflected a moment. Then, 'Why not?' she agreed. 'Call him.'

As the Marchioness was obeying, the door leading to the King's cabinet was pushed open, and Ferdinand, robed to the feet in a furred gown of royal blue, made an appearance that was none too welcome to either of Colon's sponsors. He checked on the threshold, but the Queen beckoned him forward.

'Come in, sire. Come in and take your share of censure
for our treatment of Colon. They tell me that he is leaving
Spain, and has already started for France.'

Ferdinand moved slowly forward. 'May he prosper there,'
was his careless answer.

'If so,' said the Marchioness boldly, 'France will prosper
with him at the expense of Spain.'

Ferdinand put up his brows, to stare at indignant loveliness.
Then he laughed. He almost conveyed that the news put him
in a good humour. He fingered the gold chain that hung
across his breast. 'I rather think that our expense would be
to have retained him. And an expense of dignity as well as
gold. You look glum, Santangel. You don't agree, perhaps.'

'Since you ask me, sire, I do not. I should be indifferent
to your interest if I could bear to see others profit by the
opportunity we neglect.'

The Marchioness came stoutly to support him. 'There was
the chance of glory and profit such as never yet came the
way of any prince in the world.'

'As for glory, we have found all that we need of it here in
Granada. The profit will follow. Meanwhile, as you well
know, the war has been costly, and we have no money to
set upon a gamble.'

'No, no,' the Queen disagreed. 'That is not the reason, as
I have said before. At least not a reason that would absolve
me from my promise.'

'None could suppose it, Highness,' said Don Luis shrewdly.
'Sovereigns with the spirit to launch such perilous and glorious
enterprises could not be suspected of boggling at one in which
the loss would be trifling and the gain might be incalculable.
Dare we doubt the gain?'

'There are those who do,' the King reminded him.

'Of course there are,' said the Marchioness. 'There are

always doubters for everything; timid men who will **advance**
no opinion that might be disproved by the events.'

'And what in any case,' ventured Don Luis, 'are the doubts
of our doctors worth when set against the word of Toscanelli?'
He turned again to the Queen. 'Your Highness well knows
the fame, the wealth, the credit earned for Portugal by navigators less intrepid. Colon offers Your Highnesses the opportunity to surpass all that.'

'We have heard all this before,' said the King.

'And I have weighed it all,' said the Queen. 'That is why
I deplore Colon's decision. But the conditions he made are
impossible, inadmissible. A man of unknown extraction, he
demands honours and dignities which we should be slow to
confer upon the noblest of our grandes.'

'Suffer me to ask Your Highness,' the Marchioness cut in,
'what noblest of your grandes offers such service in return?'

The King, standing now against Her Highness's dressing-
table, shook his head, smiling. 'That service is still in the
realm of dreams.'

'So are the titles he claims,' was the quick answer. 'They
remain mere shadows until, himself, he supplies a substance
for them.'

The Queen's prominent eyes reflected a sudden illumination. 'Why, that suggests a compromise. Let him have the
title of Admiral, but only after his discoveries have made
good his claims; and let him be our Viceroy, but only when
he has added to our dominions the lands over which to exe-
cute the office. That is a solution that should content all
parties. Whatever happens, none can say that our credulity
has been abused by making payment in advance.'

She looked at Ferdinand for confirmation. But his face had
darkened. Slowly he wagged his heavy head.

'You forget that the ships will have to be paid for in
advance.'

'To that we were already committed.'

He chose to deny it vehemently. 'Not I, madam. Not I. I entered into no such commitment. I engaged myself to do no more than consider the proposal. When eventually I yielded to your request that I should sponsor it with you, it was on certain conditions. These conditions Colon has refused. For me that ends the matter.'

'You have been listening to the Archbishop,' the Queen complained.

'Could you wish me a better counsellor than your own confessor?'

'In matters of the Faith.'

'By Saint James, is not this very much a matter of faith?'

'Now you make it a matter for jesting, which does not help me. Does Your Highness mean that we should let him go?'

'Or else, as you suggest, let him have his titles of Admiral and Viceroy when he shall have earned them, but with the condition that he, himself, shall find the money for his quest.'

It was an intentionally flippant answer, and she made it plain that it did not please her. 'Is that Your Highness's last word?' she asked.

'My very last,' he answered pleasantly.

'So be it,' he said, and sighed. But at once, and in a firmer tone she added: 'Since that is so, I will, myself, undertake the venture independently, for my own crown of Castile.'

It struck them all silent with astonishment for a moment, and there was almost consternation in Ferdinand's blank stare. Then the Marchioness broke out on a thrill of enthusiasm: 'Madam, the decision will bring you greater honour than has ever been earned by any queen.'

But Ferdinand was almost sneering.

'And the cost, madam?' he interjected. 'How will you provide it?'

She looked at Santangel. 'At what do you set the cost, Don Luis?'

'It is no such ruinous matter, when all is said. Colon would be willing at need to sail with no more than two ships. Three thousand crowns should cover such an equipment.'

'That, at least, I can provide.'

She set her hand upon the jewel casket that stood at her elbow.

'Take these, Don Luis, and pledge them for me for the necessary funds. They should easily yield them.'

'Highness!' Santangel was startled by the proposal, and showed it. Then he made a gesture of deprecation. 'There is no need for that. I can advance the money. From the treasury of Aragon.'

Ferdinand moved violently forward. 'Santiago!' he roared. 'You can do what?'

Don Luis was calm. 'I can advance the money from the treasury of Aragon,' he repeated, adding, 'to be refunded from the first gold or other merchandise that Colon may bring back. Thus he will, himself, in a sense, be providing the funds.'

'In a sense!' Ferdinand was grim. 'I am fortunate in my treasurer. A subtle magician in finance, are you not, Santangel? And what if he brings nothing back? What if he never returns at all?'

'I will, myself, stand surety for the money, and refund it in either case.'

His Highness glared at him a moment, still frowning. Then his features relaxed, and he shrugged and laughed.

'On my soul, Santangel, I don't know which to envy more, your wealth or your faith. However, on those terms you may make as free as you please with what's left of my treasury.'

26

THE SEAMEN

OF

PALOS

FTER years of flexibility, of bending to every influence that might prosper him, it was by inflexibility that Colon prevailed in the end. His very intransigence had made his victory complete, had brought the Sovereigns to a surrender reasonably near to his demands.

Word of it reached him at dusk, when he was already some three leagues upon his disconsolate way. As he approached the Bridge of Pinos there was a pounding of fast hooves behind him. A posse of alguaziles, led by an officer of the Queen's household, overtook him with Her Highness's command that he return at once to Santa Fé. It was not an order that he would have dared to disregard; but with it the officer handed him a note: three brief lines over Santangel's signature to inform him that he had triumphed.

On the morrow, after the felicitations of Santangel and Cabrera, and after being almost wept over by the Marchioness of Moya, he was received in audience, to be benignly chided by the Queen for his abrupt and unceremonious departure without leave, and tolerantly used by the King, who

had been manoeuvred, after all, by his astute Chancellor into
at least a partial participation in the venture. The Queen,
womanlike, having stifled her misgivings, gave herself to the
matter with an unstinting enthusiasm. From a stingy doling
of favour, she adopted, now that she was committed, a lavish
prodigality.

The needy suitor, who for so long had been an object of
scarcely veiled derision at the Court of Ferdinand and
Isabel, emerged from that audience as Don Cristobal Colon,
Lord Admiral-to-be of the Ocean Sea, who might ruffle it
on even terms with the best blood in Spain.

The journey had been long and arduous, but at last he stood
in the place to which he considered that his deserts entitled
him; and if his destiny could not be accounted fulfilled until
it had stood the test of that voyage into the unknown, yet in
his mind there was no doubt of its fulfillment.

Preparations followed, still slowly, it is true, but the season
of the year was not one that called for haste, and at last,
by the end of April, they were sufficiently advanced to permit
of his departure from Santa Fé with the capitulations setting
forth the terms on which he undertook this service.

By the odd operation of circumstances it was in the very
port of Palos, where his Spanish adventure had begun, that it
was to reach its consummation. For some misdemeanour of
its inhabitants Palos stood condemned to furnish to the Crown
two armed caravels for one year. Thrifty King Ferdinand had
opportunely perceived how the employment of those two caravels might diminish the sum of the maravedis which his
treasury of Aragon had been manoeuvred into lending to
Castile.

Thus to Palos Cristobal Colon came again in early May.

Even had this not been his port of sailing, he must still have
visited it before departing, for there was his son to be disposed

of. Not the least sign of the favour into which he was come, was the appointment by the Queen of little Diego Colon to be a page to her son the Prince Don Juan. Pursuing her policy of giving with both hands now that she was resolved to give, she bestowed here a gift that normally fell only to the highest in the land.

By the track through the pines Colon rode to the convent, no longer the needy wayfarer likening himself to Cartaphilus, who knocked at the convent gate to beg a little bread and water for his child, but Don Cristobal, the bearer of a royal commission and royal powers by which he might count confidently upon climbing to quasi-royal rank.

Here in this tranquil backwater of the world nothing had changed. The same lay-brother opened to his knock and wondered what could be the business at La Rabida of this great lord in the travelling cloak of dark blue velvet and the long boots of fine Cordovan leather, who dismounted from the tall black Andalusian mare.

He was startled to hear himself addressed by name. 'God save you, Brother Innocencio. Bear word to the Reverend Prior that Don Cristobal Colon is here.'

'Don Cristobal!' The little brother's mouth fell agape at the title, at the authority of voice and person, at so much magnificence evolved out of a remembered neediness. 'God save your worship,' he faltered at last in his turn, not daring to revert to the old, familiar terms.

But the awe-inspiring air was suddenly cast off, the lay-brother's shoulder was vigorously slapped and a hand was proffered. 'Have you no warmer welcome for an old friend, Brother Innocencio?'

Thereupon the little man wriggled and giggled and almost pranced ahead of him like an affectionate dog, in conducting him to the convent parlour, a gaunt whitewashed room, smelling of wax and dominated by a great melancholy portrait of the Poor Man of Assisi.

There Frey Juan Perez, having hurried to enfold him in a warm embrace, held him off to consider him.

'My son, you do not need to tell me that you prosper. Nor yet,' he added, closely scanning the handsome face, 'that you have suffered. The way has been long and steep, and at times your hopes may well have fainted. But there' — he broke off with his jovial laugh — 'I talk instead of listening. I guess instead of hearing. Garrulity is the sin of age. I've sent for Diego. It is he, of course, who brings you back to us.'

'I should be an ungrateful dog if that were all. I come, too, to return thanks to you for having set my feet on the path that has led me at last to my goal. And I come, too, because it is from Palos that I am ordered by the Sovereigns to sail upon my voyage of discovery.'

All was told, all but the details which were to follow later; for now the Prior's happy rejoicings were interrupted by the entrance of the fair, slim lad in a fustian tunic and grey stockings, who stared in some awe at the lordly figure of his sire until Colon went down on one knee with inviting arms flung wide. Within them Diego was strained to that aching yet dauntless heart.

'I have been long gone, Diego. I waited to return until I could come to you with full hands.' And now, still holding the child, he told him of the great destiny awaiting him as a page to Prince Juan, and in so doing added much to the little that he had already told the Prior.

He took up his quarters at La Rabida for the time in which he should be making ready for sea.

It was to prove longer than he supposed: obstacles unsuspected which not all the royal powers of which he was the bearer or which might yet be evoked could suffice to overcome.

At noon on the morrow, accompanied by the Prior and by the Alcalde of Palos, a swarthy frog-faced man named Diego Rodriguez Prieto, with a notary, and a trumpeter to serve as herald, and with a half-dozen attendant alguaziles to lend consequence, Colon appeared in the porch of the grey Church of Saint George.

An earlier proclamation by the town-crier of what was to take place had filled the square with a motley crowd, representative of every class that inhabited that thriving busy seaport: mariners, fishermen, shipwrights, caulkers, rope-weavers and the like, with a sprinkling of their women, some men of substance, merchants, shipowners and master mariners, and a background of the riff-raff of every port.

A flourish of the trumpet produced a silence, not indeed of discipline, but of curiosity, and the notary, in a rusty black gown, stepped forward to read the royal order.

It called for the supply within ten days of two armed caravels to Don Cristobal Colon, for a voyage he was undertaking in the service of the Sovereigns. The crews of these ships were to receive the ordinary wages earned in armed vessels and to be paid four months in advance. There followed an order to all concerned for the furnishing of supplies at the ordinary rates, and the proclamation closed on a recital of the penalties that would fall upon any who failed in obedience to these commands.

If the owners of vessels within the description stood in sullen resentment of the possible requisitioning of their ships, a cheer was raised by the mariners at the prospect of a four months' advance of pay, and swelled by the riff-raff from the sheer love of clamour.

Deceived by this enthusiasm, Colon went back in good spirits to dinner at La Rabida.

The afternoon brought him two visitors there. The first

of these was a stalwart fellow of thirty, rudely clad, but of an engaging easy frankness of bearing. He gave his name as Vasco Aranda, announced himself as part owner of a vessel lately wrecked, whereby he had suffered the loss of almost all that he possessed. He had followed the sea for the last ten years, having served five of these as a fighting seaman on the war galleys of Spain in action against the Algerian corsairs. In this service he had acquired a command, and it had brought him the means to acquire his half-share in the round ship now lost. This loss left him in quest of employment, but it must be of such a nature as to hold out to him the prospect of building himself up anew, and in such case he was prepared for any danger.

Favourably impressed by the man's bearing, Colon was more favourably impressed still by the readiness with which he offered himself once the nature of the enterprise ahead had been disclosed to him.

'I accept the risks,' he said. 'For who risks nothing, gains nothing, and for great gains, great risks are necessary. If you can employ me, I am your worship's man, and there are six lads of mine here in Palos who were shipwrecked with me and who would follow me to hell.'

'I trust we shall not be sailing quite so far.'

'But as far as you go, I'll answer for these lads. I am known to most of the shipowners here in Palos, and they will speak for me.'

It occurred to Colon that here was a likely recruiting officer with the nucleus of a crew already at his heels. For the rest he could trust his own judgment as well as the word of any man, and so he bestowed upon Aranda this temporary office with the promise of a more permanent one when they put to sea.

He was uplifted by what he took to be a sign of the eager-

ness to join him that must be aroused in the hearts of all good
seafaring men when his second visitor presented himself. This
was the prosperous, enterprising Martin Alonso Pinzon.

'Here,' Frey Juan announced him, 'is an old friend, who
wishes you well and whom you may find of great service.'

'You have been long gone,' said Pinzon as they shook hands,
'but it has not been time wasted, to judge by the powers with
which you return.'

The Prior retained him to supper in the convent refectory,
and at table he was affable, congratulatory and ingratiating.
They lingered on at the Prior's table after the brethren had
departed, and it was not until then that Martin Alonso came
really to the matter in his mind. He approached it deviously.

'If I may venture a criticism of your plans,' he said, 'it is
that I find an unnecessary temerity in the number of ships
with which you propose to face the unknown.'

'I must be content with what I can obtain.'

'Yet only two ships!' Pinzon thoughtfully wagged his head.
'It is fraught with risk. If one were lost, but one would remain
upon which to depend. It is too narrow a margin for prudence.
It may even deter men from sailing with you.'

But Colon, made confident by the prompt enlistment of
Aranda, could not share the doubt. 'I expect no difficulty
in getting my crews together. There are perquisites beside
the pay, a chance of wealth such as does not come the way
of sailors in a thousand years.'

'You may be right. Yet I should have fewer misgivings if
you had more ships; even one more would sensibly diminish
the hazard.'

'I agree. But as you have heard, two ships are all that
Their Highnesses concede me.'

'Why should you not, yourself, supplement them?'

Colon was reminded of what had passed between Pinzon and

himself when last he was at La Rabida. Actually there was a
clause in the capitulations by virtue of which Colon had
power to add to the equipment up to one eighth of the total
outlay in return for a one-eighth share in the yield of the
expedition. It was a clause put in to salve his pride, which
had been ruffled by the taunt that in this gamble he set no
pieces on the board. But the reasons which earlier had
prompted his cold reception of Pinzon's importunities still
governed him. The very masterfulness which he detected in
this prosperous shipowning merchant was in itself a danger
signal. To admit such a man to a share in the venture would
be to risk his appropriation of a part of the glory. And of
glory Colon was not only avaricious, but he reasonably held
the view that the whole of it belonged to the man who had
conceived the enterprise.

Because he perceived that utter frankness on the subject of
the capitulations must lay him open to further importunities,
he did not practise it. 'To do that would entail subtracting
something from the total yield which belongs to the Sovereigns.'

'To be sure it would. But need the Sovereigns begrudge
that, considering the increase in the chances of success which
another ship would bring?'

'It is possible that they might begrudge it,' Colon evaded.
If he knew King Ferdinand at all, he thought it was not
possible, but certain.

'Even so, you have still to think of yourself,' Pinzon urged.
'You are gambling your life on this; add another vessel to
your squadron and your life to that extent is further secured.'

'That is sound sense, Don Cristobal,' put in the Prior.
'I think you would do well to heed Master Pinzon.'

'Oh, I am heeding him, grateful for his interest. But it is
hardly in my power to alter the dispositions of the Sovereigns.'

'That I cannot believe. It needs but to be represented to them,' Pinzon insisted. 'You remember what faith I expressed in your project. It is undiminished, and I have the very ship for you, a trim, sound little caravel that is equal to all the hazards of the sea. You have but to say the word, and I place her at your disposal with a reliable crew of men who have sailed with me before and who will be ready to follow me now.'

There was almost an anxiety in the intensely blue eyes that watched Colon from under the black beetling brows.

'I am touched by your faith in me,' Colon answered with a courteous smile. 'Nothing could be of greater encouragement. It is regrettable that the circumstances will not allow me to accept a proposal that would otherwise be welcome.'

Pinzon's expression hardened a little in disappointment. But not yet would he yield. 'The circumstances might be shaped. I am persuaded of that. Think it over, Don Cristobal. I will not take this refusal as final. We will talk of it again. You may come to perceive that my participation could be of advantage.'

'That I perceive already,' answered Colon, courteous to the last; and then, so as to make an end, he added: 'Well, well, we will see how things develop.'

'I am content that you should,' said Pinzon, and left the matter there with a smile in which Colon imagined a certain craftiness. 'And I hope that they will develop as you would wish.'

The development, however, proved very far from this. In fact, things did not develop at all. When some two days later Colon sought the Alcalde of Palos to know what progress was being made in obtaining him the ships, the Alcalde, short, fat and indolent, looking more like a frog than ever, met him with blank distress.

'The Devil's in it,' he protested. 'The owners have got wind of the purpose to which the ships are to be put.'

Colon was haughty.

'What then? They have heard the royal proclamation.'

'To be sure they have. But they come to me protesting that the ships that Palos is under sentence to supply are to be supplied for ordinary occasions, and that the term of service is for one year only. Yours, they say, is no ordinary occasion, and that to send ships out into the unknown, from which there is little or no chance of their ever returning, is not service for a year, but the equivalent of confiscation. And that is far beyond what the sentence provides.'

'All this is idle. They have the proclamation, and the law compels their obedience. You, sir, administer the law here in Palos. I rely upon you.'

The Alcalde showed exasperation. 'You don't understand. What they answer me is good law. Excellent law. They invoke the very letter of it, and I have no answer for them.'

'I think you have. Is it not also the law that if ships under such sentences are lost or not returned to their owners within the time prescribed the Crown will pay compensation?'

The Alcalde's forefinger combed a ragged beard. 'In effect it is,' he was forced to admit.

'Then return them that answer, and if they are still recalcitrant take order to compel them.'

The Alcalde gave an ill-humoured consent. But when Colon returned two days later to know the result of the measure, he was told that there was still no progress.

'They answer me that even if they supply the ships you will find no crews to man them; that there are no fools in Palos to sail on such a voyage; and that, therefore, if we use constraint all that we shall accomplish will be to have the ships standing idle.'

Colon became profane, which was by no means his habit.

'No use to inveigh,' the Alcalde admonished him. 'The fault lay in letting it be known so soon what is the voyage you meditate.'

'Who let it be known?' Colon demanded. 'There was no word said in the proclamation.'

'Nay, I can't tell you that. All that I know is that there's not a mariner in Palos who isn't aware of your intentions, and, therefore, not a man in Palos who'll sail with you. So,' he ended, 'what good are the ships to you?'

'That you shall discover when you've secured them for me. Pray see to it, whatever the owners may say, or I'll report to Their Highnesses that you don't assist me.'

He left him to think that over, and went off to the ship's chandler's where Aranda had established his office. But at the hands of that eager young seaman he received fresh disappointment.

'Will your worship tell me what ails these lubberly dogs in Palos? They're all freshwater sailors by their behaviour. I've been labouring for four days without a single recruit. I go from the quays to the taverns and from the taverns to the quays, and everywhere it's the same. A shake of the head, and a 'Go-with-God — that's not the voyage for me.' When I ask them if they would rather crawl in their misery all their days rather than take a chance of fortune, they just laugh at me. A worthless, craven lot of dogs! And even my own lads are being infected with the pestilence of the place. They were eager enough when first I told them of the venture, and now they begin to hang back. They talk of their wives, and those who haven't wives talk of their mothers.'

Colon sat down on a barrel. 'How did the town come to know of the voyage I am going? Did you tell anybody?'

'May I die if I breathed it to a soul. I'll not say I might

not have done so. But here was no need. They all knew
more about it than I did.'

Colon uttered a bitter laugh. 'I haven't been thwarted by
fools for years to be thwarted by cowards at the end,' he said.
'I'll find you recruits to spare.'

He went back to the Alcalde. 'We must bestir,' he told
him. 'I'll have these crews if I have to pick them from the
gaols.'

It so happened that among the powers with which he was
invested was an authority, which he now disclosed, to offer an
amnesty to persons under sentence who might choose to
embark with him.

'You'll be pleased to proclaim that at once. It will also
be a sufficient answer to the shipowners.'

Conceiving that he had played a master-card, he departed
in better humour, and on the quayside just outside the
Alcalde's office he ran into Pinzon, who had with him his
brother Vicente.

Martin Alonso hailed him pleasantly with a friendly lift
of the hand. He presented his brother, and hoped that Colon's
preparations made good progress.

'So far they have made none at all. Your seamen of Palos
have no appetite for discovery. A poor spiritless lot who
prefer safe squalor to adventure.'

The Pinzons looked grave. 'I swear, sir, you do them an
injustice!' cried Vicente.

'Yet I can understand it,' said Martin Alonso thoughtfully.
'After all, you labour under the disadvantage of being a
stranger among them. Men are slow to face high risks unless
they know all about their leader. You should consider that,
and not judge these poor devils too harshly.' He smiled as he
spoke, with a flash of his strong white teeth behind the dense
black beard.

'It may be so,' Colon agreed. 'But I think we shall move more briskly now,' and he told him of the proclamation to be made.

Pinzon's face was overspread with dismay, confirming Colon's growing suspicion that he had this man to thank for the obstacles he was meeting. 'You don't approve?' he questioned with the faintest suspicion of mockery.

Martin Alonso was downright in his answer. 'I don't. It seems a mad folly to sail with a crew of cut-throats and bandits. What can you look for but trouble?'

'They'll be neither cut-throats nor bandits once they're on the high seas with me. They'll lie in the hollow of my hand, for their lives will depend on mine. You hadn't thought of that.'

Pinzon remained grave. 'It's not for me to school you, sir. All I know is that not all the wealth of the Indies would induce me to put to sea with such a crew as that.'

This, too, was the view of Frey Juan when back at La Rabida that evening Colon told him what he had done.

'Sail with a crew of criminals!' The Prior was aghast. 'It is a terrifying prospect.'

But neither he nor Martin Alonso need have wasted emotion upon the plan, for such appeared to be the fear of the unknown upon ignorant, superstitious minds that not even the gaol-birds would purchase at such a price their deliverance from the misery in which they languished. They laughed the proclamation to scorn when it was published in the prison. Like the seafaring men of Palos, they appeared to be well informed of the nature of the voyage, although it remained a mystery how the information could have reached them.

Weeks sped in waiting during the best season of the year, and Palos, broiling in the sunshine of high summer, remained inert in the matter of the royal command. Colon could no longer show himself in the streets of the town without being conscious that he was an object of sly derision. This seemed to be his fate. He had endured it from the nobles at court, during the weary season of his solicitations, and must endure it now from the scourings of the quayside.

Even Vasco Aranda's loyalty began to suffer strain.

'There are influences at work against us, Don Cristobal,' he complained one day.

'I've noticed it,' said Cristobal, with a hard laugh. 'Have you discovered whence it springs?'

'The talk in the wineshops is all that this venture is fore-doomed, that none who sails on it will ever come back. I've fought it hard. I tell them that the Sovereigns would never support it unless they knew it to be sound. I've told them of houses tiled with gold, as your worship said, and of pearls and rubies common as pebbles in Andalusia, and of how a single voyage may make them so rich that they'll never need to go to sea again. Again and again I've got men to swear they'll take a chance and sail. But when next I meet them they've altered course again, whilst of the few who have actually en-listed, taken the oath and made their mark, there's scarcely one that hasn't since disappeared. I'll stake my soul that someone else talks to them when I've done. Look to it, Don Cristobal. You've an enemy, burrowing underground like a mole.'

Glooming in his room at La Rabida, Colon sat listening to his recruiting officer, who had sought him there to relieve his mind of these suspicions. The lad's steadfastness and high courage in the face of difficulties warmed him a little.

'Great as are your powers, they are not great enough, my lord,' Aranda continued, for thus already he addressed a man who was to be Admiral, and was the better liked for it. 'What you need is a royal order to impress the ships and the men.'

There was, Colon agreed, nothing else that would meet the case. So he wrote a letter to Santangel, and when it was written chose Aranda for his messenger.

'Out of your knowledge of what is taking place here, Vasco, you will be able to furnish any fuller information that may be required.'

Aranda went off to Santa Fé, and more weeks of fretful waiting followed.

When at last he returned, however, he brought not only the order, but a brisk officer of the royal household to see that the Alcalde put it into instant execution.

A tumult followed, and Colon, venturing forth at the height of it, with intent to address the people, was suddenly and angrily beset. Under the leadership of a man named Rascon, who owned a caravel which the authorities had been examining with Colon, they set upon him in the public square before the Church of Saint George, with cries of 'Down with the adventurer! Break the bones of his body! Throw him in the harbour! Death to the Devil's mariner!'

Colon put his back to the church wall and brought out his sword.

'Devil's mariner, is it?' he roared. 'By Saint Ferdinand, I'll pilot some of you into hell.'

With a sweeping flourish of his blade he cleared a space about him into which they hesitated to venture, being armed with no more than knives. But it must have gone ill with him in the end, and he might have found his last adventure there in the square of Palos, but for Vasco Aranda and his lads who rallied to him.

Thanks to that bodyguard he came unscathed out of the press, followed by the jeers and curses of the mob he had raised.

It looked like defeat, and gloomily he admitted as much to Vasco; but the buoyant lad scorned the notion.

'In Palos, perhaps. But Palos is not the only port in Spain.
Elsewhere we'll find better hearts and less intrigue.'

'But we'll not find a sentence to supply two caravels.'
He did not add his fears that unless they came by ships on
such cheap terms, a thriftily cautious King might yet persuade the Queen to abandon an undertaking to which there
was so much manifest opposition. Considering this he came
to dread the effect upon the Sovereigns of the admission of
failure which a fresh appeal to them must entail.

He was discussing this that same afternoon with Frey Juan,
when Martin Alonso came to pay them one of his periodic
visits. They sat at a table of pine logs that bore a dish of
olives and a jug of wine, set under a trellis of vines that made
a cool arbour of the little esplanade before the convent.
In the river below a fishing fleet was homing with the flow of
the tide, and from where they sat they commanded a view
of the port of Palos, on the right, crowded with shipping,
about which there was a brisk activity. It was a sight to fill
Colon with the heartache of a caged bird, and it had brought
him to this fresh unburdening of himself.

'Just as I hold myself to be but an instrument in the hand
of God for opening up the hidden parts of the world to receive
His Holy Word, so I believe that it is Satan who labours at
every step to thwart me. Each almost proves the other.'

'If this is not just rhetoric,' said Frey Juan, 'if you sincerely
believe it, my son, then you should take heart, for you must
believe also that in the end God will prevail.'

'In the end. But where is the end?'

'In God's own time.'

It was at this moment that Pinzon came into view, emerging by the road through the pinewood.

The prosperous merchant in a dark wine-coloured surcoat
of fine camlet, which he wore with almost courtly grace,

displayed a heat of indignation at the treatment Colon had received that morning and the danger in which he had stood.

'A superstition-ridden herd of dolts, these seamen of Palos,' he condemned them. He pulled out a stool, and sat down at the little rustic table. 'They imagine that the paths to hell lie across the oceans; they people the wastes of it with fiends and goblins and basilisks, who guard them against intruders. Idle to reason with them. Idle to seek them, as I have done, who has ever seen and reported these things to warrant such beliefs. What would you?' He shrugged his broad shoulders and spread his short, square hands. 'They answer me by asking why, if I believe these seas are safe, I don't sail them myself.'

'To which,' said Frey Juan, 'the answer is that you can't sail a ship without a crew.'

'That is what I have answered them. But they mock me with the retort that I could find a crew if I were to declare myself ready to sail on such a venture in a caravel of my own.'

'Are they to be believed?' the Prior asked.

'Who knows? I cannot be certain until I have put it to the test, and I hesitate to boast. Yet my opinion is that I could raise the men to follow me.' He spoke casually, selecting an olive from the dish.

Colon was not deceived. This was Pinzon's none too subtle method of reopening the question of a partnership in the venture. Not only was he certainly an opportunist in his choice of the moment, but possibly also the creator of the opportunity, for Colon regarded it as more than likely that this merchant-mariner of such influence among the men of Palos was the hidden enemy of whom Aranda had spoken, and very possibly that it was he who had prompted the morning's violence.

The more ingenuous Frey Juan, however, harboured no

such suspicions. All that he perceived was how Pinzon might offer Colon a way out of the deadlock that was fretting him. In haste he spat out a couple of olive stones, so that he might be free to speak.

'You remind me, Master Pinzon, that when first we talked of this, you spoke of bringing a ship to it at your own charges. What should you say, Don Cristobal, if he were still of the same mind?'

Colon went cautiously, his face inscrutable. 'But are you of that mind, sir?'

Pinzon trod delicately in his turn. He raised his brows, as if the question took him by surprise. He appeared to reflect. Behind his black beard his red lips parted, his white teeth appeared in a slow smile. 'Who knows? It is no longer as easy as it was. Difficulties have been created. To-day's explosion was a sign of them.' He left it there, his blue eyes meeting Colon's, the smile still lingering on his lips.

Colon perfectly understood that Pinzon retreated so as to be pursued; and reluctant though he might be to pursue him, yet the developments no longer left him any choice.

'The question is,' he said slowly, 'do you think that your influence in Palos could overcome these difficulties?'

Again there was that 'Who knows?' He paused before continuing. 'I must not be understood to speak with certainty. But I do believe that if I were to declare for the adventure, there are enough men in Palos with faith in me to supply the crews we should need. You understand that this is no more than an opinion.'

'Will you put it to the test?'

'I should be willing,' was the slow answer, 'if you mean that my association would be welcomed, and always provided that the dispositions you have made, or could make, would give me an adequate return.'

'That is the difficulty, as I think I have mentioned,' said Colon. 'All that I have faculty to do under the capitulations is to provide up to one eighth of the cost of the expedition, taking in that event one eighth of the yield.'

'One eighth? But to provide another ship would be to provide a third.'

'True. But there is no need to provide one; no need to provide more than one eighth of the cost of the whole expedition; and for that I have power to grant one eighth of the profit. That, under the capitulations, is the utmost I can divert from the Crown. The Crown, you see,' he added cunningly, 'is reluctant to part with any of the profit it expects, and even this eighth was grudgingly conceded me, just as I should grudgingly concede it again.'

'But you are prepared to concede it?'

'Unless I should decide to petition the Sovereigns to let me seek my equipment somewhere else. After all, Palos scarcely deserves the benefits that should result from this expedition.'

Thus Colon, as shrewd as any man in the ways of bargaining, startled Pinzon into the fear that the chance so ardently desired and only half offered to him now, might be definitely snatched away again if he were not quick to settle.

Pinzon stroked his beard. 'At what,' he asked, 'would you compute an eighth share in the venture?'

Here Colon smiled and shook his head. 'Do you ask me that? Must I really tell you that the yield will be either nothing or else wealth incalculable? But it will be nothing only if I am wrong; and I do not believe that I am wrong, nor, I think, do you, Master Pinzon.'

Martin Alonso took his chin in his hand, and was sunk in thought. 'I will consider,' he said at last. 'We will talk of it again. Perhaps to-morrow.'

He spoke of sounding some of the seamen of the port, so as

to test his belief that he could find men to ship with him, and on that presently he took his leave, a certain satisfaction in his air.

'I think,' said Frey Juan, when he was alone with Colon once more, 'that this may be the end of your difficulties, and that he will make up his mind to join you.'

'And I think,' Colon answered, 'that he has made it up already; that he had made it up before he came; that he made it up, in fact, before he created the difficulties that will now vanish.'

Frey Juan professed himself shocked that any man could build idle suspicions into opinions so unflattering to another's probity.

27

 DEPARTURE

Iꜰ ᴛʜᴇ good-natured Prior of La Rabida could not at once agree to the obliquity of Pinzon's courses, yet in the sequel he came reluctantly to believe that Colon had correctly read the wealthy merchant-mariner.

Martin Alonso came punctually back upon the morrow to seal the contract. He did not come alone. He brought with him his two brothers, Vicente and Francisco, both ready to share the venture with him, and he made bold to assert that with this powerful support of the Pinzon family, of admittedly unrivalled influence in Palos, it would be odd, indeed, if all difficulties did not vanish and all superstitious obstacles melt away.

From the moment the bargain was concluded matters began to move. The powerful drive of Martin Alonso achieved with the Alcalde and the regidores what Colon had found impossible. Stirred out of their lethargy, they went ruthlessly about the execution of the royal mandate, and it was only a matter of days before two ships had been impounded, to add to the *Pinta*, which Pinzon had brought as his share into the partnership.

The work of fitting them and equipping them for sea was
briskly in hand, and Aranda no longer wandered from one
quayside tavern to another seeking to enlist a crew. In his
own words, a mysterious breath had breathed over Palos.
Where all had hung back with jeers and curses, so many hard-
bitten seamen clamoured now to be taken that Aranda found
himself under the necessity of choosing from amongst them.
As the days passed there was a cooling of this enthusiasm
which the Pinzons had whipped up. The women of Palos
may have started the process, reluctant to let their menfolk
sail on a voyage so dark and perilous. There was a defection
that began to spread. Some of those who had definitely en-
listed and could now be claimed were found to have disappeared. In the end, however, some ninety resolute fellows,
enough to man the three ships, stood firm, and lent their
labours to speed on the preparations.

Vasco Aranda, now appointed to the responsible position
of Alguazil-Mayor of the expedition, was again sent off, in
July, to Santa Fé, with letters reporting progress, and at the
same time to escort little Diego Colon to Court, so that he
might take up his duties there.

The caulking, fitting and equipping of the ships now went
on apace. For his flagship Colon had taken the largest of the
three, a rather tubby three-masted caravel of some two hundred tons, ninety feet in length, built for the Flanders trade,
and named the *Mariagalante*. She was so high in fore and
stern castles as to appear topheavy, a vessel that might pitch
badly in a heavy sea, yet nevertheless preferred by him on the
score of her comparative roominess.

Her frivolous name was distasteful to him. Having decided
to rename her, he hovered between his loves sacred and profane, between his deep adoration of the Virgin and his passionate devotion to Beatriz. He wavered long, the while

praying Our Lady to forgive this hesitation, trusting confidently in Her infinite mercy and compassion for a man distraught by heartache. The impulse was strong within him to give his ship the name of the beloved woman whom he accounted lost to him, whose dear image haunted him, whose flowing grace was ever before his eyes. But in the end his piety conquered, or perhaps it may have been the belief that his ship would more surely prosper and more safely ride the unknown ocean if placed under the protection of Our Lady, whose very name, the Maris Stella, made her the natural guardian of all those who sail the seas. And so in the conviction that Beatriz, herself, would not resent the preference were she ever made aware of it, the *Mariagalante* was renamed the *Santa Maria*.

On the more practical side, he jealously supervised the equipping, the arming with bombards and falconets, whose projectiles of stone and iron went to serve as ballast. Side by side with this there was the care of the victualling: barrels of biscuit, of salted meat and fish, bacon and cheese and beans, ropes of onions, kegs of olives, casks of wine, of oil and of vinegar. Then there was the provision of spares: sails, ropes, tow, pitch, and all other supplies necessary to ships that might have to keep the seas for six months or longer.

The purchasing of all this was mainly left to the Pinzons, whose maritime experience knew what to seek, and whose trading relations in the port told them where to find it. Colon's knowledge of the currency employed by the Portuguese in Africa for the purchase of gold and ivory made him see to it that a goodly store of such trumperies as glass beads, hawk-bells, mirrors and the like were also shipped.

By the end of July, at long last, they were all but ready to take aboard wood and water, and put to sea.

With his brother Francisco to act as pilot, Martin Alonso

took command of the *Pinta*, a vessel half the length of the *Santa Maria*, and with one castle only, in the stern, but of lines that proclaimed her the better sailor. Like the *Santa Maria* she was square-rigged, whilst the third and slightly smaller vessel of the squadron, the *Niña*, in charge of Vicente Pinzon, was rigged with lateen sails, upon which Colon looked without favour.

Of the crews it was quite evident that the more staid and trustworthy were aboard the two ships commanded by the Pinzons. They had been picked, too, for their competence as seamen, all of them lads who had sailed before with the Pinzons, which gave the latter a certain prior right to them. The hands of the *Santa Maria* were not only generally rougher and less experienced as sailors, but they included a fair sprinkling of gaol-birds, who belatedly had availed them-selves of the amnesty. Colon, however, as he raked them with a masterful, scornful eye was not at all perturbed by their quality. Their toughness he took to promise endurance in the trials that might lie before them. Their unruliness he would know how to govern should they display it once he had them under his hand on the high seas.

Besides the men of the crews, a few adventurers had come at the last moment to swell their numbers, so that in all some hundred and twenty souls were ready to embark in those three frail vessels. They were shipping a couple of barber-surgeons, and an interpreter in the shape of a Marràno named Torres, who because of his knowledge of Hebrew, Greek and Arabic it was ingenuously thought might prove useful when they came to Zipangu. Against the possibility of reaching the mainland beyond it, and the realm of Marco Polo's Grand Khan, Colon bore a letter from the Sovereigns to that po-tentate.

The last of the stores were being stowed in the hold when

towards evening of the last day of July, the town of Palos was flung into excitement by the arrival of a cavalcade such as was rarely seen in that simple stronghold of mariners and traders.

With the approach of the hour of the squadron's sailing an air of gloom had been settling upon the seaport. Forebodings dejected those with kinsfolk committed to the adventure, whilst others, from sympathy with them, were reprobating it and coming to regard as doomed those who were about to sail. Out of this dejection the town was momentarily lifted by the arrival of that glittering train. Word flew that the puissant lord, the Escribano de la Racion of Aragon, Don Luis de Santangel, was coming to utter in the name of the Sovereigns God-speed to Don Cristobal Colon, and in holiday mood the people turned out to line the narrow unpaved streets and see the show.

The Chancellor rode into Palos on a white Arab, portly, serene, imposing in his damask surcoat edged with a silvery fur, and across his breast a chain of heavy links of gold that would have kept a Palos mariner at ease for a lifetime. He was attended by an armed escort of a half-score riders, glittering in back-and-breasts and caps of polished steel. With him came the returning Vasco Aranda, and a royal notary, named Escobar, who was to accompany the expedition.

The cavalcade clattered and jangled through the town without drawing rein, and breasted the sandy slope through the pinewoods to La Rabida.

Colon was absent from the convent at the time. He had gone aboard the *Santa Maria* with some effects that were to furnish his cabin, and to make a survey of the stowage, which was now complete. Coming ashore he learnt of the passage of the train on its way to the convent, and he followed at speed on foot. Reaching La Rabida heated and a little out

of breath, he was met in the courtyard by Santangel, who engulfed him in an embrace.

'Don Luis!' had been his glad, astonished cry. And then a
sudden excitement turned him pale. As he stepped back, it
was to inquire breathlessly, 'What brings you here?'

'Did you really suppose that I should allow you to sail
without coming to utter a God-speed? Should I let you go
without a word on this great expedition which I have done
my little to promote?'

'Little? It is the little without which I should be much
where I was when last I landed in Spain.' After a little pause,
he added: 'But . . . Is that all?'

'All?' Taken aback, the Chancellor looked at him, and
became aware of his pallid air of disappointment. 'Why,
what's amiss? You are not pleased to see me.'

'How could I not be?' Colon began a protest. But he went
no further with it. He passed a hand wearily across his brow.
'You are keen-eyed, Don Luis. It is not that I am not pleased
to see you. It is that your coming raised a sudden hope.
Forgive it. There is no reason in it. I have prayed so hard
that I might have word of Beatriz before I sail. And seeing
you, I thought, I hoped, that you brought me news that she
has been found.'

Santangel shook his head, sighing. 'Ah, my son, if she had
been found, it would not have been word of her I should have
brought you. I should have brought Beatriz herself. But
don't imagine that I have forgotten. I saw Don Xavier in
Cordoba, and urged him to continue the search. We shall
find her in the end.'

Colon accounted these words as uttered merely to hearten
him. They drew from him no more than a sigh, and there
for the moment he left the subject. But late that night, when
the convent slept and Santangel sat alone with him in his cell,
other matters being disposed of, he came back to this.

'You have been so good a friend to me, Don Luis, and I owe you so much that I make bold to ask you something more. If Beatriz is found let her know of my feelings for her, of my penitence for my hasty judgment; and if it should happen that my voyage prospers and yet I should lose my life in it, then I beg you to see that a full provision is made for her out of what will then be Diego's heritage. I should wish, too, that she should have the care of Diego; that for my sake she will regard him as a son, just as I hope that in her he will find a mother. I have set it all down in this letter, which is by way of a testament. I leave it in your charge, Don Luis, if you will bear this burden for me.'

'Depend upon me,' Don Luis assured him. 'But depend upon me, too, to continue the search, so that we may have her waiting for you on your return.'

Two days later, on the following Thursday, Colon sailed.

On the night of Wednesday Frey Juan heard him in confession, and before daybreak next morning he set out alone with Aranda for Palos, which was already astir, with lights gleaming from its windows, to hear Mass and receive the Sacrament with his crews in the Church of Saint George.

At the mole, after that, he came upon just such a scene as he had expected. The women of Palos and some of its men and children were filling the air with their lamentations as they took leave of the departing sailors. Upon Colon, as he came striding amongst them, they looked without affection, and if they did not openly curse him, it was from a fear lest, by harm to him, the curses should recoil upon those whose slender chance of returning depended upon his survival and his skill.

As the sun came up over the hills of Almonte, he entered the waiting boat and was pulled out to the *Santa Maria*, where she rode at her moorings, with the other two ships of the squadron, over against the sandbar of Saltes, which there divides the Tinto from the Odiel.

From the break of the high poop he issued his first command. The trumpeter below him conveyed it in a flourish, which was the signal of departure. The boatswain's whistle shrilled, and the clank of the capstan followed. As the anchor came above water, other hands, at the halyards, were heaving to a melancholy chant, inarticulate yet suggestive of the 'La illaha illa Allah!' from which it was inherited.

The blocks creaked, the yards were braced, the sails slatted for a moment, then bellied to the morning breeze, and the *Santa Maria* quickened on the bosom of the ebbing tide.

She moved in stateliness through those calm waters under a full spread of canvas above her black hull with its towering castles at stem and stern. The Papal cross spread its arms on her foresheet, and the heavier cross of Malta on the square mainsail, with the flag of Ferdinand and Isabel, quartering in red and gold the castles with the lions, flowing from the maintruck above the crucifix. Colon's long pennon fluttered aft from the mizzen, which was rigged with a high sweeping lantern.

The men in the waist below, a motley assortment that included a few pretentiously full-coated adventurers among a bare-legged majority in shirt and breeches, were crowding the larboard bulwarks, silent and awed now that they were launched upon this voyage into the unknown, in quest of lands that might have no existence outside of the mind of that tall fanatic on the poop. Thence they waved in response to the mournful wavings from the crowded quays, from which they were receding ever more swiftly as the vessel gathered way, or to the stragglers who raced along the shore, so as to keep in touch with them up to the last moment.

Thus, with the *Pinta* and the *Niña* following in her swirling wake, the *Santa Maria* came abreast of La Rabida, and Colon, too, moved to the larboard rail, and lifted his eyes to the heights. On the promontory's edge, clear against the morning sky, in the golden light of the new-risen sun, stood the figures of Santangel and Frey Juan, the two men to whom perhaps more than to any others in all Spain he owed it that he was sailing at last upon this great adventure.

He raised his hand and held it high in a last salute to those good friends. Santangel waved his bonnet in response, and from Frey Juan's hand a scarf fluttered and was agitated with a rhythm long and slow as the tolling of a passing bell.

Thus Colon stood until the ship swung round the point at the mouth of the Domingo Rubio, and the two figures were lost to his view. Then, at last, he faced ahead, his eyes stern with resolve, and went down to the long quarterdeck, where those who composed his officers stood grouped. The deck was heaving gently now under his feet as they went through the choppy water over the bar of Saltes, and took the open sea.

With Juan de la Cosa, who was part owner of the *Santa Maria* and sailed as pilot, a squarely built, sandy-haired man with a good-humoured freckled face, Colon conned the ship. A southerly course was laid and the watch set, whereafter Colon went into the cabin that for months was to be his home. Neither cramped nor spacious, it was all plain and yellow varnished, without any carving or decoration on bulkheads or stanchions. It contained his bed, which was draped in red, a small table of plain deal, with a stool and a couple of Gothic chairs, a clothes-press set against the starboard bulkhead, a locker under the windows astern, on one side a shelf holding a few books and on the other his astrolabe and cross-staff. An hour-glass surmounted the clothes-press, and on the opposite bulkhead hung the oval brass panel with the little painting of Our Lady that once had hung in Colon's room in Cordoba.

28

 THE VOYAGE

For most of that first day they sailed south, and then altered the course to west, heading for the Canaries. But in his cabin Don Cristobal calmly commenced — *in nomine D.N. Jesu Christi* — to indite the voluminous detailed journal for the information of the Sovereigns and his own subsequent glory. He would keep it, he declares, after the model supplied him by the *Commentaries* of Caesar, in which conceit he affords you a glimpse of how profound was his own sense of the grandeur of his enterprise.

He was done with the intrigues, the treacheries and meannesses of men. With the less incalculable treachery of the sea he felt himself strong to deal, just as he accounted himself well able to deal with the hands if they should give trouble.

Of this there was to be more than enough before all was done, and a perception of the possibility, considering the rascally lot aboard, made him anxious to reach and pass the Canaries, so that once he had committed them irrevocably to the adventure, they would lie, as he supposed, at his mercy, or, as he had once already expressed it, in the hollow of his hand. But until that first stage of the voyage was overpast, should the gloomy apprehensions shed over them in the farewell tears at Palos explode in a mutinous demand to return, he would be almost powerless to impose his will.

Hence it was of more than ordinary vexation to him when, on the third day out, the *Pinta*, which, as the swiftest vessel of the squadron, had held the lead under a towering spread of snowy canvas, was suddenly taking in sail and falling astern with a rudder that had snapped from its socket.

The wind was too fresh to permit them to go to her assistance. The experienced, resourceful Pinzon, however, standing in no need of it, set promptly about effecting a temporary repair with ropes. They had to stand hove to and wait until this was done, a delay to which the morrow added a worse when the repairs gave way. Again they had to shorten sail and wait whilst Pinzon contrived to rig a jury rudder on which to stagger into Grand Canary.

They reached it on the following Thursday, and there they careened the *Pinta* whilst a new rudder was being made and fitted. Since this further delay was imposed upon Colon, at least he profited by it to have the *Niña's* rig altered to square, since with her lateen sails, which he had ever viewed with misgivings, she would be useless in close-hauled sailing.

Meanwhile, not trusting his crew ashore, he went on to Gomera, on the pretext still of perhaps finding another ship to replace the *Pinta*. Meeting with no such vessel there, he came back to Grand Canary to hasten the conclusion of the work.

Three weeks were thus lost. But at last all was ready, and on the sixth of September the voyage was resumed. They put in again at Gomera, for wood and water, and then, with the prows headed into the west, the real voyage began.

Even now, however, the start seemed to be little better than

a false one. For three days they lay becalmed, scarcely crawling over a sea as smooth as the Guadalquivir, and with the
land, of which Colon was so anxious to see the last, ever in
sight.

At daybreak on the ninth the Island of Ferro was still
visible, a vague grey mass, nine leagues away on the horizon
astern. But at last a breeze sprang up, the sails filled, and
with a welcome gurgle at the prows the ships began to go
through the water. The wind quickened to a ten-knot breeze,
and swiftly the way increased. The sea curled back in white
plumes from their bows, and the coastline of Ferro faded
from their sight. They were launched at last into the unknown, and Colon's mind knew peace.

Not so the minds of his crew. With the disappearance of
land, with the line of empty sky meeting the line of empty sea
on every side, a panic arose. It spread until boys and even
men gave way to tears as they sat dejected on the hatchways.
Lamentations resounded through the ship, and reached the
ears of Colon in his cabin, to interrupt his calm recording.

It was not the mere fact that land was lost to sight that
troubled those tough, hardy souls. Saving some odd hands
and the few gentlemen adventurers, there was scarcely one
of them who had not lost sight of land before and borne the
loss with equanimity. But they had always known the land
to be just abeam of them below the horizon, whereas now
they were headed into the empty abyss of waters which no
keels had ever ploughed, sailing right out of the world into
a desert of ocean in which land might well have no existence
outside of the untested dreams of the lunatic by whom they
were committed to this dread gamble.

Whilst in some such terms they lamented and inveighed,
hideously noisy, Colon made his appearance, calm and masterful, upon the quarterdeck, cross-staff in hand. He came for-

ward to the rail with unhurried, measured step, bare-headed, the breeze ruffling his tawny mane.

The sight of him at that moment produced an explosion. A sudden angry roar went up from the men who crowded the waist. Those who had been squatting on the hatch-coamings or astride the bombards sprang to their feet in the vehemence of their protests.

He raised his hand for silence, and as it fell one shrill voice rang out to supply him with a cue.

'Whither do you lead us?'

'Out of misery into glory,' he answered. 'Out of squalor into splendour. Out of hunger into plenty. That is whither I lead you.'

Though in the view of the Sovereigns his title of Admiral was yet to be earned, to the crews of this squadron he was in fact the Admiral already, and as their Admiral they should know him.

Dominant there above them, an incarnation of scornful strength and confidence, he awed them into attention.

'You mutter of a gamble. And if it were? What is it that you set upon the board? Your empty bellies, your crawling poverty, your bitter hardships, your unrewarded toil. Behold your stakes. Are they stakes that you need grudge to set against the chance of fortune and ease? What are your lives worth so lived that you do not count yourselves fortunate indeed to be given this stupendous chance of soaring out of them? Chance, do I say? This is no chance, no gamble. I know what I do, whither I go. Had I not persuaded the Sovereigns of that, and shamed the witlings who opposed me, do you think that Their Highnesses would have entrusted me with these ships?

'Out there, seven hundred leagues to westward, whither we are steering, the incalculable treasures of Zipangu await you, to make you the envied of all Spain on your return.'

Such was the spell he wove by his words and the assurance of his tone and manner that as he ceased he was actually answered by a cheer from some of those who but a moment since had been prostrate in dejection.

Content, he raised the cross-staff and laid his eye to the end of it to take the highth of the sun. To most of them it was a mysterious operation, impressive by its suggestion of power and skill to find a pathway across the trackless wastes of water.

Then he turned away to give attention to the helmsman, and to rate him for allowing the head to fall away to the north. He summoned Cosa for a stern injunction to be watchful that the westerly course be maintained. After that he went back to his cabin, to mark the position of the ship on the chart which he was making as they proceeded. In estimating this he depended upon dead reckoning; and it now occurred to him to provide for possible error in his estimate of the distance to Zipangu. He had asserted with such confidence that it lay seven hundred leagues ahead, that trouble would almost inevitably follow if when that distance had been sailed they should still have made no landfall. He must leave himself a margin for error. To this end he now began to falsify the log, attributing to the ship a daily run of a score or so of leagues less than the actual. The true distances traversed were secretly noted in his journal. From time to time the Pinzons, from the other two ships, would pass their charts across to him at the end of a line, so that he should mark their position upon them. Whilst his figures might not agree with the reckonings on the *Pinta* and the *Niña*, yet they were adopted out of trust in his greater skill in computation.

Graver, and calling for deeper trickery, was a variation of the compass by which they were surprised at the end of a week's sailing, by when they were some two hundred leagues west of Ferro.

The gloom which Colon's harangue had once dispelled had been descending again upon the crew ever since the *Santa Maria*, two days ago, had passed a drifting mast, which by its size must have belonged to a ship of at least an equal tonnage. It had been remarked with an apprehension which the more timorous had vigorously fanned. If storms were to overtake them, they complained, they would be utterly at their mercy here in this vast desert of water, with no land within reach to which they might hope to run for shelter. When, in addition, the variation of the needle became known, even the stouter souls were infected by the alarm. Nor was the uneasiness that of ignorant sailors only. Colon, himself, was the first to discover that instead of pointing to the North Star, the needle was pointing several degrees west of it. Prepared as he was for every risk rather than admit defeat or doubt, he would have concealed the fact had it depended only upon himself. But there were others aboard to observe it. One night Rata, the quartermaster, consulted about it by an intelligent steersman, went in his turn to consult Cosa. Others, overhearing the discussion, spread the alarm. Like a ripple over water it ran to pervade the whole of that uneasy ship, and the explosion that followed awoke the sleeping Admiral.

He sat up in bed for a moment listening. Then, already suspecting the source of this fresh trouble, he flung back the coverlet, and rose. He thrust his feet into slippers, groped for a robe, and pulling it about him came out upon the quarterdeck. Below, about the binnacle, the faces of the foremost faintly lighted by the glow of its lantern, he beheld the dark mass of turbulent men. In a moment he was elbowing his way through that noisy press.

'What is happening here?' he demanded, to add a stern injunction to the steersman. 'Steady your helm, man. We are luffing alee. What is this?'

'It's the needle, Admiral,' Cosa answered him, and instantly the clamour died down, so that the men might hear his answer.

'The needle? What ails the needle? What do you mean, the needle?'

'It's no longer true.'

Still Colon chose not to understand. 'Not true? How can it not be true?'

A hard-bitten, middle-aged seaman named Ires, said to be an Irishman, who claimed to have sailed all the waters of the known world, stood truculently forward to answer him.

'It's lost its power. It's lost its power. Here be we adrift in unknown seas without even the poor guidance of the compass.'

'That's the fact, Admiral,' said Rata grimly.

And before Colon could answer, a grey-haired sinner named Nieves was excitedly adding, 'It's the proof that we've sailed out of the natural world that God intended man to inhabit.'

'We're doomed, by hell,' groaned another voice. 'Lost and doomed.'

'May I die if I didn't always know it would end thus,' raved Ires.

The words were as a torch in a powder-barrel. Uproar burst about Don Cristobal.

'Quiet!' he thundered. 'Let me come.' He approached the binnacle, and the light from the lantern beating upon his long face showed it calm and stern. In silence now, almost holding their very breath, the men waited whilst he confirmed with his own eyes this dreadful portent. Only Cosa, at his elbow, spoke.

'See for yourself, sir. Look at the North Star yonder. The variation is at least of five degrees.'

If Colon looked, it was not, indeed, to inform himself; for, to his great secret uneasiness, he was already but too well aware of this. His pause, now that the matter was discovered to the entire ship, was to gain yet a moment for conjecture.

In the light of the lantern they saw the expression of his countenance change to one of derision. Suddenly his laughter startled them.

'You fools! You poor, lubberly fools! And even you, Cosa, even a seaman of your experience! You amaze me. How can you suppose the needle inconstant because it no longer points to the North Star?'

Cosa was bridling. 'What then?' he demanded.

'Why, it's the star that is inconstant. Not the needle.'

'The star? How can the ——'

'Observe it.' He pointed upwards. 'And see how it moves across the heavens. How should the needle guide us if it moved with it? Little service it would do us if it did not remain ever true to the invisible point that is the north.' Contemptuously he waved the hands away. 'Be off with you to your quarters, and leave these matters to those that understand them.'

The authoritative firmness of his tone, the scientific truth that he appeared to state, the scorn that was to be read in every line of him, left them in a cowed persuasion as he turned away.

But at the foot of the companion he was stayed again by Cosa, a hand upon his arm. The pilot was not as those other unreasoning kinds. He spoke softly.

'I left it there, Admiral, so as not to provoke a riot. But ——'

'That was wise.'

'But in all my years at sea I've never known ——'

He was interrupted coldly. 'You've never sailed this parallel, Juan.'

'Neither have you, sir,' was the prompt retort. 'The experience is as new to you as it is to me. So how can you know ——'

Again he was peremptorily cut short. 'Just as I know that we are sailing to the Indies. Just as I know many things that lie outside man's experience. And you'll take my word for it unless you want a panic among those rats.' Colon patted his shoulder in friendly dismissal of the subject. 'Good night, Juan,' he added, and left the pilot to scratch his head in perplexity, not knowing what to believe.

Upon the crew, however, Colon's improvisation had sufficiently imposed, as it was to impose on the morrow upon Pinzon, to whom he communicated the same plausible reassurance. For a spell now Colon knew peace.

They were in the belt of the trade wind which flows between the tropics from east to west. So steadily did it blow that for days, with the ships ploughing evenly westward, they did not shift a sail.

The men took their ease. They gambled some of the time away at dice and cards. They bathed now and then in the tepid waters whilst the ships stood hove to for them. There were trials of strength and wrestling matches to while away the time, and one or two who had brought guitars would make indifferent music for their fellows. Every evening at sunset, by Colon's orders, they would stand ranged in the waist, to raise their voices and intone the *Salve Regina*, as an evening prayer to Our Lady for protection.

Thus for a few days of calm sailing all was well. And then one night they were stirred to fresh alarm by the sight of a shower of meteors that filled the sky with fire. It awoke their superstition and the memory of dreadful tales of supernatural forces guarding the ocean spaces from presumptuous intrusion. But it proved no more than a transient alarm, as they sailed on from under clear skies into cloudy weather with drizzling rain and a diminished wind, and from that into sunshine once more and temperately warm airs, so that, in Colon's own words, it was like spring in Andalusia without the nightingales.

Presently they found themselves driving through vast and increasing patches of weed, some withered and yellow, and some so green and fresh as to suggest that it had drifted from some near land. Tunny fish came sporting about the ships, and so as to raise spirits that were again beginning to droop, Colon — who knew not, and knew that he knew not — informed them that tunny were never to be found far from land.

One or two of these great fish were caught from the *Niña*, and steaks, roasted in the brick and iron galley in the waist, supplied welcome fare to men who had been nauseated by salt fish and bacon rendered tainted by the heat and damp of the hold. They found it toothsome, although in truth, as their cook dealt with it, it was of the texture of roast horse without the flavour.

The weed patches increased until now from the ships' sides they seemed to be looking out upon wide meadows. Tangled in this, the ships laboured slowly on, and gradually alarm awoke once more in those uneasy minds. The cry now was that they were coming into shoal water, and that presently they would run aground or pile up upon hidden rocks and be held there to rot and perish.

Colon recalled Aristotle's account of Cadiz ships blown westward to great fields of weed resembling islands, from which those ancient mariners had turned back in terror. But he was careful to say no word of it. Nor dared he suggest that it heralded the approach of land because of the disappointment that must follow, since, being only three hundred and sixty leagues from the Canaries, he could not account himself more than halfway to Zipangu. So as to allay their dread of shoal water, he ordered soundings to be taken, and when no bottom was found, there was an end to murmurings.

At last they were clear of the weed fields, and sailing smoothly again, always under the same soft breezes from the east.

One of the adventurers on board, Sancho Gomez, a decayed but pretentious gentleman of Cadiz, of authoritative airs, declared that the water was growing fresher, and asserted this to be a positive indication that they were approaching land, the salt of the sea being diluted by the sweet waters of rivers. Others tasting the water were of divided opinions; the optimists yielded to the suggestion Gomez practised; the pessimists, led by Ires, violently denied any decrease in salinity.

Gomez, however, remained unshaken, and that evening just after the *Salve Regina* had been sung, he startled the ship by raising the cry of 'Land!' His outflung arm was pointing northward. 'Now, you obstinate doubters, was I wrong?'

An irregular line, vague and misty, as of mountainous country, loomed on the horizon, the summits rose-tinted by the setting sun, the base already in gloom.

Colon was on the quarterdeck, where, with Cosa, Aranda, Escobar and some two or three others whom he regarded as his officers, he had been standing for the evening hymn. Startled by the cry, he swung with them to starboard, and scanned the horizon. It is conceivable that he might have yielded to the illusion had it been less opposed to his conviction of the quarter in which land would first appear.

'That is not land!' he cried, to quench their rising hopes. 'Cloud masses. Nothing more.' And he laughed, attempting a jest so as to deflect the disappointment. 'Eagerness to earn the reward, Sancho, lends your eyes a deceptive keenness.'

The allusion was to a pension for life of ten thousand maravedis promised by the Queen to the man who should first sight land.

But none laughed with him, and Sancho Gomez flung into angry insistence that he knew land when he saw it, with a resulting clamour presently from the waist that the helm be put over.

At this Colon grew stern. 'You will save yourselves trouble if you will remember that there is one master aboard this ship, and that she will be steered as he thinks proper. The shape of that land of Master Gomez is already changing. But this I promise you, that if at dawn there should still be any such mass on the starboard beam, we'll head for it.'

They bowed to his inflexible will, and the dawn, breaking clear, with nothing to darken the line where sky and water met, settled the conviction that cloud masses had deceived their eyes.

Nevertheless, the incident was harmful. Soaring hopes led in their falsification to grim reactions, and the vanished mirage of land left behind it a renewal of misgivings. At first there were no more than mutterings, but Aranda, moving amongst the men, recognized these mutterings as the heralds of a storm, and was prompt to warn Colon.

Towards noon that day a couple of boobies alighted on the ship, whereupon Colon, whether he believed it or not, proclaimed such birds to be never more than twenty leagues from land. To lend colour to an assertion with which he hoped temporarily to pacify them, he ordered a leadsman into the forechains to take soundings. No bottom, however, was to be found at two hundred fathoms.

Later, when a flight of small birds passed overhead, flying in a southwesterly direction, Colon experienced his first mis-

givings. He knew what that flight portended. He was aware
of the guidance which the Portuguese navigators had derived
from the migration of birds, and he concluded that he was
probably passing between islands. He kept the conclusion to
himself, pondering it until nightfall. Then he decided that,
nevertheless, he must continue to run before that ever steady
wind from the east. He perceived that to turn aside might
be fatal to his credit and power. Hitherto he had acted, and
he had prevailed by acting, as one possessed of such sure
knowledge of his goal, that doubt would be impossible to him.
Let him now fumble, let him by turning aside in uncertain
questing, admit a doubt, and there would be an end to his
authority over his restive rabble of a crew.

So he held to his westward course in order to avoid trouble.

The trouble, nevertheless, was coming, black and heavy.
The persistence with which the wind held in the same quarter
began to be remarked. At first it was considered merely an
oddness in the weather. Then, because something outside of
the experience of any seaman aboard, it began to appear
uncanny. At last the mutinous Ires suggested a terrifying
explanation.

'Odd?' he chuckled in evil fear to the group about him.
'There's naught odd about it. What sailor ever heard tell of
the wind blowing steadily from the same quarter for four
weeks? I'll make oath it's never been known. I've never
known it. Not till I came on this damned voyage. Don't you
see what it means, my lads? Why it means that here, in these
seas, the wind blows the same way all the time. That's what
it means, by hell! And what I ask you is: How are we ever
to sail back against it?'

It was a staggering question.

One swore in sudden affright, 'Jesus Maria!' and another,
'By all the fiends!' and in a moment, with an explosion of

oaths, mostly of that morphological variety, in the invention
of which the Spaniard has no rival, the men in the knot about
him were violently giving him reason. Others came to join
them, drawn by the hubbub.

Ires, swollen with the consequence of a discoverer, leaned
back against the cock-boat, where it rested on its booms amid-
ships. 'Now you begin to see the pestilent plight we're in.
This wind is blowing us right out of the world. Right into
hell. That's what's happening to us, my lads. And the
farther we go, the stronger the wind gets. Haven't you
remarked it?'

Assent flavoured with more blasphemy was the instant
answer.

'Then every day we keep to this damned course, the less is
our chance of ever seeing Spain again.'

Through the clamour of agreement pierced the voice of
Rodrigo Ximenes, another of the impoverished gentlemen
adventurers, a native of Segovia. 'God rot your tongue, you
chattering jay! What are you? A sailor or a tinker? Have
you never seen a ship beat to windward?'

'Beat to windward! Ohw!' crowed Ires. 'Listen to the
landlubber turned mariner. And how many years shall we
be beating to windward if we go much farther? And where's
the victuals and water to come from whilst we're doing it?
As it is, victuals is running low and rotting in that hold. A
lot you know about the sea, my Segovian hidalgo!'

Jeers overwhelmed Ximenes; applause encouraged the
Irishman; and with the applause came a demand for action,
an exhortation to Ires to lead them.

The sounds of that swelling tumult reached Colon in his
cabin, where he was busy upon his charts, even before Aranda
came to warn him of the trouble.

'They are noisy down there,' he greeted his master-at-arms.

Aranda's brief reply was such as to bring him instantly to
his feet and out of the cabin. He reached the rail an instant
before Ires, who came storming up from the waist, the leader
of a rowdy following.

Thus suddenly confronted by the Admiral, Ires lost some
impetus, and hung hesitating.

'Down! Off my quarterdeck!' Colon rasped at him, much
as he might have spoken to a dog.

Ires, committed to that leadership, dared be no other than
bold and truculent. 'We have something to say to you, Don
Cristobal.'

'Say it from below there. Down with you!'

But Ires did not budge. He could not without loss of
prestige. Within the black hairiness of his face his skin was
livid. His hand slid to his waist, behind, where his sheath-
knife was hung. He conceived that seeing him armed the
Admiral would abate his peremptoriness. What happened
was the opposite. Scarcely had his hand begun its journey
than Colon had gripped him by the breast of his greasy
doublet, lifted him off his feet and hurled him from the companion. But for those behind and below him upon whom he
hurtled, there might have been broken bones for Guillerme
Ires.

'Speak to me now,' Colon permitted.

It was, however, Gomez who, whilst Ires spluttered invec-
tive, made himself the spokesman of the angry crew, briefly
stating their conclusions. 'And because of this, Don Cristobal,'
he ended, 'we demand to put about and return to Spain
before it is too late.'

'You demand it? Oh, you demand it. Silence, there, and
listen. These ships were entrusted to me by Their Highnesses
for the purpose of sailing to the Indies, and to the Indies we
will sail. So quiet you in that conviction, or I'll make an

example of one or two of you, patient man though I be.'

'Admiral,' cried Gomez, 'we have made up our minds. We go no farther.'

'Over the side with you, then, you and those who think like you. I give you leave. You may swim back to Spain. But this ship does not go about.'

There was fresh uproar, out of which one voice soared in an angry whine. 'You are carrying us to our death, Admiral. There can be no returning against winds that blow ever westward.'

Thus was Colon made aware at last of the source of this trouble. He perceived that if he was to quiet this alarm, he must have recourse to another of his extemporizations, and again explain something which he, himself, did not understand. He found the answer promptly, and it was so logical as to make him afterwards suspect that he had stumbled upon a discovery.

'God give me patience with such wits. Need you be told that for a belt of wind that blows fron one quarter, there must on another parallel be a compensating belt that blows from the opposite? That is the belt by which we shall return. But only after having reached the Indies. So let me hear no more of it.'

On that contemptuous dismissal he left them, dumbfounded by an answer to their fears so plausible that they could not but accept it.

As he was regaining his cabin, still accompanied by Aranda, he overheard the voice of Ximenes. 'Now, Master Ires, which of us is the tinker? Which of us knows the ocean and its ways?'

He closed the door, and crossed to the press in quest of a sheet of paper. It was his intent, with the charts that were to be passed back to the Pinzons, to send a note to Martin Alonso, informing him of the disturbance and how he had

met it, so that he might be armed with an answer in like case.
There was less likelihood of it on the other ships, however,
for the Pinzons were more fortunate in their crews. Aboard
each of their caravels there was a majority of steady men who
had sailed with them before and had learnt by experience to
trust them. These would suffice to encourage timorous spirits
and discourage mutinous ones.

'We are well out of that trouble, Admiral,' said Aranda.
'It was fortunate that you could answer their misgivings.'

'Yes. A fortunate conjecture,' Colon answered him, still
rummaging in the press.

'Conjecture? Was the belt of easterly wind a conjecture?'

Colon turned, smiling. 'What is amiss with conjecture so
that it be intelligent?'

'I see.' Aranda moved a pace or two away from the table
by which he had been standing. His face was darkened with
thought. 'Do your Indies, too, happen to be a conjecture?'

Colon stared at him for a silent moment. 'Sound mathematical deduction is something higher than conjecture, Vasco.'

'You relieve me. For a moment you set me wondering
whether this voyage is just the gamble that men call it in
their grumbling.'

'The only gamble is in what it shall profit us. That we
shall make this landfall is as certain as anything in this uncertain life can be. But why these doubts?'

Aranda pointed to the chart that had remained spread
upon the table. Colon took a quick step forward, startled.
'Ah!' he said, and his glance was steady, questioning, almost
defiant.

'I do not spy,' Aranda explained himself. 'I saw it without
intent to look. Our position as you mark it there is fifty
leagues beyond the point of your land of Zipangu.'

'True. But what, after all, is an error of fifty leagues in
such a computation?'

'But the position is not that which you have marked on Pinzon's chart. Him you delude about that, as you deluded the men about the wind.'

Colon answered with a sigh and a faint smile. 'What choice have I? If I am to prevail I must stifle doubts as best I can. But on the main issue, Vasco, I tell you again I neither cheat nor gamble. I know. As surely as I know that I am living.'

Aranda looked into his eyes, and it was a moment before he answered.

'Forgive me,' he said. 'So that your faith is honestly held, as I believe it to be, I shall never regret having sailed with you, come what may.'

'I trust, indeed, that you never shall, Vasco,' Colon answered him, and sat down to write his note.

When Aranda had left him to see the note and the charts passed across to the *Pinta*, Colon sat on grimly considering all the artifice that lay behind him and might still lie ahead for the accomplishment of his high mission, if, indeed, accomplishment were to attend it. For whilst he had been unusually frank with Aranda, he had not been entirely so. This was the sixth of October. They were nearly a month out from Gomera, and the fifty leagues by which already his computations had been exceeded was no such trifle in his view as he had represented it. On the contrary, it was the source of a secret anxiety that for all his boasted confidence was now gnawing him.

As lately as that very morning Martin Alonso, marking a flight of birds, had bawled across the water a suggestion that they alter course and steer for the southwest. Colon had peremptorily refused, again because to have yielded would have betrayed his misgivings and sapped the authority which only assurance could maintain.

That night, pacing the poop alone with his growing anxiety,

which was shaping itself into a fear that he might have missed and overshot Zipangu, he heard the flight of birds again, steadily and continuously passing to the southwest.

He paced on, his obstinacy in conflict with his reason, which told him that if anywhere in this waste of waters there was a landward course it must be the course the birds were following.

From the break of the poop he looked down into the waist. There a score or so of the men lay huddled in sleep, forms dimly visible in the moonlight, about the hatches and in the shelter of the cooking-galley and of the cock-boat. When the moon set they were lost to sight in a pit of blackness, for no lights were permitted below, save that of the binnacle, invisible from the waist.

At the summit of the poop, above the after rail glowed the big lantern within whose mica panes a wreathed rope that had been steeped in pitch was burning. By the yellow light of it anyone awake in the waist might have seen the black silhouette of the Admiral as he paced there through most of that night in his mental travail. He was still there at dawn, when the men began to awaken and stretch and yawn with a noise as of bellowing steers.

Cosa, emerging from the forecastle, where he kept his quarters, saw him, and came up to him.

'It's the birds, Admiral. All night I heard them passing in flight to the south.'

'And then?' quoth the Admiral glumly.

Cosa showed that he, too, knew the inference. 'They were small birds. Land birds. They will be flying to the land. There will be land to the south.'

'So there may be, but not the land I seek. That lies ahead.'

Cosa looked as if he would protest, but quailed under the sternness of Colon's glance. He compromised, deflecting to the crew some of the censure that might follow. 'Some of the hands have remarked it, too. They draw the same conclusion. It strains their patience, Admiral.'

'Let them strain mine no further, or by Saint Ferdinand I'll hang one or two from the yardarm as an example to the rest. Let it be known. I've been patient enough with their unruliness.'

'It's seeking trouble, Admiral,' the pilot warned him.

'Sometimes that is the way to avoid it.'

Cosa departed muttering in his sandy beard, and Colon went to break his fast on salt fish that was rank and biscuit that was mouldy, to which only the wholesomeness of the wine supplied an antidote. Afterwards, wearied by the night's vigil, he lay on his red-draped bed and fell asleep.

Whilst he slept mutiny again reared its head aboard. Cosa had fired the train in passing, by a hint of the Admiral's warning. Its effect was the opposite to that intended, and again the ringleader was Ires, his rancour in a simmer ever since the rude handling he had received.

'Hang one or two of us, would he?' Ires spat contemptuously. 'Faith, it might be a mercy to shorten the agony of some of us. For there's never a one of us'll see home again if we let him have his way.'

He stood bare-legged, arms akimbo, his hairy face inflamed, addressing a half-score men and a couple of boys who squatted on the coaming of one of the hatches. Behind him Gomez, lean and sardonic, in the threadbare finery of a gentleman, leaned against the bulwarks listening.

'By God, Guillerme,' he flung in, 'I agree with you.'

'Is there a fool aboard who doesn't?' wondered Ires. 'This rascal, this madman, is gambling away his worthless life on a blind chance of glory. His life's his own, and he may stake it as he pleases. But is he to stake yours? Are we to go sailing on to hell through this emptiness, seeking land that no living man can say exists? If we endure it longer we must be as mad as he is.'

'How can we help ourselves now?' asked one.

'Aye. Tell us that,' another mocked him.

'Do as I advised before. Put the ship about and steer for home.'

'Isn't it too late?' asked Gomez. 'Aren't the poisonous victuals already too low to last a return voyage?'

'We'll have to make them last. Better an empty belly for a while than to perish altogether.'

That elderly mariner named Nieves, sitting immediately before Ires, looked up at him and spoke softly. 'Faith, I'm entirely of your mind. But how should we be received in Spain?'

'What's to fear?' retorted Ires, and then Gomez came forward into the group.

'Nothing on that score,' he asserted. 'This upstart, let me tell you, counts for nothing among the great or the learned. Indeed, it's in my knowledge that they pushed advice against this expedition as far as they could with Their Highnesses. If we go empty home all the world will say that it's what was to be expected.'

'Maybe, maybe,' said Nieves. 'But I've not followed the sea these years without coming to know what happens to mutineers, be they right or be they wrong.' He shook an untidy grey head. 'It's a hanging matter, my lads. Don't be forgetting it.'

'Isn't he threatening to hang some of us?' another voice demanded.

Gomez edged closer amongst them. The lean, sallow face that hard living had prematurely aged was slyly wicked. His voice fell to a murmur. 'There's a simpler way. If in the dark of the night, when he comes on the poop to take the stars with his astrolabe, this Jonah were to fall overboard, what else could we do but go about and return home? The Pinzons would never go on once we had lost the guidance of the only man who pretends to know where we are going.'

There was a silence. All faces were upturned to look at him, and there was dread in the eyes of some. But not in the eyes of Ires. He bent his knee, and brought down his hand with a resounding smack upon his thigh.

'A cup of water to poor souls in hell. That's what you bring us, hidalgo.'

Aranda, emerging from the forecastle, overheard the words in their setting of raucous laughter. The sudden silence produced by his approach quickened his suspicions. He halted by the group.

'What cup of water is that?'

There was a stir of embarrassment. But Gomez was not of those who shared it. He remained at ease, smiling.

'I was cheering them with the promise that by Sunday we shall be ashore. Maybe hearing Mass.'

'Aye, just that, sir,' leered Ires. 'Cheered us mightily, it did.'

This confirmation strengthened Aranda's conviction that Gomez lied. He dissembled. 'It's no reason, anyway, to leave the ship in the foul state she is while you sit chattering. Get the buckets and swabs, and scour me this deck.'

He passed on, leaving the seamen to shamble off upon the duty assigned them. It was not, however, until some hours later that Colon received from him the day's second warning.

'Admiral, there's mischief afoot.'

'So Cosa tells me.' Colon was cool.

'I'd be none too sure of Cosa, himself.'

'What? Well, well! Let it brew until it boils over and scalds them.'

But Aranda would not treat it so lightly. 'It may be beyond mending when that happens. Ires and that rakehell Gomez are too close, and they've gathered a bunch of cut-throats about them. Give the order, Admiral, and I'll have the pair of them in irons and under hatches before the mischief spreads further.'

Chin in hand Colon considered. 'You'd need good grounds for that. Something more than suspicion.'

Aranda laughed. 'I'd soon make the grounds. A harsh order or two would do it in their present humour. I might set Ires to boy's work: cleaning out the forecastle quarters; and order Gomez to lend a hand in swabbing the decks. That should be enough to give me grounds.'

'And those whom you think they've already seduced? What if they should revolt?'

'There should be still enough loyal ones to help subdue them.'

'A risk.'

'But if we do nothing we may face a certainty.'

Colon rose in silence, still thoughtful. He took Aranda by the arm and drew him out of the cabin. From the break of the poop they saw the rebels, fully a score of them by now, gathered about the hatchway. Ires was addressing them in a subdued voice, but with a vehemence manifest in his gestures.

'It's the moment,' said Aranda. 'I ordered them to swab, and they've never moved to it. That's reason enough for action. I'll go and scatter them to it with a belaying-pin, and make Ires the scapegoat.'

His foot was already on the companion when the thunder of a gun startled every soul aboard. There was a rush for the starboard bulwarks, whilst men came tumbling out of the forecastle to swell the numbers in the waist and stare across

the blue water at the *Pinta*, a couple of cables' length away.
A pillar of yellowish smoke from one of her bombards was
wreathing her shrouds and trailing astern. On the high
sterncastle Martin Alonso stood waving.

'Land! Land!' he bawled. 'I claim the reward.'

The cry altered the direction of their gaze. Again there
was a scurrying rush, and now it was for the ratlines. Up
they swarmed, and in a moment the rigging as high as the
fighting-top on the mainmast was black with excited chattering seamen.

Away on the southern horizon they beheld the hazy out-
line of the mountainous range Martin Alonso had been the
first to descry. They judged it to be about a score of leagues
away.

'Praise God!' said Colon in devout thankfulness.

His relief at this eleventh-hour deliverance from the dangers
that must attend any attempt to suppress the incipient mutiny,
left him indifferent to the fact that he was proven wrong in
his expectations by the quarter in which the land appeared.

As he dispatched Aranda to the helmsman, to alter course,
the sounds of the *Gloria in excelsis*, chanted in chorus by the
crew of the *Pinta* came to the *Santa Maria* across the water.
Her own crew joined in it, and a heartbeat later so did the
men of the *Pinta*, until the thunders of that paean of thanksgiving hung like an incense above the empty sea.

At sunset there was more than the usual fervour in the
singing of the *Salve Regina*. That, too, from the prayer that
it had been, became this evening a hymn of gratitude to the
Virgin for having brought them safely through the perils of
the deep.

No longer did lowering looks greet Colon when he went
amongst them. Instead he was met by friendly eyes and
smiling lips, and once there was a rousing cheer, 'Long live
the Admiral!'

The Admiral! Oh yes, Admiral and Viceroy. These were no longer shadowy, anticipatory titles. Yonder in that hazy coastline lay the substance that made them real by the letter of the capitulations.

Back in his cabin he went down on his knees before the Madonna on the brass panel, to return thanks for a success which he attributed to her favour, and with his devotion in that supreme hour forming part of it almost, was the thought of Beatriz, of the pride and share that should be hers in this triumph, and of the blessings which out of the power and wealth now almost in his grasp he would shower upon her when he returned, by when she surely would have been found. If he saw himself already the greatest man in Spain under the King, he saw her set high by him and by association with him. It brought an added exultation to the hour.

His mind overheated, he spent a restless night, whilst the *Santa Maria* resounded with the rejoicings, the carolling and laughter of the men.

Towards dawn, by when the hands, grown weary of merry-making, were dropping off at last to sleep, the ship grew quiet again. Colon rose, and half-dressed came forth as one of the boys was extinguishing the poop lantern.

He stepped out upon the deck as upon another Pisgah, to rejoice in the sight at nearer quarters of the Promised Land.

Looking forth, the exultation oozed from him, and in a nausea of dismay he clutched the rail. The horizon was empty. Cloud masses which had melted in the night had duped them once again, and Zipangu was still as much to seek as ever.

29

COLON's first active emotion when his soul had recovered from the shock of that disillusion was one of anger at having been misled into changing course. Acting upon it he hastened below to the helmsman, thrust him aside, seized the tiller and brought the head of the caravel to bear westward once more.

'Keep her there,' was the short harsh command with which he left the startled seaman.

Coming up again to the quarterdeck, he became for the first time aware of the sharp pitching of the ship under his feet. The wind, he observed, had almost dropped, and the sails were slatting, alternately swelling and sagging.

Swaying to the heave of the deck he scanned the sky aft, in the weather quarter, to find on the eastern horizon a bank of sullen cloud, black with a hint of copper, coming up as a screen to the rising sun.

His sudden shout, loud and clear as a clarion call, made a stir among the sleepers below. To the several who were instantly afoot his orders were sharp.

'Aloft, there, and shorten sail. Stir yourselves. Take in every sheet on the main yards. Some of you to the mizzen, and clew it up. Hasten!'

The heave of the ship was increasing with every moment, and a passing sidelong glance showed him the sea lifting in long, oily rollers. Then his attention was drawn to what was happening in the waist, where all were by now awake and astir. A clamour of anger and dismay was rising amongst the men. Ires had leapt upon a hatch-coaming, and thence, as from a rostrum, was screaming blasphemy and incitement.

'Fools! Poor deluded fools! The land has vanished. It was never there. It was a mirage. We've been the dupes again of Fata Morgana. Of Fata Morgana and this Don Cristobal who is sailing us all to perdition. Up, you poor dupes! There is no land. I tell you there never will be land on this crazy course. We must make an end. We must put the ship about.'

It needed only this to bring to overflow for Colon the cup of that bitter awakening.

Men gathered themselves up to stare in dismay at that empty horizon. Others came aft from the forecastle to join them, and in a moment, where all had been peaceful slumber, there was now a press of men raging and ranting in this extinction of the glad hopes in which they had sunk to rest.

Led by Ires, a dozen or so of the hardier rogues came surging aft, with the proclaimed intention of taking charge of the helm.

Colon stood alone to stem the rush, armed with an iron belaying-pin which he had plucked from the rack. 'Back, you rats!' he thundered. 'Back!'

But Ires, intoxicated with fury and the pride of leadership, advanced undaunted, a dozen paces ahead of the rebels.

Colon swung the belaying-pin, and the Irishman went down with a broken head, his long body offering a momentary obstacle to those who followed. A moment later, Aranda, with Cosa, Brito the barber-surgeon, the steward and a couple more who joined them as they came, fell with fists and cudgels upon the rear of the mutineers.

'Avast, you dogs! Give way!' Aranda barked at them, as he smote and smote again. 'Give way!'

In a moment the waist of the caravel was a scene of raging battle. Colon's belaying-pin smashed the arm of Gomez as that broken hidalgo was brandishing a knife, and it sent another of his assailants rolling in the scuppers. From the forecastle and from the quarters astern, others came pouring into the fray, and soon there were few hands aboard that were not committed to it, on one side or the other. Numbers, however, were heavily with the mutineers, and to Colon it seemed only a question of time before he and those who remained loyal would be overpowered. He fought on, nevertheless, with the strength and ferocity of a lion, using his improvised battle-axe at once to parry and to strike.

Aranda, too, was wreaking savage havoc with his own lads, who had been prompt to rally to him. Gradually, however, they were being forced back to the forecastle, and for some instants Colon, with his back to a bulkhead, stood alone. Then Ximenes, with one Sanchez, a sometime gentleman of the King's bedchamber, whose fortunes had fallen into disrepair, and some four other gentlemen adventurers, brought their swords to the fray. They were men with sense enough to perceive that whatever might happen to them with Colon, the odds were that without him all would perish. By the intimidation of their blades they now clove a way through the press to the Admiral's support. They reached him, turned and formed a screen to cover him, easily holding off the unarmed rabble that assailed him. One of these swordsmen was felled almost at once by the blow of an oar. But the seaman wielding it paid instantly, for even as the oar descended, another of the adventurers, lunging on his flank, ran him neatly through the body.

Colon turned his belaying-pin into a projectile, and hurled it into the mass of the assailants, then stooped to pick up the fallen man's sword. Thus armed, and astride of the stunned adventurer, so as to shield him, he plied his blade with the rest. But although their backs were protected by a bulkhead of the poop, these swordsmen without body armour offered a barrier too frail long to resist the weight of the onslaught. And meanwhile the pitching of the ship was increasing at every moment, although in their frenzy it was scarcely noticed by the men who swayed and reeled to it as they fought.

Suddenly the stern of the *Santa Maria* was lifted so steeply that the bowsprit was under water, and the entire throng in the waist, assailed and assailants alike, went hurtling forward in a confused heap of writhing, cursing, battling men. Those who did not tumble over the hatchways were brought up sharply against the bulkheads of the forecastle, to be drenched by a cataract that poured over the bows. Colon, who had instinctively clutched a rung of the companion, found himself suddenly alone at the summit of a steep, empty deck. Thus a moment. In the next the bows rose as sharply, and the human avalanche came rolling back. The stunned and the conscious, the wounded and the whole poured torrentially down that precipitous declivity, to bring up with a bruising crash against the break of the poop.

By a leap up the companion at the last moment, Colon was no more than in time to avoid being crushed by that helpless, hurtling human mass.

A sudden short-lived puff of wind, bellying the mainsail, served to steady the caravel's recovery, and in that moment Colon, his seaman's experience supplying an understanding virtually instinctive, had grasped the situation.

The long oily rollers had grown longer and steeper. Astern of them the western sky was now all black with that sullen hint of copper, and the sun was completely obscured. Clutching the rail with one hand, whilst he still brandished the sword in the other, he let his voice ring out.

'Attention! On your lives!'

It needed no more to hold those men, who were gathering themselves up, already filled by the caravel's behaviour with a sense of imminent peril. Panic stilled all thought of turbulence. Every eye was turned for direction to the man at the poop-rail whom a moment ago they had been bent upon destroying. The very sight of his tall presence there imposed a check upon their fears, brought hope of wise direction, and eagerness for very life's sake to obey as he might command.

His orders came sharp and clear, repeating those which he had issued earlier, but which had been disregarded. 'Aloft, and shorten sail!'

A dozen hands, ignoring bruises, sprang instantly for the ratlines on either quarter. His voice whipped them on. 'Take in every sheet on the mainyards.' Seeing that in train, he shouted for the boatswain. 'Jacinto! Four hands here to the mizzen. Clew it up. You others, there, see that the hatches are tight battened. Cosa! Get the foresail reefed. Leave no more than a trysail for steering way; not another rag.'

Again he cast a glance over his shoulder at the metallic horizon. 'Hasten! Hasten!'

There was no need to spur them. Those amongst them who were real seamen, all mutinous thought abandoned in this urgency, went feverishly to work. They had outridden storms before; and given a commander they could trust, they would face the ordeal as a normal incident of their trade. Aloft in the shrouds, clinging precariously, their hold shaken by the pitching of the ship, they went resolutely about the reefing

until the *Santa Maria's* poles were bare. The adventurers and
the mere riff-raff, to whom every storm must be the harbinger
of potential shipwreck, were huddled white-faced about the
forecastle, looking on in helplessness at this arming for a
battle very different from that which they had lately waged
and which at least had been within their understanding.

Colon's next order concerned them. It was to Aranda,
bidding him herd them into their cramped quarters where
they would be out of the way and under cover.

Astern an irregular white line of foam, sweeping swiftly to
overtake them, marked the coming of the gale, and scarcely
had the last of the sailors dropped from the rigging to the
deck than it struck them with an impact as of a solid mass.
The *Santa Maria* reeled under the blow, dipping her bows to
receive a flood of water and, as she righted again, rolled like
a dog that shakes itself.

From his station at the rail the Admiral conned her, whilst
Cosa, his head bleeding from a gash he had taken in the fight,
came staggering aft.

The storm was closing rapidly about them, the sky, now a
solid black pall overhead, intermittently shot with the jagged
fire of lightnings. A torrential rain descended to add to the
waters that were breaking over the caravel and pouring in
fountains from the scuppers. Under this and the rolling boom
of thunders the *Santa Maria* staggered on with groan of timbers,
rattle of blocks and creak of straining cordage.

Away on the starboard beam the outlines of the *Pinta* and
the *Niña*, with bare poles, were barely visible through the
shroud of rain. Though but half the size of the flagship, yet
it remained that they were steadier and handier, and that
under the experienced handling of the Pinzons they should
outride the hurricane more easily than the *Santa Maria*. However that might be, in the *Santa Maria*, the seventy lives

aboard her and the jeopardy of his great enterprise, there was for Colon responsibility enough.

He came down the companion, holding fast, and meeting Cosa at the foot of it, he dispatched him to the surgeon to get his head bandaged, bidding him have a lifeline run the length of the waist, to enjoin upon Aranda that order be maintained in the forecastle, and then to see that the watches were strictly kept and that in each there should be at least two reliable helmsmen. But because in such a sea as by now was running there was no helmsman he could trust implicitly, when a momentary negligence through lassitude or stupidity might result in the caravel's being swamped and pounded to destruction, he went, himself, to stand on guard over the man at the whipstaff, so as to ensure that the *Santa Maria's* head be held steadily in the wind, and shifted promptly as the wind might shift.

It was only now, when all was done that at the moment could be done, that in what had occurred in this storm which had overtaken them and was tossing the little ship mercilessly from crest to mountainous crest he perceived, not indeed the dread visitation that it was to every other soul aboard, but a divine intervention to rescue him from a deadlier peril. Had the storm delayed long in breaking over them, it must have come too late to save him. The mutineers, vastly outnumbering those who were sane enough for their own sakes to be loyal, must ultimately have overwhelmed him, and even had Colon not forfeited his life in the struggle, his enterprise would have been wrecked beyond repair.

Never so much as in this hour — perhaps never in reality until this hour — did he see himself, indeed, the instrument in the hand of God that he had not hesitated to boast himself to the Salamanca doctors. This dreadful tempest so timely sent for his salvation was a sign to him of the Divine favour;

this raging turbulence of the elements that reminded scoundrels of their immortal souls and set them whimpering prayers for mercy, inspired him to devout thanksgiving.

So whilst the lightnings crackled in the blackened sky, the thunder boomed, the fierce blasts of the hurricane screamed through the shrouds, and the green combers broke in roaring torrents over the bows and swept through the waist of the groaning, tortured ship, Colon, beside the scared helmsman, swaying to the ceaseless heaving and sinking of the deck, returned thanks from a full heart to his protectress the Virgin for this succour sent in the form of torment.

His calm had the effect of subduing the terrors of the seaman at the whipstaff, just as his vigilant presence and his timely hand, ever ready if the vessel's head fell away ever so slightly, were of reassurance and comfort.

At the end of some two hours, another seaman, sent by Cosa, came reeling aft, clinging to the lifeline so as to save himself from being swept away. It was a timely relief, for the man at the helm was in danger of succumbing to the strain, and in the last half-hour the Admiral's hand had gone with ever increasing frequency to his aid.

As the newcomer reached them, a heave steeper than any that had gone before flung him into the Admiral's arms, and the two of them almost went over together. At the summit of the perilous lift, when half the ship was riding upon empty air, the caravel yawed away from her course and heeled over, so that for an instant her starboard gunwale was all but awash, and it needed not only Colon's promptitude, but all his weight upon the whipstaff to bring her head up again.

'Jesu Maria!' the helmsman had wailed in the dreadful moment when he felt the rudder resisting him.

'You're tired, Juan,' was all that Colon said to him. 'It is time you were relieved. Go now, but tell Master Cosa to send me the carpenter and two likely lads at once.'

The helm was surrendered to the newcomer, with an admonition from Colon to keep her steady, and when presently those he had summoned had battled their way aft, he ordered them to make a yoke for the helm by seizing a block to either side, and reeving two falls through each. With this tackle the control became an easier matter, and the yawing which lately had placed them in such peril would not easily recur.

There was not aboard a single man acquainted with the sea who had not in that dread moment bethought him of his prayers, conceiving that a little more and the caravel must founder. It presently brought Cosa, his head now bandaged, aft once more. Standing at Colon's elbow he had to shout so as to make himself heard above the crash and roar through which they reeled.

'I feared that the ballast would shift when she all but rolled over. If it had we should all be with our Maker now. And it's a miracle that it didn't.'

'A miracle. As you say. It's all a miracle.' Colon's lips were close to the pilot's ear. 'The ballast is our danger still. The lack of it. We've consumed most of it: the wine, the water, and the victuals. But we still have the casks. We're riding too light.'

He turned to the carpenter, who had been fixing the tackles. 'Fetch me the boatswain and a dozen hands of the watch.'

When they came he sent half of them down to the hold by a scuttle hatch alongside of the helm, to pass up all empty casks and barrels. In a measure as these reached the deck, he dispatched the others two by two to the waist, to fill them with sea-water, and then, when sealed, to roll them back. By a sling from the yardarm they were lowered back into the hold, there to be stowed by Cosa's directions, and made secure with coigns by the carpenter and his mate.

It consumed much time, and it was not accomplished with-

out some bruises and the loss of three casks that were swept
overboard whilst they were being filled. But it was done at
last, and to some extent this addition to the ballast served to
steady the furious pitching of the caravel.

Throughout the operation, and whilst directing it, the
Admiral had remained at the helmsman's side ever vigilant,
and there, after he had dismissed the boatswain and his crew,
he continued all that day, without nourishment beyond a
draught of mulled wine brought to him by a solicitous steward.
Nor at nightfall did he leave his post, and the following daybreak still found him there. Through every change of watch
during that dreadful night, he had been ready to repair or
correct any fault in the steering, and to direct the helmsman
in every one of the frequent if slight shifts of the gale.

Twice in the course of the night, Cosa had come aft, offer·
ing to relieve him, accompanied once by Aranda to add his
own exhortations to the pilot's. But the Admiral remained
inflexible. He could trust himself, he said, with the help of
God to bring this ship through the ordeal, but he could trust
none other.

Throughout the second day, again, it was the same. There
by the helmsman he kept his vigilant place, and more than
once in those sudden shifts of the wind it was his vigilance
alone that averted disaster. He seemed to possess some sense
that warned him of the coming of those shifts so that he was
always ready for them when they actually occurred.

Not until the late afternoon of that second day did the
tempest begin to ease. The rain ceased, the wind abated, and
green seas no longer surged up to meet and engulf the *Santa
Maria's* bows and break in deluge over her. If her timbers
had creaked ominously, at least no seam had parted, and
not a spar had gone. Gradually the wind continued to
diminish, until by nightfall, although the seas were still run-

ning high, it had become no more than a steady breeze from
the east. Only then, when in a clearing heaven the stars
were becoming visible, did Colon, grey-faced and blear-eyed
from lack of sleep, relinquish the ship to the care of Cosa,
and wearily mount the companion to his cabin on the poop.
Before entering it, he took a last look at the sky and the sea.
Less than a quarter of a mile ahead he could just make out
the other two vessels of his squadron, each already with a
spread of foresail, rising and falling on the long rollers. They,
too, had come safely through, well handled as he knew they
would be.

He glanced down into the waist. It was filling with the
men who thirty-six hours ago had been seeking his life. They
came creeping from shelter, thankful to be alive, weary themselves from their awed vigil, and with all thought of mutiny
battered out of them, realizing that they owed their survival
to the man they had set out to destroy. Thus the more devout
amongst them may have perceived in the storm as much a
divine intervention for their salvation as Colon had considered
it for his.

Within his cabin, the Admiral's first act was to go down
once more upon his knees before his little picture of the
Virgin, to return thanks for the protection which had brought
the ship named in her honour safely through the perils of the
storm. Then, peeling off his sodden doublet and kicking off
his shoes, the exhausted man flung himself dressed as he was
upon his red-draped bed, and was instantly asleep.

He was visited, he tells us, by a vision, which we, however,
need regard as no more than a dream. The image to which
he had prayed became extended to full length and grew under
his eyes to the proportions of life. Quitting the brass panel
hanging on the bulkhead, it floated to the foot of his bed,
with hands outheld.

'Sleep in peace, Cristobal,' it said, 'for I am with you, watching over you.' But the clear pitiful eyes, and the dark lips that smiled divinely, were become the eyes and lips of Beatriz.

30

 THE LANDFALL

Ｉᴛ ᴡᴀѕ high noon of the morrow
before Colon awakened from that long sleep of utter exhaustion. But at last he returned to consciousness restored in
vigour.

From the stern windows he could view the sea flooded now
with sunshine and once more calm.

Garcia, the steward, brought him food, and he broke his
long fast, his hunger mitigating the unsavouriness of the fare.

Soon Cosa came seeking him, so that they might plot their
position and convey it to the other ships. It had to be largely
a matter of guesswork, for during the storm there had been
no dead reckoning.

Coming afterwards on deck, he found the air balmy, with
a steady breeze that droned in the full spread of sail. Aboard
all was quiet. Order had been restored in the gear above
deck which the storm had battered and smashed, whilst some
that had been lost had already been replaced from their store
of spares. That had been the work of the boatswain and
carpenter with their crews. Other repairs had called for the

skill of the barber-surgeon, for between the storm and the fight that had preceded it a good deal of human gear had suffered damage.

The western horizon, towards which they continued to steer, remained as empty as ever, which now exercised Colon more than the crew. This had fallen into a sullen listlessness, as if the endurance of the tempest and the emotions it had stirred in them left them too exhausted even for resentment.

Tunny were again sporting about the ship, and again a flight of small birds passed overhead, going ever in the same southwesterly direction. Don Rodrigo Ximenes, coming to the companion, drew the Admiral's attention to them.

'If we had not seen so many already,' said the hidalgo, 'I should guess that we were nearing land.'

'You may guess it with confidence,' the Admiral answered him. 'For there goes a heron, and that's a bird that never strays far out to sea.'

He stated as a fact what was no more than another guess, although based upon a reasonable probability. Certainly he could not recall having seen a heron out of sight of land on any previous voyage.

His answer reached the ears of three or four men who were busy splicing rope, and set them staring in excitement at the slow, rhythmic flight of the great grey bird.

Later that day they saw a pelican, and later again the quick, flapping flight of a duck, which they regarded as a still more definite harbinger of land. But a more positive sign than any was a green bough laden with berries which a man fished out of the sea that afternoon with a boathook. At about the same time in the boat from the *Pinta*, which had been hove to so as to allow the flagship to overtake her, Martin Alonso came across bringing a length of cedar which he had picked up. He was bluffly affable and able to render

a good account of his ship after the storm, and in the conviction, from the signs, that land must be near, he renewed his
plea that they should stand more to the southwest.

Still, however, Colon would not yield. Zipangu, he insisted,
lay ahead to westward. He asserted it ever as if with definite
knowledge, and after Martin Alonso had ill-humouredly
yielded to his obstinacy and departed again, Aranda, who
was with the Admiral on the poop, ventured to ask him upon
what he based his certainty.

'Certainty?' Colon laughed, using with Aranda that frankness into which none other could draw him. 'My only certainty is that if I go zigzagging about the ocean I may miss
every island it contains. A straight course at least holds out
the promise that sooner or later we must make a landfall
somewhere.'

'Let me pray, then,' said Aranda, 'that it may be sooner
rather than later; for the hands are only temporarily pacified.
These signs have raised their hopes again. God help us if
they should again prove to be delusions.'

The sun went down that evening in a golden glory and
into an empty sea, and the *Salve Regina*, intoned as usual
aboard, was rendered by the crew with all the melancholy of
a *Miserere*.

Afterwards in the starlit night the crew below could see
Colon's tall figure intermittently appearing in black silhouette
against the poop lantern, as he paced restlessly to and fro.

Suddenly he checked, stepped to the rail and gripped it,
peering forward into the gloom. Immediately below him
shadows were moving.

'Olé!' he called down to them.

'What is it, Don Cristobal?' It was the voice of Ximenes
that answered him.

'Come up here.' Excitement vibrated in his voice. 'Who
is that with you? Come up here, both of you.'

Ximenes came up promptly, followed by his companion,
that Sanchez who once had been a gentleman of the King's
bedchamber.

Colon's grip was like steel upon the arm of Don Rodrigo.
'Look yonder. Straight ahead. In line with the bowsprit.
Tell me what you see.'

Peering forward, Ximenes beheld in the distance a point
of light, and said so.

'Ha! Yes. A light. I was afraid to trust my eyes. It is
either a lantern or a torch. It is being waved up and down.
Do you see?'

'I see. I see.'

Colon turned. His habitual calm had entirely left him. He
was trembling with excitement. His voice quavered. 'See,
Sanchez! See! Look!'

He was pointing in the direction of the waving light. It
vanished, however, in that instant, and Sanchez was too late
to see it.

'But it was there, as Don Rodrigo saw,' Colon insisted.
'And that light was on land. On land! Do you understand?'

'Assuredly,' Ximenes agreed. 'It must be so.'

'Land at last,' the Admiral panted. Then he commanded
himself, and sent his voice reverberating down the ship in the
stillness of the night. 'Land! Land ahead!'

The *Santa Maria* awakened to the cry. Sleepers in the
waist began to stir, and the gradually rising hum grew swiftly
into a clamour, in which men demanded more precise news.
Ximenes and Sanchez went down to tell them what had been
seen. There was no more sleep that night aboard the flagship. There was excitement and there was hope, but there
was little faith. Too often already had they been deluded,
as the rancorous Ires, nursing his broken head, actively reminded them.

'A light, forsooth,' he mocked. 'And a moving light that vanished! To the Devil with that. Why, one night the whole sky blazed with lights, and no one was fool enough to suppose they shone on land. Don't chatter to me of land. We've done with land. We'll never see land again this side of hell; not so much of it as will bury us true Christians.'

There were too many who gave heed to him. But with the rising of the moon, some two hours after midnight, came revelation. They were roused to observation by the booming of a gun from the *Pinta*, and there ahead of them, not more than two leagues distant, they beheld in the silvery radiance the unmistakable dark loom of a coastline that filled the horizon.

Upon a silence of fearful incredulity followed a roaring cheer that was mingled presently with hysterical laughter and even with sobs. Land, which so many of them had thought never to see again had, as it were, crept upon them stealthily in the night.

Then pilot and boatswain passing briskly amongst them summoned hands to obey the Admiral's order to take in sail so that they might lie hove to until daylight.

On the poop Colon, with a swelling heart, kept a tireless watch, impatient for the coming of day, to disclose to him whether this was the Zipangu of his quest where gold was used for roof tiles, or some island outpost of that auriferous land. In the need for companionship, which great joy, like great sorrow, demanding to be shared, imposes upon a man, he had summoned Aranda to his side.

'Whatever land this may be,' he said, 'I am vindicated. That which the wiseacres and doctors in Spain accounted a dream is proven a reality. To find it I have been for years the scoff of sages, constrained by ignorant mockery to sue cap in hand, like a beggar in a church porch, for the alms that would enable me to enrich a crown by great possessions. But longest laughs he, Vasco, who laughs last; and future ages shall laugh with me at the Salamanca doctors who pronounced me an impostor.'

He laughed in high boyish glee, his normal reserve cast off in a joyous excitement such as comes to few men once early youth is overpast.

'Tomorrow, Vasco — nay, this very day — I shall fully have earned my title of High Admiral of the Ocean-Sea and my viceroyalty of lands of which the coastline is yonder. They shall abate their scorn and bend their necks to me, those gentlemen of Spain who accounted me a needy foreign mountebank.'

Then his eyes suddenly clouded with wistfulness at the thought of Beatriz, and from his soul he sent up a silent prayer that Destiny might crown his triumph by permitting him to bear it to her.

 THE DISCOVERY

Leading the way for the squadron, and under a full spread of sail, so as to take the light airs of morning, the *Santa Maria* groped her way into a wide bay of amazing beauty, where like a towering green cliff beyond a wide belt of silver sand rose a mighty forest in which strange birds screeched and fluttered, glittering like winged jewels.

In the chains stood a seaman, heaving the lead and calling the fathoms, a measure almost unnecessary, for so crystal clear was the water that the eye could sound it.

At eight fathoms the anchors were let go, and there was the movement and rattle, first of taking in sail, and then of swinging out and launching the boats in slings from the mainyards.

Colon on his quarterdeck pondered the scene with fevered eyes. The trees beyond that beach upon which the waves broke with a mere silken rustle were of a size such as he had never seen. Palms that were strange to him filled the foreground intermingled with aloes of lily-like blossoms, some white, some scarlet. Behind this fringe rose the gigantic forest, in which he identified pines, but of colossal proportions, and trees which he might have supposed great elms but for the calabashes they bore, which he conceived to be a fruit. Amongst them, disturbed by the clatter and splash of the anchors, flitted those strange birds of fantastically brilliant plumage.

The October air, tepid as that of May in Andalusia, came to him laden with unknown perfumes; in the pellucid waters about the ship he beheld fishes of incredible colours. All were indications that he was come to a land of enchantment. He realized already that this was no more than an island, nor could he suppose it yet to be the Zipangu of his aims. He must regard it as an outpost of Asia, one of the thousand isles to which Marco Polo alluded. Zipangu must lie farther west, with the mainland of Cathay still farther.

As he stood there entranced he beheld human figures appearing on the beach. They were emerging from the forest, all of them stark naked, lithe, light-coloured shapes, but little duskier than most Spaniards. Taken with all the rest of that strange scene they came to persuade the amazed Colon that his discovery was not merely of new lands, but, indeed, of a new world.

He issued short orders to Aranda concerning those who were to accompany him ashore, and whilst they made ready he, too, re-entered his cabin to buckle on back-and-breast of burnished steel, to gird himself with his sword, and to don a cloak of bright scarlet camlet, so that he might do ceremonial justice to so mighty an occasion. In this splendour, and bearing the royal standard, he went over the side to the boat that waited manned by an armed crew. The notary Escovedo, the master-at-arms Aranda, the pilot Cosa, Ximenes, Sanchez and one or two others followed him, whilst from the *Pinta* and the *Niña* came the Pinzons, each with his following.

The first to step ashore, Colon knelt and kissed the earth;

then, still on his knees, with his following kneeling behind
him, he uttered a short prayer. Whilst this was doing, the
boats pulled back to the squadron, so as to bring others of
the crew ashore.

When some fifty of them were assembled on that beach,
the Admiral passed ritualistically to take possession in the
name of the King and Queen, his Sovereigns. He set up the
royal standard between those of the Pinzons, which bore a
green cross and the crowned initials F and Y. Next he drew
his sword, and pronounced the words of simple magic which
bestowed the name of San Salvador upon this island called
by the natives Guanahani, of a group — as he was yet to
learn — known to them as the Lucayas.

The deed recording on that Friday the twelfth of October
its incorporation in the dominions of Ferdinand and Isabel
was drawn there and then by Escovedo, who came equipped
for the task. To this deed the chief amongst them set their
hands in witness under that of Cristobal Colon, the Admiral.

And meanwhile the concourse of natives had been increasing. Gradually, in silent amazement, they emerged from cover
and drew ever nearer to these strange beings, borne to their
shore in the bodies of those vast birds that had now furled
their white wings. Some of these Indians — as Colon miscalled them, conceiving himself in the Indies — were armed
with spears that were mere sharpened staffs; but in none of
them was either fear or hostility to be observed. For, as the
Spaniards were to discover, fear and hostility were as alien to
these savages as was the acquisitiveness that marks civilization
and is responsible for so much of its fear and hostility. Personal
property was unknown among this people, who held in common the simple possessions of their needs, so generously yielded
them by the fruitful earth.

From this and their friendliness, a friendliness reflected in their soft-spoken voices and gentle, liquid eyes, Colon may well have come to wonder whether this new world might not be an Eden, and an Eden in which there had been no Fall, since these happy islanders were not under sentence to earn their bread by sweat. Those who now approached the Spaniards were, with a single exception, males and young, of a good height and athletic shape, well featured with lofty brows and fine eyes. Their hair, straight and coarse, was cut to a fringe across their foreheads, but left long enough to hang to their shoulders behind. Their faces were entirely beardless, the bodies of some were painted with stripes of various colours, black or white or red; others confined the paint to their faces, chiefly to the noses and round the eyes. Some few of them wore in their noses gleaming plates of yellow metal, which at a glance was to be recognized for virgin gold.

Advancing, they prostrated themselves before these strange beings with white hairy faces and curiously shaped coverings of various colours to their bodies, most of them armoured like turtles. It required no great discernment to perceive that the chief god among these gods was the tall light-eyed man in the brilliant scarlet mantle, particularly as the climax of the ceremony of taking possession closed in acclamation of him and prostrations to him by some of his followers.

These were men who had been prominent in the mutiny, Ires amongst them. They may well have feared that in the hands of one who was now a viceroy de facto, yielding a sovereign authority that included the power of life and death, and this in a land so plentifully supplied with convenient trees, they might be called to the grim account which mutiny imposes. So those unruly ones went humbly down upon their knees before him, confessing their fault with every outward sign of contrition, and imploring his merciful forgiveness.

The Lord High Admiral of the Ocean-Sea and Viceroy of this New World was, you conceive, in no hanging mood that morning. He dispensed a liberal forgiveness, imposing upon them as a penance the emptying and scouring of the casks that had held their sea-water ballast, and the replenishing of them with fresh water from the island.

Dismissing them on that, Colon faced the ever-increasing throng of natives, and by his friendly smile and gestures encouraged them to approach. If the words he used were unintelligible, at least his tone of gentle benignity was not to be misunderstood.

In each hand he held up a couple of hawk-bells, and as he agitated them the liquid eyes of the savages lighted with amazement and pleasure at the melodious tinkle. He bestowed them upon a couple of the lads who stood nearest, and had the amused satisfaction of beholding them go bounding off transported by delight at the merry music that now accompanied their movements.

A stalwart young islander, coming close, took the sleeve of the Admiral's doublet between finger and thumb to feel its texture. Next he pressed his fingers hard against the Admiral's cuirass, his eyes puzzled. Whilst he was doing so Colon fitted a cap of scarlet wool over the man's straight hair. Over the head of another he flung a necklace of coloured beads. Then he beckoned forward the solitary female in that throng, a beautifully shaped, sleek brown girl whom no paint disfigured, and with his European notion of a gift that would be pleasing to a woman, he bestowed upon her a little circular mirror. She stared at her reflection in it, at first with awe at a supposed effect of magic, and then with laughing glee. After that, whilst he and his Spaniards continued to be objects of unrestrained friendly curiosity and investigation, he carried on a distribution of hawk-bells and beads until his little store was exhausted, all to the mounting joy of those gentle, simple creatures.

One passing untoward incident marred the idyll, and appropriately it was the debauched Gomez who was responsible for it. For the enlightenment of an islander who, perplexed, was fingering his scabbard, Gomez drew his sword and displayed it to him. The savage seized the glittering blade, instantly to let it go again as the blood spurted from his hand. There was a sudden recoil, and the first display of dread at this evidence of the easy power to wound and perhaps to slay that was wielded by these strangers.

Only the Admiral's visible sternness, and the offending Spaniard's cringing under the reproof of it as he returned his blade to its sheath, effaced the momentary evil impression.

Most of that day of days was spent ashore by the adventurers, savouring the strange luscious fruits and the cakes of rather insipid but wholesome cassava bread which the Lucayans brought them. What else the natives possessed they also freely brought in token of their hospitable goodwill. But they had little to offer besides their spears, balls of cotton yarn, the value of which Colon was quick to perceive, and their tame parrots, queer, gaudy birds that puzzled and even startled the Spaniards by their raucous voices and apparently human speech, which seemed to argue the possession of human brains.

Interesting as everything was to Colon, of particular interest were the plates of virgin gold that so many of the Lucayans wore in their noses. Here was the indication of the presence of that metal, to whose abundance in these parts Marco Polo bore such emphatic witness. Fingering the plates he sought by signs to elicit from their owners whence the metal was derived. He gathered from them that it was chiefly produced from some land away to the south, which naturally he supposed to be Zipangu. Meanwhile, perceiving his interest in

these pieces of metal, the savages freely bestowed several of
them upon him. He received them in earnest of the rich
harvest of gold to be reaped at Zipangu, towards which he
must press on.

They lingered, however, on San Salvador for another day,
making a survey of the island, by coasting in their boats along
it to the northwest. As they proceeded islanders appeared to
greet them. Some came swimming out to them, displaying
in their amphibian ease a new marvel to the Spaniards. Others
paddled to escort them in canoes that were dug from single
tree-trunks, some of them so enormous as to carry fifty men.

Strange tropical flowers and fruits and birds of dazzling
plumage, the noisy parrot ever predominating, continued to
arouse their wonder; they breathed an air that was laden
with a spicy fragrance, but nowhere did they see animals of
any kind.

In token of the Spanish possession of the land and of the
conversion of it to Christianity which was to follow, Colon
set up a great cross conspicuously on a headland. Thereafter,
their water casks being filled, they took them aboard together
with a supply of wood, and that same evening weighed anchor
and stood out to sea, to resume the quest for Zipangu. They
carried off aboard the flagship seven of the men of Guanahani,
and might have taken more had they yielded to all who were
eager to go with them.

In order to render intercourse with these Lucayans easier
than by the present vague methods of pantomime, their
education in Spanish was begun at once. First each part of
the body was touched and named in Castilian, until the
Lucayans, grasping what was intended, repeated the sounds;
then came Nature's features, such as the sea, the land and
the trees; after that they passed to objects of general use.
The Lucayans proved quick and apt, their comparatively

virgin minds so receptive that within a few days simple ideas were easily conveyed and exchanged. They were also taught, parrot-like, to recite the *Paternoster* and the *Ave Maria* and to make the sign of the Cross, all of which they learnt so readily and with such manifestations of delight that Colon conceived in them a predisposition to become good Christians.

On the day after leaving San Salvador they cast anchor off another small island, which in vegetation and inhabitants reproduced all the features they had seen already. This, which Colon supposed one of the thousand isles that Marco Polo places to the east of Cathay, he named Santa Maria de la Concepcion.

Sailing on, standing now to westward, they overtook at sea a single naked Indian in a canoe. They took him aboard together with his craft, in which they found a calabash of water and a cake of cassava, with which he had provided himself for his voyage. From the fact that he bore a string of coloured beads, Colon guessed him to be travelling as a news-carrier, bearing word to other islands of the strange advent among them. So that the Indian might report upon them in a manner calculated to ensure them a welcome, the Admiral took him to his cabin, regaled him with honey, bread and wine, and then overwhelmed him with gifts: a red cap for his head, more beads for his neck, and hawk-bells for his ears. After that his canoe was hoisted out again, and he was permitted to depart.

It resulted from this that when, having lain hove to for the night, they came on the morrow to the largest island yet found, the natives swarmed about them with gifts of fruit, and yams and balls of cotton yarn. Ashore here they found the first elements of a primitive civilization, associated however with the same gentle simplicity. Whilst all the men and the majority of the women went naked, yet a notion of clothing existed amongst the latter, some of whom wore aprons woven of cotton. Their dwellings were in the shape of wigwams, fashioned of branches and thatched with reeds and palmetto leaves, and in the cotton nets in which they slept the Spaniards found a space-saving utilitarian article worth adapting to European usage under its Indian name of *hammock*. Here too they found the first animals they had seen in the Lucayas: a breed of dogs that did not bark but were as companionable to man as those of Europe; the tree coney, which the Indians called the utia; and the great lizards, five or six feet long, known as iguanas. These last the Spaniards were to find eminently edible once they had conquered their repulsion of their reptilian appearance, and their apprehension that the beasts might be armed with a poisonous sting.

In this island, which Colon named Fernandina, and in a neighbouring one which he named Isabella, they lingered for some days, hourly discovering fresh natural beauties, and ever more deeply impressed by the astounding fertility of the land. Upon each, to mark its appropriation to Spain, Colon set up a cross.

He gathered specimens of its tropical vegetation, herbs and spices; but of gold he could find none beyond the rudely wrought ornaments which were freely yielded to him.

His Lucayans by now had made sufficient progress in Castilian to answer the simple inquiry where this metal was to be found in quantity. They conveyed that it abounded in a land to the south which they called Cuba, and in another to the east of that, called Bohio. He thought he understood from what else they sought to tell him not only that gold and spices were among the produce of those lands, but that ships came from afar to trade there. It was a rash interpretation of what they strove to say, but it supplied once again a persuasion that this Cuba of theirs was, at last, the Zipangu of his quest, and thither he now laid a course.

Touching at various islands on the way, and finding each more beautiful than the last, they came on the twenty-eighth of October, just over a fortnight after making their first landfall on San Salvador, within sight of the loveliness of Cuba, with its lofty mountains, stately forests, and a coastline that spread east and west to the horizons.

Anchoring in the mouth of a noble river, he took possession with the usual ritual, and named the island Juana in honour of Prince Juan, to whom his little Diego was now a page.

The beauty and fertility of this new discovery exceeded all that they had yet beheld. That its inhabitants were not in the same state of primeval innocence as those met hitherto they suspected from the circumstance that none showed themselves. If the Spaniards had learnt anything at all in this New World, it was that fear has no place in a state of innocence; and that fear was an emotion with which this island was acquainted, they perceived when upon going ashore they found that all the inhabitants had taken flight, leaving their huts deserted. These huts were grouped into villages, and were built more solidly than any hitherto seen elsewhere. Rudely carved statues and gaudily painted wooden masks suggested rudiments of art among this people. Fishing appeared to be the main pursuit of dwellers along the coast, for in every hut they found hooks, harpoons and nets woven from the fibre of the palm tree.

At every step the extraordinary and brilliant fecundity of the land disclosed itself to their enchanted eyes in the fact that whilst some trees were in blossom, others were already laden with fruit. Parrots and green woodpeckers abounded, hummingbirds hovered over the great scented blossoms, and once a flock of scarlet flamingoes startled the adventurers by their unnatural flaming appearance against the sky.

They sailed westward along the coast of this island, which

in length exceeds that of England and is but little less than
that of England and Scotland combined; but they never
reached its westward end because from two of the Lucayans
who were aboard the *Pinta* Pinzon understood that this was
the mainland.

A little bewildered by these assertions, the Admiral nevertheless was not to be persuaded that he was here upon the
coast of Cathay, and it is probable that he would have continued westward had not his own Lucayans made it plain
beyond misunderstanding that gold was to be had in quantity
from Bohio, an island to the east. At the same time, if this
should, indeed, be the mainland of Asia, then somewhere
inland should be the dominions of Marco Polo's Grand Khan.
To resolve the matter, he dispatched into the interior a party
which included that Hebrew linguist Torres and two Indian
guides, one of whom, a native of San Salvador, was already
able in a rudimentary manner to act as an interpreter; the
other came from one of the Cuban villages with which the
Spaniards had by this time contrived to establish relations.

Whilst they were gone upon that errand Colon continued
to sail westward on his voyage of exploration along that lovely
coast, without, however, coming in sight of any end to it.
He turned back at last to the river of his first anchorage, there
to await the return of his envoys. When they came they
reported failure to discover the object of their quest. They
had penetrated some miles inland, and found a large village
with greater signs of civilization than hitherto beheld, set in
delicious groves and amid wide plantations of maize. They
had been well received and entertained, and among curiosities
observed they reported a habit of using burning brands, which
the Indians called tobaccos, made up of weeds wrapped in a
leaf, the smoke of which they inhaled, discovering in it a
stimulus that conquered fatigue. They had found, however,

no signs of wealth, beyond that of the stupendous fecundity of the soil, which, whilst ultimately it might prove as productive a source of riches as any other, was not quite the kind of wealth they sought as a beginning. Of gold they had discovered no sign, but they, too, brought back the tale that it was to be found in plenty on the great island of Bohio.

So Colon weighed anchor and they stood off to the northeast, carrying with them a half-dozen Cuban youths and as many of their women.

32

WHATEVER else Martin Alonso Pinzon may have gathered from his Lucayans in addition to the error by which he would have misled Colon, it was something that abruptly took him off on a quest of his own without the Admiral's leave.

This happened in late November, when, meeting with contrary winds and a rough sea, Colon, conquering impatience, decided to put back to Cuba. Going about, he fired a gun, and signalled to the other two vessels to follow. Vicente Pinzon was prompt to obey him with the *Niña*. But the *Pinta*, ignoring his repeated signals, held to her course. Even after night had fallen, and the *Santa Maria* lay hove to, the Admiral continued to signal with lights from the masthead. Nevertheless, when day broke, the *Pinta* had vanished completely from the sea.

So deliberate a departure in disobedience to clear command made Colon uneasy. It revived in him all those old misgivings and mistrusts of Martin Alonso, which necessity alone had compelled him to stifle. He had read this wealthy, experienced merchant-mariner for a man as domineering and ambitious as he was undoubtedly able, whence came that reluctance to admit him to a share in an enterprise of which he might take undue advantage whenever the chance offered. Had he now, Colon asked himself, perceived the chance, and seized it? Had he gone off on an independent search for Zipangu, to enrich himself with the treasures of it, and perhaps return at once thereafter to Spain, to claim for himself the credit of the discovery? It was an ugly suspicion as well as a disquieting one; but Colon accounted himself justified of it by the unscrupulous craft with which Pinzon had intrigued in Palos to obtain for himself the coveted part in the enterprise.

Whatever Martin Alonso's aim, however, it would have been idle, in view of the superior sailing speed of the *Pinta*, to attempt to overtake him even if the Admiral could have been sure of the course that he was steering. So, despite his indignation and misgivings, which he did not even trouble to communicate to Vicente Pinzon, Colon pursued his eastward voyage in a manner leisurely enough to permit him to continue the survey and charting in the direction of the coast of Cuba. Thus they were in the first week of December before he reached the easternmost end of the island, which, if Martin Alonso's inferences had been correct, would be the eastern end of Asia.

He sailed on without determined course until they sighted the loom of mountains to the southeast, and then headed for a land that once again surpassed in beauty all those that he had yet discovered. Well might he account it so, for this was Hayti, one of the most beautiful islands of the earth.

He went ashore, took possession with the usual ritual, named the island Hispaniola, and on a headland above the harbour in which he had cast anchor, which he named Port Concepcion, he erected the usual cross.

It was at once apparent that he had come to a land more populous than any yet visited, a land not only of extensive villages, but of connecting roads and other signs of social systems. As in Cuba, incipient civilization appeared to have introduced fear amongst the natives, for, again, the appearance of the ships was as a signal to the Indians to forsake their coastal dwellings and seek safety in the interior.

The Spaniards had been exploring the land for close upon a week without being able to approach any native, when one day, in giving chase to a party of islanders who fled before them, they captured a young woman and brought her to the Admiral.

Such civilization as the inhabitants of Hayti had developed had not yet reached the point of imposing even rudimentary garments, and this girl, who was beautifully made and no darker than would be a Spanish woman who had similarly exposed her skin to the sun, was completely naked.

In her terror she struggled wildly in the arms of her captors, using tooth and claw, and struggling she was brought aboard and taken before the Admiral. She was by then approaching exhaustion, and she cowered panting at Colon's feet, where her captors deposited her.

He beckoned forward one of the Lucayans, and bade him convey to her that they were good people and intended her no hurt.

Taking courage from this assurance from a man of her own race and seeing other Indians apparently on friendly terms with these pale hairy strangers, she dared at last to look up at the splendid, strangely bedizened being who stood over her. She must have found his aspect benevolent, gentle the smile on his white handsome face and soothing the voice in which he addressed her, for all that his language might be incomprehensible. Gradually her fears were allayed, and she sat up with her legs tucked under her, and took stock of her strange surroundings. Even the grinning bearded men who stood about ceased to frighten her. She was induced to go with Colon and the Lucayan interpreter to the Admiral's cabin, where he spread for her a little feast of bread and honey that she relished. Whilst she ate her large, dark, liquid eyes gazed in wonder at each of the cabin's queer furnishings. The Lucayan youth, squatting on his hams on the stern locker, jabbered gaily, conveying to her the Admiral's assurances that presently she would be set ashore again.

On her side there was no longer any anxious haste, and having eaten she moved in childish innocence about the cabin, peering at and fingering everything that she saw.

In dismissing her at last, Colon delighted her with a gift of coloured beads strung into a necklace, and hung a hawk-bell in each of her ears. She departed in laughing, childish glee, rowed ashore by Spanish sailors and accompanied by two Lucayans who, under her aegis, were to go as ambassa-dors to the people of Hayti. Colon's best ambassador, how-ever, was the girl herself. Her account of the marvels seen and the entertainment received brought the inhabitants in their thousands to the beach upon the morrow, to pay their homage to these beneficent beings from the skies.

They led Colon and a party of Spaniards inland, through a vast luxuriant forest, to a great village of upwards of a thousand houses, and there they spread a feast for them of fish, cassava bread and the strange succulent fruits of a land so bountiful that it required little cultivation.

Having in this fashion, at once shrewd and happy, set afoot relations with the inhabitants of Hayti, Colon extended them widely in the course of the next fortnight. He spent the time cruising along the coast of that great island of enchantment, and wherever he put in it was to be courted by the islanders, who flocked about the ships in their canoes, some of which were dug out of enormous trunks of the great mahogany trees. The Indians came laden with offerings of provisions and fruits, and in the course of that progress the Admiral collected no little store of gold. Ornaments of the precious metal were here so common as to proclaim its abundance in the land. With these ornaments the Haytians parted freely, and whilst seeking nothing in return — for, as elsewhere in these blessed lands in which all things were enjoyed in common, they were without any notion of traffic — they were overjoyed if they received a few beads or a hawk-bell.

Various caciques were among those who came to pay homage to the strangers, whom they regarded as more than human. One of these, borne in state in a rude litter on the shoulders of four men, was the Admiral's guest to dinner on board the *Santa Maria*, his attendants seated at his feet, his manners gravely ceremonial. At parting he presented the Admiral with a belt and two plates of gold.

Elsewhere the flagship was visited by an embassy from a still greater cacique, named Guacanagari, bringing a curiously wrought belt and a great wooden mask, the eyes, tongue and nose of which were of solid gold. These he followed up by gifts of pieces of gold and two tame parrots. He was ruler of the greatest city they had yet seen, in the northwest of Hayti, and not only was a more advanced art displayed here in the construction of the houses and an ubiquity of carved statues, but the inhabitants possessed some notion of clothing themselves, and whilst the majority still went naked, many, including the cacique himself, wore rudimentary garments woven of cotton.

To satisfy the interest in gold displayed by the Spaniards, the Haytians in their propitiatory eagerness let it be known that there was abundance of it in the island, especially in an eastern region which they named Cibao, whose cacique's banners were wrought of that metal.

It took no more than this to convince the Admiral that Cibao was no more than a corruption of Zipangu, and that in that eastern region he would find the treasures of which Marco Polo spoke. In quest of them he weighed anchor on Christmas Eve, steering eastward. But the goal was never reached, for that night he was overtaken by a disaster destined to arrest at this stage for the present the extent of his discovery.

They were lying hove to, a league or so from land, and because the night was calm and the sea as smooth as silk, not only did the men of the watch, but the helmsman with them, careless of Colon's standing orders, lie down to sleep, leaving the helm in charge of a mere boy.

The sea, however, was not so motionless as appeared. An unsuspected current bore the *Santa Maria* imperceptibly landwards, nor was the boy warned by the boom of the surf. Suddenly with a thudding scrape the caravel was aground, and held fast in a tumult of swirling waters.

It awakened the Admiral, who came in haste from his cabin, and might yet have saved the ship had he been better served.

He ordered the watch into the boat, to carry an anchor astern, by which to warp the vessel off. Cosa commanded that boat crew, but in his extreme anxiety, instead of implicitly obeying Colon, he rowed off to the *Niña*, a mile away, so as to enlist her added assistance. The delay was fatal. By the time help came the *Santa Maria* was beyond helping. The thrust of the current had set her farther upon the bank and had swung her partly across the flow, there to be helplessly pounded by the breakers. Her seams were opening under the strain, and she listed gradually until her larboard gunwale was awash and the sea pouring into her.

There was no more to be done until daylight, and, as it proved, nothing to be done then. The little caravel that had carried Colon across the Atlantic was irretrievably lost. It remained only to salvage what they could, and in this work they spent that Christmas Day, stoutly assisted by the friendly Haytians with their canoes, and availing themselves of the huts ashore that the Haytians placed at their disposal.

They began by unloading all the gear, weapons and other moveables from the ship. Later on, when they came to consider their future, and how it was affected by the shipwreck, and to perceive that it was impossible that all should return home in the little *Niña*, it was decided to build a fort that should house those who must be left here on Hispaniola until another expedition should come out from Spain.

They built solidly, using the timbers of the wrecked ship, and for protection against all comers they erected emplacements for the guns which had been salvaged. Of the need for these, however, there seemed little likelihood in a land over which peace and amity held such absolute sway.

They had the assistance of the Haytians, and Guacanagari himself did all to promote not only the work but their general well-being, signifying his regard for Colon in daily gifts amongst which there were gold plates and gold coronets and another of those wooden masks, of which in this instance the eyes and ears were of gold.

Every day new offerings of gold in the form of plates or in dust came as tokens to the Admiral of the island's great wealth. But he was no longer impatient to trace it to its source. Of its plentiful existence he had proof, and that for the moment must suffice. His impatience was to be gone. At the root of it lay the continued absence of Martin Alonso and the daily strengthening suspicion that this self-seeking collaborator had perhaps already set out to recross the ocean with the news, so that by forestalling Colon he might garner for himself the glory of the achievement.

Nor was this really the end of Colon's anxieties. The return voyage of the *Niña* alone, the smallest of the ships that had sailed from Palos, was fraught with more peril than for all his maritime audacity he could face with calm. If he were lost, his log, his charts, his elaborate journal would be lost with him, and if, as might well befall, Martin Alonso too, sailing alone, should be lost, nothing would ever be known in Spain of the discovery; it would be assumed that the fate prophesied by the wiseacres had overtaken the expedition and that Colon had been destroyed by the unchallengeable forces of an ocean that marked the confines of the habitable world. His name, instead of blazing in the lustre that would await it once he were safely ashore in Spain, would remain the synonym of a foolish dreamer, a presumptuous charlatan; and the men he was compelled to leave on Hispaniola, these first colonists of this New World of his discovery, would also be the last. They would live out their little lives in this pleasant land of plenty, and so pass out of all human knowledge.

Among his followers, however, with no disturbing vision of this, there was no lack of those who were willing to remain and devote some portion of a lotus-eating existence to the exploration of the island and the discovery and perhaps the working of the gold mines that must indubitably exist upon it.

Despite his deep reluctance to part with him, he appointed Vasco Aranda to the command and government of the two-score men he was leaving at La Navidad, as he had named the fort, in commemoration of the fact that he had suffered shipwreck there on Christmas Day, the Feast of the Nativity. As Aranda's lieutenant he appointed Ximenes, and with them he left Escovedo as the representative of the royal treasury, to receive and keep account of the gold that might be mined or collected. Among the others were craftsmen necessary to that embryo colony, a carpenter, a cooper, a smith, a tailor and a gunner, as well as a surgeon who had sailed in the *Niña*.

By the first days of January all arrangements were completed, and on Friday the fourth, Colon weighed anchor and stood eastward towards a towering promontory that he named Monte Christi. A strong headwind, however, retarded progress, and they had not sailed far along the coast of Hispaniola when on the sixth they sighted the missing *Pinta*.

If her unexpected reappearance surprised Colon and at the same time allayed his worst misgivings, both at the fear of being forestalled by Martin Alonso and of having to cross the ocean in one only, small and none too seaworthy vessel, it did not suffice to appease his indignation at the insubordinate manner in which Pinzon had left him.

The *Pinta*, riding before the wind with a full spread of sail, swept down upon them at speed; and in order to receive explanations, Colon ordered the *Niña* to be put about and run with the *Pinta* back to the bay under the headland of Monte Christi, where there was safe anchorage.

At the head of the short entrance ladder Colon was waiting for Martin Alonso when he came aboard the *Niña*. Vicente Yanez Pinzon, suspecting perhaps that his brother would need support in his rendering of accounts, had placed himself at the Admiral's elbow.

Martin Alonso stepped aboard with a lift of the hand and a smiling greeting. 'God save you, Admiral, and you, Vicente.'

Colon's countenance remained sternly set. 'Well returned at last,' he answered, coldly formal. 'It will be well to know where you have tarried, and why.'

Pinzon maintained a boisterous joviality. 'We'll begin with the why, which was outside my wishes or responsibility. The *Pinta* was driven by stress of weather.'

'Driven to windward. That is something new in sailing.'

'I accounted the coast dangerous. The booming frothing of
the surf suggested reefs. We knew nothing of the currents,
which together with the wind might have borne us to disaster.
So I held to windward, away from the land, as you yourself
were doing when last I saw you.'

'Only so that I might continue my signals to you to go
about. Why did you not obey them?'

'Your signals? May I die if I saw them.'

'What ailed your eyesight, and that of your crew?'

'You forget that the daylight was fading and that it was
misty.'

'Aye, aye, so it was,' interjected Vicente.

'And your ears? Were you deaf as well? I fired a gun to
warn you.'

'You did?' Martin Alonso's eyes widened in surprise. 'The
sound must have been lost in the booming of the surf.'

'You've an answer for everything,' Colon told him.

'I hope so, Admiral.' Pinzon smiled insolently into the
stern face. 'And as I gather that the *Santa Maria* is lost I
would seem to be justified of my greater caution.'

'It was not through going about then that I lost my ship.
She was piled up on a reef at night in calm weather by the
carelessness of a helmsman.'

'In calm weather! There's proof of how right was my judgment that the coast is dangerous. But we are wasting words,
Admiral. You've no cause to repine. The voyage I made
was not unprofitable. I discovered a bay farther to the east,
and a river which I have named the Martin Alonso. I took
formal possession of the land, and I collected there a good store
of gold in earnest of all that it may yield.'

Darker grew the Admiral's brow at this usurpation of his
own prerogatives.

'What do you tell me, sir? You took possession of lands on Hispaniola when I had already taken possession of the entire island in the name of the Sovereigns? That is of no effect. There is nothing to record. And then you bestow your own name upon a river! That also is of no effect. A singular presumption. I'll say no more of it.'

But now at last Martin Alonso's manner changed. The colour darkened in his face. 'Where is the presumption?'

'Indeed, where?' Vicente supported him. 'If he discovered it, was he not within his rights to name it?'

'With his own name? Where in all this New World of my discovery do you find a single piece of land or water that I have named Cristobal Colon?'

Martin Alonso stood silent, aloof, whilst his brother continued the argument. 'It was yours to do so, Admiral, had you wished.'

'Had I wished! Should it be my wish to brand myself an impudent fool?'

'Sir!' cried Martin Alonso, stung to the quick.

'Are there not our princes to supply names for these new lands, and when these are used have we not the Lord and His Saints to keep us in names forever? Enough! You shall chart me this river, and we will name it suitably. You found good store of gold, you say. What have you done with it?'

Less and less at their ease were the Pinzons.

'The half of it I bestowed upon my men. The other half I have retained, and this I am ready to share with you. It's a share,' he added, as if thereby he hoped to tempt Colon, 'that will come to close upon a thousand pesos.'

Colon was not deceived into supposing the offer other than made on a sudden inspiration, so as to propitiate him by a bribe into a more amiable attitude. He did not, however, incline to amiability. He smiled crookedly upon Martin Alonso.

'You had not heard, then, my enactment that all gold shall
be regarded as the property of the Crown.'

'Oh, yes. But then I, too, have an interest in this property.
You are not to forget that my contribution to the expedition
entitles me to one eighth of the profits.'

'And so you help yourself to what you please, without
waiting until the profit is ascertained. A humorous notion of
trade, sir.'

Martin Alonso sought to save his face by sarcasm. 'I am
grieved to merit your censure.'

'I am grieved that you do. As for the gold, that may wait
until we reach Spain, when I shall trouble you for a strict
account of it. We are now bound thither. But first we'll take
a look at this river of your discovery.' He was sarcastic in his
turn. 'This River of Martin Alonso.'

They reached it on the morrow without further acrimony
in the meantime, Martin Alonso having returned to the *Pinta*,
and Vicente preserving a sulky submission to the Admiral.

Colon went ashore to make an exploration, in the course of
which he announced that the river should be known as the
Rio de la Gracia. That was a small matter, however wounding to Martin Alonso's pride. It was on a graver one that the
Admiral went aboard the *Pinta* later in the day.

The natives here had proved unusually shy on the approach of the ships, as shy as they had been on the first appearance of the Spaniards off Hispaniola and before word of their
benignity had spread through the land. From one of his Lucayans Colon was to learn that this was because Pinzon had
violently seized and carried off four men and two girls. It
was this that took him aboard the *Pinta*.

His tone was uncompromising. 'What is this they tell me of
violence to six islanders, seized and held here by you against
their will?'

Pinzon's simmering resentment boiled over. 'What then? Do you presume to question even my right to take a few slaves?'

'To whom have I conceded such a right?'

'To whom? God of Heaven! Have you not a dozen Indians even now aboard the *Niña*?'

'Not as slaves. Not taken by force. All have come willingly. Throughout I have studied, as I have enjoined and as you should know, to treat the Indians with gentleness, so that they may consider us their friends. Because of this I have been able to leave forty men behind at La Navidad without misgivings. But you by your violence teach them that all Christians are not good. You teach them not to trust us, but to beware of us. A mischievous folly, for which, with your other insubordinations, I should be justified in hanging you out of hand.'

There was a sneer on Martin Alonso's livid face. 'It is what I deserve for having raised you to the honour in which you now stand.'

The retort robbed the Admiral of breath for a moment. Then his words came in a rush. 'You have raised me to honour! You! Saint Mary! I thought the summit of impudence was reached when you gave your name to a river in Hispaniola. I did not think you could exceed it. But it seems you can. Enough!' He was sharp and peremptory. 'Bring me these captive Indians of yours.'

Martin Alonso stood squarely before him in defiance. His broad proportions seemed to swell. 'To what purpose?' he demanded.

'Bring them.' Colon's eyes as coldly menacing as they were steady met Pinzon's glance and held it during a long moment in which the master of the *Pinta's* hesitation was reflected in the deepening malignity of his countenance. He could depend upon the support of his brothers, and fully half the men

aboard the ships were men of theirs, who would stand by the
Pinzons if it came to a trial of strength. Caution, however,
reminded him in time that if he were to lead a mutiny against
the Lord Admiral of the Ocean-Sea and Viceroy of the Indies,
a grim account would be asked of him once they were back in
Spain.

So in the end with a contemptuous shrug he lowered his
glance and yielded. 'The reckoning will follow later,' he said.

'Depend upon it,' Colon answered him, his voice hard.

He, too, recognized a stalemate between them. He no
more dared provoke a complete rupture because of its immediate consequences than Martin Alonso dared provoke it
because of the ultimate ones.

The six youthful captives were brought from the hold.
They cowered under the glance of the tall Admiral in a
piteous fear before which his sternness was instantly cast aside.

They could not understand what he said, but he spoke so
gently, his hand was so caressing as it stroked their dark heads,
that they were partly reassured. Under the malevolent glance
of Martin Alonso, he took them over the side to his boat, and
so aboard the *Niña*. There he gave them bread and honey
and a little wine, as he had given it to other Indians whom
he desired to comfort. He found a couple of shirts as garments
for the girls, hung beads on their necks, and sent them happily
ashore restored to liberty, to spread a tale of Spanish benevo-
lence.

33

 HOMEWARD BOUND

THE homeward voyage began in mid-January. For a fortnight they steered a northeasterly course, perhaps in the hope of discovering that belt of easterly wind, the possibility of which he had been constrained to imagine so as to allay the anxieties of his crew before the persistent westerly direction of the wind on the outward voyage. Whether he considered the easterly wind which he eventually found in thirty-eight degrees of northern latitude as a proof that he had guessed correctly, or merely as a fortunate circumstance, we do not know. Anyway, he found it and took advantage of it, steering directly east.

Up to the moment of departure from Hispaniola, everything observed or learnt of the discovered regions went to confirm Colon's conviction that these were the uttermost confines of Asia. Two additional pieces of evidence came from those who had sailed with Martin Alonso. They had heard of an island called Martinino which was inhabited solely by women, and of other islands tenanted by a race called Caribs or Canibs, who ate human flesh. Marco Polo told both of

Amazons and of human-flesh eaters off the coast of Cathay.

He heard of other marvels not mentioned by the Venetian traveller, such as a race of men with tails, dwelling in a remote part of Hispaniola, and some fresh marvels he beheld for himself before he left the coast, such as mermaids who heaved themselves up in the water to view the ship from a distance. He was in no such danger from them, however, as that which compelled the Ithacan voyager to have himself lashed to the mast by sailors whose ears he had taken the precaution of stopping with wax. There were no songs of irresistible seduction from the sirens of the Caribbean, nor were they of a loveliness to cause men to hurl themselves into the sea so as to perish in their embraces. Indeed, we gather from him that Colon found these sea-cows — which is what, in effect, they were — of an almost repulsive aspect, for he expresses the opinion that the beauty of sirens had been greatly exaggerated by the ancients.

More welcome to the mariners were the abundant tunny, many of which they caught and took aboard for food, of which their store was none too plentiful.

In contrast with the outward voyage, which in the main had been so calm and pleasant, the return was to prove one long battle with elements that almost daily threatened their destruction.

For three days of mortal anxiety in the middle of February, when they drove through the worst of those persistent storms, with poles bare of all but a trysail for steering way, they expected every moment to be their last. At every pounding surge of the mountainous seas that broke over the frail and leaky little *Niña* the forty men who were crowded aboard her looked to see her founder under their feet. Great as was their faith in the uncanny seamanship of which Colon had given proof, they felt, as he felt himself, that for their deliverance from these perils something more was needed. So vows were made, of pilgrimages to be undertaken should they survive, and Our Lady's protection was invoked by an offering to go in procession in their shirts, candle in hand, to attend a Mass of thanksgiving at Santa Clara de Moguer, near the port of Palos.

Colon's earlier anxieties touching the loss to Spain of the fruits of his discovery and the fate of the men left at La Navidad were now acutely revived. What he could to ensure against it he did. He contrived, despite the tossing and rocking of the little ship, to write a brief account, containing no more than the essentials. He enclosed it in a waxed cloth, this in a cake of wax, and this again in a barrel which was cast overboard, with a prayer that it might somewhere reach land, and so eventually come to the hands of the Sovereigns, to whom it was addressed. In it he prayed Their Highnesses that since he himself would be beyond the reach of reward, they should apply such recompense as they accounted that he deserved in accordance with the direction he had left with Don Luis de Santangel in provision for the eventuality of his death. The pension which should come to him as the first man of the expedition to have sighted land he desired should go to Beatriz Enriquez.

With a conscience eased by the thought that he had now done all that lay within his power, he resumed control of the navigation in the hope of yet riding that crazy little ship through the raging storm.

Aboard the *Pinta* Martin Alonso was applying all his skill to that same grim task. As darkness descended on the evening of the fourteenth of February, such was the fury of the wind and the wildness of the water that he had little hope of surviving the night. A half-mile or so astern of him he could still descry the *Niña* in the waning light. He watched the smaller

ship as she faced each steep acclivity of dark water, paused
shuddering on the crest, and then went lurching down into
the trough in a flying spume of the waves that broke over her.

Thus until the curtain of night, black and starless, had
blotted her completely from his view. He clung to a lifeline,
swaying to the heave of the deck under his feet, and spoke to
his brother, who was beside him. He shouted into his ear, so
as to be heard above the howling of the wind through the
shrouds and the crash and roar of waters against her timbers.

'I doubt we've seen the last of the *Niña*.'

The younger Pinzon was confirmed in the gloomy need to
make his soul as best he could without the help of a priest.
'D'ye not think we'll live the night, then?'

'Only by a miracle, and God knows I can think of having
done nothing to deserve one. But my mind is on the *Niña* and
Vicente. The miracle with her is that she has not already gone
to pieces. Leaking like a basket, every buffet of these cursed
waves must be starting a fresh seam in her. She'll be at the
bottom before dawn. God help Vicente.'

'God send you're wrong,' Francisco answered him. 'Besides Vicente, there's a deal of gold aboard her.'

'The Admiral will need it to buy water in hell.'

And so it seemed when daylight came again. The *Pinta* was
still afloat, though waterlogged, with the men taking turns at
the pumps and toiling at them like galley-slaves. But on all
that wide waste of grey-green water there was no sign of the
Niña.

Martin Alonso, heavy-eyed and haggard, his garments
sodden and stiff with brine, had never left the deck throughout
that awful night, and had kept his brother beside him, thinking perhaps that drowning would be easier for them in company.

'I was no false prophet,' he gloomed, when the light was

strong enough to enable them to scan the sea. 'The Admiral's gone, and he's taken our Vicente with him. God rest their souls!'

'Is it impossible that we should have been driven apart?' asked Francisco.

'How could it be possible? We have been driving before the same wind with bare poles. There's no hope. If she were still above water we must be still together.'

They looked at each other in dejection, their grief at the loss of their brother mitigated perhaps in the perception that a like fate might still await themselves in this raging gale.

But the *Pinta*, if small, was of a solidity of build and in good seaworthy condition saving her mizzen mast, which in any case they would not tax with sail whilst the wind held any strength. She rode out the tempest, and when two days later in weather grown comparatively calm, the Pinzons took stock of their position, they began to discover compensations for the loss sustained; so much compensation, indeed, that if they had not had a brother to mourn, they must have counted it a gain rather than a loss.

'Since the *Niña* has gone,' said Francisco, 'the discovery of the Indies becomes our own.' He made it as a plain statement without any hint of exultation.

'It had occurred to me,' Martin Alonso admitted, with the same restraint.

'It is lucky that we have a couple of Indians aboard, a goodly amount of gold and some other odds and ends to show them in Spain.'

Martin Alonso nodded. 'All the evidence we need.'

This was all that passed between them on the subject until a fortnight later, when the *Pinta* came safely to anchor in the waters of Bayona. It was by no means a happy landfall, and they might have done better had not Martin Alonso been ailing in those days, and forced in most of them to keep his cabin. The less experienced Francisco had held too far to the west, and so had missed his way.

Now, however, that they were safe and snug in this Galician harbour, Martin Alonso could look Fortune in the face, and see how benignly it smiled upon him. Cheered by the prospect, he seemed to recover some of the vigour which had been wasted in battling with the stormy seas and further impaired since by the racking, exhausting cough with which it had left him. The glories that had been Colon's were now within his grasp. As the surviving partner of that world-shaking expedition, he was heir to the honour due to the discoverer of the New World. For him now the office of Lord High Admiral of the Ocean-Sea and Viceroy of the Indies, and elevation to the ranks of the hidalguia of Spain.

There might be arguments about it. King Ferdinand was too thrifty a man to dispense gifts without demurring. But after all, that close fist could be prized open. The power was Martin Alonso's. For his were all the secrets of the discovery, knowledge of the way to the Indies and the charts so gradually and laboriously drawn. A fresh expedition must be sent out to exploit the discoveries made and to add to them, to gather the wealth of which they now brought definite tokens. It was not an expedition that would consist of three poor ships, like the first that had crossed the ocean. A mighty armament would be employed, with that liberality of expenditure justified by the assurance of a rich return. It was no longer a question of chasing a dream, but of pursuing an established reality, and to this it was now Martin Alonso who held the keys.

'I shall be needed, Francisco,' said Martin Alonso, in summing up the discussion with his brother. 'If Their Highnesses should prove stingy of rewards, why I must look to make my

profit of their need of me. And I shall see to it that my profit
is not less than would have been Colon's. God rest him.'

'God rest him, indeed,' said Francisco. 'All considered,
it's a mercy he was taken. Had he lived, his arrogance might
have found ways to deny you what is justly yours.'

'Be sure he would. We had proof of it. A judgment has
overtaken him. He has been punished for his overweening
pride and grasping greed.' His vehemence brought on a fit
of coughing that almost choked him. When at last he recovered breath to resume, he went on more quietly. 'And justice
has been done to me, too. After all, was it not I who made
this discovery possible? Was it not my faith in the project
that sent Frey Juan Perez to persuade the Queen? Was it
not the credit that I pledged that found him a crew to sail
with him? Without me there would have been no discovery.
Therefore the fruits of it belong to me.'

'And Heaven,' Francisco agreed, 'has seen fit to ordain
that they shall come to you. Yet, Martin, there are men so
wicked as not to believe in divine justice.'

Thus the Pinzons argued their consciences into approval of
the opportunism of which Martin Alonso was being guilty,
and by the time he sat down at Bayona to write his letter to
the Sovereigns announcing his return from the Indies, he did
so in the conviction that all had occurred so as to single him
out for a mark of divine favour.

He supplied in that letter of his a brief account of the lands
discovered, alluded in enthusiastic terms to their extent and
wealth, and deplored in passing the loss of the *Niña* and Colon
on the homeward voyage. He contrived to convey that the expedition rendered possible by his own munificence and credit
could hardly have succeeded so signally but for the skill and
prudence he had brought to it, and he begged Their Highnesses' leave to come and lay before them a fuller relation of

the great dominions it was his honour to have added to their crown.

Having dispatched that carefully indited letter by a courier to Their Highnesses at Barcelona, where he learnt that they then were, he weighed anchor again, and put to sea for Palos.

The sea-worn *Pinta* ran down the coast of Portugal before the blustering winds of March, rounded Cape St. Vincent in the forenoon of the fourteenth, and by the evening of the fifteenth she was crossing the Bar of Saltes and heading up the Tinto.

Martin Alonso's condition had by then grown worse. But if weak in body, he went sustained in spirit by the thought of the glory that was coming to him.

In that high confidence he sailed into the port of Palos, and he was about to order the gunner who waited, blowing upon his match, to fire a salute whose reverberations should go thundering across Spain, when a sight met his eyes which drained his face of the little blood disease had left in it.

There, before him, at anchor, with bare poles and sails clewed down, rode a battered but familiar hulk.

Francisco Pinzon laid a fierce, shaking hand upon his arm. 'The *Niña!*' he cried, and in anger, forgetting for the moment that this meant the survival of their own brother, he added: 'How the devil comes she here?'

'By the Devil's aid,' rasped Martin Alonso. He waved away the gunner, whose lighted match was become a mockery. 'Take that to hell,' he raged at him, and reeled, faint and sick and shaken by coughs, into his brother's arms.

The surviving strength ebbed out of him. His faith in divine justice was shattered. His heart was broken.

He was carried ashore and up to his fine house, and there he died within the week.

34

THE HOMECOMING

It is perhaps one of the most tremendous coincidences in history that those two caravels, blown so far apart on a stormy night a month earlier, should by widely different courses and after incredible vicissitudes have come to cast anchor on the same day in the home port of their destination.

The crazy *Niña*, guided by a master-hand, had brought her leaky timbers safely into the port of Santa Maria in the Azores on the eighteenth of February. Here there was trouble with the Portuguese Governor. A score of Colon's men were arrested as they were going in pilgrimage, barefoot and in their shirts, to hear Mass, in fulfilment of the vow they had made when at the mercy of the tempest's fury. Upon this arrest followed a comedy of threats and counterthreats passing between the Governor and Colon, in which at last Colon's swagger and high tone prevailed. Once his men were restored to him, he left that inhospitable shore again to encounter foul weather. This drove him so far north that he was compelled to seek shelter in the Tagus.

Here at Lisbon there was yet another comedy to be played.
Being challenged by the port authorities, he mantled himself,
once more mounted his awful dignity, proclaimed himself
from the deck of his battered little caravel the Castilian
Admiral of the Ocean-Sea and Viceroy of the Indies, and
announced the great discovery from which he was returning.
He well knew that this would be reported to King John and
would profoundly mortify him, and he cannot have been
blind to the dangers that might follow, but these he joyfully
incurred for the sake of taunting the King of Portugal with
the glorious chance that he had missed. The magnitude of
the discovery and the stupendous wealth to be derived from
it were not diminished in the account he rendered.

The result, as he had expected, was a command to attend
the Court. He went, bearing with him his Indians, his parrots
and his lumps of gold; and his swaggering ostentation was so
wounding to the Portuguese nobles that he was fortunate to
depart again from Lisbon with a whole skin.

Before leaving he wrote a long letter to Luis de Santangel,
for submission to the Sovereigns, in which he set forth in
detail his discoveries from his first landing on Guanahani.
He described Cuba, which he had renamed Juana, as of the
extent of England and Scotland together, and Hispaniola,
which he declared to be of an acreage equal to that of all
Spain, besides the many lesser islands of which he had similarly taken possession in the name of the Sovereigns. All this
he accounted merely a beginning of the vast dominions to be
brought to the Crown of Spain. The loss of the *Santa Maria*, he
explained, had interrupted his exploration, and he had
deemed it well to return and render an account of what so
far he had achieved. He dwelt upon the wealth of the lands
he had found, in gold without limit, in pearls and spices,
cotton and many other inestimable products. He described

the incredible fecundity of the soil, and the docility of the
race of men who inhabited those regions, in whom Their
Highnesses would find ideal subjects ready for conversion
to the Christian Faith. He spoke of the specimens he would
lay before Their Highnesses in some slight attestation of the
marvels he reported.

For Don Luis alone he added that he would sail for Palos,
where he would look for news of him, praying that there might
also be some word of Beatriz, without which there would be
little joy for him in his achievement.

Sailing from the Tagus on the thirteenth of March, he
reached the mouth of the Odiel on the morning of the fifteenth.

Until noon that day he stood off and on, waiting for the
tide, so as to cross the Bar of Saltes. As the little caravel rode
there with the Admiral's pennant trailing from her mizzen,
she came inevitably to take the eye of folk ashore. At first
they were merely the ordinary inquisitive idlers of the port,
who stood shading their eyes from the morning sun, to scan
the vessel. Soon, however, there was a seafaring man who
recognized her for one of the ships of the squadron that had
sailed thence seven months ago on a crazy voyage from which
none was expected to return.

In excitement the fellow passed the word. It flew from
mouth to mouth, from house to house, and the staring groups
ashore increased until all Palos had emptied itself to crowd
the quays, the beach and the dunes above them. In belfry
after belfry the bells were set ringing.

At noon, on the full tide, the *Niña* crossed the bar to an
excited clamour from the assembled multitude, and Colon
received a foretaste of the sensation which his passage henceforth was to create.

As the helm was put over and they swung into the Tinto, he
raised his proud eyes to the white walls of La Rabida, crown-

ing its promontory, where this great adventure may be said
to have begun. On the esplanade before the convent he made
out a little group of men in monkish habits, and in the foreground a portly figure that stood waving frantically.

Erect on the poop, in his rich red cloak, which he had
donned for this tremendous occasion, Colon joyously returned
the greeting of his benefactor, Frey Juan Perez.

They let go the anchor and swung out the boat. Other
boats came crowding about them, and presently Colon was
standing on the quay with most of his crew, engulfed in a
tumultuous, welcoming, questioning mob. There were men
of the port, bare-legged sailors and fishermen, aproned carpenters and smiths, caulkers, coopers and the like, and
mingling with them, no less thrilled and scarcely less vociferous, the shopkeepers, the shipbuilders and some of the more
affluent and normally sober merchants of the town. Noisiest
of all were the women. Those who had discovered menfolk
of their own among the Admiral's following hung rapturously
laughing and crying upon their necks, whilst others who
sought in vain, be it a husband, a lover, a son or a brother,
were shrill with anxious questions.

With difficulty the Admiral obtained a moment's hearing.
Reassuringly then he addressed them. So far as he could now
say, all who had sailed with him were safe. Two score had
remained in the lovely land of his discovery, so as to lay the
foundations of a colony by which all Spain would prosper;
two score were with him, as they saw; and two score were
aboard the *Pinta*, from which he had been parted in a storm
a month ago. But since the frail *Niña* had weathered it, there
was no cause to fear that the stouter and more seaworthy
Pinta would not have done the same, so that they might look
for her arrival shortly. He was, as we know, to prove a truer
prophet than he suspected.

Blessed, cheered, acclaimed, he won through the crowd, and took his way unescorted up by the path through the straggling pines that once he and his little son had trodden hand in hand to the Convent of La Rabida.

As he approached the esplanade Frey Juan, moving with all the speed his gown would permit, ran to meet him and embrace him, glowing with the pride and joy of a father in a victorious child.

'Come with God, my son! Here to my heart. We have heard the news already of how fully you have justified Spain's hope in you.'

'Spain's hope!' Colon laughed. 'Faith, the fingers of one hand suffice to count the Spaniards who believed in me. The rest of Spain, including your junta of learned doctors, accounted me a madman.'

'My son,' Frey Juan protested, 'is this an hour for bitterness?'

'Bitterness! I have none. That is for abashed unfortunates who are without retort. I come to cast a New World into the lap of Spain in answer to her scoffings. Should I, then, be bitter?'

35

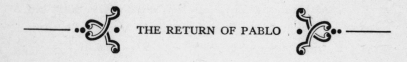

THE RETURN OF PABLO

IT HAPPENED that at about the time that Colon was tasting the first sweets of victory, at the risk of his neck, at the Court of the King of Portugal, a man was landing from a fishing-ketch at Seville in whom even his sometime intimates would not readily have recognized Pablo de Arana. A black beard unkempt and untrimmed clothed his gaunt, hollow cheeks. His black hair was tangled and matted. Abject of appearance, he was clothed in the odds and ends which he owed to the charity of the fishermen who had pulled him naked from the sea a fortnight earlier.

Venetian patience having been exhausted of its hopes of securing the Toscanelli chart, had sent Pablo to expiate his offences against God and man at the bench of a trireme.

The galley to which he was assigned had been detailed to convey an illustrious personage to the Court of the Spanish Sovereigns at Barcelona, when it was caught in one of those storms that seem to have swept all the seas of the world in the early part of that year 1493. The vessel was driven out of its course, to be ultimately capsized and lost.

With the strength of terror, Pablo de Arana had wrenched from the deck the staple to which he was chained when the vessel was in danger of foundering. When adrift, after the galley had vanished, and in danger of being shortly sunk by the iron links that dangled from his leg, another slave, clinging to one of the galley's long sweeps, had been cast against him by a wave. Pablo had clutched frenziedly at the loom of the great oar. Its original possessor, similarly weighted by his chain, protested that it could not support them both. Pablo agreed with him so thoroughly that he raised himself momentarily from the water on that length of timber and dealt the wretch so shrewd a blow between the eyes that, half-stunned, he loosed his hold.

'Go with God,' said Pablo to the vanishing head, and climbed to bestride the lightened sweep.

There were other survivors, struggling and wailing and clinging to wreckage in the storm-tossed sea. Pablo, who believed in minding his own affairs when he saw no profit in minding that of others, conceived it prudent to get away from these fellow unfortunates before any of them should be tempted to dispute with him the possession of the oar that was his by right of conquest. So he set himself to swim and paddle with it diligently, until he found himself entirely alone.

Then, at last, he came soberly to consider his case, and began to make the acquaintance of despair. Not only was there no land in sight, but he did not even know in which direction land might lie. The sky, out of which it was raining heavily, was so black that it was impossible to determine the position of the sun, which would have given him an orientation; and anyway, the sun must be near its setting. With the approach of night Pablo began to regard his oar as less of a plank of salvation than he had supposed it. He might by luck and tenacity live through to another day. But in what better

case would its dawn find him? He began to give thought
to his immortal soul, and even to deplore its immortality; for
perceiving in this hour of illumination the utter foulness of
his life, he had no cause to hope for any sort of bliss in eternity.
He had always supposed that when his time came to enter
upon it he would find a priest to shrive him, so that with the
comforting viaticum of absolution he might peacefully make
the dread journey. He was being cheated, he thought, of his
Christian rights, in being left to perish unshriven, with all his
weight of sin upon him to bear him down to hell. His soul
revolted at so monstrous an injustice. It was impossible that
the Divine Will could be concerned in this. A merciful God
would surely spare him, so that he might have the chance to
practise the better life that follows upon repentance. From
this it was but a stage to vow repentance and amendment if
he were spared. He sought to invoke Our Lady's pity, to
bribe Her with promises of pilgrimages to be made to the
nearest of Her shrines, barefoot, in his shirt, and candle in
hand, like the humblest penitent.

In such vows did the scoundrel spend a night of anguish,
tossed in the dark, astride his oar, from wave crest to wave
crest.

Towards midnight the wind eased; by daybreak it had died
down completely, and a ground swell of long, oily waves was
the only legacy of the storm. As the light grew, his smarting
eyes beheld a long, grey coastline. But the comfort the
prospect brought him was no more than momentary. That
land was anything from five to ten miles distant, and he could
have little hope of reaching it. Indeed, he could have little
hope of maintaining his hold upon the oar much longer.
Although it buoyed him up, the position enforced upon him
was one of strain, and already he was conscious of a fatigue
that was fast using up his strength.

Nevertheless, in his despair, he kicked and paddled himself along in the direction of that distant coast, until, as time wore on, his spells of activity were broken by ever-increasing spells of exhaustion.

It would be towards noon, by when he had undoubtedly made some progress, but by when he felt himself at the end of his endurance, that he sighted a distant brown sail between himself and the land. The wild hope it begat revived his expiring strength. Much of this he wasted in shouts that were lost upon the empty air, and in odd attempts to raise himself and wave an arm in signals which could not possibly be seen.

Destiny, however, had still some purpose to serve by means of Pablo de Arana. A breeze that sprang up from the land a landward drift of the current combined to bring the boat and the shipwrecked man towards each other. Late that afternoon, by when Pablo's senses were beginning to wander and he was scarcely able to hold his head above water, he was hauled, limp and nerveless, aboard the ketch.

As he lay inert upon the bottom boards, that were fishy and foul from a recent haul of the net, one of the men poured aguardiente down his throat, and a blanket was wrapped round him, for he was naked of all save a pair of cotton drawers. They could have no delusions about him. He was proclaimed a galley slave by the chain dangling from his leg and the wheals that scarred his back from the overseers' whips. Only the nature of the galley from which he had escaped remained undetermined, and here Pablo's mendacious inventiveness found its opportunity once he was sufficiently revived to give an account of himself.

He was, of course, a Christian martyr: a Spanish gentleman of Seville, a fighting sea-captain taken prisoner by Moslem corsairs and chained to the oar of an Algerine galley. Unable longer to endure torment at the hands of the Infidel dogs, he had staked his life on a chance of escaping, and last night, taking advantage of the storm, he had broken loose and flung himself overboard.

Commiserating eyes considered him as he sat propped against the mast, his beard and hair whitened by the salt that had dried upon them.

'Ah!' said the master of the ketch. 'But then the oar? How did you come by the oar?'

Pablo had forgotten to provide for the oar. He peered at them out of inflamed eyes.

'The oar? Oh, that!' The stiffened muscles of his face contracted in a grin. 'Why, it was this way: Driving as we were before the wind, the oars were not at work. My companions slept, and whilst they slept I unfastened the oar, lifted it from its thole-pin and cast it into the sea just before I leapt. In the dark and the noise of the storm it wasn't noticed. By the time I came to the surface the galley had vanished, swept along by the wind. And now by the great mercy of God and Our Lady, my desperate attempt has brought deliverance and restored me to Christian men.' He crossed himself, joined his hands, and raised his bleary eyes in piety to the firmament, his lips moving in silent prayer.

The three men of the ketch nodded understanding and grunted sympathy. There was more aguardiente, and after that, when he protested himself famished, they supplied him with an onion and a hunk of bread.

They knocked off his shackles, and spared him some odds and ends of garments, to which each contributed something, with apologies for having nothing better to offer a hidalgo.

That evening they landed him at Malaga, and the master of the ketch took him with his tale to the Augustinian monastery at the foot of the Gibralfaro. The good fathers received him with the fond solicitude due to one who had suffered

Christian martyrdom at the hands of the Moors. They housed him, fed him and provided him with a threadbare but still serviceable suit of patrician cut. In their charitable anxiety to restore him to his friends in the city of Seville, they offered him the company thither a few days later of a merchant who travelled with a mule train of his wares, and Pablo, committed to the fable of his Sevillan origin, could think of no pretext on which to decline the offer. Nor for that matter was he deeply concerned to decline it. Provided that he was not required to go to Cordoba, where too much was known about him, and where the Corregidor might possess too good a memory, it mattered little whither he went. For the purpose of living by his wits, which were now his only stock-in-trade, Seville was as good as any city in Spain, for not a doubt but it would harbour as many fools as any other.

If he had a regret regarding Cordoba, it was because he supposed it likely that Beatriz would have returned there, and Beatriz might be able to supply his needs. She had certainly shown herself able to do so before, and there was greater reason why she should do so now. He had a score to settle with Beatriz. It was to her that, after the fashion of his kind, he attributed all the misfortunes that had overtaken him. It was her failure to come to his assistance in Venice that had resulted in his sentence to the oar, at which he must soon have rotted and perished but for the miracle that had delivered him. She owed him amends for that, and he did not doubt that he would constrain her to make them if he could but find her. To seek her in Cordoba, however, was more than at present he dared. Later, perhaps, some channel would offer through which to discover and reach her.

In the meantime he must depend upon his own resources, and these took him little further than imposing upon the charity of well-disposed and pious persons by a harrowing tale

of sufferings in Moslem captivity and vaguely consequent loss
of fortune.

Using as capital such poor sums as his narrative ability
earned, he had recourse to gaming, for which Seville taverns
offered ample occasion. He was skilful with the dice, especially
when matched against the young, the inexperienced and the
naturally dull, and he was prudent enough to match himself
against no others. Thus he contrived to exist, but more or
less penuriously and scarcely consistent with the hidalguia
which he had assumed together with a sword and a plume to
his cap.

It was in the tavern that he frequented most, the Posada
de Palomares, near the Puerta del Arenal, that he came to
hear of Don Cristobal Colon. He heard that name casually
at first, and then insistently; for soon nothing else was talked
of from end to end of Spain. The fame of the man was spreading across Europe, and every day brought additions to the
epic tale of an achievement by which the size of the world
appeared to be increased. It was almost as if this Colon had
supplemented the work of creation. Fantastic accretions
came to swell the story of that voyage into unknown seas
in defiance of the monsters guarding it. Dolphins and mermaids were amongst the lesser creatures tenanting those
waters. Islands had been found inhabited by dog-faced men,
by men with tails, by pigmies who went on all fours and by
giants with a single eye placed in the middle of the forehead.
Strange animals, too, had Colon discovered, and amongst
them birds that could talk like human beings. Gold was as
common in that New World as granite in Spain, and there
were rivers that flowed over beds of precious stones. In
every palace, every hovel, every counting-house, every convent and every tavern Don Cristobal Colon and the world
of his discovery were in those days the only topics. His long

struggle for recognition made a fine theme for ballad-stringers, and in their rhymes the Salamanca doctors came at last under the scource of the ridicule they deserved.

Then, one day, word ran through Seville that the great man was coming, and the city was stirred to a delirium at the prospect of beholding this portent. The Sovereigns, so ran the report, had sent for him to go to them at Barcelona, and he was on his way thither from Palos, travelling by easy stages across Spain in a triumphal progress the like of which, for the enthusiasm it excited, had never yet been seen.

Feverishly Seville prepared herself to do fitting honour to this discoverer of worlds, and upon all this seething excitement Pablo de Arana looked with the disdain of a lofty mind for puerile and ingenuous emotions. What, after all, he asked, was it all about? A foreign upstart, a Ligurian of no birth, a common mariner with nothing to lose but his life, had adventured upon a voyage that had brought him to new lands. Since the lands were there, it followed that anyone sailing forth must have discovered them. Why, then, all this ado?

Some few there were whom he impressed by his lofty scorn; the majority, however, condemned it, and there were odd ones who, unintimidated by either his wolfish countenance or the length of his sword, cast it back with insult in his teeth.

That scorn, however, proved none so lofty as to restrain his curiosity when, at last, the great man arrived in Seville. In order to behold him Pablo turned out-of-doors with the rest of the city on that memorable Palm Sunday.

Seville had put on her best in honour of the hero. The streets through which he was to pass were carpeted with ramage, with fronds of palms, branches of myrtle and flowering boughs of jasmine, peach and lemon, whilst every window and balcony was hung with tapestries or gay cloths of velvet.

Even the religious houses lent themselves to this pomp.

One of the streets by which he would come ran on one side
along the blank wall of the garden that enclosed the Convent
of Santa Paula. A scaffolding had been set up in the garden,
so that the sisters might view the cavalcade over the summit
of the wall, from which panels of rose-coloured satin with
Arab embroideries in gold thread were hung.

The Prioress, disposed by a lingering worldliness to hero-
worship, had shared the common thrill when news of the
great adventurer filtered through the convent walls. It was
she who had borne the tale of it to her niece Beatriz, once a
cantatrice but now little more than a lay-sister, and a model
of piety, even to the professed nuns.

'There is news,' she had told her, 'as wonderful as any of
the achievements of the great Cid. A gallant sailor, a campe-
ador of the ocean, in a small, frail caravel, fronting the perils
of the seas had discovered a new world and added it to the
Crown of our good Queen Isabel. A feat to make us proud
that we are Spaniards.' Thus in a glow of worldly enthusiasm
the Prioress of Santa Paula.

'A new world?' questioned her niece, who sat by a window,
plying her needle.

'No lesser term will serve. It contains single islands that
are larger than all Spain, I am told, and yield so much gold
that Spain is become the wealthiest nation in the world.
Some of this wealth is to furnish a crusade to deliver the
Holy Sepulchre from the Infidel. Don Cristobal,' she added,
'is on his way from Palos de Moguer to the Court at Barcelona.'

'Don Cristobal?' Beatriz caught her breath, and turned a
frowning, questioning stare upon her tall, graceful and still
comely aunt.

'He is to pass through Seville.' The eyes of the Prioress
sparkled in her pale face under its rigid coif. 'He is expected

here on Sunday, and the city is preparing to receive him with royal honours. Santa Paula must bear its part. We must hang out our bravest broideries. Let me think now . . .'

'You said Don Cristobal.' Beatriz's voice was muted.

'Don Cristobal. Yes.' And the Prioress recited his full names and titles with sonorous relish. 'The High and Mighty Lord Don Cristobal Colon, High Admiral of the Ocean-Sea and Viceroy of the Indies.'

'God avail me!' Beatriz murmured faintly. Of a deathly pallor, she sank back in her chair, and closed her eyes.

'Why! What ails you? Are you ill, child?'

'Nothing.' Beatriz commanded herself, and essayed a smile. 'It is nothing. You were telling me . . . Don Cristobal Colon . . . Viceroy, you said . . .'

'Viceroy, to be sure. Viceroy of the Indies of his discovery. Does he deserve less? Who is there living who can claim more? Great was the conquest of Granada. But what is the conquest of a province to the conquest of a world? You see that we must all do him honour. Come and help me to choose the embroidered cloths for the occasion.'

Obediently Beatriz went, but her aunt found her unusually dull and absent-minded, and had occasion to chide her lack of enthusiasm in a matter that deserved so much.

It was odd, thought Beatriz, that she should be reproached with that, when her heart was filled with thankfulness that the Cristobal who was rarely absent from her loving, sorrowing thoughts, should have so heroically succeeded. To know of him raised to such honour almost consoled her for her loss of him, so pure and selfless was the love she bore him. It was as well perhaps that she had lost him; for what place could she find beside a man who had risen to such eminence? What could she ever have been to him but a let and hindrance in his ascent? Thus selflessness set her feet upon the path of resignation. Yet it was not a path to be trodden without pain. It was steep as Calvary, and the cross under whose weight she toiled was the bitter thought of the contempt in which he must hold her memory.

To see him again could but deepen her pain; yet not on that account had she the power to deny herself the opportunity. And so on that last day of March she was among the sisters on the platform that had been raised against the garden wall. Black-mantled like them, and with a black hood for coif, she would pass, if observed at all, for a lay-sister of the order.

From the Giralda Tower to San Marcos, soon after midday, the bells crashed forth in every steeple to announce that Don Cristobal Colon was entering the city.

To receive him at the Puerta de Cordoba, and to utter a brief address of welcome, stood the Alcalde-Mayor of Seville with a guard of honour of mounted alguaziles. A detachment of these went ahead so as to clear a way through the ever-swelling multitude in the narrow tortuous streets.

The Alcalde, Don Ruiz de Saavedra, would have had the Admiral follow at once, at the head of the procession. But Colon's instincts of showmanship gave better counsel. First let him display the evidences of his achievement, and thus enhance the climax which he would provide in his own person. Himself he marshalled the order of the procession, and the alguaziles were followed by a train of mules and donkeys bearing the exhibits he brought from the New World. Cases slung like panniers contained the gold, some in dust, some wrought into barbaric ornaments, whilst others were filled with gums and spices. A cage borne like a litter on poles between two donkeys contained a pair of iguanas, six feet long, giant lizards that drew gasps of astonishment and horror from the sightseers; in lesser cages there were utias and birds of fantastic plumage. A half-score of Colon's mariners led the beasts of burden and guarded their loads, enjoying a share in the triumph and breezily jesting with the Sevillians as they passed.

Next came the little troop of Indians, moving lithely in the blankets with which, for modesty's sake, their nakedness was mantled. The first pair displayed on poles the grotesque masks of wood and gold that had been among the gifts of the caciques to Colon. The crowd gaped in wonder at these savages, some of them with painted faces, others with headdresses of parrot's feathers and one with a gold ornament in his nose. Some carried the rude spears and the long bows that were natural to them, whilst each of the three girls bore a parrot like a falcon on her wrist.

The better to behold these fantastic beings the Sevillians craned their necks, with exclamations of 'God avail us!' and 'Jesus Maria!' Their greatest amazement, however, amounting to awe was produced by a large parrot on the wrist of a tall Indian who came last. To every scratch of the Indian's finger on the parrot's head, the bird responded with a screech of 'Viva el Rey Don Fernando y la Reina Dona Isabel!'

The Sevillians, scarcely able to believe their ears, asked themselves what manner of world was this that had been discovered in which even the birds could talk.

The Indians were followed by another group of Colon's mariners, and after these — now that the stage was suitably set for him — the great man himself made his arresting appearance. He came mounted on a white Arab with the sombrely splendid Alcade riding beside him. Erect in the saddle, in a crimson doublet that was cut square at the breast and laced in gold across the white froth of an undergarment, he was a figure of princely pride. He rode bare-headed, and a fulvid tone, which lately increasing strands of grey had brought into his naturally red hair, served to stress the patrician cast of his countenance.

The acclamations of the crowd brought a smile to his shaven lips and a sparkle to his clear grey eyes.

Passing the garden wall of the Santa Clara Convent, the stir and the waving of the sisters over the parapet of the wall's summit drew his glance upwards to the white-coifed faces.

Beatriz, who had watched his approach in wide-eyed wonder, worship and pain, caught her breath in sudden dread, and slipped behind the nearest nun, so as to be hidden from that raised searching glance.

With a hand lifted in salutation to the sisters he passed on, and she came forward again, and eagerly advanced head and shoulders, so that she might still follow him with her longing, sorrowing eyes.

It was just opposite that convent wall, as near as the crowd had permitted him to get, that Pablo de Arana had taken his stand to view the show. As the files of mounted alguaziles who made a tail to the procession passed, in the wake of Colon and the Alcalde, the crowd closed into the street's middle like water into a ship's wake, and flowed along, to follow to the Alcazar, where a banquet was to be offered to the Viceroy of the Indies.

Pablo, however, did not move with the mob. He remained, like a fixed object in a whorling stream, letting the human tide flow past him until he was left there, as it were — high and dry and almost alone, on the spot to which astonishment had rooted him, his breathing a little quickened by excitement. Then, with a sudden resolve, he plunged across the street and along the convent wall, now deserted by the sisters, until he came to the green wooden door embrased in it. He tore at the bell-chain as if he would pull it away, and listened impatiently to the clangour within.

A shutter opened behind a grating in the door, and the

wrinkled weathered face of the old gardener of the convent
disclosed itself at the Judas-hole. Cunning old eyes took
stock of the raffish air and rusty finery of this lantern-jawed
visitor.

'What do you want here?' a querulous voice demanded.

'Civility, to begin with,' snapped Pablo. 'Then you will tell
Mistress Beatriz Enriquez de Arana that her brother has come
from Italy and is here to see her.'

The gardener studied him suspiciously. 'Are you her
brother?'

'It's what I am telling you. Pablo de Arana is my name.'

'Wait there.'

The shutter was slammed in his face, and it was not until,
cursing that ill-mannered old custodian, he was beginning to
ask himself whether he should ring again that a drawing of
bolts came to end his impatience.

'Come you in.'

He stood in a fair garden of alleys bordered by clipped
myrtle hedges. Beyond a file of tall cypresses, and through
the burgeoning ramage of orange trees and pomegranates the
walls of the convent gleamed white in the spring sunshine.

Near a granite fountain set amid silver-bladed aloes Beatriz
stood waiting for him. Under the black mantle that reached
from shoulder to heel, the straight slender figure was sheathed
in simple grey without any ornament. She had cast back
the hood of her cloak, and the sunlight touched her rich chestnut hair to the hue of bronze. She was very pale, and there
was a look of strain almost of fear in the wide-set eyes that
watched Pablo's brisk approach.

'God be praised that you are free, Pablo,' she greeted him.

'Owing nothing to anyone for that,' said he.

'I am glad — so glad — that they let you go.'

'Let me go?' He laughed at her. 'Let me go to the galleys.
That's where they let me go. They and you.'

He made it plain that he came in no spirit of brotherliness. The implied reproach, however, she ignored. 'How did you find me?' she asked.

'By chance. A lucky one, I hope. God knows I've the right to a little luck. I've not found much of it yet in my life.'

She motioned him to the lichened granite seat by which they were standing. 'Tell me of your escape,' she asked him.

He sat down. 'That is soon told. The galley foundered in a storm somewhere off Malaga. I was a night and a day in the water, and all but dead when a fishing-boat rescued me. They landed me at Malaga. I pretended to have escaped from a Turkish galley, and that earned me the charity of a monastery. After a while I drifted here to Seville. Devil take me if I knew why until I caught sight of you on that wall this morning. Yet I'm not so sure that I know now. For it's a cursedly unsisterly welcome you give me.'

She had been gravely observing him whilst he spoke, considering his pretentiously raffish, soiled appearance with his sword and the plume out of curl in his hat; scanning the lean hungry countenance that had been handsome once, before vicious hard living had stamped it with its present wolfishness; heeding the sneeringly querulous speech with its assumptions of martyrdom. Once, out of loving pity, her every impulse had been to shelter and protect him. Because they were sprung from the same womb she had felt a duty to him. She had gone with him in his flight from Spain so that she might serve him at a time when disillusion seemed to have rendered her own existence of little account. She had sacrificed herself for him. So that she might provide for him in his idle, thriftless worthlessness she had allowed herself to be debased. But all this was over. Considering him now, she found him repellent, knew that he had been repellent to her ever since that day in the Pozzi when he had urged her to prostitute herself so as to rescue him from the consequences of his evil courses. In a measure — though, God be thanked, not in the full measure he had begged — it was what she had done, and because of that her life lay irretrievably in ruins, robbed of the one great chance of redemption that had been offered her.

Perhaps Pablo had ill chosen the moment of his visit. Perhaps that very recent glimpse of Cristobal, reopening her wounds, rendered all this too poignantly apparent to her. She made an effort to dissemble her distaste of him. She sat down beside him, but not too close.

'You appear so suddenly, so unexpectedly,' she excused herself. 'You take me by surprise.'

'And not too pleasant a surprise, you would say.'

'What pleasure can I take in your presence in Spain knowing its dangers to you?' This was true, yet less than the whole truth.

'Sh! What the devil!' He looked over his shoulder in apprehension, to make sure that there was nobody within earshot. Reassured, he flashed his teeth in a grin. 'There's no great danger so long as I keep wide of Cordoba. And even there it's doubtful if anyone troubles to remember. Still, as you say, I'd be safer out of this cursed land. And that's where you can help me, Beatriz.'

'Help you?'

'A man can't go on his travels with empty pockets. It's like my luck to be penniless in the hour of my greatest need.'

'I've never known you other in any hour.'

'Must you sneer at my evil luck?' He broke again into that self-pitying whine. 'God knows I've never had good fortune in all my sad life.'

'Have you deserved it?' she asked him.

He scowled annoyance. 'That comes well from you. By

my life, it does. You are to reproach me now, are you? Do
you think I don't know what I have to thank you for? Do you
suppose they didn't tell me in Venice why I was being sent to
the galleys?'

'You were sent to the galleys for a theft,' she coldly reminded him.

'Rot your pert tongue! Had you kept faith I should have
gone free. Oh, they told me. You were given a chance to do
a service to the State as the price of my deliverance. But you
cared so little for your brother that you played them false
and played me false; delivered me to death, for aught you knew
or cared. Me, your brother. Your brother! A noble, loving
sister you, Beatriz. Our sainted mother, whom God have in
His holy keeping,' he added, crossing himself, 'must have
turned in her grave at your treachery. And yet you dare to
reproach me. It's ... it's unbelievable.'

She looked at him in wonder; and the wonder grew to see
that he was not acting. He was sincere in his grievance. She
had made him very angry. The sheer unreason of it made her
angry in her turn.

'Did they tell you what it was they required me to do?
Did they tell you that so vile did I become on your account
that I actually set out to do it — that I came to Spain to
practise the arts of a decoy upon Cristobal Colon?'

'Colon! Cristobal Colon!' His jaw fell in stupefaction.
Then his face contracted in a grimace of disbelief. 'Colon?'
he repeated.

If in the heat of the moment she had said perhaps more
than she intended, she did not now retract. 'Colon,' she replied. 'I was to steal a chart from him, so as to prevent the
great discovery he has now made for the glory of Spain. That
is what I was required to do, what I came to do.' Anger made
her hoarse, blazed at him from her clear, hazel eyes. 'Now
you know.'

But as her anger had flamed up, his own had cooled. 'Indeed, I do not. You came to do it, you say. And then? What failed?'

She spoke in scorn. 'My vileness. That is what failed. That and my heart. I came to see my loathsomeness. But it had already gone far enough to ruin me. Because of you, Pablo, I have damned myself in this world whatever may be in store for me in the next.'

This, it seemed to him, could have but one meaning. Yet that was something not to be believed. He probed cautiously. 'Damned yourself? You set me riddles. You were doing this thing, and then you broke off and did not do it. Faith, to me it seems that mine was the only soul you damned by that stupidity.'

'Can't you understand? I came to care for Colon. We loved each other.'

'The devil! What are you telling me? That you were his mistress?'

She felt her colour rising under his searching contemptuous glance. 'That shocks your purity, of course.' Defiantly, in self-defence, she added, 'He offered me marriage.'

'Marriage! Lord God! Marriage! The Viceroy of the Indies!' He looked at her with widening eyes. 'You were never a liar, Beatriz, and I must believe you. But marriage! Mother of God!' Reflecting, he twirled the point of his black beard between finger and thumb. 'But why not? Why not, eh?'

'That I already have a husband is, of course, a trifle not worth remembering.'

'A husband? Basilio? Pshaw! He's as good as dead.'

'But lives.'

'On the galleys, for life. What need to publish it? You fool, Beatriz! Could you not have forgotten it and taken such a chance? We must take chances in this life if ever we are to accomplish anything. And what a chance was this! You'd be Vicereine of the Indies now, and easily able to help a poor devil of a brother. It's like my cursed luck that you should have wasted such an opportunity. Of course you never gave me a thought; never saw the difference this would make to me' — he seemed on the verge of weeping.

It made her laugh despite her pain. 'For once I did not.'

'For once? When did you ever think of me? When did you ever think of any but yourself? You left me to perish like a rat in the Pozzi.'

'Better for me had I never thought of delivering you from it.'

'There you go again. Better for you. Always yourself. Never another. Never me. And you dare to say it to my face!'

She stood up suddenly. She was profoundly affronted. He filled her with horror. She burned with shame at the thought of the intimate thing she had told him merely to provoke the selfish reproaches of a mind that could take no heed of her agony.

'You had better go, Pablo. Indeed, I don't know why you came. There is nothing for you here.'

He looked up at her in blank amazement. Never yet had she used so cold and hard a tone with him. This was proving a morning of surprises for Pablo.

'May I die, but you're a sweet loving sister. Have you no heart at all, Beatriz? I have told you that I am penniless, and you ... and you ... ' Indignation stifled him. 'It's more than a man can endure.'

'Is it money that you want? Is that why you sought me?'

'No!' he thundered indignantly. 'I came because with me blood is thicker than water; because you are my sister, and I owe you a brother's love; because I am not a cold, unfeeling fish like you, Beatriz. That's why I came.'

'I am sorry that I disappoint you, Pablo. Had it been merely money that you sought ——'

'I've said I didn't seek it. No. But I am come so low in misfortune that I cannot refuse help from anyone, not even from my worst enemy. For when it's a choice between pride and hunger, pride must founder. A neck can't remain stiff when the belly's empty.'

'I understand. Wait here.'

She left him with his thoughts, which were not pleasant. Whatever he had come for — and he could scarcely define it even to himself — disappointment was his portion. It was bitter for a man to find himself unwelcome to his own kin, to discover a sister so frigidly indifferent to one's misfortunes. But then, Beatriz had always been a prudish fool. Had it been otherwise she would never have disregarded such an opportunity as Fate had offered her. It was one of the ironies of existence that God gives nuts to those that have no teeth.

Her return disturbed his melancholy musings. She held out a little purse of green network, through the meshes of which there were gleams of silver and of gold. 'Here is what I can spare you, Pablo. It is the half of what I possess.'

'It will be something,' he admitted, by way of thanks, balancing the purse in his palm. 'How do you live, Beatriz?'

'By teaching music, by needlework and other little services in the convent here. Aunt Clara has been very good to me.'

'Aunt Clara? To be sure. I had forgotten. She is the Mother Abbess, is she not?'

'The Prioress of Santa Paula here.'

'And I never thought of her.' He displayed genuine regret. 'I must recall myself to her. She is our mother's sister, after all.'

'Better not,' Beatriz advised him. 'Her views are strict, and she has heard of your . . . misfortunes in Cordoba.'

'And you mean...?' Here was yet another unpleasant surprise for him. 'The devil! What a family to belong to!'

'It is certainly regrettable that you were born into it. Come, Pablo. I will let you out.'

He went in surly humour. Halfway to the door in the wall he paused, detaining her. 'This is a poor lenten life you lead here, Beatriz. Needlework and teaching music to children.' He made a wry face of disgust.

'It is enough. I have peace.'

'Peace and poverty. A revolting combination. And a girl of your looks! With your voice and your legs you needn't want for gold. There's riches for you in singing and dancing. With me to protect you, we might go to Italy again. I should be safe there so long as we kept away from Venice. What do you say to it?'

'So that is why you came?'

'I've only just thought of it. May I die else. And it's a good thought. You can't deny that.'

'Oh, I thank you for it.' He did not like her smile. 'But here I have all I need.' She moved on, and he, perforce, must follow.

'Devil take it, Beatriz, it's mean-spirited to be so easily content.'

'I am content to be mean-spirited. It's in the Beatitudes, Pablo: "Blessed are the meek."'

She unbarred the door.

'Devil take the Beatitudes!' he exploded in irreverence. 'With me to look after you, you could live in plenty. At your ease.'

'Never more at my ease than here.' She opened the door. 'Go with God, Pablo. I shall pray for you. I am thankful that you are free again. Be prudent so that you may continue free.'

'Saint Mary! What good is freedom if . . . Oh, think it over. I'll come again.'

She shook her head, her face set. 'Better not. It is not very safe. There is Aunt Clara. Go now.'

He stepped out in evil mood, reviling her selfishness.

She closed and barred the door upon him and all that he stood for.

36

 TE DEUM

From the King and the Queen
 To the High and Mighty Don Cristobal Colon, their Admiral of the Ocean-Sea and Viceroy and Governor of the Islands discovered in the Indies.

T HUS ran the superscription of a letter from the Sovereigns handed to Colon by a royal envoy who met him at Seville on the morrow of his arrival there.

He had paused in that city, housed in the palace of the Count of Cifuentes, who entertained him as if he were royal.

In itself the superscription conveyed a foretaste of the more than flattering terms in which the Sovereigns wrote to him. Never perhaps was royal letter to a subject penned so lovingly and gratefully, or with such unmeasured acknowledgment of the debt in which his achievement placed the Crown. For nowhere was the delirium of wonder at this acquisition by Spain of an empire of illimitable possibilities higher than in the hearts of Queen Isabel and King Ferdinand. It was a letter to intoxicate a man less eager than Colon for the pomp and vanities of the world. But if his heart swelled and his pride was inflated, he suffered no sign of it to appear. There was no need now for jactancy in an attempt to magnify himself. Sufficiently had his achievements magnified him. There was no need to stand upon his dignity so as to increase his stature, for already the events had lent him in the eyes of the world a stature more than royal.

The terms of the Sovereign's letter were not merely gracious; they were affectionate. He was bidden by them to hasten to the Court at Barcelona, there in person to render an account of this new empire. He was urged to take order at once for the equipment of a fresh and vastly greater expedition, and the treasury, from which erst a few maravedis had so laboriously been wrung, was now virtually placed with all else in Spain at his command. With an assurance of the welcome awaiting him, the letter closed on a promise of new titles and dignities.

He reached Barcelona by the middle of April, after a progress across Spain which Las Casas likens to the triumph of a returning victorious Roman emperor.

Nothing, however, on that journey could match the arrival.

Out from Barcelona to meet him and escort him into the city, came by command of the Sovereigns a courtly cavalcade, including representatives of the best blood in Spain. Triumphal arches, draped balconies, blaring of trumpets, booming of guns, and blossoms showered upon him marked his passage through the crowded streets to the Palace.

Under a canopy of cloth of gold, set up in the main hall so that his reception should be as public as possible, the Sovereigns awaited him. The entire Court was in attendance: grandes of Spain in velvet and brocades, mantled knights of Calatrava and Santiago, prelates in purple, the Cardinal of Spain in scarlet, captains in glittering steel were ranged in a crescent broken by the canopy, the ladies ranged at the foot and to the right of the dais, beside the Queen.

A flourish of trumpets heralded his coming, and sent a rustle of expectancy through the brilliant assembly.

The arras was drawn aside from the arched entrance by two tabarded ushers, and he appeared, tall, commanding, his head high, his countenance a mask of composure upon his inward agitation. He was studiedly dressed for effectiveness in two shades of red, his wide-sleeved surcoat edged with sable.

With calculation he paused a moment on the threshold, focus of every eye in that vast hall.

Immediately behind the Queen, the Marchioness of Moya considered him with a heightened colour and a sparkle of excitement in her fine eyes, exulting in this supreme triumph of one who, had she so willed it, she might once have claimed for her own. Near the King, Santangel found his sight dimmed by a tear of pride in this man who so richly had repaid his affection and support. At the side of Prince Juan, a well-grown stripling of a dozen years, young Diego Colon, much petted in these last days for his great father's sake, grinned broadly as he looked upon that princely figure.

After that moment of impressive, unembarrassed pause, Colon came forward towards the throne, with a brisk, elastic step, and then occurred a thing without precedent in the memory of the oldest courtier. Their Highnesses rose from their gilded chairs of state, to receive the Admiral standing.

It made him quicken his step to the royal dais, where he knelt to kiss the royal hands so eagerly extended to him, whilst royal eyes smiled benevolent welcome. By those hands, he was immediately raised, and not only from his knees. The Queen turned to Fonseca, the yellow globe of whose hairless head and face was craned forward the better to view the upstart whose achievement marked the presumption in which the priest had once opposed him.

'Don Juan,' was her incredible command to him, 'be good enough to advance a chair for Don Cristobal.'

The yellow face grew yellower, the beady eyes were baleful with disgust. Not only was this foreign adventurer to be seated in the royal presence, but a gentleman of Castile, a hidalgo born, was to play the lackey to him and set a chair. Perforce Don Juan must swallow his resentment, and obey.

'Pray sit, Don Cristobal,' the Queen invited, as she, herself, resumed her chair.

Even Colon's audacity was daunted. 'Too great an honour, Highness,' he deprecated.

King Ferdinand smiled, as warm to-day as Colon had ever known him frosty. 'Too great for any but the greatest. Be seated, my Lord Viceroy.'

Colon conquered his awe, a transient emotion to which, you will have gathered, he was not subject. He sat, and his glance, spuriously calm, swept round the semicircle of standing nobles and prelates, more than one of whom was on the edge of consternation. Meeting at the end the smile of the Marchioness of Moya, there was in his light eyes the suspicion of a mischievous irresponsible twinkle.

'We are here,' said the smiling Queen, 'to hear you, Don Cristobal, on your great adventure.'

His answer had been well rehearsed. 'May it please Your Highness, by the grace of God, in whose hands I am but an instrument, as I have always protested, without always being believed, I am to lay at the foot of your noble throne an empire of a vastness and wealth that are still incalculable.' Having thus, as he was ever careful to do, pointed to his own consequence, lest any part of it should be overlooked, he collected himself for a moment, and then began his tale.

His achievement was certainly one to make men marvel, and he would not have been true to himself had he permitted that to be overlooked or lessened. He spoke at length upon the islands discovered, giving — as he had done already in his letter — the size of Cuba as that of England and Scotland combined, and of Hispaniola as equivalent in area to the whole of Spain, besides the lesser islands, such as San Salvador, where he had made his first landfall. He told of their delicious climate, the amazing fertility of their soil, the richness, abundance and variety of their fruits, of their great forests yielding magnificent timbers, of cotton, gums and spices to be had in incredible plenty, of their inhabitants who went naked in a state of primeval innocence, so meek of nature as to offer themselves as docile subjects ready for dominion and conversion to the Christian Faith. Then, having kept the best for the last, thus, cunningly, to provide a climax, he told of the inestimable wealth of those lands in gold and pearls and precious stones. The gold, he conveyed, was to be dug from the ground as readily as clay in Spain. There were mines to be established and worked with the abundant and ready labour Their Highnesses' new Indian subjects would supply. Pearls he implied were to be gathered by the bushel. And so far, he reminded them, no more than the fringe of his discovery had been touched, interrupted as it was by the loss of the *Santa Maria* and the propriety of returning home to report upon the lands of which he had so far taken possession. A multitude of islands, from what he had gleaned from his Lucayans, as primitively peopled, awaited occupation, together with the mainland of Asia beyond them.

Of the fact that he identified Hispaniola with the Zipangu of Marco Polo he cautiously made no mention yet. An element of doubt must have lingered with him to restrain him from an assertion that subsequent discovery might disprove.

Having at great length, heard throughout in hushed awe, painted in dazzling colours that astounding word-picture of his new world, he begged leave to present to Their Highnesses the few tokens which he had brought home, so that they might obtain a glimpse of the actual substance of the marvels he had related.

If he had cast a spell upon his audience by his words, he was further to astound them now by his exhibits.

Six Indians, three men and three girls, were marched in. Regrettably, as he explained, respect for Their Highnesses and the Court prevented him from displaying them in their native nudity. The blankets mantling them had been supplied aboard. Even so they remained sufficiently startling to Spanish eyes.

The coarse, lank black hair of the men was adorned with parrot feathers, red and green. The red and black paint in circles round their eyes and in stripes along their cheeks lent their mild countenances an aspect of ferocity. The girls, slight, straight and golden-skinned, aroused a more admiring wonder.

Stalwart and lithe as cats, the men advanced until Colon's raised hand arrested them. Then they knelt and prostrated themselves before the Sovereigns so that their foreheads touched the ground.

When this was over, and these savages were ranged aside, to be stared at and to stare, a seventh was introduced. A stalwart, handsome youth this, without any disfiguring paint on face or body. Save for a loincloth he was naked, his limbs like gleaming bronze. There was a tuft of parrot's feathers in his black mane; round his right arm a flexible length of gold was coiled like a strap, and he bore a green parrot hawk-wise upon his wrist.

He went down on one knee at the foot of the dais, and scratched the head of the parrot, murmuring softly to it. Under that stimulus the bird swayed on his wrist a moment like a dancer, and then gave tongue.

'Viva el Rey Don Fernando y la Reina Doña Isabel.'

At the miracle of a bird with human speech, the Queen shrank back startled, and there was a stir of amazement amounting almost to consternation in the courtly throng.

The white teeth of the Indian flashed in a wide smile as he came erect again.

'Viva el Almirante!' screeched the parrot. 'Viva Don Cristobal!'

'Viva,' replied the King, dumbfounded into that polite echo of the bird's salutation. 'This is a strange, uncanny marvel, Don Cristobal.'

'A marvel in appearance only, Highness,' Colon said. 'Others of which I bring you word are marvellous in reality.'

He dismissed the Lucayan to join his fellows, and introduced now a troop of his men, bearing panniers. From these he took in handfuls gold in dust, gold in crude lumps, gold wrought into barbaric ornaments, and auriferous stones which in turn he proffered for Their Highnesses to handle and admire.

'These are but specimens.' Colon gave a free rein to his optimism. 'To bring you enough to fill this hall from floor to ceiling all that I require is ship-space in which to carry it.'

'That, by my faith,' said Ferdinand, 'it shall be our care to provide.' With glowing eyes he fondled a handful of those precious lumps.

The Queen's voice trembled with emotion. 'What a power for good have you delivered into our hands, Don Cristobal.'

'In that, Highness, I count myself the most fortunate of men.'

So, too, thought the Court. And not all of it with satisfaction. To the jealous soul of many a courtier it was no pleasant sight to behold this foreign upstart exciting the wonder of the Sovereigns and winning honours which they, for all their hidalguia, could never hope to reach. More than one noble brow was darkened as Colon continued to spread his marvels: the grotesque masks, the statues rudely carved in a wood that was as hard as iron, the balls of cotton, the hammocks, the bows and arrows, brilliant stuffed birds and the rest, like a pedlar, they thought, spreading his wares to gull a foolish housewife, whilst the Sovereigns purred over Colon, petting him and flattering him with boundless praise.

When they could praise him no more, they bethought them of praising God. They went down on their knees on the dais, compelling by that pious example the entire Court to kneel with them. With tears in her eyes the Queen uttered a short prayer.

'Humbly we give Thee thanks, O Lord, for a bounty which we pray Thee teach us to employ to the greater honour and glory of Thy Holy Name.'

Inspired by this, and the more fully to give expression to what he divined to be in the Queen's heart, Talavera raised his voice to intone the *Te Deum laudamus*. Instantly it was taken up by the entire assembly, and the hymn of thanksgiving reverberated through the great hall, awakening the echoes of the vaulted ceiling.

 THE ZENITH

It was over at last. The great reception had reached its climax in that *Te Deum*, which addressing men's words to God had served to focus their thoughts more closely upon Colon.

After that the Admiral had been held awhile in intimate talk by his grateful Sovereigns, friendly, intoxicatingly familiar talk which seemed to place all the resources of Castile and Aragon at his disposal.

Prince Juan was with them, and with Prince Juan was little Diego, who, emboldened by his father's manifest eminence, stood close, holding his hand even whilst Colon conversed with the Sovereigns. Then others had come with friendly greetings for the man whom Their Highnesses honoured: that greatest of Spanish nobles, Mendoza, the Cardinal of Spain; Hernando de Talavera, Archbishop of Granada, ascetically formal, yet with compliments enough to make amends for past mistrust; the bluff Admiral Don Matias Rezende, frankly to confess the dullness of his sometime scepticism; and many others who when he was last at court had looked askance at

him. Of these were not, at least, Cabrera and his handsome
wife. In felicitating Colon they could felicitate themselves
upon a faith that had never wavered.

The Marchioness, with a warm pressure of her jewelled
hand upon his arm, enveloped him in the affectionate regard
of those languorous eyes that once had played such havoc
with his senses.

'In justifying yourself you have justified us, Cristobal. So
to us belongs a little of the satisfaction that must be yours.'

Cabrera's yellow goat's eyes twinkled at him. 'Beware of
her. Before all's done she will claim a share in the discovery
of the Indies.'

'She will thus claim no more than is her own,' Colon
acknowledged. 'Is she not the discoverer of the discoverer?'

The pressure upon his arm increased. 'That is generous.
Too generous. But I did what I could.'

'And here are the golden fruits of it,' said he.

Later, however, and to Santangel alone, he was to allude
to those fruits in very different terms.

He was regally lodged and served in the palace itself, and
in those apartments aglow with splendid tapestries and carpets
from Persian looms, he sat that evening with the old Chancellor, who was indulging a limitless joy in the occasion.

'You know the faith I had in you, my son,' he was repeating.
'But what you have accomplished goes far beyond all that I
could have believed, and, I dare swear, beyond all that you
expected yourself.'

Colon laughed freely. His mantle of magnificence was cast
aside, and in this intimate hour he used Don Luis with the
simple frankness that true affection prompts. 'It is that and
more. Fortune has been bountiful to me beyond my deserts,
and, between ourselves, beyond my knowledge. May I die if
even now I know what I have discovered.'

'One thing you know, at least,' Don Luis fondly approved him. 'You know how to carry the burden of greatness. It asks a natural nobility.' He grew thoughtful. 'You will meet envy and malice. They may be very active against you. But I believe that you are of a stature to confront them calmly and defeat them.'

'Bah! What do they matter? Whatever other things may be in store for me, of those I can be certain. But they shall not fret me.'

Yet as he spoke his tone became so heavy and sombre that Don Luis, who was pacing the chamber, paused to look at him. He was sitting with his elbows on his knees, staring gloomily at nothing.

Reaction was descending upon him. From the zenith to which it had that day been lifted by the enthusiasms of which he had found himself the object, the pendulum-swing of human emotion was now approaching the nadir.

'Why, Cristobal, what ails you now? What are your thoughts?'

Colon stirred. He smiled wistfully. 'What would you? I have permitted myself to get drunk on the wine of adulation. It's a draught for which I have thirsted, and the intoxication of it has been falsifying my outlook, magnifying the mean, glorifying the worthless. As the fumes pass off, vision becomes truer. That is what ails me, Don Luis.'

The Chancellor blew out his cheeks and made eyes of astonishment. 'Now, here's stark ingratitude! Caressed by princes, with everything at your command, money, ships, friends, the service of all men, and, faith, the smiles of all women, and you find grounds for repining! You are voracious if you are not satisfied.'

'In other circumstances I should be that, and more. But of what avail all this when a man is ... lonely?'

'Lonely! At such a time?'

'Aye, lonely. To sustain me out there in the perils of the ocean, to add to the glamour of my discoveries, there was the conviction that whilst I toiled afar, your search at home would not fail.'

'Beatriz?' Don Luis interjected.

Colon nodded. 'Your letters at Seville crushed that hope. Pride and gratified vanity have sustained me, intoxicated me and momentarily dulled the pain.' He rose. 'Oh, it was a fine thing to be acclaimed wherever I passed, to hold the Sovereigns spellbound by the magic of my tale to-day, to lay my trophies at their feet, to know that I was dazzling a world by the marvel of my achievement. I was dazzled myself by the reflection of the wonder that I caused. But now, now that I am, as it were, alone with myself, I ache to think how poor a thing it all is compared with what it might be if I could lay it at the feet of my Beatriz. Without her, my glory becomes a handful of ashes.'

'She means as much to you as that!' Santangel's eyes were compassionate.

'Just so much.'

The Chancellor came and set a hand upon his shoulder. 'But why despair? The search goes on. Somewhere in Spain she must be, and sooner or later she will be found.'

'Somewhere in Spain? Why? The world is wide. She has been abroad before. Why should she not be abroad again, now that there is nothing to hold her here? Does she even live? And if she does, how does she live? Do you conceive the torture of that question to a lover? Without resources, to what shifts may she not have been driven; and by me, by my so ready unfaith.' For an instant he sank his face into his hands. 'The horror of it! Who will assure me that she is not dead, or that living she would not be better dead? Will

you still wonder that when the incense of adulation ceases to
drug my senses, I count my gains cheap when set against my
loss?'

'Courage, my son! Courage!' Santangel said. 'You torment yourself with imagined fears. You have no evidence of
all this. Continue to have faith that Beatriz will be found.'

He had courage enough at least to let none but Santangel
suspect the cankering pain that marred his triumph. In the
days that followed he divided his time between the honours
continually offered him and the society of his little son, in
whose gentle, pious, affectionate nature he found a measure
of solace for his unsuspected loneliness amid so much adulatory
companionship.

He was much in the company of the Sovereigns in those
Barcelona days and the object of their flattering affection.
A grant of arms was made to him, in which the Lion of
Aragon and the castle of Castile were quartered with the
device of his own choosing, a grant this to dismay some of
the proudest of Spain's stiff-necked hidalguia.

Often he was seen riding through the streets at the King's
side, with Prince Juan commonly on his other flank, and
acclamations arose wherever he passed. The great Mendoza,
the Spanish Primate, the very Pope of Spain and popularly
known as the Third King, gave a banquet in his honour,
attended, whether they liked it or not, by all who were noblest
in the realms. The Marchioness of Moya sat on his right and
flattered him by an engaging solicitude that defied evil tongues.
His response was a model of courtliness. His esteem for her
was deep and sincere, but gone was the magic of her glance
to disturb his pulses or the white curves of her breast to
quicken the flow of his blood. That power belonged now
only to a ghost.

In attendance upon the Queen, the Marchioness was often

present, too, during the long hours he spent closeted with the
Sovereigns, when plans were laid for the discovery of those
farther lands to be included in the great empire he bestowed
upon Spain. Details of their colonization were discussed, and
details of the great armament preparing at Seville; no little
penurious matter this, of two or three small caravels, but a
mighty fleet, of twenty or more ships, that should carry a
thousand men to the New World.

There came a day when Santangel was called in to discuss
the financial arrangements. The discussion was interrupted,
to the great vexation of the Sovereigns, by urgent matters
concerned with the Fueros of Aragon demanding King
Ferdinand's instant attention.

'You may leave me to continue the arrangements,' said the
eager Queen, out of her reluctance to postpone them.

'By your leave, madam,' His Highness pleaded, 'let me beg
you to suspend until I can again be present. Take pity on
my interest.'

Her amiability would not deny him. 'As Your Highness
pleases. At noon to-morrow, then, Don Cristobal. And you
shall stay to dine with us.'

Ferdinand smiled, well pleased. 'That will be excellent.
You are gracious, madam. Until to-morrow at noon, Don
Cristobal.'

Colon bowed. 'I kiss Your Highnesses' feet.'

38

 SATISFACTION

Later that same afternoon, as Colon was taking his ease, a chamberlain brought him word that a certain Don Pablo de Arana solicited the honour of being received by him.

It was notorious that Colon, despite the eminence to which he had climbed, remained easily accessible. With his greatness he had put on none of that exclusiveness which in so many is greatness's only sign. Although the name conveyed nothing to him, he ordered this stranger to be brought.

He beheld a man still young, of middle height, spare and of a rather disreputable exterior in a shabby pretension of gentility. A pair of dark eyes, nervously intent, met his glance out of a lean, pallid face that ended in a blue-black, pointed beard.

Colon found his tone and manner as little prepossessing as his appearance.

'You are Don Cristobal Colon,' said the stranger, between question and aggressive assertion.

Colon was all urbanity. 'To serve you, perhaps.' He sat

down, and waved his visitor to a chair, which the man disregarded. 'What do you seek of me?'

He was answered in a word, delivered with explosive
truculence.

'Satisfaction.'

Colon put up his brows, beginning to wonder whether he
had to deal with a madman. 'Satisfaction, do you say?' His
tone was mild. 'Pray for what?'

'For the wrong you have done my sister.'

This was more than Colon could accept with gravity. The
charge was as preposterous as the man who brought it. He
burst into laughter, and rose.

'You'll be mistaking me for someone else. I do not think
I have the honour to know your sister.'

'The seducer's common denial,' said the fierce Pablo. 'It
will not serve you with me.'

'Will it not? What will, then?'

'Satisfaction. That is what I am here to demand. Satisfaction.'

Colon began to find him tiresome. 'My good sir, the door
is behind you. Take advantage of it before I summon a
servant to rub you down with a cudgel.'

The fellow sneered. 'That were, indeed, unwise. You're
a great man these days, are you not, Don Cristobal? Lord
Admiral, Lord Viceroy, and Lord other things. But not all
your greatness shall shelter you. Show me violence, and the
world shall know your villainy. We shall see if you'll stand
as well with Her Highness the Queen when ——'

'Enough!' Colon flung at him in a tone that checked the
minatory flow. 'I do not find you amusing. Out of this,
before my patience wearies.'

Pablo recoiled. He cringed, he sighed, he flung out his
arms and let them fall again. 'So be it. I had hoped that for

your own sake, for the sake of your fair name, for the sake of
decency, you would be reasonable. Oh, I am going!' he cried,
retreating again before the anger gathering in Colon's countenance. 'But you'll not be surprised if I go elsewhere with the
tale of the cruel wrong you have done poor Beatriz Enriquez.'

'Who?' Startled by the name, Colon leapt forward, flinging
out the question in a roar.

Pablo retreated yet again. He had almost reached the door.
But suddenly he perceived that there was less reason to fear
violence. He recovered. 'Beatriz Enriquez, I said. I see that
you had not understood me. That is my sister.'

He stood waiting now, observing that Colon had lost colour,
that his breathing had quickened.

'Where is Beatriz?' Ignoring all the rest he disclosed to
Pablo another advantage.

The rascal's wits were quick to seize it. He shook his head.
'I am not to disclose that.'

'Why not? How else am I to make the reparation you
demand?' His voice had fallen to a humble note. 'That I
have wronged her, I know. How I know! I have suffered
for it, but perhaps no more than I deserve. But — praised
be Our Lady! — you bring me the means to end it. Come,
man: where is she? Tell me.'

Dumbfounded, Pablo stood and gaped. Unaccountably
things had taken a turn in a direction quite other from what
he had expected. Somewhere his calculations had been at
fault. It was necessary to readjust his views to what he
found. 'Why should I tell you?' he asked, at last, groping
his way.

'Why? So that I may go to her at once, of course.'

'Can you be supposing that she wishes to see you?'

Colon showed him a face of dismay. 'Do you mean that
it is beyond her to forgive my error?'

'Does that surprise you?'

Colon did not answer. He stood gloomily considering, his eyes on the ground. Then he took a turn in the room, closely watched by the other's crafty, probing eyes. He came to halt before Pablo presently, and threw up his head. Whilst pale and in prey to manifest excitement, yet his voice was level. 'I must take my chance. I must go to her. I must see her and explain myself. After all, man, her happiness is as much concerned as mine. Where is she, then? Tell me.'

'I should be breaking faith with her,' Pablo lied impudently.

'She'll forgive you that. Come, man. Don't keep me waiting.' He spoke with a fresh, increasing urgency.

Pablo was baffled, cheated of advantages that had seemed so full of profit. He had not reckoned that Colon would have discovered the error of his judgment of Beatriz; nor could he conjecture how Colon had discovered it, since, as Beatriz had told the tale, there was no such error. It was infernally inconvenient to his plan. It shattered his line of attack. He could only keep to his evasions, and see what came of them.

'You do not know her if you still think so.'

Standing squarely before him, Colon was pondering him now with penetrating eyes, whose expression changed slowly from intercession to something that Pablo found disquieting.

'What was it,' he asked slowly, 'that brought you here? You spoke of satisfaction, of reparation, did you not. What was the reparation that you had in mind?'

Uncomfortable under those stern searching eyes that were as grey as steel and as cold, Pablo shifted on his feet, shrugged and put on a sneering brag. 'What is the usual reparation to a woman one has wronged and abandoned?'

'I do not know. It is not in my experience.'

Pablo grew sullen. At every point this man checkmated

him. He shrugged again, ill-humouredly, offensively. 'Yet it should be plain. If she is without means...' He left it there, his glance defying those dreadful eyes.

'Ah! Money. That is what you came for?'

'What else in such a case?'

'I see. I see.' His tone made Pablo's blood run cold. 'And you dare, you miserable pimp, to say that Beatriz sent you?'

Colon's hand was suddenly raised. To avoid the blow, Pablo not only stepped back, but answered quickly, 'Of course not.'

'Ah!' The hand was lowered again.

Quickly Pablo ran on: 'Beatriz would perish of want before she would touch a maravedi of yours. But that,' he blustered on, 'is no reason why I should not make you provide for her.' He thought that he began to see his way at last. 'I account it no less than a brother's duty.'

'Rightly. And you need employ no compulsion. All that I have is at her disposal. But she shall hear of it from me. So tell me where to find her.'

'That I will not. I have told you that she will neither see you nor accept anything from you.'

'So that you are to be her unsuspected almoner. I understand. But are you to be trusted?'

'What choice have you but to trust me?'

'I might still turn you out-of-doors.'

'And have me publish the infamy of the great Don Cristobal Colon? Petition the Queen's Highness for justice upon the seducer of my sister? Is that what you would prefer?'

But now, in the very moment in which Pablo thought that he had found the sure way, Colon actually laughed at him, actually had the air of being amused, but with something sinister in his amusement.

'You're an impudent dog. I begin to remember you. You

are — are you not? — the noble brother for whose sake, so
as to save you from the Venetian galleys, she lent herself to
the treachery that parted us.'

This was worse and worse. Pablo asked himself how much
more this man might know, and cursed Beatriz's tongue. But
he would play his hand to the end. 'What then?' he demanded
truculently. 'You are not to blame her for obeying the instincts
of a good sister.'

'Or was it the promptings of a bad brother? However,
you've escaped from the galleys to begin again, it seems.'

'From the Venetian galleys.' Pablo was strident. 'The arm
of Venice does not reach to Spain.'

'You start at shadows. I was not suggesting it.'

'I start at nothing. Let us keep to the point.'

'What is that?'

'What are you prepared to do for my sister?'

'Everything once you tell me where to find her.'

'We go round in circles. I shall never tell you.'

But Colon, he could see to his disgust, was not taking him
seriously. There was still that disquieting mockery in those
cursed eyes.

'You are not brotherly, my friend. You show no proper
concern for your sister. Whatever you may say, I can bring
happiness to her in finding my own. Perhaps you had not
thought of that. Come, sir, come. Where is she?'

'You make me repeat myself. I have said that I shall not
tell you.'

'Not even at a price?'

Pablo blinked in surprise, incredulous. Then his heart
leapt within him for satisfaction in his own craft. He had
played his victim into a corner, and in that corner the great
Colon lay at his mercy. He fingered his black beard. He
stood for a moment affecting reflection.

'Devil take you for tempting a poor wretch. But...Oh, well, since that's your mood...a thousand gold florins would be nothing to you. And you need have no fear that you'll not find her as you left her. She's been shut up in a convent ever since. May I die if that's not the truth. A thousand gold florins, then, and I'll tell you where she is.'

'You are modest. I had in mind a much higher price than that.'

'Eh?' Pablo stared a moment, then swept him a bow. 'I'll leave myself to your generosity.'

'How wise you are! For the price I propose to give for your information is nothing less than your own life.'

'My life!'

Colon smiled upon his sudden change of countenance, his wide-eyed consternation. 'You see, I am well informed about you. I happen to know why you went to Italy, taking your sister with you, so that you might prey upon her, living upon her earnings as a cantatrice. You were in flight from your native Cordoba, having killed a man. I don't know his name or station. But that's no matter. They will be known to my good friend, Don Xavier Pastor of Cordoba, the Corregidor, who will thank me to send you to him, as I shall unless you tell me where to find Beatriz. The choice is yours, my shameless friend.'

It was with Arana's recovered assurance as with a lamp that is suddenly blown out. He fell visibly to trembling. His eyes bulged in his leaden face. His lips twitched. It was a long moment before they recovered the power of utterance, and then what came was merely an ejaculation of obscene blasphemy. Rage and fear struggled within him, and his rage was not all against Colon. Some of it he reserved for Beatriz, and for this shameless incredible betrayal of him by which he was now undone.

'Come, sir,' Colon prodded him. 'We have wasted time enough. Make your choice.'

'Malediction!' growled Pablo. 'May I die, but that's unworthy. Cowardly. It's no choice at all.'

'More choice than you deserve. More than I need give you. The Corregidor has arts to make men talk, even valiant men; and I do not think you are very valiant, Master Pablo. So answer my question. And lest you should attempt any of the tricks you deal in, I'd better tell you that you will be held here under guard until I return. So that should you lie to me, the Corregidor shall have you. You are warned.'

'How do I know that you'll keep faith with me when I've told you?'

'You don't. You'll have to trust me. But if I didn't mean to keep faith I should not waste time with you. I'd send you at once to Cordoba, where the rack would wring the information from you.'

It was the end of the encounter for Pablo. Abjectly the rogue surrendered. 'You'll find Beatriz in the Convent of Santa Paula in Seville.'

Colon's eyes flashed. 'That is the truth?'

'As I've a soul to be saved.'

'I doubt if you have. But no matter. You would not dare to lie. On my return you shall have fifty florins to take you out of Spain. But if ever you set foot in it again, or if ever again you venture to approach your sister, I'll see to it that to Cordoba you still find your way.'

He clapped his hands as he ended, and into the care of the chamberlain who answered the summons he delivered his visitor. 'Until my further orders this man is to be kept here under strict guard, but without other hardship. You may go, Master Arana. And a last warning: no subtleties.'

It was a superfluous admonition. That unlucky man, Pablo

de Arana, went out broken in spirit and more persuaded than
ever that he was the sport of a malign fortune.

Colon sought Santangel's apartments, and thrust himself
without ceremony upon the Chancellor.

'Great tidings, Don Luis.'

Santangel, who was at work, laid down his pen, to gaze in
wonder upon this transfigured man who seemed to have
grown younger by ten years.

'God avail me! What's happened? You look as if you had
made another discovery.'

'I have. A greater discovery than the Indies.' He loosed
a boyish laugh. 'I have discovered Beatriz. She is in Seville,
at the Convent of Santa Paula.'

Don Luis stood up, his eyes reflecting the joy in Colon's.
'Praise the Lord!'

'I do, and I am leaving at once for Seville.'

'At once?' Santangel's satisfaction was checked. 'You don't
mean to-day?'

'Within the hour. As soon as a horse is saddled.'

Santangel approached him. 'But you can't.' His protest
was vigorous. 'You are to sup to-night with the Duke of Arcos.
The banquet is in your honour.'

'They shall honour me in my absence. Make my excuses
to the Duke.'

Santangel was distressed.

'He'll never forgive you.'

'I should never forgive myself if I delayed.'

'But . . .' The Chancellor's distress increased. 'Devil take
you! Have you forgotten that you are commanded to dine
with Their Highnesses to-morrow?'

'Their Highnesses will dine very well without me. Wish
them a good appetite for me, and explain that vital matters
have taken me to Seville.'

'Are you mad?'

'It is possible,' laughed Colon.

'But you can't do this. A royal command ——'

'Must give way to a command from Heaven.'

Santangel was appalled. 'Will you treat it lightly? In God's name, come to your senses. Their Highnesses are impatient to settle the details of this new expedition.'

'I was impatient to settle the details of the old one. But I had to wait. The Sovereigns and I have changed places. That's all.'

'But Cristobal, my friend!' The Chancellor was wringing his hands. 'This is stark madness.' He caught Colon by the arm. 'Listen, listen, you madman. Such a thing will make enemies for you, and envy has made you enemies enough already. You conceive what will be said, the poison that will be uttered against you. And if you leave Their Highnesses affronted by this disregard of their commands, they may lend an ear to it. Princes are jealous folk. Most jealous of their rights over their subjects. Think what you may jeopardize.'

But he expostulated in vain. Colon laughed irresponsibly. 'I am thinking only of Beatriz. I can think of nothing else. The lover is greater than the discoverer. But the discoverer is still great enough to brave the frown of royalty and the malice of courtiers.'

He took the troubled Chancellor by the shoulders. 'Serve me in this like the friend, the dear friend, you have always been. Whisper the exact truth to the Queen. She is a woman and tender-hearted. She may understand.'

'And the King?' Don Luis was emphatic. 'What shall I say to him?'

'Persuade him that I am saving money for him by this sudden journey,' laughed Colon. 'He'll forgive anything on that score.'

'You make a jest of it!' cried Santangel in despair.

'What else?'

He caught and wrung Santangel's reluctant hands. 'God keep you, Don Luis,' he said in exuberant farewell, and was gone like a whirlwind.

THE END